Blaze of Glory

m. garzon

For my brothers, L.G. and I.G.
Thanks for always being there.

"Blaze of Glory," by m. garzon. ISBN 978-1-60264-810-4.

Published 2011 by Virtualbookworm.com Publishing Inc., P.O. Box 9949, College Station, TX 77842, US. ©2011, m. garzon. All rights reserved. No part of this publication may be reproduced, stored in a retrieval system, or transmitted in any form or by any means, electronic, mechanical, recording or otherwise, without the prior written permission of m. garzon.

Manufactured in the United States of America.

Acknowledgments

My unending gratitude goes to the following:
To my children, for giving mommy time to play with her
make-believe friends.
To Stéphanie Roy, osteopath extraordinaire and friend through the
ages—if you hadn't been my first fan, this story might never have
seen the light of day.
To my proofreaders: Stéphanie Garzon, Jennilyn Robbie, Sasha
Malashenko, and Jean-Marc Miousse, for their priceless enthusiasm
and input.
To the Club Polo Nacional, especially Dan and Arlene, for being so
welcoming and answering my many questions about the game of
polo.
To all the Inspiration Montessori moms, for your sympathetic ears,
unfailing support, and childcare during time crunches (this means
you, Lise!).
To my mom, for being a great Oma.
To Jack Habacon, for all the design, website and technical stuff.
For the fantastic cover photograph, thanks to Weltina (Velvet),
Kaida, Elaine, and Natacha.

Lastly, my gratitude goes out to all horses, those wondrous
creatures who inspire and uplift us.

Prologue

I squished my way through the water-soaked grass to the pasture. The sudden downpour had cooled the air, and I shivered slightly in my wet clothes. The worst of the storm seemed to be over, and when I reached the pasture fence I paused, debating whether I needed to bring the horses in. The rain had abated to a fine drizzle, and there hadn't been any lightning or thunder since I'd left the barn. It was such a relief to escape the tense atmosphere there that I lingered, leaning on the fence and watching the dark wet patches creeping down the horses' coats.

I didn't hear the footsteps until they were right behind me. I knew whose they were without turning; only Jaden's presence would raise the hairs on my body like that.

"Tea," he said my name like a caress.

I was about to duck away, but he knew me too well—his hands shot out and gripped the fence board on either side of me, though he didn't touch me, of course. He was so close now that I could feel the heat from his body searing the back of mine, but this heat made me shiver all the more.

"How long are you planning on not talking to me?" His voice was subdued.

I shrugged. I felt, rather than heard, his sigh.

"You're angry with me."

He was wrong about that. It wasn't anger that was making me avoid him, it was self-preservation.

"I don't blame you. I know I've made a mess of things. I came to give you a choice... I was planning to leave at the end of the season." He paused, but my brain was already frozen. As though it couldn't process the word 'leave'. "But if you'd rather I left now, I'll understand. I'll find a spot for my horses closer to Toronto."

My chest constricted painfully, and my breath started coming in sharp, raw gasps. Either way, he would be gone. My only option was whether to prolong my suffering. It was always the same impossible choice: the pain of his presence versus the torture of his absence. I didn't say anything. I don't think I could have spoken even if I'd wanted to.

"Let me know what you decide," he continued quietly. He hesitated, then dropped his head close to mine; I felt the *zing* of current from my face down to my shoulder. He whispered his parting line in my ear.

"I miss you."

I waited until his footsteps faded to surrender to the wracking sobs, and they shook me for a long time before I pulled myself together and went back to work.

Part One: Forbidden

One

Weekends were always busy.

I rushed out the door after a hasty breakfast and headed for the familiar weathered beige of the barn. It was a warm day for September, the sky intensely blue with only a few small puffy clouds. The most time-consuming parts of my weekends were the riding lessons I taught, although I also had horses to ride, a few for clients, and some of the barn's own. Also on the weekends, my brother Seth and I did the evening feeding, and the last check of the barn before lights-out at night. And then there was homework... I was starting grade eleven; the workload this year meant I'd probably have to study a bit more.

"Hey, shrimp," Seth greeted me as I almost ran into the barn. He was sweeping the aisles, cleaning up after the morning feed. "Nice of you to finally drag yourself out of bed."

You learn early that life isn't fair when you grow up with a twin brother like mine. Seth had always been the sweet-tempered, beautiful one, while I was the scrawny, mercurial one. Things hadn't changed much over the years. At sixteen, I was five foot two and a half—don't forget the half—with a slight frame, average looks, and colored in boring monochrome: brown hair, brown eyes, and skin that tanned easily. By now, after a summer spent working outdoors, it was a smooth... well, brown. Seth, on the other hand, was blessed with shaggy light blond hair, clear blue eyes, and skin that seemed to alternate between red and white all summer without perceptibly darkening. Even worse, he was six feet tall—I hoped that he was done growing now, or his smugness would become unbearable.

"Hi, Tea!" a high voice piped up.

I smiled at the little girl skipping toward me. Eight-year-old Emma was the first student to arrive for my nine a.m. lesson.

"My dad came to watch me today!" Emma almost squeaked with excitement.

Her father was almost as blond as she was. "Hi," he said, smiling, "Tia, right? We've heard a lot about you."

"It's Tay-a, actually," I corrected as we shook hands.

4

Once my students were ready I led them out to the smaller ring, stifling a yawn. I enjoyed teaching, but the beginner lessons were a bit boring. After getting them all mounted I asked them to walk and began correcting their positions.

"Push your heels down, Emma. Cassandra, remember to sit up straight. Sebastian, you're looking good, just shorten your reins a bit, okay? Chip looks like he's about to fall asleep," I said. On hearing his name, the pony turned and ambled toward me, little Sebastian's ineffectual pulling on the reins not diverting him in the slightest. He pushed his head against my chest, and I patted his dark brown neck for a minute.

"Okay, boy, time to get back to work." I gave the pony a push, and he meandered willingly back to the track.

"Is everyone behaving themselves this morning?" Dec's voice called out cheerfully. All four kids giggled and greeted him; my stepfather was very popular with our students and boarders. Blue, Dec's Australian Cattle Dog, ran to me for a pat; they'd gone out to the hayfield early that morning—thankfully before I'd gotten up. Seth would be heading back with them later.

"How's the haying?" I asked.

"Not bad. We should be done with the cutting by tomorrow." Dec's pale blue eyes, which contrasted starkly with his dark hair, squinted up at the sky. "Hopefully the weather will hold and we can get it baled this week. Oh, don't forget that Jaden's coming for dinner tonight—Gran's coming to cook, so make sure you help her."

I suppressed a groan as I turned my attention back to my students; I'd forgotten that Dec's nephew was coming. I hadn't done any homework yet, and today was Sunday. A dinner guest meant that I'd be losing sleep to get my homework done—or, if I was being honest with myself, trying to finish it up during school tomorrow. I wrapped up the lesson with relief.

"Tea!"

I was hailed the minute I walked into the cool shade of the barn; Teri bounced up to me, looking both smug and secretive. She was my closest friend.

"Last week of September, right?" she said in a low voice.

"Shh! Are you trying to get me killed?" I hissed, but I grinned at her all the same. "Let's talk about it later."

Teri pulled her hair back and tied it in a ponytail. She had hair I'd kill for, the color of burnt caramel, falling in thick waves to her shoulders when it was down.

"Okay," she said, "but we have a lot to organize."

I hung out with her while she got her Appaloosa pony, Picasso, ready to ride.

"Hey girls," our friend Julia's voice rang out.

"Hey, Jules," we responded, and Teri added, "Yay, you can ride with me—I thought I was on my own today."

"What am I, chopped liver?" I protested.

"No, but Blaze is out of Picasso's league. At least Jules and I can set up one course to jump."

The mention of my pride and joy made me smile; riding him was always the highlight of my day.

"So what's new, Jules?" I asked.

She spoke over her shoulder as she went to retrieve Jasmine, her black mare.

"Well, I went on a date yesterday. Total train wreck!" She began recounting the horrors of her date while Teri and I listened, and occasionally snickered. Julia went on a lot of first dates, but few subsequent ones. She had very exacting standards, but she could afford to be picky: she was stunning. She was half Japanese and half Caucasian, but at five foot six, she was much taller than Teri or me, with a willowy physique that we tried hard not to envy. Her brown-black hair fell in a glossy curtain down her back and as heavy bangs in the front, but her eyes were her most striking feature—they were a stormy gray, thickly fringed in long black lashes. You couldn't help but stare at Julia; it was really no wonder that her parents sent her to a private girls' school.

After teaching my next lesson it was time to ride Blaze. I stepped into his stall and he turned to me right away, whickering a greeting. As always, I felt a warm swell of affection for him. I leaned my forehead against his and spent a few minutes just stroking his silky head and neck; he would stay that way for hours, never pulling away. Blaze was *my* horse. My mom had convinced Dec to buy him for me when I was thirteen, the year before she died. He'd been a yearling then, but had shown incredible potential, and now as a five-year-old he was more than living up to that promise. That wasn't why I loved him so much, though. I would have adored him even if he couldn't jump over a garden hose.

A small crowd had assembled in the aisle. Four of my students, plus Julia, Teri, and a couple of boarders—Jennifer and Stephanie—were staying to watch me ride. I was taking things slowly with Blaze, laying the groundwork for us to have a long, successful career together. I had only brought him to five shows this year, and at those five shows he had won third place once... and first place every other time. So naturally, we had started attracting some attention, and he already had some die-hard fans in his home barn.

I cross-tied Blaze and started grooming him while multiple hands came to pat him hello. Blaze never minded the attention. In fact, he seemed to consider it his due. I couldn't help admiring my Dutch Warmblood as I led him out of the barn; he was the most gorgeous light copper bay, and the sunlight danced red and gold on his glossy coat. All four of his legs were black from the knee down—his only white marking was the wide blaze down his face. His black mane and tail were so smooth and shiny you'd think he was hiding a flat-iron in his stall. All in all, he took my breath away. Even after four years, I could hardly believe he was mine.

I mounted easily; Blaze was sixteen-one hands high—not that big for a jumper, though big enough for me. After warming up in the large paddock, we started jumping a small gymnastic combination. It used to make me horribly self-conscious to ride in front of people at home, but I was getting used to it now, and it was nice to have help making changes to the jumps, rather than me having to dismount every time.

"Okay, baby, we're going to trot over nice and quietly... don't get excited," I murmured to Blaze. He flicked his ears back and forth, listening. He liked it when I talked to him while I rode, so I usually did. Sometimes I even sang to him, though I was way too embarrassed to do that in front of an audience. Of humans, anyway.

We trotted in: jump the large X, one canter stride, over the vertical, another canter stride, and over the oxer, which had a squarish shape since it consisted of two parallel poles. I stayed as quiet as possible, and revelled in the raw athleticism I felt under me. We went over it perfectly twice more, and then it was time to put the fences up.

"Could you raise them all a bit, please? Make the oxer about three foot six."

Another few trips over the combination, and again it felt like Blaze was barely trying. Suddenly, I wanted to feel him really jump—I wanted to know at what point he'd have to expend an actual effort to get over.

"Ter, can you raise them again, and adjust the distances for cantering, please? Put the vertical at four feet and the oxer at four-six," I said, trying to be casual. I could hear gasps from the watching crowd, but I ignored them, focusing on Blaze.

"Okay, baby, this one's going to be a lot bigger." I didn't talk to him on our approach this time. He raised his head before the first fence—he had noticed the increased size. He popped over the X, took a carefully measured stride, bounded over the vertical, one more stride and I held my breath as he rocked back onto his hocks and gave an enormous leap over the oxer, landing handily and cantering away gaily as though he did it every day. A cheer went up as I slowed him to a walk, patting him joyfully over and over.

"Oh my God Tea, you should've seen him, he looked unbelievable!" Julia yelled.

"Yeah, his knees were around his ears," Teri added, grinning widely.

"We need a camera next time," someone added to the happy chatter. I walked Blaze around on a loose rein; I couldn't get the huge grin off my face.

"Hey, who's that?" Teri asked suddenly.

I followed her gaze to a tall, lean figure leaning with one hand against a black SUV.

"Wow, is that an Armani suit?" Julia asked, impressed. I snickered; trust Julia to recognize a label at that distance. Though it did look like a nice suit, light grey and sleek. As I watched, the figure took off the jacket and tossed it into the car before strolling over to the fence.

"Hi, Tea." He smiled, a flash of white in a tanned, angular face.

"Jaden!" I exclaimed, suddenly recognizing him. "Welcome back."

"Thanks. Nice riding, by the way. That's some horse." His eyes travelled over Blaze appreciatively.

I was about to thank him when I realized what his presence meant.

"Oh no," I groaned, "You're here... which means I'm late. I'm supposed to be helping Gran with dinner."

"Don't worry about it, I'll give her a hand." He headed for the house, covering the ground quickly with a long-legged, athletic stride.

An excited babble arose in his wake.

"Who was *that*?" Julia demanded.

I continued walking Blaze as I answered.

"Um, that's my cousin, Jaden." It didn't feel quite natural to call him that, since I barely knew him. We'd only seen each other a few times as kids, and lately he'd been playing polo in other countries. Seth and I heard about him often, though, because he was Dec's favorite— and only—nephew.

"You didn't tell us your cousin was gorgeous," Teri said accusingly. "You've been holding out on us!"

"Give me a break! I haven't seen the guy in three years." I laughed. "Now, can you get a handle on your hormones long enough to give me hand? I've got to get Blaze cleaned up quick or I'm in trouble."

As soon as Blaze was taken care of, I dashed into the house and straight to the kitchen. Gran was at the stove, her white hair escaping from its usual bun as she turned to smile at me. I gave her a quick kiss on the cheek. She smelled like talcum powder.

"Sorry I'm late... though it looks as if you've found a far more competent helper than me," I commented.

Jaden was chopping vegetables with a speed that would have left me short a fingertip or two, the sleeves of his charcoal grey shirt rolled up to his elbows. He shot me a grin.

"Can I have a quick shower?" I asked Gran.

I'd been working all day, and was feeling decidedly grubby, a feeling exacerbated by the fact that Jaden looked as though he'd just stepped from the pages of a fashion magazine. Gran shooed me out, smiling.

I showered at lightning speed, threw on the first clean clothes I found and bounded down the stairs, my wet hair trailing down my back. I was just in time to see Dec and Seth walking in. My stepfather shook his head at me in disapproval, and I shrugged apologetically—it was clear I hadn't been helping Gran as I was supposed to.

At the sound of the front door, Jaden emerged from the kitchen. Dec took his outstretched hand and, to my surprise, pulled him into a hug.

"It's good to see you, son," he said gruffly. He looked Jaden up and down. "You're looking good—you didn't get dressed up on our account, did you?"

"I had a date earlier," Jaden admitted.

9

Dec gave a chuckle. "Some things haven't changed," he said. "You remember Seth?"

Jaden shook Seth's hand, then clapped him on the shoulder. "Wow, Seth, I almost didn't recognize you."

I wasn't surprised. Standing next to our cousin, Seth's recent growth spurt was even more apparent. Jaden used to tower over him, but now Seth didn't have far to go to catch up. In height, anyway... though I'd thought Jaden was lean when I'd seen him outside, he was considerably broader than my lanky teenaged brother.

Seth slung his arm around my neck. "Yeah, Tea's the only one who's still puny."

Jaden considered me. "Maybe in size, but certainly not in talent. I saw her riding earlier, it was impressive." His smile warmed me almost as much as his words. My warm feeling was quickly doused, though, by the cold look Dec gave me on his way to the stairs. I guess he'd seen the jumps too.

"I'm gonna shower," Seth said, turning away. I suddenly registered his appearance and grabbed his arm, stopping him.

"Dude!" I exclaimed, planting my hands on my hips. "You're crispy! Didn't we talk about the sunscreen?"

Seth put a long red arm around my shoulders and grinned down at me.

"You worry too much, Sis. I'm tough as an ox."

"You'll worry too, when you get skin cancer," I grumbled.

"Worrywart here puts sunscreen on the horses' nosies," Seth told Jaden, rolling his eyes.

They both had a good laugh at that while I stomped off to set the table. I didn't care what anyone said—the horses' white markings had pink skin underneath, which reddened in the sun. On sunny days I sunscreened those parts that were only thinly covered in hair; sunburn hurt and I didn't want my horses suffering from it if I could help it.

Seth was ultra-fast in the shower, as usual. Within minutes, he came into the dining room.

"Why didn't you take the combination down?" he murmured. "Now you're in trouble."

Jaden came in while Seth was talking and put a plate of carrots on the table. He stopped to listen to our exchange; I caught a subtle waft of some alluring scent as he moved.

10

"I don't care, Seth," I said smugly. "Blaze jumped a four foot six oxer like it was fallen log. You should've seen him!"

"No way!" His warm blue eyes shone with excitement. "Do you think-" He fell silent as Dec came in, and I scurried to the kitchen to see what I could do there.

Dinner was festive; a bit like the return of the prodigal son, I mused. Dec had only seen Jaden a few times over the past three years, and I hadn't seen him at all; he'd been attending university in British Columbia. Gran seemed thrilled to have him back, too. It must be nice, I grumbled mildly to myself. I doubted they'd be as pleased to see me after a long absence, but then, I was clearly the odd-colored sheep in my family flock.

"Tell us why you haven't been home in so long, dear," Gran requested. "What have you been doing with your summers?"

"Well, normally I play in the States over the summer, but since I took last year off school, I went to Argentina for the winter, and then England for a few months, which was incredible—polo has a much greater following there."

We spent a while discussing what England had been like. Gran in particular had a lot of very specific questions; she had grown up there, and retained more than a trace of the accent.

"Well, it's lovely to have you closer to home," Gran said.

I wondered if it was too early to excuse myself and go take a stab at my homework, but fortunately Seth chose to do just that a minute later, and we headed upstairs.

Later, Dec came into my room while I was doing my biology reading.

"I saw the combination you set up today," he began. He looked frustrated, but less angry than I'd expected.

I turned in my chair wearing an apologetic look.

"I know it's bigger than I'm supposed to jump alone, but there were lots of people around, you know, in case... and Stephanie's a doctor." I added the last part hopefully, since Dec's main worry was that I'd get hurt jumping too high without my coach.

"Stephanie's an osteopath," he growled.

"Sorry, I'll wait for Karen next time," I promised.

He leaned his muscular frame against the wall by the door; he seemed to be in a good mood.

"I don't know why it's so hard for you to listen, Tea," he said. "When I was a kid I did what my father told me to, period. Or I suffered the consequences."

I sighed; I'd heard this speech before. So I chose 'suffer the consequences' more often than I did 'listen'. Sue me. Dec saw it differently. His father had been in the military, and had raised his kids according to its principles; I suppose Dec was following in Grandad's footsteps. I wished he wouldn't. It would make our relationship so much easier.

I shrugged. "I just got carried away, Dec." I felt a flutter in my stomach at the thought that I'd forgotten to wear a helmet again. I knew that if he found out about that, the tenor of this conversation would change in a hurry. He seemed to be over it, though.

"I'm glad you and Seth got to spend some time with Jaden. I always thought the three of you would get along... I think we'll be seeing a lot more of him, now that he's back in Toronto." The thought obviously made him happy.

"Yeah, that would be great." I didn't really care; I had more pressing concerns than a long-lost cousin, like pulling off my secret job, the details of which Teri had yet to share. Not to mention finishing my homework.

"Well, goodnight, honey." He smiled at me before leaving—Jaden's visit had certainly lifted his spirits.

"G'night."

I stayed up late doing homework, so I started off my week tired. Life at our rural Ontario school this year was the same as always—I didn't love it, but I didn't hate it either. I was pretty good at academics, but I wasn't particularly popular. I hung out mostly with Teri, Seth, and Kabir, Seth's best friend. When I wanted one, Seth was my 'in' to social events; he was Mr. Popularity and got invited to everything worth going to.

I found Teri at lunchtime.

"Okay," she began as soon as we'd found seats, "I got us the job! Are you sure Dec will be away that week?" Her light green eyes sparkled with excitement.

"Yeah.... wow, we're really doing this." My pulse sped up at the thought, though whether with excitement or fear I wasn't sure. I turned to give her my full attention. Barely five foot two, Teri was tiny, yet also curvaceous in a way that I wasn't. Her small size had drawn the attention of a girl named Lori who, it transpired, was an exercise rider at a nearby racetrack. Lori had taught Teri the basics of galloping racehorses, and now Teri had managed to finagle us both jobs as fill-in exercise riders for a week.

"We'll need to leave by 4:45 a.m.," Teri was saying.

I groaned aloud and she nodded, looking glum.

"Yeah, it sucks, but we'll be getting on our first horses by 5:30. That gives us a couple of hours to work, and still be at school on time—but we'll make about $500 for the week!"

"Woohoo!" I whooped, "Royal Winter Fair, here we come!"

Thanks to numerous wins at horse shows over the summer, Teri and I had both qualified for the Royal Winter Fair that November. The Royal was a big deal; it was the last indoor show of the season, the prize money was substantial, and it was prestigious. Unfortunately, it also cost a lot. Dec normally covered half of my costs—I competed a lot more than he considered necessary—but we were already way over budget this year, so Teri and I had hatched our brilliant exercise riding plan to make up the deficit in our funds. There was only one slight drawback: I was absolutely, completely, without question, forbidden from setting foot on the racetrack. To hear Dec go on about it, you'd think the track was a cross between a gang clubhouse and a crack house. But since he was fortuitously leaving for a week on business, I felt as though the heavens had finally conspired with Teri and me to get us to the Royal. The excitement of that prospect helped me ignore the little voice in my head that was squeaking in panic at the thought of defying Dec.

We finished working out the details, which included having Lori coach me in exercise riding techniques. Teri had already shown me the basics, but we didn't have the proper equipment or an actual racehorse to practice with, and as I needed to be reasonably competent in order to avoid killing myself, it was worth putting in the effort to learn.

The dry weather held, so we'd be putting the hay up into the barn's loft that weekend. Even though it was only the second week of school, I already had less time to ride. I taught two nights a week, which left only three weeknights for riding, and I had two horses in training—Blaze and Zachary, the horse I was bringing to the Royal. I hoped we'd get the hay done quickly so that I could ride them both over the weekend... not that I was that useful at haying time. The bales weighed anywhere from fifty to seventy pounds, and on a good day I might hit a hundred and five, so I couldn't exactly toss them around.

I decided to ride Zac early Saturday morning, before we got to work. I was almost done and had just set up a fairly large combination when a voice made me jump.

"Won't you get into trouble for that?" Jaden was leaning on the fence, watching me. I wondered how long he'd been there.

"Not if you don't tell." I grinned at him. I was surprised he remembered; we had barely mentioned it in his presence. When he didn't answer right away I added, "Okay, this is the part where you say 'Tell on you? I wouldn't dream of it.'"

He smiled then. "Actually, I'm torn between wanting to stop you and wanting to watch you."

"Well, good luck stopping me," I muttered. I glanced at him; the sun created a golden halo around his light brown hair—not very fitting, I thought. I found his presumption irritating. I turned back to Zac, who was standing with the reins hanging loose on his neck. He was great that way, sometimes following me, but usually standing quietly and waiting. I mounted, and patted his sandy bay neck.

"Okay boy, let's show Jaden what you've got," I murmured to him. We picked up a canter and Zac bounded over the three fences with ease. I patted him enthusiastically as we landed.

"Nice," Jaden commented. "Did you start riding after Dec married your mom?"

"No, the year before, when I was nine," I said as I walked Zac on a loose rein to cool him off. "That's how they met, did you know that? Seth and I wanted riding lessons, and we came here."

"Well, you've definitely got natural talent," he said.

"Um, thanks." I wasn't too sure about that. I worked very hard at my riding.

By the time I'd put Zac away, everyone was laboring at putting the hay up. Dec was on the wagon chucking bales onto the conveyor, and I went up to the hayloft to lend a hand there.

"Hey, sweetie." Kabir grinned at me as he heaved a bale onto a stack that was already four bales high. I sighed. That was something I could never manage, and it irked me. He came over and gave me a one-armed hug. Seth and Kabir had become instant friends when we moved here six years ago, and he and I had grown close, too. He was of

Indian descent, with milk-chocolate skin, wavy black hair, and two huge dimples that made him look like a little boy when he smiled. That little-boy visage was at odds with his body, though, which could only be described as huge. He was a few inches shorter than Seth, but stocky, with enormous bulging muscles that came in very useful at the barn.

"We don't need you up here, Sis," Seth pointed out. "We've got this covered." He, Jaden and Kabir were very efficiently taking the bales off the conveyer and piling them; I'd probably get in their way.

I found Teri and Julia in the barn when I went back down.

"I see your handsome, rich, international-polo-playing cousin is back," Julia giggled.

"Come on, Jules." I rolled my eyes at her. "What makes you think he's rich?"

"Uh, hello, polo player?"

"Yeah," Teri added, "doesn't he need at least four horses for that?"

"He's only got two now, he sold four when he got into law school," I corrected.

Both my friends watched me with their mouths hanging open. I sighed.

"Yes, Mr. Perfect just started law school," I said. "And Dec's been throwing that in our faces at every opportunity. It's getting pretty annoying. As is Jaden himself."

"So he's smart, too?" Julia's perfect eyebrows got lost under her bangs. "And you haven't introduced us yet because...?"

"Because I'm a thoughtless, inconsiderate friend." I grinned at her. "I'm sorry I didn't immediately consider him for your dating pool."

"Apology accepted," she sniffed theatrically. "Are you coming on a trail ride with us?"

"I can't, I've got to help with the hay."

"By the way, Lori said this weekend would be perfect," Teri confided. "She's got time to teach us."

I shook my head. "I don't know how I'll get away; today there's the hay and tomorrow I'm teaching lessons all day."

We wandered outside to get Picasso, who was in a paddock.

"Hi girls," Dec greeted them cordially. "Tea, can you take over here for a little while?"

I ran to get some gloves from the feedroom, then climbed onto the wagon and took over from Dec. The job here was easier than in the hayloft—I just had to place the bales, one at a time, onto the conveyer that trundled them up to the loft. I heard a sharp intake of breath from either Ter or Jules, who were standing by the wagon with Picasso in tow. I followed their gaze up to the loft's open double doors.

"What?" I demanded.

"Wait..." Teri murmured.

I shrugged and kept heaving bales.

"Look up," Julia said in a low voice.

Jaden was taking a bale off the conveyer. He'd taken his shirt off... and I had to admit the view was impressive. His muscles weren't huge like Kabir's, but there seemed to be so *many* of them—you could have used him for anatomy class.

"Now that's vampire hot," Teri breathed. The three of us exchanged a grin; it was our highest form of praise. A minute later we all jumped as Jaden rounded the corner, pulling on his shirt as he approached.

I decided to make Julia happy.

"Jaden, these are my friends, Teri and Julia." I indicated them in turn, and battled a smirk at their wide-eyed expressions as he greeted them.

He turned and hopped onto the wagon in one easy bound.

"Why don't you let me take over here, Tea." He was tossing a bale onto the conveyer as he spoke; it looked effortless for him. "These bales are almost as big as you are."

I dithered a minute. I knew I was probably good for about an hour of lifting.

He saw my hesitation. "I'm sure you can find something better to do than lug haybales around."

I met Teri's gaze with a smile. Indeed, I could find something better.

So we spent my serendipitously free afternoon at the Thoroughbred farm, and Lori taught us to gallop racehorses. It was unbelievably hard, exhilarating, and terrifying all at once. I loved it. I wished I could get in more practice before I had to face the real thing in a week's time, but these few hours were all I could manage to sneak away.

Dec was on the hay wagon when I got back. "Where have you been?" he demanded.

"We went to Ter's to do homework," I replied innocently. "I wasn't needed with the hay."

"You shouldn't have left without telling me." He frowned.

"Sorry, I couldn't find you," I said, trying to look contrite. My stomach twisted uncomfortably at the lie, and I was glad he would be away during my week at the track. I didn't think I could pull it off if I had to lie to him every day.

Our first day at the racetrack was brutal. It started off tense for me; Dec was leaving on his business trip that morning, but I had to sneak out before he got up—the birds weren't even chirping yet, for crying out loud. I wouldn't know whether Dec had noticed my absence until I saw Seth at school.

We arrived at Fort Erie Racetrack, heavy-eyed and clutching our Tim Horton's coffees; the first fingers of light were just poking over the horizon as we stepped out of Teri's car. My heart picked up its pace. Thoroughbreds were walking up and down the dirt road, voices called morning greetings in the barn, and from behind us, I heard the distant thunder of galloping hooves—an exhilarating sound. Also a bit scary for me right now. We paused uncertainly in one of the doorways of the barn.

"Can I help you?" A big blond head emerged from a stall, followed by a massive, muscular body.

"We're looking for Mike," I told him. "We're the new exercise riders."

"Oh, right. I'm Ben," he said. Ben helped us find the trainer, a dark-haired man with a mustache, and we introduced ourselves. As usual, my name took a couple of tries.

"Tay-a," Mike said finally. "Okay, let's get you started. Lori said you're not very experienced, right?"

We nodded our assent. I wondered if Teri was feeling as suddenly petrified as I was. 'Not very experienced' was so inaccurate it was almost a lie... I'd done it once.

"All right, we'll start you off on some quieter horses, see how you do."

We followed Mike down the shedrow; he disappeared into a stall while Teri and I waited in the doorway.

"Who's gonna get on this one? His name's Danger Bay."

Teri and I exchanged a glance. Her green eyes were wide in her pale face.

"I'll take him," I volunteered, praying that his name wasn't indicative of anything.

"Come on, then." Mike waved me forward cheerfully. "I'll give you a leg up, then we'll get Teri mounted. One of our regular riders will go out with you to keep you outta trouble."

He tossed me expertly into the saddle. Or what passed for a saddle at the track—it was tiny and thin; I pulled my legs up to put my feet into the ridiculously short stirrups. My hands were clammy inside my gloves, and I hoped my trembling wouldn't show. It seemed only seconds before Teri and Rob, the regular exercise rider, joined us and we headed toward the track. Rob chatted with us in a friendly way; he was cute, not much older than us, and seemed to understand our nervousness.

"Don't worry, we won't let nothin' happen to ya." He grinned as we got close. "Just stick with me."

My mount tensed as soon as his feet hit the track, and I felt weak with fear. I shortened my reins and trotted off after Rob's horse, feeling unfamiliar muscles working already. As we started to canter I thought frantically about what I'd learned. Rob's horse was pulling ahead; I crouched a bit lower over my mount's neck, and felt a rush of pure exhilaration as he smoothly lengthened his stride into a gallop. The wind was freezing on my face, and my eyes were streaming. I could feel the pounding of my horses' hooves reverberating through my chest. It was a good feeling, despite the fact that I was also gasping for air.

By the time Rob slowed his horse to a jog, my arms, back and legs were all screaming in protest. I didn't how I was going to get through the morning—this was only my first horse.

"That was pretty good." He smiled at us. "How do you feel?"

"Petrified." Teri grinned at him.

"Yeah," I laughed my agreement. Petrified, but also electrified. We laughed and joked our way back to the barn, riding the high of having survived. It hit me for the first time that there was a very real risk of getting injured doing this job. And if that happened there wouldn't be any way to hide it... which would mean definite follow-up injuries for me. Oh well, it was too late to worry about that now, I reasoned.

By the time we left for school, I had ridden four more horses. I pulled off my gloves in the car to find that my hands were bleeding. Teri was hurting too; we were both pretty fit from riding, but the physical demands of galloping were on an entirely different level. I fell

18

asleep during my last afternoon class. On the bright side, Dec hadn't noticed my absence that morning, so I was probably safe for the rest of the week. Gran was staying with us, and she wasn't an early riser.

The next morning we were better prepared. I wore more layers; I had underestimated not only how cold it was at five a.m., but also how hot I would get while galloping. We were less nervous, too, and got acquainted with the riders, grooms and hotwalkers. Rob was especially nice, as helpful and kind as he'd been the day before.

By the end of the morning I was starting to suspect that maybe Dec had a point about the racetrack. For one thing, I'd walked into a stall to find a groom casually rolling a joint.

"Don't worry, it's not for now," he'd said, grinning. "There's no smoking here. You're welcome to join me afterward, though."

I was also learning a lot of new words, mostly of the kind that I wouldn't dare use at home. My biggest concern, though, was the horses. They were worked so hard at such a young age, it was a miracle that any of them stayed sound. And from what I had heard, many of them didn't.

On Wednesday I could barely crawl out of bed when the alarm went off, and when I did, everything hurt. I was on my second horse before my muscles loosened up; Teri and I were walking our horses back to the barn, having just galloped without Rob for the first time.

"Oh, crap," I muttered, trying not to transmit my sudden tension to the filly I was riding. "What is *he* doing here?"

"Who?" Teri looked around; I nodded in the direction of the shedrow. Jaden was planted outside it, his arms crossed and his posture rigid.

"Uh-oh... he wouldn't tell on us, would he?" She looked only slightly less apprehensive than I felt.

"I don't know—I don't actually know him that well," I said worriedly.

We dismounted at the shedrow. I patted my filly before the groom took her, then jumped as a low voice spoke behind me.

"Can I have a word with you, please?" He sounded tense.

"Um, sure." I glanced at Teri. I wished her face didn't look so guilty.

My mind was working furiously, but I didn't come up with any brilliant cover stories as I followed Jaden to the parking area, where he turned and resumed his arms-crossed stance. I made an effort not to let

19

his disapproving look raise my hackles—losing my temper now would be the opposite of helpful. Instead, I tried to affect nonchalance, hooking my thumbs into my chaps and looking him straight in the eye.

"Hey Jaden, what's up?"

He didn't say anything at first, his eyes roaming over my face searchingly. I noticed they were a very unusual color; mainly a light, limpid brown, but brightened strikingly by numerous flecks of gold. I didn't know what to call it—hazel didn't seem exotic enough.

"What are you doing here, Tea?"

The question startled me. I'd gotten distracted by his remarkable eyes... how could I never have noticed them before?

"Galloping some horses... why?" I tried to look innocently confused by his question.

"So you have permission to be here?"

"What are you doing here?" I took the offensive, eyeing him suspiciously.

He rolled his eyes. "*I* came to look at a horse. A polo prospect." He was still watching me, unsmiling. The girls are right, I thought, he really is good-looking. In a superior, aggravating sort of way.

"Tea, the track isn't a safe place. And I'm not just referring to the riding, though that's exceedingly dangerous. The backstretch itself is... sketchy. I'm willing to bet that Dec doesn't know you're here."

I gazed at him appraisingly. "What if he doesn't? Are you planning to enlighten him?"

"Unless you promise me you'll quit, then, yes." The threat in his tone was unmistakeable; I could see the beginnings of anger sparking in his eyes.

"Why? What business is it of yours?" I demanded. Despite my efforts, my nervousness was giving way to my temper now. "I need this job, and I'm old enough to handle the risks, thank you very much."

"You don't know what you're talking about," he said coldly. "There are far safer ways of earning money. And I'm family—therefore you *are* my business."

We were both leaning in, our faces a foot apart, glaring at each other.

"Tea!" Mike's voice broke the standoff. "Are you getting on any more horses this morning? Or are you too busy with your boyfriend?" He grinned at me.

20

"Sorry, Mike. Be right there." I took a deep breath and tried a new tack. "Look, Jaden, this job is really important to me. And I won't be doing it much longer-"

"Let me guess—just until Dec comes home?" He raised a brow, daring me to deny it.

"Can't you just be reasonable about this and look the other way for a few days?"

"No, I can't," he said flatly. "That wouldn't be a 'reasonable' response at all, given the risks involved." I gazed at the hard angles of his face and felt a surge of intense dislike toward him—what gave him the right to meddle in my life, anyway?

I considered quickly. I could only see two options: Option One, quit the job, and forfeit my chance to go to the Royal. I didn't like the sound of option one at all. Option Two, keep the job... which meant I'd have to lie, because Dec simply could not find out about me working at the track. Ever.

I threw up my hands. "Fine," I said in a low, curt voice. "I'll quit. But I can't very well leave them stranded... just let me finish up today. Please." I tried to soften my voice at the end.

He considered me silently for a moment, while I attempted to keep the nervousness out of my face. His expression relaxed as he finally conceded.

"All right. As long as today is your last day."

I sighed in relief as we turned and headed back to the barn. I was counting on the fact that Jaden would believe me... I mean, he did live over an hour away. Surely he wouldn't drive all the way back here. I waited until we were driving to school to tell Teri about Jaden's ultimatum.

"Oh no," she exclaimed, looking scared. "What are we going to do?"

"Nothing." I shrugged. "I've already talked to Mike about it, he says he'll play dumb if anyone calls asking for us. I'm going to risk it, personally. I'm pretty sure Jaden won't tell on you, in any case—it's me he's harassing. Stupid, self-important meddler." I spat the last few words.

School today would have been slightly better—I was getting used to the insanely early hours, though my muscles still ached—but for the new, gnawing worry that Jaden would somehow realize my deception. I told myself it wasn't likely... after all, why would he expend the energy to check up on me? He barely knew me. Yet I was still uneasy.

The next day passed uneventfully, except that I got bitten on the arm by a big colt. My attention had lapsed because I was looking over my shoulder, worrying about being discovered, and I irrationally blamed the blooming dark bruise on Jaden. After work, the school day seemed endless. I was too tired to pay attention in class.

I was relieved when Friday arrived; not only would I be getting a lot more sleep after today, but the odds of my being safe from discovery were improving by the minute. Dawn was just breaking as we got to the racetrack, the barns and a few horses exquisitely silhouetted by pink and coral streaks low in the sky.

We were greeted cheerily by all the grooms, who propositioned us as usual, and by now we could easily joke back. Ben threw me up onto my first mount. My soreness from earlier in the week was beginning to fade, and I trotted off happily to follow Mike's orders to gallop Bailey, a chestnut filly, for six furlongs.

Bailey went well, and I walked her back to the barn alone, humming. But as we came within sight of the barn, my humming—and my heart—stopped. Jaden was leaning casually against the outer wall, watching me. I tried to pull up the confused filly, but she skittered sideways and tossed her head up. She knew her routine, and she wanted to go home to her breakfast. My heart was banging loudly against my ribcage now. Dec was going to find out. I was as good as dead. Bailey, who had been dancing around in increasing agitation, suddenly decided she'd had enough and stood up on her hind legs. I threw myself forward onto her neck; when she came down I kicked my feet out of the stirrups—much safer on a rearing horse—and tried to drive her forward, but she reared again, higher this time, standing straight up until I was scared that she would go over backward. All at once a hand grabbed my wrist and yanked me out of the saddle. I fell sideways; Jaden broke my fall with his arm and shoved me out of the way in one motion. He turned to deal with Bailey, whose reins he held in his other hand; the force of his push propelled me to the ground.

It didn't take him long to gentle the filly, and he turned to survey me irately. Without a word, he extended a hand to help me up. I felt a jolt when I took it, as though he was so angry his very skin wanted to shock me. He jerked hard; I flew upward and nearly overbalanced again, but his hand steadied me. My fear and adrenaline made me aggressive.

"You scared my horse," I accused him.

"I didn't make the horse rear, Tea. Your own guilty conscience did that," he said scornfully. His eyes were blazing—I actually took a step backward before I caught myself. When he headed for the barn I followed reluctantly.

Back at the barn, Ben stepped out to take Bailey.

"It's never a good sign when the rider comes back on foot." He laughed. "Did she give you a hard time?" He spoke to me but eyed Jaden curiously.

"No, she galloped really well, it was my fault," I said as normally as I could. I noticed Teri staring at us, looking shocked and pale.

Jaden turned to me and grabbed my arm.

"Let's go," he said, his voice hard.

"No, wait..." I struggled to free myself and he tightened his grip, digging his fingers painfully into my fresh bruise.

"Ow! Let go!" I yelped.

He dropped his hand; at the sound of my cry, Mike, Ben and a Jamaican groom whose name I couldn't recall stepped out and advanced on us. I noticed with surprise that they looked rather menacing, but Jaden seemed entirely unfazed.

"What's going on here?" Mike demanded. "You okay, doll?" He peered at me in concern.

"Yeah," I muttered. This was getting embarrassing.

Jaden extended his hand. "It's Mike Lambert, isn't it? I'm Jaden Foster. I think you know my uncle, Declan Foster?"

Mike gave a curt nod as he shook Jaden's hand. "Yup, I know him. What's that got to do with Tea here?"

"She's his daughter. Dec isn't aware that Tea's been working here, and I know he wouldn't approve, so I think it's best if she comes with me."

Surprise crept into Mike's expression while Jaden spoke. He looked at me somewhat accusingly. "Is that true?"

I nodded glumly.

"Well then, kid, I think you'd better go with your cousin here, before you get yourself into trouble."

The men disappeared back into the barn, and after I'd shrugged at her apologetically, Teri followed them, avoiding Jaden's eye. When

Jaden took my arm again I jerked it away furiously. He was self-righteous, interfering, and arrogant, and I'd had enough.

"I'm not going," I fumed. "You're going to tell Dec anyway—there's nothing I can do about that—but there is absolutely no reason for me to go anywhere with *you*."

He exhaled sharply and glared at me. "Tea, I'm not discussing this with you. You have two options: you can leave under your own power, or I'll carry you. Which will it be?"

"I'll take door number three. Staying," I argued stubbornly.

He didn't say a word, just grabbed me and threw me over his shoulder in one easy movement. I was stunned, mortified, and didn't want to make an even greater scene, so I didn't struggle. I did make use of my new vocabulary, though, and kept up a satisfying stream of profanities in a low voice that only he could hear, until he tossed me into his car. He didn't speak during the drive, other than to spend a few minutes castigating me for lying to him. Besides those pleasantries, we spent the time in seething silence.

He pulled up to the school; I was reaching for the door handle when he spoke.

"Tea."

"What," I muttered without turning.

"Look, I know you think I'm a huge jerk for doing this-"

"That's an understatement."

"-and this is beyond cliché, but it's for your own good. Really."

I faced him. "It won't be for my good if Dec finds out," I said bleakly. I couldn't bring myself to ask him, again, not to say anything. I had too much pride, for one thing, and in any case something about his expression told me it would be futile.

I got out, not even bothering to slam the door. My anger had burnt itself out, and I felt a cold dread settle into its place. Thanks to Jaden's meddling I was insanely early for school, and my schoolbag was still in Teri's car, so I couldn't even fill the time by catching up on my neglected homework.

Seth got to school before Teri did, and I moped over to meet our bus. He took one look at my face and guessed what had happened.

"Aw, neeps," he said, and I had to grin. Only Seth could make me smile at a time like this. We weren't allowed to swear at home, so we had developed our own vernacular of made-up oaths; 'neeps' was the worst one—our childhood version of the "F" word. I had told Seth about

Jaden's surprise appearance on Wednesday—Seth and I shared everything—and he had agreed with my assessment that the risk was small.

He put his arm around my shoulders and gave me a reassuring squeeze.

"Well, it ain't over yet. Maybe he won't tell," he said hopefully.

I didn't have the heart to disabuse him of that happy notion, but I was sure he was wrong. We set off to our separate homerooms, Seth giving me an encouraging smile first. Teri ran into our class at the last minute, breathless; she handed me my bag and threw herself into the seat next to mine. We were in the back row, so we could manage a careful, whispered conversation.

"Is he going to tell?" she asked worriedly.

"I think so." I couldn't help wincing as I said it. "But don't worry, I'll keep you out of it. I'll tell Dec someone from the track drove me, if he asks."

Two

When we got off the bus I spotted Dec's truck in front of the shed. He was home, then... at least I wouldn't have to wait for hours, riddled with anxiety about whether I was busted. I glanced at Seth.

"If he knows, leave the house, okay? Please?"

There was no reason for Seth to suffer along with me. He nodded dumbly, his face completely serious for once.

We had barely stepped into the house when Dec came out of the kitchen.

"Tea." The low, menacing way he said my name sent a chill down my back. Yup, he knew.

"I want you in my office. Now." He stalked away without a backward glance.

I dropped my schoolbag and slowly kicked off my shoes. I looked at Seth; his face was pale.

"Maybe I should talk to him," he suggested.

"No! You know it won't work... you'll only get yourself in trouble. Just go. I'll be fine." We both knew the last part was a lie, but he wheeled and went out, slamming the door behind him.

I squared my shoulders and reminded myself sternly that I'd known full well what the consequences would be if I were caught, so there was no reason to panic. I'd made my money—if this was the price of getting to the Royal, so be it.

I went through the living room and into the office. Dec was in front of the desk, hands locked on hips, his glare following me as I moved to stand before him. I took deep breaths, trying to stay calm, but I could feel adrenaline starting to make me shake. I kept my eyes down.

"Jaden called today," he said, his voice without inflection. I felt a flare of outright hatred at the sound of the name. "He told me something so implausible that at first, I didn't believe him."

Dec paused, maybe to assess my reaction, but I didn't move.

"He told me you've been working at the track this entire week," he continued. His voice was a growl now. "Every morning. Risking your life, without us even knowing where you were. Lying to me, and to your grandmother."

Please God, I thought, let Jaden not have said anything about lying to him, too. If Dec knew that I'd been caught once, and had insisted on going back... that would be almost worse to him than going to the track in the first place. A repeat offense, in a sense.

"Is it true?" he demanded.

"Yes, sir," I whispered. I didn't bother trying to make excuses; there were none, and it would only make him madder.

Dec unbuckled his belt. He didn't make a production of it, the way some people would have. My shaking increased as I walked to the end of the desk and braced my hands on its dark wood surface. I clenched my teeth hard—I didn't want to make any noise—and tried to distract myself from the blows by reliving the adrenaline-soaked rush of galloping hell-bent down the racetrack. The memories were still vivid, thank God—I was starting to think that Dec was trying to set a new world record. When it was over I turned away from him. I hated crying when he hit me, but I couldn't help it this time. I did my best to keep it quiet.

"One more thing, Tea," he spoke behind me. His voice was cold. "Jaden says that he warned you on Wednesday to quit, yet you persisted in going back anyway. So you can forget about the Royal this year—you're not going."

I gasped and whirled around, furiously blinking away tears so that I could see.

"But, Dec... the Royal... you can't! Please..." I pleaded, my voice breaking.

His face was implacable, his eyes like chips of ice. "I can and I am. Now get out of here."

I stumbled up to my room. Once there I started pacing; I was adrenalized, and my mind whirled chaotically. I wasn't concerned about the strapping, though it was obviously ridiculous. I was sixteen, not six. Seth and I were resigned to it; Dec had given us the 'as long as you're under my roof' speech often enough that we knew he wouldn't change. What killed me was the Royal—I couldn't believe he was serious. For the past two years I'd had virtually no social life; all I did was ride and work in the barn, and he knew how hard I'd been training. He also knew I wanted to make a career of riding jumpers, although he didn't approve. I wondered how much his decision had been influenced

27

by his desire to see me go to university instead of ride horses for a living... but no matter the answer, this was a disaster. He could not have imposed a worse punishment, and all because of that pretentious ass, Jaden. Of course someone like him, moving in the prosperous circles of polo, would have no idea why I'd taken the risk of going to the track, I thought bitterly. I doubted that he had ever struggled or suffered a day in his life. A caustic hatred for him seared through my veins; I could taste it, hot and metallic, in my mouth.

That evening I was lying on the bed, trying to read, when Seth came in and threw himself into the chair. He crossed his arms over his chest; he looked uncharacteristically grouchy.

"So I'm grounded for two weeks," he announced.

"What?" I yelped. "Why?"

He considered me carefully for a moment.

"For not telling on you," he said finally.

"I—but—that's so unfair!" I was overcome by chagrin. The last thing I wanted was to get Seth in trouble. He nodded.

"I'm sorry, Seth," I said fervently. "I'll talk to Dec, I'll make him take it back. I'll beg if I have to."

"Whoa, let's not get crazy here." He grinned, suddenly himself again.

As luck would have it—mine, anyway—I had a lesson with my coach, Karen, the next morning. I was almost more afraid to face her than I had been of Dec. Karen was an old friend of Dec's, which is why we were lucky enough to have her teach at Shady Lane Stables. She was a former National Team member, one of the youngest ever selected, but the pressures of success had driven her down the path of substance abuse. When she was clean again she stuck mainly to coaching. She was a very gifted coach, but extremely tough and demanding—she had been known to make grown men cry in her lessons. She was thrilled that I had finally qualified for the Royal with a jumper. I'd qualified before, in the pony hunter divisions, but I hadn't gone because that was the year my mother got sick. My chances always depended on the horses we had in training, since I hadn't had one of my own to show, until Blaze this year.

I made my way stiffly down to the barn the next morning.

"Hey Ter, hey Jules," I greeted the girls unenthusiastically. They were in the aisle, grooming Jazz and Picasso.

28

Teri looked at me in alarm. "I guess I can assume the worst, huh," she said sympathetically.

I nodded glumly.

"What would that be?" Julia queried.

"Dec found out about Tea working at the track," Teri told her when I didn't answer.

"Omigod—so are you grounded for life, or what?" Julia asked.

"Worse," I said miserably, "I'm grounded for the Royal."

My friends' expressions of horrified shock had barely formed when a sharp voice behind me demanded, "What?!"

I turned slowly to face Karen. For a woman of average height and build, she could be remarkably imposing sometimes. Like now.

"I'm really sorry, Karen, but I can't go to the Royal," I muttered, not looking at her.

"Why the hell not?"

"I'm being punished," I mumbled.

"What for? What can you possibly have—oh, never mind, I'm going to talk to that man." She marched away, grumbling.

"Oh, Tea, I'm so sorry," Teri said. She put her arm around me. "But on the bright side, at least you didn't get your butt whupped."

"If you call that a bright side," I said darkly. I felt bad about the fib, but I thought the humiliation of telling the truth would feel worse. "Oh, and you'll never guess—Seth's grounded too, for not telling on me."

"Dec's really strict, isn't he," Julia said, her flawless features thoughtful. "It's like he's from another century or something. Have you ever thought about sitting down with him and discussing discipline options? You know, things that would work for both of you?"

I gazed at her in disbelief. "Yeah... that's not going to happen," I said with finality.

I couldn't imagine Julia's cultured, progressive parents ever laying a hand on her, so maybe the suggestion was within the realm of possibility in her world. My reality, though, was obviously different.

Karen tramped back in, looking harassed.

"Way to go, kid. The racetrack?" She scowled at me. "He won't budge."

At my dejected look, she softened a bit.

"Well, you never know. Maybe a miracle will happen and he'll change his mind... try to be an absolute angel for the next couple of weeks, okay?" she wheedled. "Who are you riding today?"

"Oh, um, I can't ride today. I hurt my knee."

Teri gave me a startled look of sudden understanding, but I knew she wouldn't say anything until we could speak in private. I wished them a good ride and trudged back to the house to do some homework. I had lessons to teach that afternoon and most of Sunday; I figured I might as well put my extra time to good use.

I'd been avoiding Dec since the day before, but on my way inside I bumped into him. He was irate.

"Did you send Karen in here to try to change my mind?" he asked accusingly.

"I... no, of course not," I stammered. It hadn't even occurred to me that he would see it that way. "It was her idea to come talk to you."

"Well, I hope you realize it was a pointless attempt," he said. He was frowning, his stocky form tense. I felt a piercing pain at his words, but I nodded and headed for the stairs.

Dec and I barely spoke for the next three days. Seth, always the peacemaker, did his best to lessen the tension, but with only spotty success. When Gran came to make dinner on Monday she noticed too; I overheard her and Dec in the kitchen.

"Declan, what's going on? You and Tea seem to be at odds."

He explained what I'd done and that as a consequence, I wasn't allowed to compete at the Royal. I put on my shoes while I eavesdropped, then stood poised by the front door, ready to run out.

"That seems rather severe," Gran was saying. Hope raised its head feebly within me. "After all, Tea showing at the Royal will benefit us all. The stable needs the exposure."

"That may be, but what *I* need is to know those kids will obey me, and not behave outrageously the minute my back is turned. It may seem cruel, but I need to make this point very clearly. We don't want another Jaden on our hands."

Jaden again. I had no idea what he'd done, but apparently my missing the Royal was thanks to him in more ways than one.

By Wednesday I was riding again; I had to get Blaze ready for a show that weekend. As we were cooling down, though, I felt a moment of doubt. I found Dec in the kitchen making coffee, and kept the counter between us as I spoke.

"The Talbot Fall Fair is this weekend," I informed him unnecessarily. He was driving the trailer, I was sure he hadn't forgotten.

30

"I remember," he answered normally. He looked at me but didn't smile.

"Am I still allowed to ride Blaze?" I muttered.

"Sure. It's only the Royal that you're grounded for." Only the Royal. He said it so matter-of-factly. Only the show that I'd been striving toward for my entire competitive career—about seven years. I felt pierced afresh at the thought.

"About that... Dec..." I looked up, suddenly, into his eyes. I couldn't maintain my pretense of toughness anymore. He watched me impassively. "Isn't there any way I can still go?"

He walked around the counter to face me. My heart plummeted before he spoke; I could read the denial in his expression.

"Punishment is supposed to hurt, Tea. I wouldn't be a very good parent if I let you get away with that kind of dangerous behavior."

"But... what's the point? It's not like I'll do it again." I stared unseeingly at the floor tiles as I spoke.

He hesitated. "I've seen where this type of recklessness leads, Tea, and I don't want you going there. The grounding stands." He sounded almost sympathetic, but I didn't look at him, and after a moment he walked out. I felt nearly more dejected than when he'd first dropped the bombshell on me; this time, there was no hope of appeal. I remembered belatedly that I should have pleaded Seth's case, but I didn't have another attempt in me. I resolved to try the next day.

Teri and I stayed up late the night before the show, braiding the horses' manes and tails. The next morning we groaned our way out of bed at five-thirty to go feed the horses who were competing.

At the showgrounds, we unloaded the horses before Dec unhooked the gooseneck trailer from his truck; he didn't usually stay at the shows unless they were too far to drive back.

"Good luck." He smiled at Teri and the two students who had arrived so far.

He approached me; his smile disappeared before his eyes found mine. "Tea—stay out of trouble. I mean it."

I nodded, trying to ignore the disappointment I felt at his parting words. He hadn't wished *me* luck. My mood soon lightened, though, because I loved the Fall fair. It reminded me of the reasons I'd started competing, at age ten: for the sheer fun and excitement of it. At the fair there was no pressure, no points to accumulate toward year-end standings, and no big-name riders and trainers watching my every move. And it was good experience for Blaze, because of the strange sights and sounds that he wouldn't encounter at most shows, like a midway with loud, wild rides, and an assortment of farm animals parading by at regular intervals. It was an ideal place to teach a young horse to focus no matter what was going on around him.

The day started off well when Emma won the short-stirrup class aboard Chocolate Chip.

"I'm going to get us some lunch," Seth announced around midday. "Can I get you something?"

"Yeah, a hot dog and some fries would be great, thanks," Teri said.

"Can you get me the large fries, please? And don't forget the ketchup," I reminded Seth. Blaze absolutely loved those greasy horse show fries, especially with ketchup. It used to worry me that he ate them—horses have sensitive stomachs and French fries are far from their ideal diet—but he convinced me over time. He was sneaky and relentless; he would stick his head over my shoulder or around my body and grab some fries when he thought I wasn't looking, and since they never seemed to make him sick, I relented and allowed him some at every show. I untied him and he hung out next to me, sharing our fries, while I coached.

The show was a first-time experience for some of my students, so I had to explain the basics. "You're all riding in Hunter classes, so you'll be judged on style. The judge will look at how consistent your horse's pace is, how they use their bodies when jumping—even their grooming and tack, and your clothing, counts. In the jumper classes, on the other hand, only performance matters—how many rails the horse knocks down, how fast they go, and whether they refuse any obstacles. You need more experience to compete in the jumper divisions, because the courses are bigger, more complex and more technical."

Blaze was in a good mood as we warmed up for his jumper class. I worked on keeping him focused; he was such a happy, confident horse that his approach to jumping was downright brazen, especially considering how green he still was. I loved his courage, though, and I trusted him implicitly. He had never refused a fence. Our trust and confidence in each other probably stemmed from the fact that we'd been together since he was a year old; we'd done a lot of growing up together.

When it was our turn we walked into the ring like we owned it.

32

"Number 372, Tea Everson, riding Blaze of Glory," the announcer said. I felt the usual spurt of adrenaline as we picked up a canter, but also, for the first time, an oddly calm sense of assurance. As though Blaze and I were more than equal to this course. We jumped the first fence and turned to approach a line on the diagonal. I had to shorten Blaze's stride to squeeze in three of them, but he compressed his body easily and sailed over the oxer at the end. The next fence was an odd-looking wall, but he barely noticed it, just bounded over as though he had one at home, too. My heart was soaring. It felt as though Blaze and I were one being, reading each other's every intention perfectly and adjusting to each other's bodies instantaneously. There were twelve fences in all, and as we approached the last one I wished the course were longer—this feeling of oneness was so incredible that I wanted to prolong the moment. I barely registered the cheer that went up as we flew over the final vertical; I was too busy patting Blaze over and over as he ambled out of the ring, my heart overflowing with love for him.

We won the class.

There wasn't much prize money, but somehow this win felt significant to me. We'd won classes at bigger shows, but I'd been anxious and tense while riding those courses. This was the first time that I truly felt we could handle the big time, when it came. I'd gotten a taste of what it must feel like to be a seasoned performer on a 'made' horse, and I loved it.

After Blaze was cooled off I tied him up at the trailer with some hay in a net, and set off with Teri to explore the fair. We got some mini doughnuts to celebrate our day—our barn had cleaned up at the show. I was looking forward to showing Dec all the ribbons we'd won. In the back of my mind shone a glimmer of hope that if he saw how hard I'd worked and how successful we'd been, he might reconsider his Royal ban. It was a faint glimmer, though, and I did my best to ignore it.

We went on a couple of rides before concluding that violent motion was not the ideal follow-up to greasy doughnuts. We decided to go investigate the auction instead. The building was run-down, the wooden pens chewed up by generations of nervous teeth, and the entire place was pervaded by the acrid smell of urine. We walked through the holding pen area, patting pigs and calves and goats and even a llama. Eventually we came to the wooden bleachers above the ring where the animals were auctioned off. We didn't stay long; we had to prepare the horses for the journey home.

"What the hell, Tea?" Seth's voice snapped loudly as we came into sight.

I started at the sound. Seth so rarely got upset about anything that it was a shock to hear that tone coming from him. He was glaring from me to the small, woebegone donkey I was leading. Teri threw me an "I told you so" look and hurried off to get Picasso ready.

"I had to, Seth," I began apologetically.

"No, you didn't!" he interrupted angrily. "In case you've forgotten, I'm still grounded from the last time you ticked Dec off." My talk with Dec about un-grounding Seth hadn't gone well.

I averted my gaze, feeling guilty.

"I know, li'l brother. And I'm sorry about that, but the meat man was going to buy this little guy. And he's so young, only a yearling, I think..."

Seth was still glaring. "Do these words ring a bell for you at all? 'We are not going home with any more animals than we left with'."

Those had, in fact, been Dec's exact, sternly delivered words to me that morning. I sighed and gave Seth a beseeching look; his glare slowly dissolved.

"Aw, crap, Sis," he muttered. "I just don't want you to get hurt... and I'd rather not be grounded till I'm thirty, either."

It wasn't so bad, really. Dec's face went through a few color changes when he first saw the donkey, but we were in a public place, so he kept his voice in the low bellow range. However, the strain we'd experienced over the past week was something new to us, and he didn't seem inclined to exacerbate it. He kept the lecture short, and I ended up grounded for the rest of the month, or until I found the donkey a new home, whichever came first. Worst case scenario, I was looking at three weeks—I could live with that.

Romeo, as we named him, adjusted quickly to life at the barn, and had a very nice personality, inquisitive and affectionate—even Dec could be caught petting him. My relationship with Dec was essentially back to normal, and even though he was peeved by Romeo's presence, he didn't often bring it up.

"Gran, what do I put in the potatoes again?" I called out.

It was Thanksgiving Monday, and we were expecting most of our family for dinner. Gran had stayed over the previous night, and Seth and I were helping her; luckily Monday was the school horses' day off. I

34

was making mashed potatoes—probably because it was hard to mess up.

"Just some butter and milk, dear. And then you can get some fresh air, if you like."

I was relieved at the prospect of getting outside, but as I headed for the front door, someone came in. Someone I really didn't want to see.

"Hello, Tea," Jaden greeted me pleasantly.

I appraised him coldly. "Judas."

"Tea!" Dec's exasperated voice came from right behind me. Of course. "Apologize," he commanded.

"It's okay," Jaden said, watching me. "I deserve that much."

I noticed that his mouth was twitching. My temper flared—he had practically ruined my year, yet he apparently found the whole thing amusing. I felt a momentary but powerful urge to slap that arrogant face, and thought I'd better remove myself from temptation before I ended up in more trouble. I pushed past him and stomped out of the house.

The crisp air was calming. I strolled around aimlessly, admiring the fall colors, until Romeo's incessant braying got annoying and I went to see him.

"Hey buddy," I said as I gave him a scratch. "Sorry you can't come out today. We're expecting too many people who don't understand about closing gates."

My extended family weren't used to thinking about such things; none of them were used to dealing with animals larger than housepets. Well, except for Jaden, I remembered reluctantly, and I wished I didn't have to count him as family. His mother, Paloma, was my favorite aunt—she was smart, vivacious, beautiful, and always interested in what Seth and I were up to. I didn't know how she had managed to produce such an irritating son.

I heard Seth coming down the aisle with our cousin Stacey and her parents.

"It's time to go in, Sis," Seth informed me, "but Stacey wanted to see Romeo first."

And heaven forbid Princess Stacey not get what she wants, I thought. She leaned gingerly into the stall; I doubted she'd actually set a designer-clad foot inside it, but her startling aquamarine eyes moved over Romeo with interest. Her brown hair was looking almost blond

35

from all the highlights. She reached out and gave Romeo a tentative pat, her long, manicured nails contrasting sharply with my short work-roughened ones. She really was very pretty, I mused. She didn't need that always-perfect makeup and hair. In both style and appearance she took after her mother, my Aunt Penny, who was Dec's younger sister. The effect was markedly different, though, since Stacey was only fifteen—a year younger than me.

"What made you get a donkey, Uncle Dec?" Stacey asked as soon as we sat down. "He's really cute."

"He may be cute, but he's not staying. Tea got him, and she has to find him a new home," Dec said. He briefly recounted the story of my purchase.

"Oh! I forgot to tell you—the Donkey Sanctuary of Canada agreed to take him," I said. "So... does that mean I'm un-grounded?" I added hopefully.

Dec shook his head. "Not until the last hoof is off the property."

"Come now, Dec, don't tell me you grounded her for that?" Uncle Robert, Stacey's father, chided. "It sounds like it was just an impulse."

"And a charitable one, at that," Jaden added.

I didn't look at him; I hoped he wasn't trying to suck up, because if he was, it was a pathetically weak attempt.

"Well, Tea needs to learn some impulse control," Dec growled. "Last year she came home from the fair with sheep. Sheep, plural. This isn't a petting zoo."

"But Dec, she won't be grounded on our birthday, will she?" Seth asked. I stole a glance at him; his face was all wide-eyed innocence, but I knew better. He was putting Dec on the spot so I'd be liberated.

Dec knew when he was outmaneuvered; he grinned at me ruefully. "Looks like you're free on your birthday, kiddo."

All eight of us were squeezed around the table in the dining room. It was the same number as usual, only Jaden sat in his mother's place, as Aunt Paloma had gone to visit her daughter. I could feel Blue stepping on my toes periodically as she scavenged, and I waited for the chance to sneak her something.

"It's too bad your mom and sister couldn't be here, Jaden," amiable, balding Uncle Robert said. "It's nice to spend Thanksgiving in the country. Do you go into the city much, Dec?"

"Once in a while. But I don't really enjoy going, to be honest."

"Yeah, Tea's the only one who likes the city," Seth offered.

Out of the corner of my eye I noticed Jaden glance at me with interest. I ignored him.

"What do you like about the city, Tea?" Uncle Robert asked.

I tried to put my attraction into words. "I don't know, exactly... it's so vibrant. I like the energy, and all the things to do, and the diversity—walking through the city is like going on a mini world tour. After all, Toronto's the most multi-cultural city in the world; we're fortunate to live close enough to experience that, I think."

Jaden gave me a doubtful look. "I don't know about that."

"I suspect there's a lot you don't know," I told him icily.

His eyes narrowed. "What I mean is, I've never heard that Toronto is the most multi-cultural city in the world. Where did you unearth that little factoid?"

I just stared at him in disbelief—his hubris seemed to know no bounds.

"At a loss for words?" he taunted.

It was my turn to narrow my eyes. "No. It's just that your arrogance is leaving me breathless."

Seth kicked me under the table and made a face to lighten my mood. I took a deep breath before turning back to Jaden.

"Is the United Nations a credible enough source for you?" I asked him. I tried to filter the scorn out of my voice as much as possible.

He nodded slowly. "If they really said that, then yes."

Seth snorted. "I wouldn't question the walking encyclopedia here, dude," he told Jaden. "I swear our mother should have named her Britannica."

There was a smattering of laughter, and the hum of conversation resumed. I met Jaden's speculative look with a contemptuous one, then went back to ignoring him.

After dinner I volunteered to clean up—I didn't feel much like socializing. I had just started the dishwasher when I heard the sounds of an argument outside. I went to the door that led outside from the kitchen. The angry voices were nearby, and when I recognized one of them as Seth's I yanked the door open and stepped quickly onto the small deck.

Seth was standing with his fists clenched at his sides, looking angrier than I'd seen him in a long time. Jaden was facing him, distraught. He was running his hand through his hair. He glanced at me for a second, his face pained, before turning and striding away.

"What's up, bro?" I asked, watching Jaden's hurried pace carry him quickly around the corner. "Are you okay?"

Seth was already relaxing as he loped over to join me; he never stayed mad for long. We sat on the steps.

"Yeah, I'm cool. I was just giving our dear cousin a piece of my mind for squealing on you."

"Oh. So what, was he telling you how justified he was?" I couldn't help the derision that leaked into my voice.

Seth glanced at me. "No. He didn't believe that Dec took his belt to you."

"What?" I yelped, "You told him about that?"

He shrugged. "Why not? I thought he should know all the trouble he caused."

"Because it's embarrassing, that's why! And anyway, I don't care about that nearly as much as missing the Royal."

"Oh, I told him about that, too. To be fair, he did seem to feel really bad about it... I don't think he'll be tattling again anytime soon." He grinned at me, his eyes sparkling like a kid's, and I couldn't help smiling back.

I taught a lesson after school the next day. I was headed back to the house when the sound of galloping hoofbeats made me spin around, and I laughed as a big black and copper blur dug in his feet and slid to a stop in front of me. I reached out to pat him; he had stopped near enough for me to touch.

"You cut it kind of close there, don't you think?" I asked Blaze, smiling. It was a trick he liked to play on me—he'd gallop up as though he was going to run me down, then sit on his haunches and skid to a stop just in time. It took him a while to get the timing right; when he was younger he'd actually knocked me down a few times, much to Dec's consternation. I hadn't minded, though. I knew it was all in fun.

Blaze didn't seem to recognize the purpose of the paddock fences. When he got bored in one, he simply jumped out and wandered wherever he wanted to on the property. Dec hated it. He thought it was risky to have a large horse loose among the boarders, students and cars. But I had taught Blaze not to go down the long driveway toward the road, so I didn't worry about his little treks. The only time it became an issue was when I was teaching—he sometimes jumped into the ring to see me—or when I was riding Zac, who he hated. Blaze was

38

very jealous of Zac, so I made sure the two were never out at the same time.

We had barely started dinner when Dec cleared his throat.

"There's something I need to talk to you about, Tea," he began.

I looked at him in surprise. There was something odd about his tone, he sounded almost... nervous.

"We have a possible buyer for Zac," he went on. I felt myself blanch. "She's coming to see him next Saturday. I thought you could ride him first so she can watch him go, before she gets on him."

I stared at my plate, only distantly aware of a buzzing in my ears. Zac sold. I'd been training him for a year and a half, riding five days a week in every kind of weather, all so I could compete at the Royal. Of course it was part of my job—we bought and sold horses that I trained in order to make a profit on them. I understood that, but we'd had Zac so long that I'd grown very attached to him. Too attached, apparently.

"Excuse me," I muttered. No one tried to stop me.

I ran to Zac's stall. I took deep, steadying breaths while he rested his chin on my shoulder the way he always did. I could only hope the buyer wouldn't like him, though the chances of Dec keeping him until next year's Royal were so slim as to be invisible. It was all up to Blaze now.

Saturday dawned sunny and clear, a perfect late October day. I'd met the potential buyer, Anne, briefly before mounting. She was a thin, rather mousy-looking woman in her thirties who wanted a horse to ride in amateur jumper classes. I took an instant dislike to her, naturally.

Zac went well for me, as always. Once Anne was mounted I went and sat on the fence to watch. She seemed to be a decent rider, but she was a bit stiff, especially for someone riding in the jumper divisions. She had just asked us to set up a small fence when a commotion broke out—a bay streak shot over the fence toward Zac.

"Blaze, no!" I yelled, jumping down and running toward them.

Blaze heard me and put on the brakes, but Zac had seen him coming, and Blaze had once bitten Zac on the neck while I'd been riding him. He shied violently out of the way, almost unseating his rider. She yanked on the reins and screamed—about the stupidest reaction I'd ever seen from a seasoned rider. Not that I was biased in any way.

I grabbed Blaze's halter and led him to the barn, avoiding Dec's eye. Anne didn't ride much longer; when she thanked us and left Dec walked her to the car. As he came back I braced myself, but to my surprise he put his hand on my shoulder and walked Zac and I to the barn.

"What did you think, Tea?" he inquired seriously.

I shrugged. "I didn't like her," I told him truthfully. "I think she's too nervous a rider for Zac, he needs someone calm and confident."

He nodded. "Well, she didn't say much, so I suspect she's not very interested in him. You can relax for a while."

October ended pretty well, considering. Seth and I went out for a fun, lively dinner with friends on our birthday. Dec announced that he'd match whatever we saved up toward the car we wanted. The Donkey Sanctuary people came and picked up Romeo, so I was officially free. Teri was getting excited about competing at the Royal in three weeks' time, and I tried hard to share her happiness without tainting it with my despair.

Three

I went to the Royal, in the end, as a groom for Teri. It was evening when we arrived at the stabling area, which was aptly named the Horse Palace. It was an enormous, two-storey stable housing everything from gentle, gigantic draft horses to tiny ponies, with virtually every variety of harness, breeding and jumping horse in between. Once Picasso was happy we wandered the barns and watched our idols—international jumper riders from several different countries, and their magnificent equine partners. Later we sat in the Coliseum to watch the glamorous evening event, with its attendant pomp and ceremony.

Early the next morning we were walking Picasso down the cavernous, echoing aisles to the shower stalls when we ran into Alex, a fellow competitor.

"I'll catch up with you," I told Teri. Her dad was off getting some coffee.

"I didn't see your name on the list of entries for our class," Alex said. "What happened?"

Alex was my age; we competed in the same division, with one big difference—his parents were wealthy and fully supported his riding goals, with the result that he had two well-schooled horses on the circuit, and was doing very well.

"I had a... personal conflict," I said uneasily.

"There's going to be no competition without you here," he joked, smiling. He was good-looking, slim, with dark hair and hazel eyes, and half the girls on the circuit were chasing after him. He was a bit shy, though, and he and I often hung out at the shows.

"I can't tell you how much I wish I were here to kick your butt, dude. Maybe next year. Good luck."

I was thoughtful as I joined Teri in washing Picasso. For some reason, running into Alex had driven home for me the fact that I should have been riding here—I went up against him at all the shows. I sank further and further into gloominess as the morning wore on. Karen arrived to coach Teri, and we watched, hearts racing, as Teri and

41

Picasso collected three ribbons. I was happy for Teri, but as we cared for her pony I couldn't help brooding.

I decided to get a ride back with Teri's mom rather than wait for Dec and the trailer. I asked Mrs. MacLeod to drop me off in Julien, the tiny town where the MacLeods and Kabir's family both lived—our place was only ten minutes outside of it. I wasn't sure what I was doing, exactly... I just knew that I needed some time alone to think. I went into the town's only diner, ordered hot chocolate and some fries, and tried to settle my thoughts. I couldn't, though. The more I thought about Dec's Royal ban, the angrier I got. It wasn't right that he could so easily sabotage not only the years of work I'd already invested, but also my future career. And that he could do it so cavalierly. Things would have to change, I decided, although I had no idea how I might orchestrate it. I had just noticed that it was dark outside when Kabir walked in; he sat across from me.

"Are you okay, Tea?" he asked, concerned.

"Fine, why?"

"Everyone's out looking for you. Seth asked me to check for you in town."

"Oh." I was probably in trouble, then.

"C'mon, I'll drive you home."

Seth greeted me with relief, and we were still on the porch when Jaden's car pulled in. I went into the house, determined to avoid him. I wanted to go hide in my room but I knew Dec was on his way and would want to see me... I was wrong, though. When Dec got home we were in the living room, Seth joking with Kabir and Jaden while I sat with my arms crossed, saying nothing. I jumped when I heard the door; my heart started racing while I tried frantically to remember the carefully rehearsed arguments I'd come up with that day, and which my brain now seemed to have misplaced.

Dec walked up next to me.

"Tea, go to your room," he barked.

I looked up at him in surprise. Yup, he was angry—his hands were on his hips and a scowl adorned his face. I got up, confused.

"Now, Tea," he rumbled. Seth gave me a nudge, and I decamped upstairs.

Dec avoided me the next morning before school, but my feeling of having dodged a bullet didn't last; I wanted to have this out with him. When I got home that afternoon his truck was gone, though Jaden was apparently still around. I grimaced as I trudged into the barn, but once inside I froze in shock. Anne was there—and she had Zac on the crossties. Seth came up and put his arm around me.

"I didn't want to tell you yesterday, Sis... but she bought him," he murmured.

That explained why Dec had been so lenient the day before. I stumbled to Blaze's stall and leaned against his comforting, solid warmth. At least I still had him—he was my true love, after all. Anne's nasal voice floated down the aisle, and I quickly slipped Blaze's halter on and led him outside to escape it. I climbed the fence and slid onto Blaze's back; I wanted to canter down the trail and escape the pain for a while, but it was already getting dark. And chilly. I shivered slightly as we walked aimlessly around, and hid my hands under Blaze's mane for extra warmth. I don't know how long we perambulated before Dec came into the ring. We turned to face him.

"Come inside, Tea," he said gently. Oh, no, I thought angrily. He doesn't get to start being understanding *now*.

"You should have told me."

"I didn't want to upset you before the Royal."

"Do you honestly think I could have had a worse time at the Royal?" I snapped. "Do you think it wasn't torture, knowing that Zac and I could have won that class, that you could have sold him for way more money, and that you denied us all of that just to make a point?"

"That's enough," he said sharply. "Now get off that horse—you know very well you shouldn't be riding without a helmet, especially when he's only wearing a halter."

You had to hand it to Dec; he was predictable—put him on the spot and he'd change the subject by getting mad.

"Why? You know Blaze won't do anything!" It was just more control, more orders for the sake of them, and I was not in the mood. I had meant to stay calm while we talked—so much for that strategy. Again. I took a deep breath and tried again more quietly.

"I just think we need to talk about this, Dec."

"This is neither the time nor the place."

Everything had to be on his terms, as usual. Jaden and Seth emerged from the barn and the sight of Jaden was the only spark my simmering anger needed to explode.

My eyes flickered to the paddock fence—it was about four feet high, easy enough for Blaze to manage, but I had never tried jumping

43

him bareback and bridle-less before. Dec saw my intention and started toward me.

"No, Tea!"

"Come on, baby," I whispered to Blaze, pushing him into a canter.

For once I was happy that Blaze had always disregarded the paddock fence's purpose of keeping him contained. He sailed over it easily; I heard gasps as I turned quickly to avoid the fence to the next paddock, right in front of us. Of course the smart thing to do would have been to keep going down the trail as fast as possible, and stay away until Dec had a chance to calm down. Several weeks, possibly. But I wasn't exactly known for doing the smart thing; I rode over and jumped off Blaze to stand before him. Bet he'd talk to me now.

Dec's face was brick red. He glared at me, nostrils flaring; when he tensed I was surprised to see Jaden's hand come down on his shoulder. I held Dec's stare, and was feeling the first ripple of doubt about the wisdom of my action when Seth gripped my arm and started towing me toward the barn.

"I feel like I'm trapped in a really corny after-school special," he grumbled as we stepped inside. "What was that about?"

I shook my head, sighing. "I don't know, Seth. But I'm sick of being treated like a child."

He laughed. "Oh, so that move was designed to demonstrate how mature you are? Keep it up, T, and you'll be back in a playpen in no time."

I groomed Blaze in his stall, though he didn't really need it; I wanted to draw as little attention to myself as possible. From the astonished looks on the boarders' faces, I suspected some of them had seen my ill-considered feat. I was already feeling embarrassed at the drama I'd created. Seth was right, it had been a bonehead move.

Before I was done, Jaden planted himself in the doorway.

"Why do you push his buttons like that?" he asked, his voice heavy with disapproval. "You know where it will lead."

"Mind you own business," I snapped.

"Need I remind you—we're family. You are my business."

I felt a rush of anger as I recalled the last time he'd said those words to me, at the racetrack. None of this would have happened if it weren't for him. I shot him a look of loathing and turned my back on him.

I heard him sigh.

"Look, Tea, I've been in your position, or pretty close..."

"I seriously doubt that," I muttered.

"...and there are better ways of dealing with it, more constructive ways."

I was done brushing; I stalked up and faced him in the doorway. He was blocking my way.

"Well, excuse me for failing to emulate your standard of perfection. Now let me out."

His jaw tightened, and he matched my glare for a minute before turning and marching off. I heaved a sigh. I was glad to be rid of him, but not particularly looking forward to going into the house. It couldn't be delayed indefinitely though, so after sweeping the aisle and tidying up in the tackroom I trudged morosely through the dark toward the warm yellow squares of light.

There was no sign of Dec when I went inside, but I heard Jaden's voice from the kitchen. Sheesh, I couldn't even get away from him in my own house. I stopped in the doorway; Jaden and Seth were at the table eating some of Gran's peach pie.

"Hey, peewee, come join us." Seth smiled.

He was choosing to ignore my intense dislike of Jaden, obviously.

"No, thanks. I'm going upstairs... I should probably talk to Dec first, though." My attempt to keep the worry out of my voice was only partly successful.

Jaden spoke up. "He's with my mom in the office. I think they'll be a while, actually." The look he gave me was thoughtful.

I was surprised—I had thought that Dec would be pacing the floor waiting for me.

"Well, goodnight then." I only looked at Seth.

I got a day of hard labor for my trouble. I'd been cleaning stalls for an hour when Seth ambled in, pitchfork in hand, and went into the stall across from mine. He started mucking out.

"You know you can't help me, Seth," I reminded him.

"Dec went out."

"Still, you shouldn't risk it."

"Less talk, more work, half-pint." He grinned at me.

I stole glances at my tall blond brother as we worked, and wondered whether we could possibly be less alike. He'd always been a cute kid, but now his face was losing its childish roundness, revealing

45

my mom's good bone structure. They had shared more than looks; Seth and my mother had the same relaxed personality—as opposed to mine, which was anything but. They'd been very close, and he had been devastated by her death. Since we lost her, Seth had gone from laid-back to almost lackadaisical—as though refusing to take anything seriously could prevent him from ever being hurt that much again.

Jaden arrived shortly afterward, followed by Teri, who kept me company while I worked.

"What are you doing your assignment on?" she asked.

"The economics of slavery," I said.

"Like in the old days?"

"Nope, modern-day slavery. I stumbled across it by accident. Can you believe there are more slaves in the world today than at any other time in history?"

"Hold on," Jaden broke in. "You can't make those kinds of sweeping claims without substantiating them."

I rolled my eyes. "I've researched the subject," I said scathingly. "I've got references to back it up."

"Well, would you mind sharing your references? If they're valid, I could use them for a project I'm working on." He sounded doubtful that they would measure up.

"Okay, lawyer boy," I told him. My tone wasn't friendly. "Leave me your email and I'll send it."

That night I went into the living room to use the old computer Seth and I shared, and found a sticky note with Jaden's email address stuck to the monitor. I ignored it for about a week, my annoyance with him warring with my desire to prove myself, before finally relenting and sending him the documents. I got an email from him the next day.

Subject: Research Materials
From: "Jaden Foster" <fosterPolo@gmail.com>
To: "Tea" <rainbow.dash42@yahoo.com>
Thanks… where did you get this material? I have access to an enormous university library, not to mention the law school resources, and I couldn't find half this info. I have to confess I'm impressed.

46

Subject: what can i tell you
From: "Tea" <rainbow.dash42@yahoo.com>
To: "Jaden Foster" <fosterPolo@gmail.com>
learn to surf, dude

Subject: I don't think so
From: "Jaden Foster" <fosterPolo@gmail.com>
To: "Tea" <rainbow.dash42@yahoo.com>
There's no way that you got this material from the Internet. Not all of it, anyway. What you sent me is referenced, somewhat arcane, and recent. Plus, I couldn't find it ☺

Subject: well, duh
From: "Tea" <rainbow.dash42@yahoo.com>
To: "Jaden Foster" <fosterPolo@gmail.com>
ok, so i wasn't going to send you random interweb flotsam. that would have been a waste of time. mine, especially.

Subject: Not bad
From: "Jaden Foster" <fosterPolo@gmail.com>
To: "Tea" <rainbow.dash42@yahoo.com>
No offense, but I'm impressed that you know the difference. A lot of kids your age don't—in fact a lot of the people in law school still haven't learned.

Subject: excuse me?
From: "Tea" <rainbow.dash42@yahoo.com>
To: "Jaden Foster" <fosterPolo@gmail.com>
precisely how should your last statement be taken for it NOT to be offensive?

Subject: My compliments
From: "Jaden Foster" <fosterPolo@gmail.com>
To: "Tea" <rainbow.dash42@yahoo.com>
You know, you write extremely well for seventeen.

Subject: nice diversion
From: "Tea" <rainbow.dash42@yahoo.com>
To: "Jaden Foster" <fosterPolo@gmail.com>
that should read: "You write extremely well for a seventeen-year-old." and btw, i suspect that my writing would measure up even for an aged twenty-two-year-old such as yourself. but don't change the subject.

Subject: Sorry
From: "Jaden Foster" <fosterPolo@gmail.com>
To: "Tea" <rainbow.dash42@yahoo.com>
You're right, that statement was offensive. Please accept my abject apologies. And thank you for the documents. Which you acquired...?

Subject: fine, then
From: "Tea" <rainbow.dash42@yahoo.com>
To: "Jaden Foster" <fosterPolo@gmail.com>
all right. i'll tell you, if only to stop you from harassing me virtually. i know someone at "imagine canada". she provides me with articles, and contact names, and generally gives me the scoop on whatever I need. happy now?

Subject: Yes
From: "Jaden Foster" <fosterPolo@gmail.com>
To: "Tea" <rainbow.dash42@yahoo.com>
Extremely.

December brought freezing weather to southwestern Ontario. I shivered while teaching lessons, while turning out horses, and while feeding. I was in the arena setting up some jumps for my advanced students one afternoon when Marcus, one of our boarders, marched in.

"Can I give you the board money? There's no answer at the house," he said abruptly.

"Um, sure, I guess," I said absently. The boarders were all supposed to pay Dec directly, but Marcus was a bit whiny, so I placated him. He handed me a wad of bills and I stuffed them into my pocket before continuing to shiver my way around the arena.

48

As I headed to the house before dinner I remembered the board money and put my hand in my pocket—and found nothing. Frantically I searched all my pockets; I couldn't find a single bill. I retraced my steps to the barn, the tackroom, and the arena. Still nothing. My heart was beating fast now. A month's board, in cash, was a lot of money to lose.

I trudged inside. Seth was in the living room, and I picked his sweatshirt up off the couch and threw it at him. Dec was almost obsessively neat; he cleaned up a lot himself, but he expected us to keep the house tidy too. I had managed to train myself—with some effort—to be relatively orderly, but unfortunately Seth was one of those people who littered a trail of cast-offs everywhere he went. You could practically find him by following the path of keys, school stuff, and clothes he discarded. So, in order to keep the peace, I ended up picking up after him quite a bit. I didn't want Dec upset by anything else before I told him I'd lost the board money.

"What's up, Sis?"

Seth shrugged after I'd told him. "Well, it was an accident."

"What was an accident?" Dec's voice came from behind me.

I explained what had happened, fidgeting. Dec took a deep breath before walking over and sinking onto the couch; he pulled me down next to him.

"You know this is why the boarders are supposed to pay me directly, right?" Dec reminded me.

"Yes, I know," I said quietly. "It's just that it was Marcus, and you know how he gets... but I should have insisted, I guess." I was looking at my knees.

"Well, these things happen."

I looked up; there was barely a trace of irritation in his features.

"You know, Dec, I still have the money I made at the track," I admitted. I'd been surprised that he hadn't confiscated it at the time; I wondered if he'd forgotten. "I'll give it to you to replace the board money."

"No, you keep it. You and Seth will need it once you buy your car." His tone was gentle, and I felt a swell of confusing emotions rising up inside me.

"Dec... I never told you, but I really am sorry about the whole racetrack thing." I apologized without looking at him.

I heard him sigh.

49

"So am I," he said in a low voice. Wait, had he just said what I thought he did? That was definitely a first. "You know, for the record, I would have given you the money for the Royal," he added, "But you didn't ask me."

I nodded, trying not to feel bitter as I absorbed this news. It hadn't occurred to me to ask. I knew that money was tight, and Seth and I tried to pull our own weight as much as we could. We knew that Dec had loved our mother, but he married her and four years later, she died. And left him with two fourteen-year-olds that we weren't sure he had bargained for.

We went to my cousin Stacey's on Christmas Eve; they lived in a big house in Thornhill, north of Toronto. Seth was sulky on the drive because he wanted to go to his girlfriend's; they had been together for six weeks, a record for Seth. Although he had a lot of girlfriends, you couldn't call Seth a womanizer—he genuinely liked all the girls he dated, and he never meant to hurt their feelings. He rarely stayed interested long, but while it lasted, he was his usual sweet, funny self; that, combined with his good looks and popularity, ensured him a steady lineup of girls. It was pretty amusing to watch.

Dec had asked us to be on our best behavior because my Uncle Peter, Jaden's father, would be in attendance. We hadn't seen him in five years—in fact, we barely remembered him, and we were curious to see what he'd be like. Dec had had some sort of falling out with his older brother, but we weren't privy to the details.

Aunt Paloma and Jaden arrived shortly after us. Jaden promptly strolled over and plunked himself down on the couch next to me, but I didn't bristle this time—after our email exchange I had given up my grudge.

"Hey, fosterPolo," I greeted him.

He responded with a teasing smile. "So, My Little Pony, seriously?"

"Hey, you recognized the name—that's almost worse than my using it, seeing as how you're a boy and all," I taunted.

"Hmm, you may have a point. Why the 42?"

I shrugged. "Because it's the answer, you know-"

"To life, the universe, and everything," Jaden finished, grinning. "How does someone your age end up reading offbeat sci-fi from the eighties?"

"The same way you did, I guess—I read a lot. Anyway, dude, you're only five years older than I am."

"True," he said thoughtfully. "I guess it's just your attitude that makes it seem like you're ten."

Without hesitation, I tossed a punch toward his shoulder, but his hand caught my fist instead.

"Ow," he said in a perfectly flat voice. His smile was mocking. "You have sharp little fists, but you're not very fast."

"What?" I was indignant. Physically, there were not many things I could claim—I wasn't tall, or strong, or beautiful—but I was speedy. That much I knew.

He was still looking at me, though he had released my hand. Without breaking eye contact, I surreptitiously threw another punch. Again, my fist smacked into his palm. His amber-flecked eyes hadn't left mine.

"Sneaky." His smile grew even more mocking.

"So it's come to blows this time, has it?" Dec asked in amusement. "It's getting worse, Paloma," he called over his shoulder to my aunt, who appeared in the doorway. "Now our kids can't even make it till dinner without fighting."

Jaden's mom shook her head at us in mock disapproval, but she smiled at the sight of us side by side.

"Tea, this is the first time in four years that my son is home for Christmas. Please, be nice to him."

I sat across from Uncle Peter during the meal. He was taller and less stocky than Dec, his hair a lighter brown, but they could easily be marked as brothers. Jaden took after his mother more, I decided, except for the height.

Dinner was interesting. Uncle Peter was some sort of high-powered executive, and he was very charming, in a superficial kind of way. Huge platters were making their way around the table, and I piled my plate with potatoes, greens beans with almond slivers, some mushrooms in pastry, and glazed carrots. Uncle Peter noticed my choices.

"What, no meat?" he asked. There was both turkey and ham on the table.

"No, thanks," I replied.

"Are you a vegetarian?" It sounded like he was accusing me of a crime.

51

I peered over at Dec. "Not yet."

Uncle Peter laughed. "I'm glad to hear you're not letting her get away with that, Dec."

Dec had told me I was free to be a vegetarian as soon as I did my own shopping and cooking. And since about the only thing I hated more than grocery shopping was cooking, for the moment I ate meat. I did try to minimize my consumption, though, and since this meal offered me the option, I left out the flesh.

"Why would you want to be a vegetarian?" Uncle Peter went on.

I sighed. The rest of my family had heard this all before, and Dec would not consider it appropriate dinner table conversation.

"It's a personal decision."

"Meaning that you can't explain it?" Uncle Peter insisted.

"No, I can probably explain a lot more than you'd care to hear. But I have no interest in converting anyone; I think it's fine for anyone who wants to eat meat to do so. I just don't want to, myself."

"But why?"

"Because I love animals. Hence, I don't want to kill and eat them."

Uncle Peter snorted. "That's ridiculous," he scoffed.

"Dad," Jaden objected, frowning at him.

"Really, Jaden, would you buy that argument?"

"Just because it wouldn't be sufficient to convert me to vegetarianism doesn't mean it isn't a perfectly valid reason for Tea," Jaden argued.

"So that's it?" Uncle Peter challenged, looking at me.

I tried another, slightly longer explanation.

"Many famous people throughout history, from Socrates to Albert Einstein, have advocated a vegetarian diet, and they're all a lot smarter than me. There are social, environmental, ethical and health arguments supporting a vegetarian diet," I said carefully, aware of Dec's eyes on me.

"If there are so many arguments for it, why can't you give me even one?" Uncle Peter's tone was mocking, his eyes challenging. I felt my chin come up.

"You're eating meat purely for the hedonistic and temporary satisfaction of your taste buds. What's your argument for that?" I snapped at him.

Uncle Peter's eyes widened in surprise for an instant. Then he frowned at me.

"I don't have to justify my dietary choices to you," he spat.

"Then neither do I."

"It's not the same," he argued, "I have tradition and culture on my side."

"In some cultures, people of color are considered inferior. In others, women are expected to be submissive and stay at home. That was even the case here, not so long ago—culture is a fluid and evolving thing. And just because something is culturally accepted doesn't make it ethical. We used to think that boiling someone in oil was cool."

Uncle Peter opened his mouth, but Aunt Penny spoke first. "Peter, can we please talk about something else? I'm trying to enjoy my turkey here."

"Sorry, Aunt Penny," I told her, abashed.

"Don't worry, Tea, it's not your fault." She smiled. I was glad she wasn't upset; I often felt that Aunt Penny disapproved of me. I was too unruly, too much of a tomboy for her taste. I didn't say another word during the entire meal, just to be safe.

Later, I was sitting on the basement stairs watching Seth set up Stacey's new game system.

"Hi, rabble-rouser." Jaden settled onto the step next to me.

"Hey."

"Are you always so outspoken?" he asked.

"Sadly, yes. I'm always getting into trouble because I can't keep my mouth shut."

"I thought you got into trouble because you don't listen?"

"Yeah, that too." I grinned at him.

"Well, now that you don't have to censor, will you tell me what you really think?"

I hesitated for a minute, but he looked genuinely interested, so I tried to verbalize the uneasy feelings I sometimes had, a suspicion that I didn't differentiate well enough between humans and other species.

"All I'm saying is, I prefer the company of animals to that of some people," I tried to sum up. Too late, I realized how that might sound and added, awkwardly, "Um, present company excepted, of course."

He chuckled. "Thanks. Although," his face grew grave, "I wouldn't be surprised if you lumped me in with the other group."

He shifted toward me and looked into my eyes. I felt a slight lurch in the region of my stomach, as I was reminded of how mesmerizing his gaze could be.

"Look, Tea, I haven't had the chance to apologize for what I did in September," he said in a low voice. He didn't mention that I hadn't given him the chance, since I'd been rudely avoiding him these past three months, and I thought that was generous of him.

"That's okay," I mumbled.

"No, it isn't. I would never have said anything if I'd known how harshly you'd be punished. I'm very sorry. Please forgive me." His warm voice was utterly sincere; his eyes, which never left mine, were repentant. I couldn't even blink; I just gawked at him like an idiot. I'd never received such a heartfelt apology in my life, and I couldn't imagine anyone being able to resist forgiving him—he probably got away with a lot.

We played video games for the rest of the evening, Seth and I against Stacey and Jaden. Seth and I were totally destroyed, mostly due to my complete lack of gaming skill, but it was still fun.

Later, I was standing back from the crush at the front door while everyone was leaving. Jaden was making the rounds, saying goodbye. When he got to me his face was serious.

"I'm glad you forgave me," he said quietly.

I smiled at him. "Me too—imagine missing the opportunity to get my butt kicked at Super Mario for two hours."

He grinned, then ducked his head quickly and kissed my cheek; I smelled the same enticing scent I'd noticed the first time he came for dinner. There must have been a draft from the door, because as he turned away I shivered, and noticed I was covered in goose bumps.

Four

Even though January hadn't brought any relief from the cold, I was still excited about the first horse show of the year. No one else from our barn was going, so Karen said she'd pick me up with her two-horse trailer. She was bringing a client's horse to ride.

I had a good schooling session with Blaze the day before the show; he was in excellent spirits as he bounded over the fences I'd set up, and I felt mine soar correspondingly. That night I groomed him carefully and picked out his stall so he wouldn't get dirty overnight.

"This is going to be our year, Blaze," I reminded him with a hug when I was done. "This is the year we really get noticed. Let's start if off right tomorrow."

But the next day didn't start off right at all. Somehow I had set my alarm wrong, for six p.m. instead of a.m. I awoke to pounding on the door downstairs; I leapt up and staggered down the steps half-asleep, twisting an ankle as I went. It was Karen, naturally.

"Why aren't you ready? Dante's in the first class," she said impatiently. "Get dressed, I'll feed Blaze."

I ran upstairs and threw on my clothes, then rushed to the barn, hobbling a bit on my twisted ankle and still muddled from sleep. I wrapped Blaze's legs with shipping bandages while he ate; the sound of grinding grain was making me hungry.

"Man, I am beat," Karen yawned as she helped me put on Blaze's blanket. He was so good-natured, I thought with a doting smile. Some horses would have hated to be rushed through their breakfast, but he took it in stride, perking his ears up with interest as he stepped into the trailer next to a large chestnut horse. I examined Karen as I came out; she did look tired—she was pale and had purple circles under her eyes.

"I think I'm coming down with something," she continued as she tried to stifle another yawn.

"Why don't you let me drive?" I suggested. "That way you can have a nap."

She looked at me narrowly. "Are you legal to drive a trailer on the highway yet?" she demanded.

"Um, not technically... I only have my learner's permit. But we're not going far. It's not like I can't manage it."

Karen looked torn.

"It's six-thirty in the morning, Karen. The roads will be practically deserted," I encouraged her.

"Oh, all right. Just make sure you drive slowly, then."

We climbed into the big gold pickup. Karen laughed as she helped me adjust the seat so that I could reach the pedals, but once we got underway she was asleep within minutes. I debated going through a drive-through to get some coffee, but I was worried about maneuvering the truck and trailer through it, so I decided to skip it. I yawned as I merged cautiously onto highway 403.

We only had to go a few exits, and I felt a mild sense of relief when I pulled off the highway. The lights at the off-ramp were green, and I was thinking of my upcoming jumper class as we glided slowly through the intersection. And then my world ended.

Sharp, stabbing pains woke me. The first thing I noticed was the taste of blood in my mouth; I was surprised at the effort it took to swallow. My eyelids fluttered open to an unfamiliar view. I tried to move and found I couldn't, but the effort sent more stabbing pains through me, and I groaned weakly. I wasn't exactly conscious of where the pains were located, other than my head. The pain in my head was very clear.

"Don't try to move," a male voice said. He sounded bored. "You're in an ambulance and we're taking you to a hospital."

"No, wait—my horse! What about Blaze? And Karen?" My voice sounded feeble even to my own ears.

"I'm sorry, I can't tell you much about that. Your friend stayed at the accident site, she's not badly injured."

A confused memory was starting to emerge: a sudden loud roar to my left, followed by a vicious wrenching motion. There was nothing after that, only blackness. I could feel panic ballooning inside me—I had to know how Blaze was. But I started to turn my head, and the blackness rose up and claimed me again.

The next time my eyes opened I stayed conscious longer. Not that I wanted to, after the first minute. I looked around blearily; a dull throbbing started in my head as soon as I turned it.

"Hey," Seth murmured. He was sitting on the edge of my bed, and looked as though he'd been crying.

"Is she awake?" Dec walked to the other side of the bed, frowning in concern.

"What happened?" I croaked. I cleared my throat, sending shooting pains through my forehead and ribcage. I noticed an IV tube running into the back of my right hand; the left one felt weird and when I lifted it I saw a splint on my ring finger. Damn, that was the finger that held the reins.

Dec put his hand on my arm gingerly.

"How do you feel?" he asked. I noticed he hadn't answered my question.

"I've been better... what happened?" I asked again. "How's Blaze? And Karen and the other horse?"

Dec didn't answer right away. He swallowed hard, then met Seth's eyes across my bed. Seth turned his head away quickly so I couldn't see his face. All of a sudden I couldn't breathe—my heart felt like it was staggering to a halt. Something was very, very wrong.

"Tell me," I whispered. "Tell me what happened."

Dec looked back at me, his face haggard. My heart went from stumbling to sprinting.

"There was an accident. A truck—an eighteen-wheeler—crashed into you. The driver was asleep, he went through a red light," he said quietly. He paused, while the pain in my chest grew more and more unbearable. Suddenly I didn't want him to go on; I knew what he was going to say.

"No." It wasn't even a whisper. I shook my head, ignoring the pain. My brain was already trying to shut down. "No..."

Seth turned then. He hugged me, hard, but I couldn't move. Over Seth's shoulder, I met Dec's eyes. He tightened his grip on my arm.

"Karen is okay. The other horse will likely recover. But Blaze was on the wrong side; the truck ran directly into his side of the trailer. I'm sorry, honey, but he's gone."

I had to move, to run, as if escaping from those horrendous, impossible words would mean escape from the truth. I struggled to get up, ripping the IV out of my hand and sending lancing pains through my body. Seth tightened his hold, and Dec pushed my shoulder down, both of them murmuring words of comfort I didn't hear. I struggled for another minute, welcoming the pain and praying for unconsciousness,

57

but now that I desperately wanted it, it wouldn't come. I lay back and screwed my eyelids shut tight. At that moment, I never wanted to see daylight again.

Five

I was always in pain. At some point every day I would suddenly feel as though someone had sunk a cleaver into my head. The pain tended to radiate out from my forehead, over my left eye; I guessed that was the spot that had spidered the glass and given me my concussion. It was so intense at first that, whatever I was doing, I would just sink to the ground and press my forehead into my hands, trying to hold my skull together.

My broken finger and ribs didn't bother me as much; they were just nagging background pains, except at night when the ribs kept me from sleeping. When I wasn't already awake from the nightmares, that is.

But worse by far than any of those was the constant raw wound in my gut. I felt as though a sharp-clawed, razor-toothed animal had tried to rip its way out of me. I couldn't eat; not only was I completely lacking in appetite, but whenever I did manage to get a morsel down, stabbing pains in my stomach immediately made me sorry I'd tried. It was so bad that I worried they'd missed something at the hospital, though I didn't say anything. After a week of watching me sit around holding my stomach, though, Dec dragged me back there. The doctor palpated and ran tests—nothing was wrong. Except for the fact that I felt lacerated inside.

I refused to talk about Blaze. In fact, I barely spoke at all. I was allowed home after two days in the hospital, and Dec let me stay home for another week before suggesting I try going to school. I shrugged. I really didn't want to face anyone, but I knew Dec wouldn't let me stay home forever.

I dutifully went to school the next day. Seth hovered solicitously most of the time, but we didn't have all our classes together, and in any case he couldn't prevent people from talking to me entirely. So I did my best to avoid eye contact, slinking around with my shoulders hunched and answering in monosyllables if I was cornered. I was grateful for Teri's presence. She was also suffering over Blaze's death, and I could feel her unspoken support whenever she was near. When I got home that night I was exhausted. It was Wednesday, which meant that I had a lesson to teach, but I didn't feel up to it. I asked Seth to cancel it, and collapsed into bed.

I woke up screaming. Seth burst through the door seconds later; he rushed over and put his arms around me.

"It's okay, it's okay. Shhh."

I cried into his t-shirt for a few minutes before managing to get myself back under control. The only times I cried were after waking from nightmares. This wasn't the first time Seth had run into my room in the middle of the night; Dec had come in too, the first two or three times, but he seemed at a loss for what to say. After that he'd let Seth handle it. I was a bit surprised that Seth woke up to my screams, because he usually slept like the dead, but then maybe he wasn't sleeping soundly these days either. It reminded me piercingly of the time after our mother had died... that was the last time I'd cried in anyone's arms, and Seth had been the one to hold me then, too. Only then we'd cried on each other.

I pulled away from him and wiped my tears on my sleeve. His fair hair was dishevelled, and he was in pajama pants.

"Sorry I woke you."

"Don't be dumb, Sis. I'm here for you." There was a furrow between his brows, and his eyes, which looked almost black in the dim light, were troubled.

"I think I'm going to stay home tomorrow. School's still too tiring for me," I muttered.

"Good idea, give yourself time. I'll tell Dec in the morning, if you want."

I accepted his offer gratefully; the more time I could spend hiding out in my room, the better. Unfortunately Dec had other ideas about my hiding out. He let me stay home Thursday and Friday, but made it clear that starting Monday I'd have to go back, and keep going. Gran agreed with him.

"It's not healthy, dear. Your injuries are healing; if you're to get past this, you need to return to your normal routine, your normal life," she told me one afternoon when I'd ventured to the kitchen for a drink.

I looked at her incredulously. Normal life? Life would never be 'normal' for me again. Not that my life had been that normal to begin with.

"I know it's terribly difficult, dear, but really—your friends call, and you won't speak with them. Your students arrive and you don't teach them. And you're going to fall too far behind in school." She came over and put her arm around me; I tried not to cringe. I didn't like anyone touching me these days.

Karen showed up the next morning to teach our usual Saturday morning lesson. I forced myself to go outside, more to get away from Dec's worried glances than to see anyone. It was a bright, sunny day, not too frigid for late January, and my boots crunched in the snow as I made my way slowly to the barn. This was the first time I was venturing in there since the accident, two weeks before. I wasn't sure whether anyone realized that—normally I almost lived in the barn; I don't think it had occurred to anyone that I was avoiding it. But I had been. I didn't want to see Blaze's empty stall, the physical symbol of the immense emptiness left in my heart, and in my life.

I stepped slowly into the familiar, horsey-smelling warmth. The sounds of chewing, rustling, and snorting were the same as ever, the most homey sound I could imagine. The glow of the polished wooden surfaces welcomed me, and it wasn't until I relaxed that I realized how tensely coiled my posture had been. I followed the sound of voices into the main boarder aisle.

"Tea—how are you, honey?" Karen came over immediately and draped her arm around my shoulders.

"I'm... okay, I guess," I mumbled. What could I say? That I wished a big hole would open up in the Earth and swallow me up? "How are you feeling?"

"Like crap, mostly. Dante's recovering well, though, so I can't complain." I flinched at the mention of the other horse's name—not that I wasn't pleased to hear he was improving. I noticed Teri and Julia hovering a few feet away, watching me with sorrowful expressions.

"Hey," I acknowledged them.

They both came and hugged me then, and I had to grind my teeth and then bite my tongue to keep from crying. I tasted blood in my mouth, and pulled away as soon as I could.

"Nice day for a lesson," I commented, drawing attention away from myself. And hopefully forestalling any questions.

"Yes—how long until you can ride again?" Julia asked.

"Another four weeks," I responded morosely. Not that I felt any desire to ride, anyway. That was the strangest thing of all; I couldn't remember a time in my life when riding wasn't the most fervent desire of my heart. I considered it a basic need, right up there with eating—which I admittedly wasn't doing much of, either. I made an effort to talk for a few minutes before I escaped to the school horse aisle.

My friends there were all happy to see me. They greeted me with soft whickers, pressing their noses against the bars or reaching out over their half-doors. I went from stall to stall, petting a neck here and a nose there, and being nudged and rubbed against. Their touch didn't bother me; on the contrary, it was a relief to be in their warm, sweet-smelling, completely accepting presence. After seeing all the school horses, though, I knew whose company I really wanted.

I let myself into Zac's stall as quietly as I could. He pricked his ears and ambled right over, leaving his hay, and as usual he came to rest with his chin on my shoulder. I stood with my arms around him for a long time, until I began to get tired.

Karen found me as I was exiting the stall.

"I wanted to ask you, Tea," she began in a low voice, "are you still okay with telling everyone that I was driving?"

"Sure." It made no difference to me, and as she had pointed out when she came to the hospital, it would save us both considerable trouble. I wouldn't lose my learner's permit—and my chance at a driver's license—and she would be able to collect the insurance for her truck and trailer.

"I just want to make sure it's not stressing you out."

"No. I'm fine."

The concern in her brown eyes was already too familiar to me. "Call me if you ever want to talk about it."

I nodded, but I knew I never would. I'd heard all the platitudes, and I didn't believe them. I'd had my heart broken before, I knew it wouldn't heal—scar tissue would just form around it, and make it a little harder.

Jaden showed up the next day. I was in the house, staring blankly at the computer screen, and he headed straight for me. I shrank back slightly as he got close. He stopped, but didn't look offended, as some people did. He settled his long frame onto the arm of the couch a few feet away from me. He'd gone to Florida to play polo the day after Christmas, and was tanned from his time there.

"Hi." His tone was light, but his eyes examined my face carefully. I looked away.

"Hey."

There was a pause. When he went on, his voice was quiet, and rougher than usual.

"Tea—I'm, so, so, sorry, honey." I heard him take a breath; he went on slowly. "I had to have a horse put down once. She went down under me in the middle of a match, at a full gallop. She couldn't be saved. The pain and guilt I felt over it were... excruciating. I'm not saying it's the same as what you're feeling. Blaze was special; I think everyone who saw him knew that, and the two of you had a tremendous bond. But I do have an inkling of what you're dealing with. If there's anything I can do, or there's anything you want, no matter how minor—or major—just ask, okay?"

I glanced at him; the pain on his face was real. I nodded. He nodded back before heading outside. He didn't come near me, to my relief, but I'd been surprisingly touched by his words. It sounded like he understood, to a degree, about Blaze. But there was nothing he could do. My life was empty.

School on Monday was hell. I attracted unwanted attention twice by sinking to my knees in the hallway and clutching my head. One of those times I was sent to the nurse's office; I was happy to miss a class but then I feel asleep on the cot and woke up screaming, as usual, which caused the nurse to call Dec, who came to pick me up. He seemed almost at his wit's end on the drive home. I was pretty sure he thought I was on the verge of some kind of breakdown, an eventuality that would petrify him. I resolved to keep it together a bit better.

The weeks passed in a fog, getting marginally better as people moved on to fresh topics of gossip. I hardly spoke at school, and my teachers had mostly stopped calling on me. I had always been a good student, so they probably wouldn't worry until they saw my grades, which I suspected would be dropping precipitously. Not that I cared. I was teaching riding again, though without much enthusiasm. Seth had taken over some of my lower-level classes, and he continued to teach them to lessen my workload.

It was mid-February. I hadn't ridden in five weeks and was beginning to feel the first faint whispers of desire to get on a horse, which I thought was encouraging. Aunt Paloma and Jaden had just arrived for lunch, but before heading to the house I had to change the dressing on Splash's leg—somehow he had managed to cut himself while he was turned out the day before.

Marcus came around the corner. "Hey, I want to ride and there's a horse in the arena," he complained.

"Oh, right. I'll get him in a minute, just let me finish up here," I said absently, applying ointment to the gash.

"I don't have much time," he said impatiently.

I sighed. Marcus always found something to complain about. I couldn't very well leave Splash half-bandaged, though.

"Feel free to bring him in yourself," I hinted.

"Oh, all right," he said petulantly, turning on his heel.

I was just smoothing down the bandage when a commotion made my head snap up. Through the open arena door, I saw Zac rear up while Marcus swore loudly and jerked on the lead shank. Searing heat flashed through me. I was already running before I registered the chain over Zac's nose—my sensitive baby never needed that extra control, and Marcus had obviously hurt him.

I launched myself at Marcus from three feet away; the impact from my body sent him down flat on his back. I had just gotten onto his chest and drawn back my fist when I was jerked upward by what felt like an iron bar around my middle. A lancing pain shot through my injured ribs. I struggled instinctively, and my arms were quickly pinned down by more iron.

"Get Zac and get into the barn, *now*," a low voice growled in my ear.

I only hesitated for a second; Zac was short distance away, tossing his head up and down in distress. I gave a curt nod and Jaden released me. I could hear Marcus starting to swear as his breath came back.

"Whoa, baby, it's okay. Let me see your poor nose," I murmured to Zac as I unclipped the chain. There was a welt forming across the bony bridge of his nose, and I rubbed it as I led him into the barn. I heard Marcus's heated voice and Jaden's smooth one arguing as I passed, my eyes locked on Zac.

Jaden came in as I was closing the door to Zac's stall. He grabbed my shoulders; I thought he was going to shake me but he just spun me around to face him.

"Tea, have you looked in a mirror lately?" He said it with painful restraint, but his eyes were scorching.

"Um..." I was confused by his question, and his unblinking glower was making it hard for me to think.

"You—are—a—small—girl," he bit off each word distinctly. "For you to attack a full-grown man like that is insane."

"Did you see what he did to Zac?" I demanded. My power of speech returned in a rush as my temper began to flare again; small flames were erupting inside my chest, but they felt good. It had been too long since I'd felt anything.

"That's irrelevant-"

"Not to me!"

"What if he had hit you back? What if I hadn't been nearby? Did you pause for one second to consider what would happen *after* your daring rescue?" His intensity was oddly intimidating, considering that he didn't raise his voice.

I was saved from answering by Seth's arrival.

"Nice move, Sparky," he grinned, shaking his head. For once I couldn't blame him for using my hated nickname.

I couldn't think of a witty riposte, so I settled for, "Shut up."

"Seriously though, what are you going to tell Dec when we lose a boarder because he was assaulted by an elf?"

I'd been trying not to think that far ahead, but now I was gripped by worry. It eased a bit when Jaden answered, "I don't think that will be a problem. For one thing, I pointed out to him that he could be held responsible for any injuries to Zac. And honestly... can you see him admitting publicly that Tea was able to take him out?"

He and Seth both looked at me and howled with laughter.

"If you're quite done..." I turned away, miffed, but a hand caught my elbow.

"Come on, little Defender of the Downtrodden," Jaden said, snickering, "let's go inside and plan your defense. We still have to tell Dec."

The brief flare of emotion I'd felt while avenging Zac didn't last. I drifted through the days in a haze, doing the absolute minimum I had to. About a week later I decided to try riding again. I was supposed to wait another week, but I felt okay. I would just have to be careful of my splinted finger. I tacked up Winter, Seth's horse, and spent half an hour doing some leisurely riding in the arena. I popped him over a few small jumps at the end; my ribs hurt a bit, but the effort felt good all the same. It was the first thing that had felt good to me in a long time.

So I started riding again, but I didn't have a particular horse in training, and I really missed it. I missed building that bond of trust, imparting knowledge and in turn learning from each horse, and enjoying the flowering of what was, every time, a unique relationship.

Seth had taken our pooled money and bought us a car, an old Toyota that he claimed would run for a long time. I was happy not to be taking the school bus anymore. We got home almost an hour earlier this way, so it was still light out when we got home one afternoon and saw the trailer parked near the barn. We headed straight there.

Dec was in front of a stall in the school horse aisle. Circling nervously inside it was a smallish palomino horse; he stopped only briefly to regard us suspiciously before continuing his inspection of his new home.

"Who's this?" Seth inquired.

"He doesn't have a name, as far as I know," Dec said. "I got him from Rodney."

I grimaced. Rodney was the type of horse dealer that gave horse dealers a bad name. "What's his story?" I asked, interested despite myself.

"I don't know much, but apparently he's fairly well schooled, and can jump a small course. He was outside when I saw him and he's a nice mover. You've been saying we could use another school horse—I know he'll probably have issues, but I'm sure you can sort them out. In any case, he was cheap."

That raised my suspicions even more, but he was very attractive, I had to admit. His body was almost the exact color of gold, and his mane and tail, though dirty, were a silvery white. He had a stripe on his finely chiselled face, and good conformation.

"Is he a Quarter Horse?" I asked, noting the well-developed hindquarters.

"Appendix registered, apparently—half Thoroughbred, too."

That was surprising, given his size—he wasn't much over fifteen hands, I guessed.

"By the way, we have some more changes coming," Dec announced as we turned away from the stall. "Marcus is moving his horse out."

I stiffened. Dec knew about the arena incident, but Jaden had told him that we'd smoothed it over. I raised my eyes cautiously to find Dec watching me.

"It's okay, Tea, I'm not going to mourn his loss. We all know what a pain he was."

I relaxed.

"And in any case, we already have someone new moving in—Jaden." He smiled, obviously happy with his announcement. "He's going to be a pro at the new polo club next summer."

"But doesn't he play in other countries during the summer?" Seth voiced what I'd been wondering, too.

"Normally, yes. And the level of play at the Killean club will be far beneath what he's accustomed to, but he wants to stay closer to home this year." The nearby polo club had opened only two years earlier, and I wasn't familiar with it—I didn't know anyone who played polo. Well, besides Jaden.

The next day I went to see the little palomino after school, and discovered the reason for his cheap sale price. The minute I opened the stall door he lunged at me with ears pinned and teeth bared; I staggered backward as I slammed the door, and heard his hooves crash against it.

"Whoa," I panted. That was the least friendly reception I'd ever gotten. No wonder he'd ended up at Rodney's—since he was on the smaller side he would have been sold as a kid's horse, and no one wanted an aggressive horse for their child. This was going to take some work, but I was intrigued; it's quite rare for a horse to be aggressive, and I'd never encountered one like this, that would actually try to attack in his stall.

I went and got a handful of grain and cautiously opened the door only wide enough for my hand to fit through. The little gelding had smelled the grain, but he still pinned his ears back and shook his head menacingly.

"There's no need for that," I chided, carefully extending the grain toward him. "I'm just being friendly, see? You'll like it here, if you give it a chance."

He seemed interested in my voice, so I kept murmuring to him as he took a hesitant step forward and started eating the grain. I was careful to hold absolutely still while he ate, breathing a sigh of relief that he hadn't tried to bite my hand.

The pattern varied slightly over the next week. After two days I'd managed to get inside the stall and put a halter on him, and I left it on. We normally took them off in the stalls, for reasons of both comfort and safety, but it was safer for me to be able to catch him easily. I asked Dec to make sure no one else handled him, explaining that he was a bit tricky. It made a fair amount of extra work for me, since I had to clean his stall after school. I didn't want Alan, whose job it was to clean the stalls and feed, to be injured. By week's end the little palomino had made some progress, and wasn't trying to savage me every time he saw me. He would consent to eat some grain and let me lead him outside to stretch his legs in a paddock. I didn't tell Dec the extent of his behavior problems. If Dec knew the horse was that aggressive he would have gotten rid of him right away, and I wanted the chance to work with him a bit first. A horse who threatens people stands a very good chance of winding up dead. Changing his behavior could save his life.

Jaden's horses arrived the first Saturday in March, and Seth and I went to help unload them. Seth came down the ramp first with a pretty, leggy chestnut mare, and headed inside.

"You'd better stand back while I take Kermit out," Jaden warned. "He doesn't trailer well."

I moved away a safe distance, interested now. Jaden came down the ramp with an obviously stressed horse—he was wringing his tail and sweating, looking anxiously left and right as he backed down the ramp.

"Wow, is he always like that?" I asked as Jaden led his horse into a stall. He left the blanket on, which was a good idea considering how wet Kermit was.

"Unfortunately, yes. He's an incredible horse, but polo ponies travel a lot, and it's a nightmare going places with him. Usually he's tranquilized but this was such a short trip, I didn't want to drug him."

I watched Kermit carefully. This was probably something I could help with, but I didn't say anything; I'd almost used up my quota of talking for the day. Seth came over and checked out Kermit too.

"Nice horse," he complimented Jaden. "What would you call his color?"

"Mouse dun," I answered at the same time as Jaden said, "Grulla." He smiled at me. "You're right."

68

"You're right too. I know it's Spanish, but that's what the Western people call it, also. I've never seen it on a full-sized horse, though, only on ponies... what's his breeding?"

"He's Argentine bred—a mix of Thoroughbred and local breeds; they make the best polo ponies in the world." He looked at his horse with obvious pride. It actually made me smile, for a second.

We left Jaden's horses to settle in, and I went to collect Schweppes, the little palomino. Some of the barn rats—the lesson kids who hung around a lot—had named him after a ginger ale brand, and it had stuck. Today he greeted me by swinging his hindquarters my way. As I was about to go in I felt a hand on my shoulder, ready to yank me back. I sighed as I turned to see Jaden.

"It's okay, he's only bluffing."

"How do you know?" His eyes were on Schweppes, his hand still tense on my shoulder.

"Look at him—sure, his ears are back, but his tail is clamped down, not swishing, and his feet are quiet, not stamping. That's a defensive posture, though he's pretending to be aggressive. He's psyching me out."

Jaden's face relaxed. "Hey, you're right."

I shrugged. "You might still get a show, though. I'm riding him for the first time today."

I tacked up carefully; Schweppes was touchy, swishing his tail and sidestepping on the crossties. He snapped at me twice when I got close to his head. Jaden insisted on standing nearby.

"You know, Jaden, this is my job—I deal with difficult horses all the time. You don't have to hover," I said. I was a bit annoyed by his lack of faith in my abilities.

"You're seventeen, Tea," he replied shortly. "You shouldn't have a job that warrants danger pay."

Normally I would have argued, but I was too tired. I let it drop. He could take it up with his uncle, if he wanted.

Schweppes was a surprise under saddle. He was athletic and balanced, and fairly well-schooled. It seemed we'd found a good school horse for our more advanced riders—though I might have to supervise when they were handling him on the ground.

Jaden spent the night so he could get his horses settled. After I was done with Schweppes he spent most of Saturday studying, which made

69

me feel a bit guilty for the lack of effort I'd been putting into school. I figured if an international polo player—who was doubtless used to a much more glamorous lifestyle—could buckle down and study, then I should be able to slog through some prosaic grade eleven material. I went to my room and made an effort for a couple of hours, but I couldn't concentrate, especially with the puzzle of a new horse to figure out.

I had trouble sleeping, so I stayed in bed as late as possible on Sunday. Unfortunately I had a lesson to teach at nine, so a few minutes before the hour I dragged myself into the kitchen for some coffee.

"Hey guys," I yawned. Seth and Jaden were at the kitchen table.

I finished adding cream and sugar and headed out with my travel mug; I nearly fell over when a hand caught the back of my sweater.

"Where are you going?" Jaden asked.

"I have a lesson to teach," I said blankly. Where did he think I was going?

"You didn't eat anything," he pointed out. He looked disapproving.

I shrugged. "I don't have time; I'm late already."

He let go, shaking his head.

"You shouldn't worry so much," I teased on my way out. "You'll get wrinkles on that pretty face."

Jaden came to find me in the cold arena a few minutes later. He handed me a cheese sandwich wrapped in a napkin, and I looked up at him in surprise.

"Eat," he ordered.

"Thanks," I mumbled. I took a bite; the grin he gave me made me smile in response. A real smile—I actually felt lighter, for a minute. I turned back to my students, bemused. I wasn't used to being taken care of.

We all had lunch together, Dec, Seth, Jaden and I.

"Can you bring me copies of your horses' Coggins tests and vaccination papers?" I asked Jaden before I could forget. "I'll set up a file for each of them."

"Sure. You're the one who does that?" He glanced at Dec questioningly.

"It's easier that way," I explained while Dec was chewing. "I usually coordinate with the vet, and I organize the show papers."

On top of managing the stable, Dec also took contracts as an efficiency consultant, which had been his career before he'd returned to the barn after Granddad died. Seth and I picked up the slack as much as possible while Dec worked on those projects.

"Tell us about Piba and Kermit, what are they like?" I asked.

Jaden was so animated when he talked about his horses, his whole demeanor changed. It reminded me of... well, me. He gave us each horse's background and told us about their likes and dislikes. I was surprised to hear that Piba was eight; her leggy build made her look like a filly.

"Yes," Jaden laughed when I told him so, "and she's the girliest mare you'll ever meet. Hates to be dirty or walk through mud, and loves to be groomed for hours."

"What's the deal with Kermit and the trailer?" I asked him.

He sighed. "I'm not sure. He's always been petrified of it, and he actually copes better than he used to, if you can believe it. For a while I even considered retiring him because the travelling is such an issue. I've tried practically everything."

"Well, if you're interested, I can probably help," I offered.

"I don't know," he said skeptically. "I don't think this is something I want to revisit with Kermit. We have a workable arrangement now."

"Maybe it's workable, but it's hardly ideal—especially for him, if he's still getting off the trailer all sweaty and freaked out," I said.

Jaden didn't look convinced. Dec spoke up.

"I'd let her give it a shot if I were you, son. And I would watch and learn—she's got quite a way with problem horses."

"That's because I don't believe there's such a thing as a 'problem horse'," I said with some asperity. "Only horses that have been messed up by bad handling or unrealistic expectations."

"You're in for a surprise, buddy," Seth added with a grin.

Jaden chuckled. "Well, now I've got to say yes—I have to see this magic for myself. When do you want to start?"

"As soon as we can clear the snow out of the round pen, I suppose."

"Well then, I'll get right on it." He smiled at me, and I felt suddenly warm.

We went outside; in between the barn and the square, red-brick house was a rectangular building, finished in the same beige and navy as the barn. Most of it was devoted to a two-car garage, but on one side, a separate section served as a storage area. We called it the shed. I went in and found us some shovels and we plodded through the fresh snow to the round pen.

"What are you going to do with him?" Jaden asked once we'd started shovelling.

"Some round pen work for a start, to establish trust, and then I'll use clicker training to actually get him on the trailer."

"And you really think it'll work?"

I shrugged. "Every horse is different. I've had good results with that combination in the past, though." In fact I'd never seen it fail, but I didn't want to get Jaden's hopes up. I didn't know the extent of Kermit's trauma. I tried not to think about the fact that he was a very valuable horse, who had travelled to more countries than I had. Or that he was Jaden's pride and joy. Those thoughts would only make me nervous, something I couldn't afford to communicate to Kermit.

"Why don't you let me shovel, Tea? It's harder for you than for me." It was true; he was clearing the space with ridiculous ease.

"I don't mind, it's keeping me warm. And I'm used to hard work."

"Unfortunately," Jaden said under his breath. At least that's what it sounded like.

It didn't take us long to clear the pen. Jaden brought Kermit out, and at my request stayed outside the fence to watch.

"Please don't talk to me until I'm done," I said. Not only would I need to concentrate, but I didn't want Kermit to focus on Jaden's voice.

I led Kermit into the pen and started the process of driving him forward and away from me. He trotted around the ring; eventually, he dropped his head, his inside ear angled toward me, and began working his jaw. I softened my body language, bringing my hands close to my body and angling away from him slightly, and he tightened the circle he was making around me. At that, I turned and took a few steps away from him, and within seconds he walked up beside me. I stroked his neck gently, went to stand on his left side, and tried walking away. He followed closely, now acknowledging me as his leader—and therefore, not a predator or someone to be feared.

I walked Kermit back to the barn without the lead shank. He stayed glued to my side the entire way, nudging me occasionally and keeping his near side eye on me.

"Wow," Jaden commented. "I've never seen him behave that way with anyone. How does it work?"

I explained how join-up inspires trust because you are using body language, which is the horse's own method of communicating, as well as telling him that I was assuming the role of 'lead mare'—the real leader in an equine herd, as opposed to the stallion, who is essentially there for protection and to fight off challengers. We were headed back to the house; I was dying for a hot drink. My hands were frozen inside their gloves.

"And what does clicker training involve?"

I smiled at his enthusiasm. We got to the kitchen and started making hot chocolate as I explained.

"It's really classical or operant conditioning by another name," I said. "You know, based on B.F. Skinner's work."

"The salivating dog and the bell, right." He nodded. I was glad he was familiar with the premise, at least.

"Could you pass me the milk, please?"

As he handed it to me his hand brushed mine.

"You're freezing!" he exclaimed. He promptly lifted the milk away and took my hand between both of his. He started rubbing it gently; his hands felt downright hot.

"So how does classical conditioning work?" he continued without missing a beat. His unusual eyes were alight with curiosity as they rested on my face. I felt suddenly strange; my breathing had faltered when he had taken my hand... probably from the shock of his warm hands on my frozen one. He changed hands now, starting on my other one.

"Um," I struggled to remember what I'd been saying. "Oh, right. Clicker training rewards every partial step toward a desired behavior. For instance, if Kermit took one step toward a trailer—even if he was still fifty yards away—then he'd be rewarded for that."

"Hmm..." He was lost in thought, still rubbing my hand absently. My hand was tingling; it must have been more frozen than I'd thought. "It must take a long time, then."

He released me, finally, and I went back to making our drinks. My mind was clearer now that I had my hands back.

"It's a lot faster than you'd think. The great thing about this method is that it allows you to communicate so easily—you can almost see the lightbulb going on over their heads. You may be surprised at how smart Kermit is." I couldn't contain my own enthusiasm either. I always loved sharing this gentle, positive training method, but it was especially nice now, with Jaden so interested and attentive.

We sat at the table, hot chocolates in hand.

"Nothing Kermit does would surprise me," he said. "He's the best. Did you know I've had him since I was fifteen? And he was three?"

"No, I didn't." I felt a sudden, unreasoning stab of jealousy. Though I longed for it, constancy had never been a big part of my life. I'd thought that would change with Blaze... I thought we'd be together for the next twenty years, at least. I gazed into my mug, feeling the raw wound in my gut again, not wanting to show it.

"I'm sorry," he said softly. "That was thoughtless of me."

"No, it wasn't."

He hesitated. "Look, Tea, if you ever want to talk..."

I shook my head without looking at him. I swallowed hard, and forced myself to raise my head. His face was sympathetic rather than pitying; I was able to hold his gaze.

"Where did you find him?" I was determined to be able to carry on a normal conversation.

He only hesitated for an instant. "In Argentina. He was a birthday present from my mom."

My jaw dropped. He grinned at my look of amazement.

"I was spoiled rotten, I know." He paused, thinking. "I was going through a hard time, and I think my mom hoped that polo would focus my energies on something positive... and it worked. At least, it delayed the worst of the trouble."

I couldn't believe that I was related to someone with that kind of lifestyle—who could jet down to another continent to buy a horse. Seth and I considered ourselves fortunate, but we were always working, and Dec worked two jobs. I managed to close my mouth while he was talking.

"And what made you pick Kermit?" Attraction—whether between or within a species—is so subtle, yet also so definite. I always found it fascinating.

His whole face softened; his eyes were liquid with affection as he thought about his horse. I felt a sudden rush of warmth toward him— he truly was a kindred spirit, in some ways.

"There were so many things... the Argentineans breed the best polo ponies in the world, so some things you'd expect: he's very fast, he has good endurance, and he's agile. But Kermit himself is something else. It was his color that first made me notice him, and as I got to know him I discovered he's intelligent, and courageous, and tough... he's got a very strong personality. I liked that about him. He's quirky. For instance, the first year I had him he bucked every time I got on him. I checked his tack, had the vet check him from nose to tail, tried changing our routine—but it was just his way of making me take him seriously. That's how he got his name; he bucked like a frog." He chuckled at the memory.

I nodded, smiling. It was the kind of thing that would attract me, too.

Jaden headed back to Toronto, and I headed upstairs to do homework, but two hours later I'd gotten very little done. I sighed; I didn't know what I was going to do about school. Dec was going to have a fit when he saw my report card.

I found myself engaging less and less with my classmates, except for Teri who, bless her, was the same down-to-earth, supportive friend as ever, despite my grim moodiness. The only points of light were at the barn, when I worked with Kermit and Schweppes. I initiated clicker training with Kermit; since it began with me feeding him treats every time I pressed the clicker, Kermit, like most horses, was happy to cooperate. As we progressed, though, he proved to be very inquisitive and intelligent—I enjoyed working with him. Jaden was right about his horse, he was a character. I also brought Schweppes out to the round pen. It took a lot longer to achieve 'join up' with him than it had with Kermit, which just confirmed my theory that Schweppes had trust issues.

On Saturday morning I had Catherine, one of my best students, ride him in a lesson, and within minutes he had bucked her off. I got on him, worried, but he seemed to be fine when I rode him. I was still shaking my head when I went into the barn and saw Jaden. Piba was on the crossties.

"I saw some of the action," he commented.

"Weird, isn't it? I'm not sure what's bothering him."

"Well, this isn't my area of expertise, Tea, but you're a very soft, fluid rider. It looks to me like he simply prefers your riding style."

"Well, I hope you're wrong there," I said, shaking my head, "because he's supposed to be a school horse. Dec won't keep him if I'm the only one who can ride him."

Jaden tacked up while I put Schweppes away.

"Wow, that's a lot of gear," I remarked. Piba was wearing way more tack than I was used to seeing.

"You'll have to come watch a game this summer," he said. "You'll see why we need it."

I'd been curious about Jaden's riding. To be honest, my expectations weren't high—the horse world is pretty hierarchical, and showjumpers, like me, are generally considered to be the top of the heap, although every discipline naturally thought highly of its own style. What I'd heard of polo players didn't lead me to believe they were particularly skilled riders, though they were certainly tough. But Jaden surprised me. He rode languidly, his natural athleticism becoming evident right away. I noted the differences in riding style, but mostly I analyzed Jaden with the skill honed by many years of teaching riding. He was relaxed, balanced, and effective, and—most importantly—Piba appeared to be a happy and willing partner in their efforts. I mentally revised my opinion of polo players upward by several notches.

When he was done with Piba I asked Jaden to follow me. I went into Kermit's stall and patted his neck.

"You've got a very smart boy here," I told Jaden. "He's learning a lot. Why don't you take a bow for all your hard work, Kermit?"

Kermit promptly sank onto one knee, his other foreleg extended, and bowed his head down. I almost laughed aloud at the astonished look on Jaden's face.

"That's amazing," he exclaimed.

"I'm not trying to turn him into a trick pony or anything, but I wanted to start with something basic to help him grasp the concept of the clicker. And he learned very fast, didn't you, Kermit?"

I gave my head a tiny nod, one that would be almost imperceptible to the human eye, and Kermit nodded his sleek head up and down. This time Jaden laughed aloud. He had a nice laugh, I noticed—it was very carefree. He stepped into the stall and patted his horse.

"I can't believe you taught him that so quickly," he said, turning to me with his eyes shining. It took me a minute to look away.

"This type of thing is easy," I assured him. "The hard part is still ahead of us. I was going to start today, in fact."

The horse trailer was parked in a small paddock near the house. I collected the clicker and some treats, and we led Kermit toward the paddock. Halfway there he raised his head, snorting—he had spotted the trailer. His breath started coming faster, his tail went up and he started jogging and pulling on the lead shank. At the gate Jaden turned him loose. Kermit hugged the fence and did a high-stepping trot to the far corner, while I headed for the trailer. The fear came out of nowhere. It slammed into me, rooting me to the spot even as my limbs trembled and my breath came in rapid, shallow gasps. The sheer panic made it impossible to think; all I knew was that I had to get as far away from that trailer as possible. I backed away a few steps, then turned and headed for the fence. It took an incredible act of will to force myself not to run; I slipped through the fence boards and waited as my trembling lessened and my breathing slowed. Jaden loped over, frowning.

"What happened?" Damn, he'd noticed. This really wasn't something I wanted to get into with him... or anyone for that matter, other than Seth, who obviously knew.

"Nothing." Fortunately that came out sounding pretty casual. I was regaining my composure.

Jaden looked skeptical, but thankfully let it drop. I turned to watch Kermit. I pressed the clicker occasionally but soon called it quits; Kermit was agitated and I didn't want him associating too much fear with the paddock, since he'd be back here frequently.

"He's a tough case, isn't he," Jaden remarked as he led Kermit back to the barn.

"Yes, but don't give up hope. It's only our first try."

The week at school was tortuous. Not only was I behind in everything, but I just couldn't find it in myself to care. I hated being there, hated having to talk to people and try to act normal. Maybe it was because my mind wandered in class, and lately it had begun venturing into forbidden territory—Blaze. Right after the accident the pain had been so sharp, so overwhelming, that it had been relatively easy to shy away from any thought of him. My mind seemed to instinctively know what kind of suffering would follow thoughts of my dead horse, and it protected itself accordingly. Now, though, stray memories began to infiltrate my consciousness when my defenses were down. It was agonizing.

The only thing worse than school was Zac's decline. As I had predicted, Anne wasn't the right rider for him, and I watched with increasing dismay as he became a less confident jumper, and eventually started refusing. It was absolutely infuriating, but she refused all offers of help from me. It was the one thing I still felt some strong emotion about, so maybe it wasn't surprising that I made a foolish decision one night.

It was Friday evening, and I was alone. Seth was at swimming practice; Dec had gone out somewhere and told us not to expect him back until midnight or so. I wondered idly if he had a girlfriend. I was doing a last check of the deserted barn around nine, and stopped at Zac's stall when he whickered to me.

"I know, baby, I miss you too," I told him, stepping into the stall. He rubbed his soft nose against my cheek. "What's been going on with you lately, huh?" I asked him. "You're not yourself out there. You don't like Anne much, do you? Sorry, buddy. I'm so sorry you got sold to her." I continued talking as I stroked his neck. The idea hit me with a sudden, blinding sense of rightness—I could ride Zac. Everyone was gone, no boarders would show up this late. I could actually jump some real, jumper-sized fences again.

I was in the arena warming up within minutes. Zac seemed thrilled to have me on his back again. He was going as well as ever, and it wasn't long before I was jumping a line that I'd set up along one wall. He bounded over so joyfully that before long I raised it, then raised it again. Each time, he jumped it beautifully, and each time, I felt a small shift within me. It was as though, as my body moved in tune with Zac's, something that had been tightly bound was being slowly released. For the first time since the accident, I felt like opening my eyes.

Six

I patted Zac's sweaty neck over and over as we cantered away from the last fence. With a shock, I realized I felt... happy. I slowed to a walk, trying not to think about why joy was now a stranger to my life. It wasn't as hard as it should be, with my hand still on Zac's warm shoulder.

A furious word broke through my reverie.

"Tea!"

Oh, crap, crap, crap, I thought wildly. Dec wasn't due back for hours—why was he suddenly in the middle of the arena, hands on his hips, looking murderous? I cudgelled my brain for an inspired excuse, anything that might mitigate what I was doing in some way, but it remained obstinately blank.

"Come here," Dec snarled.

I dismounted and shuffled slowly toward him. I knew better than to stop out of range; I walked up close—close enough to be touched. As soon as he moved I closed my eyes. I expected a blow, but all I felt was his hand grabbing the front of my jacket. I was about to peek when Jaden's voice rang across the arena.

"Dec."

My eyes flew open to see Jaden striding toward us. I'd never been happier to see him, but he didn't meet my eyes at all; instead he raised a brow and looked straight at Dec. It was hard to tell who looked more disapproving. Dec glanced at me.

"Go cool off that horse. On foot," he ordered curtly. I turned quickly to run up my stirrup irons, my heart thudding from my close escape.

"What's going on?" Jaden demanded.

Zachary and I stumbled toward the track.

"Take a look at that combination—she was jumping *that* when I came in. No helmet in sight," Dec growled. Something that sounded suspiciously like a strangled oath escaped Jaden, and I was glad I had my back to him.

"And that's not all—that horse has a nasty stop in him," Dec went on.

I ground my teeth at the slur against Zac; hadn't I just proven the refusals weren't his fault?

"Also, his new owner has made it very clear that she doesn't want Tea riding him. In fact she hired another trainer."

"Has the other trainer been doing this with Zac?" Jaden's voice sounded amused as he indicated the jumps.

"Not even close."

I gazed at the jumps once more, and felt a warm glow of pride. I'd been positive the problem wasn't Zac... whatever I had coming for this, it was worth it. I laid my cheek on Zac's neck and hugged him as we walked, my arm under his neck. I heard the murmur of Dec and Jaden's discussion as we circled the arena, but I didn't look their way until Dec addressed me.

"Make sure you get every mark off him." He glared at me as he headed for the door. "And come into the house as soon as you're done."

I gulped at the thought of what would await me there.

To my surprise, I found Jaden waiting in the barn. "Thanks for before," I said. "Nice timing."

"Anytime." He smiled slightly, his eyes warm. "I thought I'd help you groom."

"I'm not really in a hurry to be done." To put it mildly.

"We'll take our time, then." He grabbed some brushes. I could hear him pat Zac's neck and murmur to him as he worked. We groomed in silence for a few minutes, the soft swishing of our brushes added to the comforting background sounds of horses chewing hay and rustling in their stalls. Even though the barn was older now, it had been a high-end show barn in its day, and it was still beautiful.

"I was wondering," Jaden said casually, "I know another trainer's been riding this horse. And from what I understand, you've got a low opinion of her skills."

I was surprised, and glad my face was hidden by Zac's body. How did he know that?

"So why are you doing this?" he continued. "Getting yourself into trouble, especially when she'll get the credit for Zac's improvement?"

I sighed. "It's not about her, it's about Zac," I said. "I wanted to make sure he was okay, that he hadn't lost his confidence."

"And to prove to yourself that you're better than the new trainer?" he guessed shrewdly.

"Maybe that had something to do with it," I allowed.

Jaden came and stood in front of me; his face was grave as his eyes searched my face. I was struck again by how ridiculously handsome he was.

"I can understand that. But jumping without a helmet—really, what were you thinking? And so soon after-"

"You know," I cut him off angrily, "in about ten minutes Dec will be giving me the same speech, only his will be delivered a lot louder and followed by a few good smacks to get his point across—so you can save your breath." I scowled at him.

He didn't look at all perturbed by my outburst. A small smile played around the corners of his mouth. "Oh, I don't think you'll be punished too severely."

I snorted. "Then you don't know Dec very well."

"Do you know what I saw in his eyes just now?"

"Other than homicidal rage, you mean?"

"I saw pride. Yes, he's angry—and he has a right to be, frankly—but he's proud of what you were able to do. And I think he's relieved, too." He didn't expand on why Dec might feel relieved, and I was glad about that.

We finished grooming, and I put Zac in his stall with a final hug. Riding him again had been great, but I was afraid I'd start missing him all over again now. Jaden walked me to the house, and I appreciated the company—I didn't want to face Dec alone. I paused on the porch, nervous now.

"Are you coming in?" I asked somewhat hopefully. I could hardly see his face in the dark; only the sharp angles of his cheekbone and jaw were visible.

"Do you want me to?"

"Yeah," I admitted, ashamed to be such a chicken.

I felt his hand on my shoulder; it was very warm. Comforting.

"Can I give you some advice?"

"Sure," I said suspiciously.

"Tell Dec the truth. Tell him how you're feeling, why you wanted to ride Zac so badly."

My voice was very low as I answered, "I don't think he'll care." I was surprised at how painful the thought was.

81

"Humor me," he said softly.

I shrugged. It couldn't hurt, I supposed.

We found Dec in the kitchen, drinking coffee at the head of the table. I stopped at the other end, and stood uncomfortably with my hands gripping the back of the chair. Jaden went and got himself a drink. He stayed by the counter, but gave me an encouraging nod when I glanced his way.

I looked at Dec; his expression was impassive. Better than mad, anyway. I examined the surface of the table while I spoke.

"I'm sorry, Dec," I began nervously. Might as well get the apology out of the way first, then maybe he'd hear me out. "I know I shouldn't have done that."

"Why did you, then?" he demanded. I risked a glance at his face; he didn't look angry as much as... frustrated.

"I—well, I really miss jumping, for one thing," I told him hesitantly. My eyes were back on the table, my voice quiet. "And I also miss Zac, I was worried about him, he's seemed so unhappy lately. I wanted to make sure he was okay."

I heard Dec clear his throat. I looked up to find him watching me thoughtfully.

"Well, I'm assuming you know better than to pull a stunt like that again."

I nodded quickly.

"You're still grounded, though. Two weeks," he said gruffly. "And Tea, if I ever catch you jumping without a helmet again..." He let the threat hang. I nodded again, relieved to be getting off so lightly.

"Good night." I was anxious to make my escape to bed. Jaden winked at me when I caught his eye, and to my surprise I had to suppress a smile.

I used Schweppes in another lesson that weekend, and although he looked irritated from the beginning, he didn't do anything drastic. Erin was a rather stiff rider, and her aids weren't that smoothly applied. I could understand why Schweppes would object, but as a school horse he would have to get used to less-than-perfect riders.

My students started jumping, queuing up their horses to go one at a time. Out of the corner of my eye, I saw Schweppes shake his head in anger, grab the bit, and take off. He galloped across the arena straight for an oxer that remained from a previous lesson, it was too big for these students, but before I could react he had jumped it. Erin fell off as he landed, and I ran over anxiously to check on her.

"Are you all right?" I knelt next to her; she was crying.

"Yes," she sniffed. She got up and started brushing herself off.

Seth and Jaden strolled in as I worriedly went to collect Schweppes. "Hey, T," Seth called out. I turned, distracted, just as I grabbed Schweppes' reins.

"Ow!" I jumped and spun toward him; he had bitten me hard on the forearm. He stepped back quickly and flung up his head, frightened. He'd obviously been hit for this kind of behavior before. I shook my head, disgusted. This was one of the things Dec and I argued about—he thought nothing of hitting a horse that bit, even though it rarely changed their behavior. As I had repeatedly pointed out to him, it only made them head-shy. Erin decided to call it a day, so I finished teaching while sitting on Schweppes. It seemed safer than standing next to him.

Jaden came and found me while I was untacking.

"Why is Dec keeping that horse?" he asked, frowning.

"Dec doesn't exactly know," I admitted. "Schweppes just needs a bit more time and kindness; he'll come around."

"He's a menace. I saw him bite you."

"It's nothing," I insisted.

He grabbed my arm and pushed my sleeve up. The bite mark was already red and swollen—it was going to be a bad bruise.

"That's not nothing. And you can't fix a bad temperament."

"Why are you assuming he's innately bad?" I demanded angrily.

"Why are you assuming he's not?" I could tell he was getting angry too, but he kept his voice lower than mine.

"Because I prefer to give others the benefit of the doubt, until such time as they prove to me they're not capable of change," I growled at him. His eyes narrowed; I lifted my chin and gave him a challenging look. "I'm asking you not to tell Dec about this horse. Let's see if you're capable of change, Jaden."

A spasm crossed his face. "I won't make the same mistake twice," he said in a flat, low voice, "but you'd better pray this horse doesn't really hurt someone. Including you."

Seth, Jaden and I went to clean tack after dinner. The barn was empty, since most people came during the day on weekends. It was cozy in the tackroom; we turned the radio on and took our time cleaning while we talked.

"This brings back memories," Jaden remarked. "I've spent many an evening in here."

"How come I only remember seeing you a few times, then? Dec claims you were always underfoot, but we barely saw you after we moved here," Seth said.

"I used to spend most of my summers here—Dec and Gran are the ones who taught me to ride. But you arrived right before I moved in with my dad; I was sixteen, so you two would have been what, ten?"

"Eleven," I recalled. Dec had been upset about Jaden moving; I remembered overhearing him talking to my mom.

"So your parents were already divorced by then... how old were you when they split?" Seth asked.

"Thirteen."

"Do you know what happened?" Seth continued, hanging up a bridle.

"Yes. My mom left my dad because he hit me."

"And..." Seth looked confused.

Jaden looked up. "A lot."

"Oh. Sorry, man," Seth offered. He looked abashed.

"No worries. It's in the past."

"So your dad was following the Foster family tradition, then." Seth grinned. I sighed; Seth couldn't stay serious for more than a minute.

"Family curse, more like," Jaden countered. "You must have heard about Granddad—all the Foster men tend to strike first and question later."

"But you're not like that," I said suddenly. It was clear from his horses' behavior that he never handled them roughly.

There was a pause before Jaden looked at me. "It took time, and a lot of effort, for me not to be that way," he said quietly.

"So maybe it's not too late for Seth..." I joked.

We all laughed; Seth was the least violent person I knew. Far less so than me. The conversation turned to lighter matters—much of it seemed to involve cars—but I was still thinking about Jaden's revelation. I had assumed he'd lived some sort of charmed, cosseted life. I was ashamed of how far off I'd been.

School wasn't getting any better. You'd think that, being grounded, I'd have more time to study, but I just couldn't seem to concentrate for any length of time. So, as usual, I focused on horses instead.

I started using the clicker to try to change Schweppes' attitude, by rewarding him for greeting me in a friendly way rather than threatening me every time I opened his stall. It was the first time I'd attempted to change something as nebulous as attitude—usually I employed the clicker to teach specific behaviors. But it gave me an idea.

I hadn't had any luck in getting Kermit near the trailer, and it struck me, as I mulled over the problem, that I was going about it backward. In the end, all I wanted was for him to be calm in the trailer, so I set about rewarding him for calm behavior, not knowing if it would work at all.

During our next session I started off rewarding Kermit as soon as I led him outside. I headed slowly toward the paddock, where the trailer was still ominously parked. Kermit noticed; his head came up, and his body tensed. I allowed him to stop, and backed him up a few steps. As soon as he began to change his hyper-alert stance I pressed the clicker, and he actually looked at me in surprise. I felt a swell of pride—he understood what I was saying. I kept at it for another few minutes, reinforcing my point, and then put him back in his stall with lots of treats and encouragement. I had a good feeling about Kermit.

Monday morning I was exhausted. I slumped down the stairs dragging my bag, and in the kitchen I dropped heavily into a chair. Dec was away on business for two days so it was just Seth and I.

"Did you make coffee?" I yawned.

"No, and we don't have time now, either. Here's some toast, though." He handed me a plate. "Hurry up, we've gotta go."

The thought of rushing off to another endless miserable day at school was suddenly too much for me.

"You know what? You go ahead. I'm going to stay home today," I said decisively.

Seth looked at me, aghast. Dec had strong feelings about school—surprise, surprise. We weren't allowed to miss any unless we were practically on our deathbeds. If he were here, I knew without a doubt that I'd be going. But he wasn't here, and I couldn't face another day.

"Tea-"

"Let's not argue, Seth. You won't win this one."

He looked at me carefully and sighed; he knew when I was serious.

That night, we chatted about our days while doing chores in the tackroom. I was looking forward to getting to bed.

"I'm not going tomorrow, either." Missing school was the best idea I'd had in a long time.

"What? Are you *trying* to get Dec to kill you?" He threw me a worried look as he transferred clean saddlepads into the dryer.

"I don't care, Seth." It was true, I really didn't.

He blew his breath out noisily, frustrated. "You know, all this death wish stuff would go over better if you were goth."

"Who's got a death wish?" Jaden's voice startled me; I hadn't heard him come in.

"Hey, dude. Shrimpo here is ditching school. Hence the death talk, 'cause she's toast when Dec finds out."

I was afraid that Jaden would launch straight into lecture mode, and I had no patience for it, so I kept my eyes on the bandage I was rolling, prepared to tune him out. I saw him in my peripheral vision as he came and picked a clean bandage from the pile in front of me. He sat down a few feet away to roll it.

"So," he said conversationally, "how much time are you planning to take off?"

I looked at him in surprise—it certainly wasn't the response I'd been expecting. He kept his eyes on his work.

"I don't know," I said in a low voice.

He nodded thoughtfully. "Would the rest of the week be enough?"

"Hold on here—she's in enough trouble already. She can't be taking *more* time off," Seth objected.

"She can if she has a doctor's note," Jaden said reasonably. "And my mother is a psychologist, remember?"

I stared at him in disbelief; my heart felt lighter at the mere suggestion of escaping the drudgery of school for a few days.

"But... would she write me one?" I asked him doubtfully.

"I think she will. She knows you're grieving." He said it with surprising gentleness, but I still flinched at the word. "And if she won't," he added with an impish smile, "I sign her name as well as she does... and I have access to her stationery." He winked at me.

"But-" Seth's objections were drowned out as Jaden and I started planning.

"Go to school in the morning, and I'll meet you in the office."

"But where will I go after? I can't hang out in town."

"Come to my place—you can take the car, right?"

"Yeah." I was getting almost excited.

"Hey! Time out!" Seth interrupted loudly. Jaden and I both looked around in surprise. "This is risky, Sis," Seth reminded me. He was unusually serious these days, I realized with a pang, and I was pretty sure that my withdrawal and constant sadness were the cause.

"I don't care," I reiterated. "I'll go insane if I have to sit through another day of school right now."

He shrugged, giving up, but the troubled look on his face made me feel even guiltier. I went over and put my arms around him.

"Don't worry, Moo. It'll be fine. I *need* this." I rarely used my childhood nickname for him anymore; the look I gave him was pleading.

He smiled, finally, and ruffled my hair. "Well, good riddance, then."

The plan went off without a hitch in the morning. I fidgeted nervously on a bench in the office while waiting for Jaden to arrive, but I needn't have worried. He walked in wearing a suit, and every single person in the office, male and female, turned to watch as he loped over to me. The secretary didn't even glance at the letter; she was far too busy gawking at Jaden. Just like that, I was free.

I waited until we were outside before I risked looking at him.

"Thanks—I owe you big."

He shook his head. "You don't owe me a thing."

I followed Jaden into the city. His place was on the second floor of a brick building that looked like it might have once been a factory. He unlocked the door and let me in first, and I stopped inside the doorway and looked around curiously. It was a loft-style space, very open, with high ceilings. The kitchen was right in front of me; only a counter separated it from the living room to my right. There was a hallway to my left.

"Make yourself at home. I've got to get changed for school." He disappeared through a doorway at the end of the hall.

I wandered into the living room, feeling a bit awkward now that I was actually here. A large window dominated the far wall, with the rest of the wall covered by canvases of all sizes. On the wall near the kitchen counter were grouped some pictures of polo ponies. I recognized

Kermit and Piba; I assumed the rest were the horses Jaden had sold. I was admiring them when he rushed back into the hall, dressed in jeans, sneakers and a cool jacket I'd never seen at the barn.

"I've got to run. I'm leaving you my laptop, so you can surf if you feel like it." He pointed it out on the kitchen counter. "Help yourself to anything in the fridge." He slung his bag over his shoulder and paused by the door. "Oh, and, you're not planning to go out, are you?"

"I hadn't thought about it—why?"

"I'd rather you didn't go wandering around the city by yourself, that's all."

"Okay." I shrugged. It really made no difference to me; I was equally miserable anywhere these days.

"I'll see you at lunchtime," he called over his shoulder on his way out.

I had a sneaking suspicion that he was only coming home to check on me.

Once Jaden was gone I explored a bit more. When I got to the bedroom I went in a bit timidly. The walls were a light brownish color; I couldn't name it, but I liked it. There were two windows in here, and more pictures of horses on the walls. As I turned back toward the door I stopped in surprise—hanging in the corner was a punching bag, the kind you see in gyms. I smiled; that helped explain the fantastically toned body. There was a good picture of Jaden with his mom and sister by the bed, but as I sat down to look at it, I felt a sense of wrenching dislocation. The clawed animal—the one I'd hoped had moved to a new burrow—was back, and my insides were once again shredded by its razor-sharp talons. I wrapped my arms around my stomach in anguish and lay on the bed, curled into a tight ball, and waited for the pain to pass.

I awoke sensing a presence. My eyes flew open as I remembered where I was, and I sat up in a rush.

"Hey, sleeping beauty," Jaden greeted me. "I hope I didn't scare you."

"Oh—uh, no. Sorry... I don't know how I ended up here." I was disoriented, and a bit embarrassed that he had found me on his bed.

"I'm glad you had a nap. You looked exhausted."

I felt exhausted, too. I still wasn't sleeping well; I suppose it wasn't surprising that I'd fallen asleep during the day, now that I had the chance.

"I'm going to make lunch." He headed for the kitchen, and I went to the washroom and washed my face, trying to wake up.

"So why the suit this morning?" I climbed onto a stool and watched him in the kitchen.

"Because it's important to look the part. I was claiming to have the authority to take you out of school—I thought they'd be less likely to question me if I looked respectable."

I didn't think 'respectable' quite covered it. 'Spectacular' would be more accurate.

"Very clandestine. Thanks." I noticed that he was preparing two plates. "Um, Jaden, I'm not really hungry..."

He looked at me thoughtfully.

"Sorry, Tea—my place, my rules. If you want to hang out here, you're going to have to eat." He dropped a plate in front of me, then walked around the counter to stand next to me. He ran his hand down my back, then across my ribs. It wasn't a caress; it was purely appraising, the way I might run my hand over a horse's ribs to assess her weight. "You're way too thin."

I started to protest, but wilted instead. I inspected my plate with a sigh. On it was some kind of wrap, along with a bowl of sauce for dipping.

"Try it," he encouraged. "It's vegetarian."

I smiled. It felt odd, like I was out of practice. My eyes widened in surprise when I tried the wrap—it was really good.

"Wow," I said, "I can't believe you made this... you can cook?"

He gave half a shrug. "Well, I have to feed myself, and I like to eat well."

When I couldn't finish my wrap he polished it off happily, making me feel right at home, since Seth usually finished what I didn't.

Before he left he handed me a key and a piece of paper. "You'll be leaving before I get back, so here's a map. And this is the key to my place. I'll see you at lunch tomorrow."

After he left I spent most of the afternoon on the couch, reading a novel. I couldn't go on this way indefinitely, I realized sadly—my homework was piling up—but it was a nice break.

As I was getting out of the shower the next morning I caught sight of myself in the mirror. I'd lost some weight, I had to admit—I could see ribs on my reflection. I stepped onto the bathroom scale. Dammit, I thought. I'd really wanted to prove Jaden wrong... but the scale said ninety-eight pounds. I tried getting off and stepping back on, but the number remained stubbornly the same. I resolved to make an effort to eat; I'd have no stamina for riding if I stayed this thin.

When I got to Jaden's I tried to sort through my assignments. By now everything was urgent. I got tired just thinking about it, so I pulled out my math—the subject I least needed to work on, but the one that would take the least effort.

Jaden found me still absorbed in it at lunchtime. "Calculus?" he queried, looking over my shoulder.

"Trig. Calculus is next year."

"Ugh." He shuddered. "I'm glad that's behind me."

I was surprised. From what Dec had told us Jaden was a very bright student. "You don't like math?"

"Not really," he admitted. He had moved into the kitchen and was putting a pot on the stove. "I hear you're a whiz at it, though. What other subjects do you like?"

"Now? I couldn't tell you," I answered, suddenly subdued again as I realized the truth of those words. Jaden just nodded. He made pasta with vegetables and some kind of cream sauce; it was as delicious as yesterday's wrap. I ate a bit more than I had the day before, and was rewarded by his smile of approval. He finished my leftovers again. When I started doing the dishes he got a dishtowel and dried.

"I'll do that, Jaden—don't you have to go?"

"Soon." He perused my face as he wiped a bowl. "How have you been sleeping?"

I shifted uncomfortably under his scrutiny. "Fine," I lied.

"You still look tired." He hesitated, then went on gently. "Tea, have you considered talking to someone? A therapist, I mean."

I shook my head vehemently. "I don't need to. I'm fine."

"Well, you don't seem fine," he said bluntly. My eyes flew to his face, startled. "Your behavior's been erratic, you're exhausted, you've lost weight—those are all classic symptoms of depression."

I shrugged noncommittally. I didn't care what he thought my symptoms were, I wasn't about to talk to some stranger about Blaze.

He sighed. "Sometimes I think living with Dec has made you feel like you have to be tough all the time."

"I do have to be tough." It just slipped out; I didn't know what made me say it, but I kept washing the pot without looking at him.

90

I felt his arms go around me. He pulled my hands out of the sink and cradled my head to his chest with one hand. To my shock, I found myself shaking violently, sobs threatening to burst from my throat. We stayed that way for a minute, Jaden holding me while I struggled to control myself.

"I wish you'd just let it out, Tea," he murmured.

I pulled out of his embrace and backed up until I felt the counter at my back, keeping my eyes down and grinding my teeth against the sobs. I thought I heard him sigh again, but to my relief he didn't come any closer.

"Will you be okay if I go back to school?"

"Yes." My voice was rough.

"All right. I—I'll see you tomorrow." He sounded subdued. I listened to the sounds of his exit before returning to the sink.

Exhaustion crashed over me while I finished the dishes, so I went and lay on the bed again. I was shivering, and I pulled back the covers and got under the comforter. As my head sank into the pillow I caught a hint of Jaden's scent—I didn't know why it made my throat constrict, but suddenly I couldn't hold back the sobs any longer.

I awoke with a start. It was late, and I dashed around frantically grabbing my stuff before running out to the car, still half-asleep. It wasn't until I was on the highway that I remembered what had happened at lunchtime; I felt a hot flush of embarrassment at the memory. I wasn't sure how to account for the intensity of my reaction, but upon reflection I still couldn't figure it out, and after a while I gave up.

The next morning I impressed myself by working on biology and English. I was somewhat worried about seeing Jaden; I didn't want to talk about my almost-breakdown. To my relief he acted as though nothing had happened when he arrived at midday.

"Hi cuz," he said. "What do you feel like eating?"

"I don't know. I have no imagination when it comes to food," I admitted.

Jaden made sandwiches while I quizzed him about what law school was like. His descriptions of his professors and fellow students made me smile; they were insightful, and not always complimentary. I had trouble picturing him in that kind of environment, though, and told him so while we started eating.

"Why?" he asked curiously.

"I don't know... 'lawyer' just sounds like too stuffy a term to apply to you."

He grinned. "At least I'll be able to get you out of trouble when you're arrested for radical activism."

"All right, so you'll come in useful," I conceded. "But what made you choose law in the first place?"

"Well, I've had the opportunity to travel quite a bit, and though I work in wealthy countries, when I travel for pleasure I like to stray off the beaten path. I've made my way through most of Central and South America, as well as a bit of Asia, and many of the people there have very little in the way of protection. I saw enough outrageous and flagrant abuses to make me want to be a human rights lawyer, so I could help people protect themselves."

"But what about playing polo? Won't you miss it?" I couldn't imagine giving up riding for an office job.

"I'll still play, just not professionally. But yes, I'll miss it, and the transition is hard. I've had to do a lot of adjusting this year already."

I checked the clock. "Hey, don't you have to be back at school by now?" I asked him.

"In theory—but I thought I'd hang out with you this afternoon."

"You're gonna get in trub-ble," I sang.

"Nah. There's a girl in my class with a crush on me," he said easily. "She'll give me a copy of her notes."

"I doubt there's just one," I muttered under my breath.

He didn't seem to hear. "What do you want to do? Walk around downtown? Catch a movie? Go shopping?" he rattled off suggestions.

I started to perk up; an afternoon outside, doing something different, sounded great.

"How about we start off walking and see where it leads us?"

It was a nice day for March, and wandering the city with Jaden was like having an insider's guide. We window-shopped, ate some Vietnamese food when Jaden inevitably got hungry, and browsed through a bookstore. We were at a coffee shop, warming up, when the conversation turned back to horses.

"Remember that day we put Kermit in the paddock with the trailer?" he asked.

"Yes." I tried to say it as normally as possible, but I wasn't likely to forget that day.

"What happened? Why were you upset?"

"I—what makes you think I was upset?" I equivocated.

He gave me a 'what do you take me for' kind of look; I raised my brows back at him. I wasn't admitting anything.

"All right, then," he said, watching my face. "When he ran from the trailer, you started shaking like a leaf. You backed away from it also, and your face was white. You didn't even want to get near it on your way out, you went through the fence instead. And you had me catch Kermit later."

I leaned back in my chair and stared at the ground, stunned. I was grossly underestimating his powers of observation, that much was clear.

"And up goes the wall again," he muttered. I glanced at him. "You have more defenses than the Pentagon, Tea."

I assessed my posture—arms tight over my chest, teeth clamped together—and had to smile slightly.

"You can trust me, you know." He leaned toward me over the table, his gaze locking onto mine. Its intensity was like a physical force; I could feel its pressure on my skin. "I know I haven't always given you reason to in the past, but... I'm on your side. Really." There was no doubting the sincerity in his eyes.

"I *do* trust you." And I found, as I said it, that it was true. "It's just that—what happened—it's not something I talk about."

He smiled, and the intensity evaporated.

"Okay, how about I go first. I'll tell you something private about myself." He paused, and the smile faded. "Something that's not easy for me to talk about, because... I'm ashamed of it."

He definitely had my full attention. I picked up my coffee cup so I'd have something to do with my hands, but I was watching his face closely. He swallowed before he went on.

"A few years ago, I was arrested, and charged with assault."

I struggled to keep from showing how shocked I was. Dec's golden boy *arrested*?

"That's really not what I expected," I admitted. "What happened?"

"I was at the racetrack—Fort Erie," he started. I felt my eyes widen, but didn't want to interrupt him. "I found two guys beating up a man I knew, and I stepped in. They were injured, and they pressed charges." He was looking down, folding and unfolding an empty sugar packet.

"Were you hurt?" He certainly didn't look like a fighter, not with that perfect face.

"No." He looked at me. "I've told you I went through a rough patch in my teens, right?" I nodded. "Well, I did a fair amount of fighting during that time. I was...practiced." He looked away again.

"Does Dec know about this?" I couldn't help asking.

To my surprise, he grinned. "Dec's the one I called to come and get me out of jail."

My mouth fell open. "Because... you were also suicidal?" I asked faintly.

His face softened. "I'm sure it must seem that way to you. But you might be surprised at what Dec's capable of. In any case, I didn't have a choice. I was too ashamed to call my mother, and I couldn't call my dad."

"What did he—what happened?"

"He didn't touch me, if that's what you're wondering," he said. "I did get the worst dressing down of my life on the drive home, though." His expression was troubled when he went on. "That's why... well, I never thought he'd be abusive toward you, Tea."

I stared at him in shock. "Dec's not abusive."

His eyes tightened in pain. "Yes, he is. He hits you."

"Well, yeah, but... it's not frequent. Or completely unjustified." I couldn't believe I was actually defending Dec to Jaden. I felt like Alice in Wonderland.

"It's *never* justified, Tea." He leaned forward; the intensity was back in spades. "You never deserve that—no matter what you might think."

I averted my gaze, feeling distinctly uncomfortable with the turn the conversation had taken.

"Okay, you win," I conceded, changing the subject. "Your secret is definitely bigger than mine."

His look of confusion only lasted a second, and then he grinned.

"So you'll tell me why you looked almost as freaked out as Kermit that day?"

I nodded. I was nervous now that it was my turn on the hotseat. "I looked as freaked out as him because I *was*," I began uncertainly. "Because—I don't know how to say this without sounding like I'm crazy."

"Just say it. I solemnly swear not to think you're crazy."

I searched his eyes. There was only curiosity there, no judgment. Not yet, anyway.

"You asked for it. Sometimes, when I'm close to a horse—usually only when I'm riding—I can feel what they're feeling." I blurted it out in a rush, not looking at him.

"Hmm," he said thoughtfully. I chanced a look at his face; he was frowning in concentration. "That makes sense, I suppose."

"It does?" I said blankly.

"Yes. You're very sensitive—though you hide it well—so maybe you have the ability to sense more than the average person. It would certainly help explain your great subtlety as a rider."

I felt my heart lift. Not only did Jaden not think I was crazy, he thought I had 'great subtlety'. I smiled at him.

He checked the time on his phone. "We'd better head back. Say, can you make an excuse to be home late tomorrow?"

"Sure, I don't teach on Fridays." And I didn't have any horses to ride. Sigh.

"I'm having some friends over after school, and I'm going to your place for the weekend. If you'd like, you can stay and meet my friends, and I'll follow you home afterward."

"Okay." I was a bit surprised that he'd asked, but he was good company. It would be better than moping around at home.

We started walking back toward Jaden's.

"So, what happened with the assault charge?" I asked him, a bit hesitantly.

"It was dropped, fortunately. You know, that whole incident ended up being a turning point in my life." He glanced down at me thoughtfully. "I got some counseling, I let go of my anger, and everyone—including me—was a lot happier."

"If that's your oh-so-subtle plug for therapy, I'm still not buying it," I told him.

"You're just as stubborn as Dec," he muttered. "Who knew that was a learned behavior?"

I looked at him quizzically.

"Dec's been getting counseling. Did you know that?"

I stopped dead on the sidewalk; he pulled me out of the way to let other pedestrians pass.

"I take it you didn't," he said.

I shook my head. I was speechless. Jaden leaned one shoulder against the storefront wall and watched me absorb the news.

"Why?" I finally managed to ask. "And since when?"

"It's been a few months now. I tried to convince him to start last fall, after Seth told me... after the racetrack. But he flatly refused. Then, when I saw you try to goad him into hitting you after the Royal-"

"That's not what I was doing," I denied indignantly.

"It is and you know it. I'm familiar with the dynamic, Tea. Anyway, at that point I called in the big guns—my mom. She convinced Dec, and he's been undergoing therapy ever since, with her. It's not ideal, given their relationship, but he refused to do it any other way."

"Dec's getting counselling... because of us? Seth and me?" I still couldn't believe it.

"Yes. And he's made changes, I think," Jaden replied seriously.

"Why are you doing all of this?" I demanded suddenly.

"We're family, Tea. That means something to me."

"Oh, that's right," I replied, fighting a smile. "Carte blanche to meddle in my life—I almost forgot."

Fortunately all the unaccustomed quiet time during my drive home gave me the opportunity for reflection, because I had a lot to think about. I considered Jaden's characterization of Dec as abusive; I was doubtful. Dec rarely hit Seth, other than the odd cuff to the head. And as for me, well, I could have driven Gandhi to violence. I tried to pinpoint changes in Dec's behavior, but I'd been so blinkered by misery these past few months that I couldn't be sure. He'd been more reasonable than I expected when I rode Zac, but I had chalked that up to Jaden's presence. Maybe there was more to it than that. Then there was Jaden's admission of his arrest. I had a hard time imagining it, he always seemed so... controlled. I'd never seen him lose his temper.

Seth missed the bus the next morning, so I drove him to school. He wasn't back to his usual blithe self yet; he wasn't even dating. We went to a drive-through for coffee on the way. As he was pulling his wallet out of his schoolbag a pack of cigarettes fell out.

"What the hell, Seth?" I exclaimed, shocked.

He shrugged. "Don't freak out, Sis, it's not a big deal. I just needed something to steady my nerves a bit."

"What do you *mean* it's not a big deal? It's a huge deal—you're an athlete, for crying out loud! And you know what will happen if Dec ever catches you."

Smoking was at the very top of Dec's list of 'zero tolerance' activities—if he ever caught either of us with a cigarette we would be flayed half to death, therapy notwithstanding. Of that I had no doubt.

"I'm quitting, anyway, so don't worry about it."

"How long have you been smoking?" I felt as though I'd just stepped into a parallel dimension; that Seth could be doing this without my knowledge seemed impossible.

"Just a couple of weeks."

We got our coffees and I went and parked in the lot.

"Hey, I'm gonna be late," he protested. I grabbed his arm and waited for him to look at me. His eyes were troubled.

"Moo... look, I'm sorry I've been so messed up lately..." I began awkwardly.

"This isn't about you, T." He averted his eyes, sighing. "I'm on probation with the swim team. My coach says I'm not 'committed', whatever that means," he said bitterly.

"Oh." I knew Seth loved swimming, but secretly I thought maybe his coach had a point... it wasn't just the swimming, though. Seth ran hot and cold with everything. "I'm really sorry to hear that, but I don't see how smoking-"

"Look, I told you, I'm quitting. Promise." He flashed me a smile, and I relented enough to drive him to school.

I barely noticed driving into the city, consumed as I was by worry and guilt. I'd been wallowing so deeply in my own grief that I hadn't even noticed how much Seth was being affected. He was undoubtedly troubled by the probation, but I was sure there was more to it than that. I wasn't picking up after him at home, which caused some tension between him and Dec. I also normally kept Seth organized—I reminded him when his library books were due, when to pay his swim meet entry fees... I supposed I hadn't been doing those things either. I hadn't really noticed. And Seth had loved Blaze too.

I got another surprise when I arrived at Jaden's: he was home, unshaven and drinking coffee in front of his laptop.

"Did I miss the memo?" I asked.

"Hey, you're taking the whole week off, can't I take a day?"

"I thought law school was supposed to be hard," I grumbled.

"'Hard' is relative."

I dumped my bag on the couch and went to sit by him. He studied my face for a moment before asking, "What's wrong?"

I hesitated, wondering how far I could trust him. The desire to share my worry won out over caution. "Promise not to say anything? To anyone?"

He nodded.

"Seth started smoking." The sorrow was clear in my voice.

"Damn." He turned to face me. "This has been a bad time for both of you, hasn't it?"

I shrugged. I really didn't know what was going on anymore.

"You know, when you grow up with a psychologist as your mom, eventually some of their reasoning starts to rub off," he said. "Sometimes you'll hear how someone is feeling and guess how they'll behave, and other times you can look at a person's behavior and guess at the feelings driving it."

I frowned at him. "What are you talking about?"

He took a breath before continuing. "One of the basic tenets of psychology is that guilt demands punishment. So if you're feeling guilty about something, you'll subconsciously act out in ways that will hurt you. Or that will get you caught."

I stared at him in confusion. "But—what would Seth have to feel guilty about? He's a wonderful person." A way better person than I was.

It was his turn to shrug. "Guilt isn't logical. We can feel it over things we have no control over, things we're not responsible for."

I suddenly knew where he was going with this, and I felt abruptly angry.

"Would you please give the psychoanalysis a rest?"

"Sure," he said easily.

I went to the couch and tried to work on a chemistry assignment for a while, but I couldn't concentrate.

"Can I ask you something?" I said finally, when I couldn't look at another formula.

"Of course." He came and sprawled on the couch next to me. "I'd rather talk to you than study, anyway."

For some reason I found myself unreasonably flattered.

"Why did you do all that fighting, in your teens?"

"It's kind of a long story."

"I'm not really in the mood for homework today."

And so we talked. He started off telling me about his dad—I could tell he was censoring a lot there—and we moved on to his parent's divorce, his relationship with his sister (good, but not especially close),

98

his troubled teens, and finally, as always, back to polo and horses. Somehow, along the way, a lot of other things emerged too... by mid-afternoon I found myself talking about my mom, and Blaze, and my aspirations as a jumper rider.

"Why did you move in with your dad?" I asked him at one point.

"My mother and I were always fighting. My behavior was getting increasingly wild; she was doing her best to help, but I resented her efforts. I felt she was trying to control me. I thought I'd have more freedom at my dad's."

"But... weren't you worried about living with him?" I would have thought, considering their history, that it would be awkward at best.

He smiled. "What, about him getting physical? No. I was sixteen; I was as big as him by then. And in any case, the balance of power had shifted—he knew full well I wouldn't tolerate that anymore."

"How was it, living there?"

"Well, I did have more freedom. My dad worked a lot, and he wasn't too concerned about keeping track of my comings and goings."

"Sounds great." I grinned.

"I enjoyed myself for a while," he agreed. "I partied, drank, experimented with drugs... but eventually, I also crashed my car and totalled it, and almost got expelled from school. Only my dad's influence and, I suspect, a generous donation kept me there. In the end, I'd say it's nice to have someone around who cares enough to put their foot down, when that's what you need."

I wasn't convinced that I wouldn't prefer the freedom, personally. He had questions for me, too.

"How was life with Dec while your mom was still with you?"

"It was great. Seth and I thought we'd died and gone to heaven when we first moved. We went from a small townhouse in the suburbs to a whole farm to tear up." I smiled at the memory. "And my mom was so happy, her joy just kind of spilled over onto us, you know?"

He nodded. "Yes, I can imagine your mother having that effect. She was a beautiful woman, inside and out. When they got married Dec was the happiest I've ever seen him."

"To be honest, I didn't understand the attraction at first—they were so different. My mom was so open and easygoing, and Dec's so... not. Of course now I understand better. She was a single mom to two wild kids, and she was easily overwhelmed... stuff like bills and taxes and big decisions just freaked her out. And you know what Dec's like. When they started dating, he just took over everything."

We got up to get a drink; I leaned on the counter while Jaden poured orange juice.

"Level with me, Jaden—why all the psychology talk this morning?"

He handed me my juice.

"Because I see myself in you. You're behaving the way I did when my life started spiraling downhill, and I don't want you to go through what I did."

I was puzzled by his assessment. His problems mostly stemmed from his dad's abuse, and mine... well, I was just sad. Not only did I miss Blaze himself, but with his death I'd lost my last link to my mother, as well as a potential future career. I didn't see how those two things compared. I didn't want to tell him that, though, so I changed the subject.

"Who's coming over later?"

"My good friends Chris and Ryan—Ryan painted most of the pieces in the living room; Brianna—she's in my class at school, and Jesse. Jesse and I used to be in a band together."

I looked at him, startled. "You were in a band?"

"Yup. I was the drummer." He beat out a rhythm on the countertop with his fingers, then laughed at the face I was making. "What, can't picture it?"

"No, I can, that's the problem." I shook my head, striving to put my discomfort into words. "You're just so... accomplished. It makes me wonder what I've been doing with my time."

"I'll tell you what you've been doing—you've been *working*." As usual he looked frustrated when the subject came up. "I've led a much more privileged life than you have, Tea; I had the luxury of developing other interests."

I loved Jaden's friends. Chris and Ryan arrived first; Chris was part-Asian, good-looking, and very friendly. We were soon talking animatedly on the couch. Ryan was tall and slim, with loopy reddish-brown curls and a shy smile. I liked him instantly. Then came Jesse, with brown eyes and hair and a more mellow vibe. And lastly, Brianna. I wondered whether she was the girl who was crushing on Jaden, and I moved from the couch to a chair on her arrival, so that I could watch.

100

Brianna was not what I expected. She was black, with striking features and gold highlights in her hair. Jaden took her coat; he leaned close to her with a half-smile and spoke low in her ear. Her lips curved upward in response. He didn't touch her, but his expression was one I'd never seen before, almost... predatory. It made me uncomfortable, for some reason. Jaden introduced her to everyone; she looked even more exotic close up—her very skin seemed to exude a subtle shimmer. I felt very plain and provincial next to her, but I didn't have time to dwell on it because everyone—Brianna included—was so interesting. The conversation and laughter flowed freely while the music from Jaden and Jesse's old band played in the background. I was genuinely sorry when it was time to go.

Jaden walked me to my car.

"Are you dating Brianna?" I asked before I got in.

"Not yet." He grinned at me. "What do you think my chances are?"

"Excellent," I assured him. "Her body language was all 'go'."

"Thanks, kid." He ruffled my hair, and for some reason that irked me too.

Seven

On Saturday Jaden was going to the polo club. When he invited us along I accepted eagerly, but Seth had swimming practice. I wondered sadly whether the smoking had damaged his lungs yet.

It was a short drive to the club. It was my first time in Jaden's car since that ill-fated day at the racetrack seven months before, and I couldn't help reflecting on how our relationship had changed. Back then I'd barely known him, yet I had hated what I knew. And now, I thought he was not only the coolest cousin anyone could hope for, I also considered him a friend.

We drove down a wide driveway flanked by enormous stone lions and through tall wrought-iron gates; I assumed the huge building on the right was some sort of hotel until Jaden said, "That's the owners' house. I'll introduce you later."

The stable area was immaculately kept and dotted with barns; we went into the largest one and were immediately approached by a stocky, black-haired man. As he shook Jaden's hand he said something I didn't understand; for a second, I was mystified... until Jaden responded in what sounded like perfectly fluent Spanish. I gaped at him in shock. It made sense, of course—his mother was from Argentina. I knew Aunt Paloma spoke Spanish, but it hadn't occurred to me that Jaden would, too. He was looking at me now, taking in my open-mouthed expression.

"What?" he asked, grinning.

"It's just... I didn't know that you spoke Spanish." One more accomplishment to add to his already overly long list, I grumbled to myself.

"Tea, this is José. He works as a groom for the club; I was just telling him that you're my cousin." José looked at me with interest, and answered my tentative smile with a shy one of his own. We were admiring the horses in their stalls when a shriek rent the air behind us. I turned in time to see a black-haired girl throw herself at Jaden.

"Jaden! It's about time, I've been languishing here all morning," she said as she hugged him.

He laughed as he hugged her back. "I'm sure you found plenty of other people to annoy while you waited," he teased.

He kept his arm around her while he introduced us.

"Caley, this is my cousin, Tea. Caley's my long-time friend, sometimes-adversary, and a pretty fierce polo player. I'm looking forward to playing with her this summer, it's been too long."

Caley snorted. "Yeah, because you got too damn good." She looked at me. "Do you play, Tea?"

"No, I ride jumpers. I can't wait to see a match, though."

We wandered around as Caley and Jaden caught up on news. I watched them obliquely, wondering at their relationship. I'd only heard of one of Jaden's ex-girlfriends, a girl named Summer Davenport that he had dated for about a year. I'd overheard about Summer from Gran and my aunts, but Caley and Jaden also seemed close. I shook myself. So what if they were? I had close male friends, too. I supposed that seeing them together just made me realize how little I still knew him.

We progressed around the stable area, chatting with people along the way. I noticed that Jaden was treated with respect, almost deference at times. I guess he really was good. Another friend, a man with salt-and-pepper hair called Dan, was just setting out on a trail ride and invited Jaden along.

"Thanks, but I've got to drive my cousin home," Jaden told him.

"Are you in a rush to get back, Tea?" Caley asked me. I shook my head. "Why don't you go, J. I'll hang with your cuz," she told him, throwing an arm around me.

Jaden looked at me. "Would you mind?" I could tell he wanted to go.

"Not a bit. Have a good time."

Caley was a riot. She was hyperactive, irreverent, and talked almost non-stop. She wasn't at all what I expected of a polo player, and I told her so.

"Yup, I'm a freak. Don't expect the rest of them to be like me."

Horsepeople are a pretty traditional bunch, as a rule, and I wasn't surprised to hear that polo players were no exception. Caley, however, was something else—she had a sheet of chin-length black hair, but on the right side of her head she was rockin' a perfect violet circle. She told me it was dyed that way but I couldn't imagine how they did it. She also had a pierced eyebrow, and was wearing a lot of heavy black jewelry.

"Hey, I'm going to a big party soon if you're interested," she said after we'd been talking for a while. "Some of my friends are throwing it; they're renting an awesome space and they got some kick-ass DJs."

"I'm not nineteen yet—would I be able to get in?"

"It's not the kind of party where people drink." She winked at me.

"Oh... so they do other things?" I guessed. "Like a rave?"

She laughed. "I guess so, although I don't know anyone who'd call it that. And don't worry about supplies. I can hook you up with some great E, if you want."

I didn't want to sound like a total rube by checking whether she meant what I thought she did by 'E', so I didn't say anything. Caley gave me her number, though privately I thought there was no chance I'd be going. Jaden got back soon after; the trails had been too muddy for a long ride.

"How did you and Caley get along?" he asked on the drive home.

"Great. I love her look—she's like a punked-out Botticelli. Though I get the impression she uses the punk to distract from the Boticelli-ness."

He glanced at me. "You know, that's a very astute description of Caley.'"

"You don't have to sound so surprised."

"I'm only surprised because you're young."

I rolled my eyes at him. "Just because seventeen *rhymes* with philistine..."

He laughed, and I couldn't help joining in.

School that week was tolerable, but the weekend was way better. On Saturday I skipped into the house and dialed Jaden.

"Can you guess where your boy is right now?" I asked him smugly.

"Out on a date?"

"Better. He's standing in the trailer, cool as a cucumber, eating some hay," I told him airily.

"No *way!*" He sounded shocked.

"Uh-huh. I believe your trailer troubles are behind you. All you need to do now is take him for some short, stress-free test drives to make sure he's okay when it's moving."

"Tea, you are absolutely, without a doubt, one of the most incredible people I know. Thank you," he said fervently. "That is the best birthday present I've ever gotten, after Kermit himself."

104

"When was your birthday?" I asked in surprise. Dec hadn't mentioned anything, but then Dec, for all his efficiency, wasn't great with things like birthdays.

"Two weeks ago."

"Oh. Well, happy birthday."

"I'll be there tomorrow. I have to see this for myself."

Dec hooked up the trailer in preparation for Jaden's visit. Jaden went and got Kermit; once outside he stopped and held the lead rope out to me.

"Do you want to take him? Since he's used to you doing it?"

I smiled. "No, you go ahead. I want to you to get the full experience."

Jaden turned toward the trailer. He looked relaxed enough on the surface, but I noted his tight grip on the lead rope and his frequent glances at Kermit as they neared the ramp. Kermit made me proud, though; I felt my heart swell as he stepped nonchalantly onto the ramp and practically led Jaden inside. When Jaden came out he strode quickly up to me and before I knew it, he was hugging me tightly. My pulse quickened, and I broke into an instant sweat. When he released me I looked away, flustered.

"Thank you," he said again, sincerely.

"Maybe you should wait until after the test drive to thank me," I suggested.

We didn't take Kermit far; a ten-minute ride was plenty for the first time. Dec, Seth and Stephanie were waiting when we returned, and gave a cheer at our thumbs-up sign. Kermit seemed perfectly comfortable when he came out of the trailer, and looked at me expectantly.

"I didn't forget," I laughed, feeding him an apple and petting his sleek mouse dun neck. It was such a pretty color.

"Well, I'm taking everyone out for dinner," Jaden announced. "As for you—I owe you, Tea. If there's anything you want, just ask."

Over dinner I decided to take Jaden up on his offer. Everyone was in a good mood, and I thought Dec would be more likely to agree with Jaden there.

"I have a favor to ask," I told Jaden.

"Anything," he replied promptly. He turned his full attention on me, and I felt my heart react again. Must have been nerves over what I was about to suggest.

"Would you teach me to play polo?" I asked. Dec glanced at me sharply.

"Of course," Jaden answered, smiling. "I'd be happy to."

Dec didn't look happy, and I hastened to explain before he could start objecting. "Schweppes isn't working out as a school horse, Dec. He's not reliable enough; he's a bit... touchy." It was the truth. Just a very sedate version of it. "But I think he'd make a good polo pony, and then we could resell him, and still make money on him."

Dec looked unconvinced. "Polo is pretty dangerous, Tea. Jaden's been hurt many times."

"It's not as though she'll be playing in high-goal matches, Dec," Jaden persuaded. "She only needs to learn the basics in order to train the horse. I promise I'll take care of her."

I could tell that Dec was sold before the sentence was finished; he seemed to think the sun rose and set on Jaden. And for once, I was glad of it.

April sucked.

The show season was swinging into gear, and though I was preparing my students, I had no horses to ride, which left me feeling empty and irritable. There was no further need to work with Kermit, and I couldn't start training Schweppes without Jaden's help.

In early April we got the results of our mid-terms back, and as I had feared, I did badly in everything except math. The principal called Dec to discuss the dramatic drop in my grades. When he got off the phone, Dec sat me down and yelled at me until I was almost in tears. Blue, sensing my distress, jumped into my lap; for some reason the sight of me hugging his dog stopped Dec in his tracks.

I could feel myself sliding back into the dull grey half-life I'd led for three months. Teri noticed too, and so did Julia when she came to ride that weekend.

"Come on, T," she encouraged, giving my shoulders a squeeze. "Cheer up. We should do something together. Hey, why don't we go out?"

"Out where? It's not like we can get into anyplace interesting," Teri grumbled. Julia was a bit older than us, but still only eighteen.

106

"Actually," I said slowly, "I know of a party we can go to."

The girls looked at me in amazement—I wasn't exactly a social butterfly.

"A friend of Jaden's told me about a party that we won't need ID for. She said most people will be doing E. Is that what I think it is?" I checked with Julia.

"Yup—'E' is for Ecstasy." Julia grinned. "Yay! When's the party?"

"Next weekend."

"Great!"

Teri and I exchanged a worried look. Julia was a lot more cosmopolitan than we were; she had tried Ecstasy once before, but neither Teri nor I had ever done anything remotely like that. After discussing it with Julia, though, we both started to get excited at the prospect. I called Caley and got the details.

"Um, Caley, I was wondering, will Jaden..."

"Don't worry." She laughed. "It's been years since he's come to any of these parties. He won't be there, and I won't tell."

The only disappointing thing about the party being that weekend was that Seth couldn't go; he had a swim meet. I'd always assumed that if we ever tried drugs, it would be together. While I was worried about not sharing the experience with him, Seth was more concerned about my safety. I reassured him as best I could; we were planning to take all possible precautions.

"Just pray the party doesn't get raided," he'd said grimly, "because if Dec finds out, you might as well ask them to keep you in jail, in protective custody."

Our cover story was a sleepover at Julia's. Once in Toronto, we left our jackets in my car and ran the short distance to the building, shivering. Inside, we hesitated, feeling self-conscious—at least, I was. It was very dark, and the music was unbelievably loud. The space was large and rectangular, with doors leading off one wall. It didn't take us long to find Caley.

"Tea!" she exclaimed, hugging me. "Follow me, I'll get you your stuff."

She led the way into a smaller room; there were couches around the perimeter and a bar at one end. We followed her behind the bar.

"Here you go," she said, handing me three small pills. "And don't forget these." She handed us each a bottle of water. "Make sure you keep drinking all night; the E will make you really hot so it's important to stay hydrated. You can refill your bottles in the washroom if you want. Have fun!"

I handed each of the girls a pill. My hand was shaking; I couldn't believe I was really about to do this. Teri and I exchanged an anxious look.

"Don't worry," Julia reassured us, seeing our nervous faces. "After this kicks in, you'll have the best night of your lives."

I took a deep breath. I wasn't looking for the best night of my life, just one that was free of constant heartache. I swallowed my pill, and quickly chased the bitterness with a mouthful of water. Julia followed suit. At the last minute Teri decided to break hers in half before taking a portion.

"What now, Jules?" I asked.

"Now, we wait."

We went back to the loud, dark main room and chilled in a corner. I don't know how long we stood there before I noticed that my stomach felt weird; when I looked up the lights seemed to be pulsing differently—they were very compelling, somehow. I glanced at Teri and Julia.

"Are you ready to dance?" Julia asked, grinning.

We headed out onto the dance floor. Suddenly, everything else ceased to exist—there was only the music, the bass pounding through my bones, reverberating deliciously throughout my body. We danced for a seemingly endless time, until Caley came and joined us.

"Hey, your water bottles are empty," she said. "Come on, let's go fill them up."

Julia and Teri went with her, Teri taking my bottle first, but I didn't want to leave the dance floor. I simply stood for a minute, my gaze wandering aimlessly.

And then my heart opened up.

Everything rushed at me. I thought of all the events of the past few months, but somehow, nothing hurt. There was no judgment attached to any of my thoughts. No matter what passed through my head, it all seemed... fine. For a minute I desperately missed Seth, and wished he could be here, sharing this with me. I thought about Blaze, but the anger and pain and sense of injustice were missing. For the first time since his death, I could focus on how much I had loved him, on what he had brought to my life.

The girls rejoined me then, and we all exchanged a long hug. I was overcome by my love for my friends, too, but I needed some alone time. I wanted to think some more, now that my thoughts were separated from the agony that normally flavored them.

"I'm going for a little walk," I said.

Teri handed me my refilled bottle and I wandered off. I ended up in the room with the couches, and curled up on one of them, prepared to take stock.

I wished that Jaden could be here, too. Although I suspected he wouldn't approve... I didn't know how I would have survived the past few months without him. It seemed incredible that I'd barely known him eight months ago; he was such a significant part of my life now. I thought about the risk he had taken, arranging for me to have time off school, and how much I'd appreciated his company that week. Of how much I always enjoyed his company. And I couldn't help admiring him. After all, he was an admirable person. Not to mention unbelievably good-looking... was it strange to think that way about your cousin? I felt mildly surprised as the realization blossomed—I was crushing on Jaden. I was thinking of him as a boy, not as a relative. It was okay, though. Everything was great, now.

"Hi," a voice said next to me.

I blinked, and looked up slowly. A dark-haired boy sat next to me, smiling.

"Um, hi," I replied.

"I'm Charlie." He held out his hand, and I shook it, feeling inordinately happy to be meeting him. "Do you want to go dance?" he asked.

I suddenly missed Teri and Julia. I nodded and led the way back out to the booming main room. It seemed to have gotten larger and more confusing, because it took me a while to find my way back to the girls. I introduced them to Charlie. He was tall and slim, I noticed, and quite attractive, although my standards for that kind of thing had been conclusively altered. Caley was right, we'd all gotten very hot, and I folded up my black tank top so that my waist was bare. I was happy that I'd worn the short black skirt that Julia had talked me into buying, but I wished I'd worn flat shoes—the ones I was wearing had a heel, albeit a low one. Even the heels couldn't really bother me, though; everything felt wonderful to me now.

I had no idea how long we danced. I thought about Jaden a lot. I felt unbelievably lucky to know him, and I couldn't wait to see him again. It seemed like no time at all before Julia said we'd have to leave soon; we had to be at her house before her father got home.

Charlie wandered off, and Teri and Julia went outside to get some air, but I wanted to dance some more. I'd only been alone a few minutes, however, before Charlie reappeared and wrapped his arms around me. It wasn't that I minded, exactly, but I wanted to dance and be in my own space for a while, so after a few seconds I managed to get my hands onto his chest and pushed gently. He didn't let go, though. I was about to try again when his body was suddenly yanked away from me; he was lifted off his feet, staggered a few steps, and was luckily caught and helped upright by the dancers next to us. I looked around in confusion—and froze.

Jaden was standing in front of me. I was thrilled to see him, but fortunately the expression on his face registered in time for me to squelch my impulse to throw myself at him. He looked... I couldn't think of a word that sounded mad enough.

"Come," he spat, grabbing my arm.

I don't know why I resisted. I *wanted* to go with him. In fact, I couldn't believe my luck in seeing him after thinking about him all night. But it was all happening so fast, and my brain was slow and bleary. I needed to find Ter and Jules, and I wasn't done dancing yet... I dug in my heels. I was about to ask him to give me a minute when I found myself, once again, hanging over his broad shoulder.

"Not this again," I muttered.

It was much more disorienting this time; my head swam until I barely knew which way was up. The bouncer's deep voice brought my focus back somewhat.

"Hold on, buddy. Who have you got there? Is she okay?"

"This," Jaden growled, "is my very under-age cousin, and she's coming with me."

"Let me see her," the bouncer insisted.

Being put down was even more disorienting. I swayed and Jaden caught my shoulders, cursing.

"Is this your cousin, miss?" the bouncer asked kindly. "Do you want to go with him?"

"Yes," I said, gazing, starstruck, up at Jaden's face. I wanted to explain, to make him understand that everything was fine—wonderful, even—but he didn't give me the chance. He dragged me outside, where Teri and Julia were huddled by the door.

"I've got her. Come with me," he told them brusquely.

He started walking, but Teri ran ahead and blocked me.

"Wait," she pleaded. She started pulling down the hem of my tank top, covering my exposed waist. My arm was freed instantly, and I looked over to see Jaden pulling off his jacket. He helped me into it and started unbuttoning his shirt. I watched, wide-eyed, until he pulled it off, revealing a T-shirt underneath. Julia and Teri were standing with their arms linked; he draped the shirt around both of their shoulders. Then, without a word, he yanked me along again.

Jaden marched me down the street, gripping my upper arm tightly. His long hand overlapped easily around it—my hand was starting to go numb. Teri and Julia had to trot to keep up with the pace he set; I didn't notice that we had reached his car until he opened the door. He barely waited for Ter and Jules to climb into the back seat before shoving me into the front. He slammed his door but said nothing as he pulled out of the parking space, and when I glanced over his face looked livid in the low light. I felt a twinge of nervousness. My high was definitely wearing off.

"What did you take?" he demanded.

"E-excuse me?" I stammered. It couldn't be that obvious, could it? I felt like I was getting back to normal, except that I probably should have been cold in what I was wearing. My mouth was dry... where had I left that last water bottle?

"I'm not an idiot, Tea," he spat from between clenched teeth. "Tell me what you took so I know what to watch out for. You *have* heard of bad trips, I assume?" he added scathingly.

His anger was dissipating the last of my beautiful, floaty, happy feelings, and I felt irritation begin to take their place.

"Fine then, I dropped some E," I snapped.

"How many?"

"Just one," I responded, too startled to remember to snap. Did he think I was some kind of drug addict? "I don't do this a lot, Jaden... I mean, it's not like I have a problem or anything," I tried to explain.

"DO NOT TELL ME THAT YOU DON'T HAVE A PROBLEM!" he roared.

I cringed back against the seat, shocked. I realized I'd never heard him yell before; his usually smooth voice was staggeringly loud in the confines of the car.

"Three teenaged girls wandering the streets barely dressed at five a.m. is unquestionably a PROBLEM," he ranted on. "And three girls alone downtown under the influence of drugs is downright idiotic!" He glared into his rearview mirror.

"Are you both high too?" he demanded, still very loud.

I turned to peek at Teri and Julia in the backseat. I'd almost forgotten they were there. They looked wide-eyed and pale under their makeup, and I wondered if I looked as young and frightened as they did right now. I felt a wave of remorse for getting them into this.

"Um... yes?" Julia whispered.

"Tell me exactly what you took, and how much," Jaden ordered.

If it occurred to either girl to refuse him, it didn't show.

"I took half a pill... I didn't want to take a whole one... I didn't know how I'd react, I was afraid to get sick or something..." Teri blurted out. She always talked too much when she was nervous, and I tried to reassure her with a quick smile.

"I took one pill, like Tea," Julia said. "And hey, where are you taking us?"

I guess the drugs weren't completely out of my system because that question jolted me into sudden alertness; I hadn't even wondered where we were headed.

Jaden's voice answered harshly, "Home to your parents."

I stared at him uncomprehendingly for a minute before the little bubbles of panic rising inside me burst open.

"Home? No, NO, you CAN'T! You can't bring me home looking like this, at this hour—DEC will be home! Do you have any idea what he'll do to me?" It was my turn to yell. "And it's not fair to Ter and Jules, they only came out because of me..." I felt angry tears welling up and stopped talking so my voice wouldn't give me away.

Jaden's face looked like it was set in stone. Alarmed whimpering from the backseat indicated I wasn't the only one panicking.

"Jaden please, *please*, just drop us all off at my house. That's where we were headed anyway," Julia begged.

"I don't feel safe leaving you alone in this condition." At least he wasn't yelling anymore.

"My dad's a doctor, he's coming off the nightshift at the hospital soon. We'll be totally safe with him there," Julia persuaded softly.

Jaden hesitated, then shook his head.

"I'll drop you and Teri off, but Tea's coming with me." He gave me a look that quelled my argument in my throat.

The drive to Julia's was quiet after that. Other than her occasional murmured directions, no one spoke. The girls shot me anxious glances as they got out of the car, and I tried to smile at them. Jaden walked them to the door, then got in and resumed driving without a word.

I couldn't stay angry in the afterglow of the Ecstasy, but I did manage to sulk for a while, until I realized we were headed back into the city.

"Where are we going?" I asked timidly. I didn't want to set him off again.

"I'm taking you to my place," he answered tersely.

A wave of relief washed over me, and I looked down to hide my smile. I could deal with whatever came tomorrow; right now I was exhausted. I just wanted to sleep—preferably for a few days.

We ascended to the loft in silence. I kicked off my shoes, very happy to be rid of the heels, and turned to look at Jaden, my stomach clenching with sudden apprehension. He was in the kitchen.

"Sit," he commanded, indicating the couch.

He joined me a minute later and handed me a glass of water and two Tylenols. I didn't ask any questions, and drank all the water after swallowing the pills. I hadn't realized how thirsty I was. He got up without a word and refilled my glass.

"Thanks," I mumbled as he sat back down.

He sat with his elbows on his knees and stared at the floor. I could see a muscle working in his jaw despite the dim light; my anxiety increased as the silence wore on.

"Are you going to tell Dec?" I finally whispered.

"I don't know," he answered in a low voice. He didn't look up. "Honestly, I'd rather not, but I'm worried about you. This self-destructive behavior has to stop."

"Since when is going out considered destructive?"

At that, his head whipped around and he leaned toward me, eyes blazing. Uh-oh.

"Do we really need to recap the utter insanity of your behavior tonight?" he retorted cuttingly. I shrank away from him, wide-eyed, and shook my head slightly. I'd never seen Jaden really angry before; I felt suddenly very conscious of the fact that he and Dec were related.

"I wasn't trying to hurt myself," I explained in a whisper. "It's the opposite. I wanted to feel... alive again."

His expression softened, along with his tone. "Tea, I appreciate that things have been very difficult for you lately, but it's not just tonight. Ever since the accident, you've been struggling. I understand that."

I seriously doubted it, but elected to keep quiet.

"The level of grief you're dealing with would be hard for anyone to handle," he went on. He was watching my face carefully now. "But the accident was *not* your fault."

Something snapped.

"Stop it!" I yelled, jumping up from the couch. "I am so SICK of everyone telling me it's not my fault!" I shouted down at his startled face. "It IS my fault! I'm the one who wanted to go to the stupid show! I'm the one who slept in and made us late, and put us in that intersection at exactly the wrong time. And-" I bit back the rest of my sentence, clamping my teeth together.

I watched several emotions flicker across his face: surprise, understanding, dismay... then suddenly he was towering over me, an absolute glare on his face.

"You're lying," he hissed.

I started to recoil from his anger, but he grabbed the tops of my arms and held me in place.

"Tell me what happened." It wasn't a suggestion.

I gave my head a small shake, too stunned to speak.

"Tea," he growled furiously, "for months now your entire family has been sick with worry, watching you try and fail to deal with Blaze's death-"

I flinched at the words.

"-and now I find out you've been *lying* to us? No wonder you're not coping!"

I stared at the floor. He had a right to be angry, but this wasn't only my secret. I didn't want to betray Karen.

"Tell me," he ordered again, giving me a shake.

"I can't," I whispered.

114

"Let me make myself clear." His voice was hard now, as unyielding as granite. "You tell me what's going on, or else."

My head shot up at the threat. The obvious retort—'or else, then'—died on my lips when I caught sight of Jaden's face. His expression was coldly furious.

"Jaden?" I said his name uncertainly.

He blinked, then shoved me away from him and stalked down the hall. The bedroom door slammed behind him.

I dropped onto the couch and curled into a ball, my face in my hands, and found I was sobbing. I was dumbfounded, as if Chocolate Chip had suddenly tried to savage me. I didn't know how much time passed, but I felt him sink onto the couch next to me. He didn't say anything, but started rubbing my back gently. Despite my wildly fluctuating emotions I was hyper-aware of the warmth of his touch.

As I controlled my crying he spoke.

"Look, I know you probably hate me right now, but you need to stay here tonight, okay?" His voice was low, and rough with emotion. I nodded into my hands. How could he think I would hate him? That was impossible, but I was still too chagrined to look at him.

I felt him start to rise, and reached out blindly to grab his arm. I looked up at him warily, feeling the tears still wet on my face. His expression jolted me—I expected anger or frustration, but there was none. He looked absolutely shattered, the pain in his eyes unmistakeable. But I had no time to wonder at it, because at the sight of my face he sank back down quickly and gathered me in his arms.

"I'm sorry," he whispered against my hair.

Eight

I awoke slowly the next morning. I didn't know how long I'd been sleeping, but I felt surprisingly good. I recognized the familiar warm brown walls of Jaden's bedroom. Memories of the night before—well, earlier this morning, really—began to return to me. We hadn't talked much, after our intense but confusing exchange. I was so exhausted that I'd almost fallen asleep in his arms. He had supported me into the bedroom and found me a t-shirt to sleep in. Crawling into bed was the last thing I remembered.

I stretched, expecting to be sore from all the dancing, but except for a twinge in my legs from the heels, I was fine. I got up; I really needed to use the bathroom. I was nervous about seeing Jaden, but my body's needs wouldn't be denied, so I tiptoed out quietly. After peeing and swishing some mouthwash around in my very dry mouth, I realized I was thirsty again and hazarded a trip to the kitchen. As I was getting a glass of water I noticed Jaden's feet hanging over the edge of the couch. I padded over and gazed down at his sleeping form. The lines of his face were softened in sleep; he looked younger, and so beautiful it made my heart ache.

I took a deep breath. These were not thoughts I could afford to be having. Last night, while I was high, anything had seemed possible, but in the cold light of day it was clear that these were feelings I had to deny. I cringed at the very idea of what Jaden would think of me if he knew.

I decided I might as well shower. I took my time, enjoying the feeling of the drops hitting my skin... it seemed that some of my heightened sensory appreciation was lingering. I wondered if that was normal—I'd have to ask Teri and Julia how they were feeling. For a moment I wished I was with them, comparing notes in the aftermath of our crazy experience instead of dealing with the emotional drama of being at Jaden's, but that wish quickly passed. It was right for me to be here.

I wrapped myself in a big towel and was headed for the bedroom when Jaden's voice made me jump and whirl around.

"Good morning."

He was standing in the hallway, holding a glass of orange juice, the other hand shoved into his pocket. He was wearing wrinkled clothes from the night before, stubble darkened his jaw, and his hair was sticking up in all directions, yet my breath still caught in my throat at the sight of him. Damn, I was in trouble.

"Hi," I stammered.

"How do you feel?" His eyes were appraising, wandering over my face. I felt a rush of warmth go through me and ducked my head so he wouldn't see my blush.

"Fine," I responded. Though confused, tormented and guilty would have been closer to the truth. "How are you?"

"I'm in dire need of a cup of coffee and some breakfast, actually. And the fridge is empty, so I'm taking you out." He went into the bathroom and I heard the shower start. In the bedroom I realized with dismay that I had nothing to wear—my clothes were back at Julia's house. I didn't want to put my sweaty things from last night back on, and in any case I'd freeze in them. I put Jaden's t-shirt back on in the meantime, and went out to the living room so he'd have some privacy to dress. He was faster than me in the shower; it was only minutes later that he dropped onto the couch next to me, fully dressed and smelling faintly of soap. I was shocked at how much I wanted to touch him, suddenly, now that he was so close. I leaned away slightly and didn't look at him, just to be safe.

"How are you, really?" he asked quietly.

"I told you, I'm... good. Only I don't have anything to wear," I said, happy to steer the conversation in less thorny directions.

"Oh, right. Well, let's go see what we can find—everything of mine is going to be huge on you."

I followed him to the bedroom, where he started ransacking his closet and tossing potential items my way. There was a grey sweatshirt that looked promising, but pants were an issue; I swam in all of them. I finally ended up in his smallest pair of jeans, folded up at the bottoms and cinched up tight with a belt that fortunately had holes all the way around.

"You look like a little kid playing dress-up," he chuckled.

"I feel like a scarecrow," I complained. "All my stuff is at Julia's."

He handed me his phone. "Why don't you ask them to join us? Then she can bring your clothes."

Neither Julia or Teri answered their phones, though, so I left them messages with the name of the restaurant Jaden gave me, and we headed for the door.

"Does Julia have her car?" he asked as he strode around scooping up keys and wallet.

"Yup."

His sudden frown made me cringe mentally. I could practically see where his thoughts were headed.

"How were you planning to get to Julia's if I hadn't shown up?"

I shook my head, not looking at him. "Please don't ask, Jaden."

A hand caught my arm and pulled me forward; hard fingers forced my chin up.

"I'm asking." His voice was hard, too.

"Well, I drove us there..." I couldn't bring myself to continue while his eyes were burning into mine.

His face tightened, and the grip on my arm increased uncomfortably, but he didn't say anything, just kept searching my face with those incredible eyes.

"What are you thinking?" I whispered finally.

"I'm debating how irresponsible I'm being by letting you get away with this," he admitted. He took in my confused look and clarified. "Consider it from my perspective, Tea. If I tell Dec, I'm afraid he'll hurt you. If I don't tell him, I'm afraid you'll hurt yourself."

His hands on my arm and chin were warm, and his eyes were lit by concern. I heard the murmur of his voice continue, but I didn't absorb his words... instead I noticed how beautifully the amber and limpid brown tones in his eyes complemented each other. I wondered how those scolding lips would feel pressed against mine... a tremor went through me, and I gave myself a mental shake. What was I thinking? This was wrong, so very wrong. Was it just the lingering effects of the Ecstasy that were making me think these patently twisted things? Or had the drugs merely revealed what had been brewing in my subconscious all along? I trembled in earnest at the thought.

He released me, and I snapped back to awareness.

"Are you okay?" he asked. His brows were pulled together.

"Um, yes." I swallowed and tried to focus. "It's just a lot to think about before we've even had coffee."

He grinned suddenly, and steered me toward the door.

We picked a booth in the restaurant's rather dim interior. We had just ordered coffee when Jaden's phone rang; he handed it to me after answering and mouthed 'Teri'.

"Hey girl," I greeted her warmly. I noticed that I still felt very affectionate toward my girlfriends too—maybe my reaction toward Jaden would fade, become more reasonable. I could only hope.

"Are you okay, hon?" she asked in a rush. "We felt *so* bad for you yesterday, Jaden looked absolutely grim. Was he mean to you?"

"No, don't worry, it was... fine. Are you coming?"

Teri assured me they were on their way—along with my clothes—but told us to go ahead and eat, as they'd be a while. Jaden stared into his coffee for a minute, stirring it needlessly.

"They were afraid I'd be rough on you," he guessed. He glanced up; I shrugged. "I *was* rough. I'm sorry—I shouldn't have tried to force you to talk to me. Especially when you were exhausted and coming down."

"You apologized already," I pointed out, "and you really don't need to, because you didn't *do* anything."

"The fact that I could even threaten you is inexcusable. I know that." He paused, running his hand through his hair so that it fell, tousled, into his eyes. I leaned across the table toward him.

"Don't be stressed about it, Jaden," I told him sincerely. "I'm not."

"It's that obvious?"

"You always start messing up your hair when you're upset."

His eyes flew to mine, startled.

"Oh come on," I said doubtfully, "I can't be the first person to tell you that."

"The first since my mother, years ago," he said. He was looking at me strangely.

"Well, I hate to break it to you, but you haven't kicked the habit."

He responded with a small, fond smile, and I could only gaze at him in a stupor while my heart swelled mightily inside my chest. Fortunately our food arrived at that moment, or my secret might have been spilled right then.

"Eat, Tea," he said gently a few minutes later.

I realized I'd been picking at my food without really noticing.

"It's my fault, isn't it—I made you think about Blaze, I pressured you, and now you're anxious again." He looked disgusted with himself. I didn't know what to say. I didn't want him to blame himself, but I couldn't exactly tell him the real reason I had no appetite was that I had a crush on him. A huge, embarrassing, illicit crush.

"No, don't feel bad. It's not you. Not a day goes by that I don't think of Blaze, anyway, and... if I could talk to anyone about what happened, it would be you."

"What do you mean? Haven't you even talked to Seth, or your girlfriends?"

I shook my head. I was getting into dangerous territory here, but I couldn't stand to see Jaden looking so troubled. He opened his mouth, then determinedly closed it again, frowning in concern. He obviously didn't want to upset me further. I stared down at my plate. My hands formed fists in my lap. I tried to tell myself that I was doing this because I trusted Jaden, trusted him completely, but the truth was that I simply wanted to make him feel better.

"Jaden." I took a deep breath; my heart was racing. "The day of the accident... I was driving. I'm the one who didn't see that truck coming." I barely mumbled the words, but his sharp intake of breath indicated that he'd heard me. I heard him start to get up; that made me look up swiftly. I caught his harrowed expression and shook my head.

"Don't," I said desperately. If he tried to comfort me now I would go completely to pieces. He sank back down unwillingly and reached his hand across the table, palm up. I hesitated, but I couldn't help myself—I put my hand in his and felt a shiver go through me as his warm hand wrapped tightly around my cold one.

"Tea, honey, you know it's still not your fault, right? That truck went barreling through a red light. There was nothing you could have done." His voice was passionate, persuasive. "No wonder you've been having such a hard time... but why the secret?" He was rubbing his thumb across the back of my hand; it felt as though every nerve ending in my body was somehow attached to that skin.

"Because," I explained haltingly, "I wasn't supposed to be driving. I only had my learner's permit. But Karen was sick, so I talked her into it... and after the accident she didn't want me to get into trouble for it."

"She would have been in just as much trouble as you," Jaden said grimly.

I made myself look him in the eye. "You can't tell anyone, Jaden. Promise me."

He didn't hesitate. "I promise." He squeezed my hand, and held my gaze while he continued gently. "But you should tell Dec, honey."

120

I stared at him in disbelief. He had obviously taken leave of his senses.

"Tea, don't you see? You've been struggling with this massive guilt because you haven't been able to tell the whole truth about what happened. It doesn't matter that you're completely innocent. On top of the grief, and survivor's guilt, you have this big secret to carry around... this misplaced sense of responsibility for Karen. Poor baby, it's no wonder you're overwhelmed."

His sympathy was too much for me. I pulled my hand away and leaned back against the seat, my head hanging. I gritted my teeth and dug my nails into my palms to keep from crying—it worked, after a minute I was able to breathe normally again. I picked up my fork and stabbed a potato with unnecessary force, and glared at him as I chewed.

"Happy now?" I demanded.

He smiled slowly. "Yes."

I studied him surreptitiously as we ate. I loved the curved lines on either side of his mouth. They made him look like he'd just been smiling, or was about to smile. I also remembered how much I used to dislike him; it seemed inconceivable to me now.

"You're smiling," he commented. He looked happy to see it.

"I was just remembering how I used to think you were an arrogant jerk," I said, grinning.

He laughed. "I'm glad you phrased it in the past tense, at least," he said. "I, on the other hand, started out with a fairly high opinion of you. And it's only increased as I've gotten to know you better."

"Oh. I, um... thanks," I stammered, feeling a rush of blood to my face. "Even after last night?" I added hesitantly.

"I can't judge you for that—I made a lot of mistakes during my teens. I only hope I can help you avoid some of my more painful ones." He looked uncomfortable. "Who was that boy you were with last night?"

It took me several seconds to understand what he was asking. "He's just a boy we met at the party; his name is, um... Charlie," I remembered.

Jaden's jaw tightened. It looked as though he had more to say on the subject, but right then Julia and Teri arrived. I clambered out of the booth and hugged them both for a long moment. Jaden got up too, and as I released the girls he gave each of them a kiss on the cheek. I grinned at their identical, mildly stunned looks.

When we sat back down Jaden pulled me onto the seat next to him. I was electrically aware of his body only a few inches from mine; I tried hard to act natural.

"What did you guys do when you got home?" I asked the girls after they'd ordered.

"We sat around and talked until the sun came up, then we fell asleep," Teri said. "How about you?"

"About the same," I said wryly.

"How do you feel?" Julia asked me.

"Um..." I stole a glance at Jaden; he rolled his eyes at me.

"I already know what you've been up to, Tea. You might as well talk about it." He noticed Teri and Julia's doubtful faces. "I'm done yelling," he promised.

Teri, Julia and I compared notes. They both had the ongoing heightened senses. Julia, though, had also woken up with a splitting headache.

"Is that why you gave me the Tylenol?" I asked Jaden. I was surprised, and touched, to remember that he had given it to me while he was still angry.

He nodded. "Some people seem prone to headaches or vomiting when they're coming down... but you never know what's in those drugs. That's what makes it so dangerous." He paused. "That was your first time, wasn't it?"

At my nod, he sighed. "Look, I'm doing my utmost not to lecture all of you, but I hope you didn't walk into that party and buy drugs from a complete stranger, because that's the epitome of dangerous, high-risk behavior."

I glanced over quickly and caught the girls' eyes, hoping they could read the message on my face—I didn't want to get Caley into trouble, and the way Jaden was behaving almost guaranteed he wouldn't be happy with the truth.

"Well, you can relax, I got the pills from a friend of mine," Julia assured him coolly. I was relieved she'd spoken up instead of Teri, who was looking decidedly nervous in the face of Jaden's questioning.

"All right. Then there's just one more thing-"

I groaned, and he flashed me a quick grin. "Here it is: if you ever find yourself in an altered state again—whether you've been drinking, doing drugs, even if you're just tired—don't even consider driving home, okay? Call me, and I'll come get you. No questions asked, I promise."

We agreed. He made Teri and Julia hand him their phones so that he could put his number in. He looked at me and I rolled my eyes.

"I know, I'm the last person in the civilized world without a cell phone."

"I still expect you to call me."

We stayed a while longer, talking and drinking way too much coffee, but I had to be home to feed that evening and it was getting late. I went and changed into my own clothes before we went outside, into the glorious spring sunshine.

Jaden opened the car door for me. It was warm and comfortable inside, and I leaned back and enjoyed the rich tones of the sound system as he drove. He always seemed to have music on.

"Don't think I didn't notice you telling Julia to lie," he said suddenly.

"'Lie' is a bit harsh," I protested.

"So that's the unvarnished truth—the drugs came from her friend, and you had nothing to do with it?" He sounded severe; it aggravated me.

"Can't you just let it drop already?" I asked testily.

He looked surprised for a second, then said slowly, "I'm not sure that I should."

"Sorry. It's just that... I don't need another father figure in my life trying to control me, Jaden."

There was silence for a minute; I started to worry that I'd offended him.

"What do you need, Tea?" he asked quietly.

The question caught me by surprise. I needed a lot of things—my mother back, Blaze back... but what sprang to mind first was Jaden. The one thing I definitely could never have.

I gulped. "Just be my friend."

"I will always be that." He pulled into the lot where my car was parked. Julia and Teri were following behind us.

He turned to me. "Will you think about what I said? About telling Dec?"

Truthfully, I had filed away his request as soon as he'd made it, under the heading of 'not in this lifetime'.

123

"Why is it so important to you?" I asked a question rather than lie to him.

"Because I think it will help to extirpate your feelings of guilt," he said.

Only Jaden could use a word like 'extirpate' and not sound like a total geek, I thought with a smile. I turned toward him, still smiling, and found myself being pulled into a hug. I hugged him back fiercely, my heart breaking into a mad dash. His body was hard, but very warm. I pulled away first—I liked being in his arms far, far too much to stay there. This was something I'd have to get under control, and quickly.

The rest of the day had a dreamlike quality. Teri fell asleep during the drive, but I didn't mind. I pondered the unlikelihood of Jaden having found me. It felt like fate, somehow. He'd gone to see Jesse's band playing down the street, and on his way home he had seen Teri and Julia standing outside—what were the odds? I was alone in the house until Seth came in after dinnertime.

"How was the swim meet?"

"Awesome. I was second in the hundred meter backstroke and I won the fifty meter crawl. And I met the most amazing girl!" he said. "How was your night out?"

I filled him in on the details, and heard about his weekend with Melissa, the girl from Montreal who he'd met at the swim meet. It was nice to catch up with Seth, to sit and laugh and share everything... well, almost everything. For some reason, I didn't tell him about my drug-induced epiphany. That was something I wanted to squelch on my own.

I was tired, and went to bed by nine, but I couldn't sleep. There was too much to think about, not the least of which was Jaden's request. I heard Dec come home around ten, and I waited a while, giving him a chance to unwind. And gathering my courage. Then I climbed out of bed and went downstairs, shivering slightly in my PJs.

"Hi honey, how was the sleepover?" Dec asked from the couch. He looked tired.

"Great, thanks."

I perched on the edge of the couch, as far away from him as possible. I stared at my hands, clasped in my lap—now that I was actually doing this it seemed considerably harder than it had from my warm bed.

"Is everything okay?" he asked, sounding concerned. I sighed. I was tired of being the object of everyone's worry.

"Dec, I need to tell you something. But I'm hoping you'll promise me something first," I began hesitantly.

"What?" he asked suspiciously.

"Please don't take this out on anyone else. This is my fault—just remember that, okay?"

"All right," he answered tensely.

I swallowed hard. "It's about... the accident." I clasped and unclasped my fingers; this was a lot more difficult than telling Jaden had been. My heart was pounding painfully in my chest. Dec leaned toward me, and I could feel the anxiety rolling off him.

"What about it?" he demanded.

"I... well, when it happened... I was driving," I whispered. I was too nervous to look at him, and he didn't say anything right away; by the time he spoke I was trembling.

"Why the hell would Karen let you drive?" I flinched; he hadn't spoken loudly, but the fact that he would swear was a clear indication he was furious. Haltingly, I explained the events of that day. I went into more detail than I had earlier, each one stabbing painfully into my gut as I dredged up the memories I'd tried so hard to bury. Dec listened more quietly than I would have thought possible.

"Well," was all he said at the end. He leaned back into the couch.

"Please don't blame Karen," I renewed my plea after a few minutes.

"Tell me something," he said quietly, "have you been keeping this quiet for so long to protect her? Or because you were afraid to tell me that you drove?"

I thought about it. I'd been keeping the secret for so long that I barely remembered. At the time, amid so many other crushing emotions, not revealing who had been in the driver's seat had seemed a minor detail.

"I don't know. It seemed pointless to tell... I mean, it wouldn't have changed anything." It wouldn't bring Blaze back. "I don't think I was that worried about your reaction, to tell you the truth." I hazarded a look his way; I was being unusually honest with him. He nodded, looking relieved.

"Well, I'm glad it wasn't because you were... nervous about what I would say." He paused. "Or do."

125

I stared at him, wide-eyed. This was something we never talked about. And I didn't want to start.

"Listen, kiddo, I have to talk to Karen about this. Now, don't panic," he tried to appease me, and I bit my lip so he could finish. "This isn't something I can just let go. I need to be able to trust her—our friendship goes back a long way. I expected better of her than this."

I hung my head, feeling the sting of his words as though they were directed at me. I was sure he had expected better of me, too.

"Why did you decide to tell me, after all this time?" he asked.

"I guess... I was feeling guilty."

He cleared his throat. I was surprised at how gentle his voice was when he went on. "Tea, you made some bad choices, but you've suffered a lot. I forgive you for whatever you may have done—the driving, the lying, all of that. It's not important anymore. Do you understand?"

"Okay," I said uncertainly.

He nodded. "That said, I'm still going to punish you. This isn't a minor offense, Tea—you're grounded for a month."

That would mean almost to the end of May. I sighed and started to get up, but Dec's hand on my arm stopped me.

"While we're here... there's something I've been wanting to tell you, too. About last fall—I regret not letting you go to the Royal. I shouldn't have done that."

I gazed at him in surprise. It was the closest thing to an apology I'd ever gotten from Dec. I didn't know what to say. I settled for a nod, and went to bed.

I left Jaden a voicemail next day. "Hey cuz. Hope you got a better night's sleep last night. I suspect I got some sort of minor brain aneurysm on Saturday, because I actually took your advice and told Dec. He took it well, I'm only grounded for a month. Thanks again, for everything."

He called a few hours later. "He *grounded* you?" he said incredulously.

"Yes, but... wait... are you done?" I asked when he paused in his tirade.

"I suppose."

"Good. Because, as weird as it sounds, I'm okay with it."

"Oh. Well, alright then."

"Please note this does not mean that I subscribe to any of your other crazy pop-psycho ideas."

"So noted. I've got to go study for my exams, but I'll be done after next week, and then we can start schooling that pony of yours, okay?"

I had never looked forward to training so much in my life.

The following Saturday was such a gorgeous spring day that Teri and I decided to go for a hack. Technically, I probably shouldn't have been going on a hack for fun while I was grounded, but riding was a grey area for me, since much of it counted as work. I decided this fell under the heading of 'training', since I was riding Schweppes and he needed to get a lot fitter if he was going to be a polo pony.

We set out gaily, admiring the fresh green tones and the baby-blue, wispy-clouded sky. The sun was warm, but a fitful breeze kept us comfortable in our T-shirts, jeans and half-chaps. We were riding side by side down a wide path. It would be ceilinged by trees in the summer, but at this time of year the sun shone patchily through the bud-laden branches.

"Are we going to the Thomson's show in three weeks?" Teri asked. I felt a tightening in my chest as I thought about Blaze and my big plans for this year's show season, but the pain was manageable now. I took a few steady breaths and shook my head.

"No, I've got to go to Stacey's birthday party. I wish I could skip it and do the show instead," I groused.

"Bummer," Teri sympathized. "But you're taking Winter to the Spring show, right?"

I nodded. We were both quiet for a while, and I'm sure Teri was thinking about Blaze, too.

"How's the polo training going?" she asked finally, indicating Schweppes' golden form.

I grinned. "I have no idea, really. So far I've just been brushing up on his flatwork—you know, tight turns and rapid stops, that kind of thing. Jaden's going to help me now though, he just finished his exams."

"That's right—law school. He's so smart... I guess it runs in your family, you lucky duck."

I chuckled, but I was uncomfortable with the way she mentioned Jaden. I reminded myself that of course everyone thought of him as my cousin—he was—and that it didn't matter, anyway. But I felt compelled to remind Teri of our status, all the same.

"Remember, Jaden and I aren't related by blood. So there's no correlation between our intellects—not that I'm in his league, anyway."

"Oh, right. You know, I always thought Jaden was kind of intimidating, until we went out for brunch," she said thoughtfully, "but he's really nice, isn't he?"

I tried to shrug nonchalantly, but I felt my cheeks warming. Anyway, I couldn't disagree, because it was the truth.

"Yes, he's been really.... supportive, since Blaze died."

"And man, he's good-looking! I didn't think anyone who looked like that could be so nice, too—it's not fair," she went on animatedly.

"Um, yeah, I guess so," I stammered. It was even more unfair when that person is your cousin.

Teri looked at me curiously.

"Hey, let's canter," I suggested brightly, "the footing's good here, not too muddy."

"Hold on a minute." She looked at me, frowning slightly. "What's up with you?"

I leaned forward and played with Schweppes' white-blond mane, carefully keeping my eyes down.

"Nothing," I said lightly.

Teri had been my best friend for seven years. She knew me well, and she was very perceptive. I scrambled to change the subject, but before I could speak she asked, "Is it about Jaden?"

"Is what about him?"

"Why can't you look at me?"

I looked at her, frowning.

"Oh my God! You *like* him, don't you?"

"Of course I like him, he's my cousin," I retorted, flushing.

"Come on, Tea! It's me—why didn't you tell me?"

I scrutinized her face. There was no judgment there, only a slight smile. Her light green eyes were bright with curiosity.

I sighed. "It's just so... embarrassing, you know? Don't you think it's weird, that I'm crushing on my cousin?"

"I have news for you, Tea, I think the whole barn's crushing on your cousin." She giggled. "Why should you be any different? Anyway, like you said, you're not really related."

I felt myself getting lighter and lighter, as though I was inflating with happiness. Teri didn't think I was some twisted, weird sicko. The relief was intense.

"So when did you know? And what are you going to do about it?" she questioned excitedly.

"It's been creeping up on me for a while now, but I think I was in denial." I grimaced. "And I'm not doing anything about it. To tell you the truth, I'm pretty sure he thinks of me as a kid. And an irresponsible one, at that—I mean, look at all the trouble I've gotten into this year."

She nodded, looking pensive. We got to a stream and let our horses splash their way across.

"You know, you may have gotten into a lot of trouble this year, but Jaden's actually helped you out of it a few times, hasn't he?" she said suddenly.

"I guess so. Except for the track," I said thoughtfully, seeing where she was headed.

"But you said he felt really bad about that."

"Yes, so maybe all the subsequent help was just prompted by guilt. Maybe he was just atoning for the racetrack blunder."

"Well then, maybe you just need to let him atone some more," she countered.

We looked at each other suddenly and giggled. It seemed so normal now, like all the other times we had discussed whether a boy liked us.

We enjoyed our hack, and so did Schweppes and Picasso. We were walking them home when Teri brought up Jaden again.

"You think that he sees you as a kid, right?" she asked.

"Uh-huh."

"So if we could get him to see you differently," she said, "then you could find out how he feels about you."

"I'm with you in theory... but how do I do that?"

Teri eyed me critically.

"To be honest, you do look young—it's not just you," she added quickly as I made a face. "I have the same problem; it's because we're short." She made it sound like a dirty word, and I snickered. "But also... well, you never wear any makeup. Not that you need it—but it'll make you look older. And you don't dress up much, either... you know what you need?" she exclaimed, practically bouncing in her saddle, "A makeover!"

We locked eyes, grinning, and spoke simultaneously. "Julia!"

Back at the barn we sent Julia a text message—not mentioning Jaden by name—and asked if she could help with the makeover project. By this point I was fairly enthusiastic about the whole idea. Within a few hours I had gone from shame and discomfort about my hidden feelings, to—well, not exactly joy, since I was still conflicted—but tentative hope.

Julia called that night and was, predictably, thrilled at the thought of orchestrating my makeover. She was also burning with curiosity about my mysterious crush, but I refused to give her any clues over the phone. I was a bit nervous about telling her—sure, Teri had taken the news in stride, but then Teri was a very accepting person.

As I hung up the phone in the kitchen it occurred to me that I hadn't even spoken to Seth about my feelings. I thought that was a bit odd, but reflected that maybe some things are easier to share with a girlfriend than with your brother, no matter how close you are to him. I decided to give him a heads-up, though, before this makeover scheme made him curious. I wandered into the living room where Seth was sprawled on the couch, his long legs crossed at the ankle, watching t.v.

"Hey, d'you have a minute?" My voice sounded unnatural in my ears.

"Sure."

He heaved himself off the couch and followed me to my room, where he flopped on the bed. I started pacing, not sure where to begin.

"Dude—what's up? Why the caged animal routine?" He was watching me curiously.

I sat next to him. "Look, I have to tell you something, and it's a bit... well, don't freak out, okay?"

He nodded.

"I'm... interested in someone," I started hesitantly. Seth's expression brightened. "But I'm not sure how he feels about me. And he's a bit older-"

"How much older?" he interrupted.

"Almost six years."

"That's not too bad," he said encouragingly. Then, as an afterthought, he added, "Do I know him?"

"Yes," I almost whispered, gazing at the floorboards. "You know him very well."

"Aaand..."

130

I swallowed. Why was this so hard? Seth was the one person I was closest to on the entire planet. He knew everything about me.

"C'mon, Sis, the suspense is killing me here," he joked.

I looked at him anxiously, wanting to gauge his reaction.

"It's Jaden," I said quietly.

Seth's eyes flew wide. He looked dumbfounded. I waited nervously for him to say something; the seconds ticked by.

"Jaden, our cousin?" he specified finally, as though hoping I might have a spare, unrelated one tucked away somewhere.

"Yes."

Seth dropped his face into his hands.

"Just say it, Seth—tell me what you're thinking, no matter how bad it is," I urged.

He looked up. "What I'm thinking is that you're nuts."

I looked away from him. The happy bubble inside me burst, leaving a dull heaviness in its place. I must have known, subconsciously, that Seth would react this way, because there was no surprise mingled with the weight.

"Aw, come on, T, don't look like that," he pleaded. "You know I want you to be happy—if it was any other guy, I'd say go for it. But Jaden? Think of what's at stake here. D'you want Dec to be sorry he kept us?"

I understood what Seth meant. For a time, after our mom died, we had felt insecure about our living arrangements. It wasn't rational, really—Dec had never given any indication that he didn't want us—but we lived with a feeling of doubt until Seth confided in Gran one day. She reassured us that there was no question of our leaving, and when Dec found out he said the same. His grief at my mother's death was intense, and he hadn't noticed our preoccupation the way Gran did. Seth and I were vastly relieved, and we remained grateful that our 'Foster family', as we jokingly called it, had embraced us so completely... so it would be the height of ingratitude to cause dissension in that family. I understood Seth's feelings, and even shared them. Sitting here in my bedroom, I could try to pretend that what I felt for Jaden wasn't that strong, but I knew the minute I saw him again, all those carefully constructed arguments would melt in the heat of his presence.

"So you think I should just ignore it, and hope it goes away?" I asked.

"Sure, why not?" He shrugged. "It happens all the time."

"To you."

"What are you saying, that what you feel for him is... serious?"

"Honestly, Seth," I said with a touch of impatience, "do you think I would even bring it up if it weren't serious? This is no passing crush, it's... well, it's deeper than that." I felt my face coloring as I tripped over the end of my sentence.

"Come on, T, how many people have serious relationships at seventeen? I mean relationships that last?" He was speaking quickly now, trying to persuade me. "Even if things were alright while you guys went out, think of what would happen when you broke up. What if you hated each other?"

"That wouldn't happen," I protested. "I can't imagine ever hating him."

"It's a pretty common occurrence. And you're both intense people—look at the spats you've gotten into already, when there's nothing at stake."

I fell silent, thinking. Seth was giving voice to all the doubts and misgivings I'd been struggling with since acknowledging my feelings for Jaden. And moreover, he was right. What was I doing? I couldn't risk the family harmony of my entire extended clan just to gratify my own desires; that would be appallingly selfish. And I couldn't risk alienating them, they were the only family—and only home—that I had. I turned the question over in my mind, but no matter what angle I viewed it from, the answer remained the same. My only option was to learn to suppress my feelings.

I looked into my brother's clear blue eyes, and the love and concern in them only strengthened my resolve. I couldn't do anything that Seth was so opposed to.

"You're right," I conceded, my voice hushed. "It's too big of a risk."

He looked enormously relieved. "So you'll try to get over it?"

I nodded glumly.

"And you haven't said anything to him, or dropped any hints?" he pressed.

"No, nothing. In any case I suspect he only thinks of me as his bratty little cousin, so you have nothing to worry about."

"Thanks, Tea," he breathed sincerely. "And hey, cheer up. If you want, I'll set you up with some of my buddies. And don't forget Kabir's standing offer of matrimony."

He put his arm around me, and I gave him a small smile in response. I figured I'd better get used to acting.

Julia and Teri were brimming with enthusiasm the next day. We climbed up to the hayloft, one of our favorite hangouts—it was a secluded, fragrant place to sit and talk. They both curled up on haybales, but I was too wired to sit; I paced back and forth in front of them.

"Okay, here's the thing," I began, looking only at Teri. "Remember what I told you yesterday? Well, it can't happen. Just forget I ever said anything."

"Why?" Teri asked with a frown, just as Julia piped up, "Come on, that's not fair—at least tell me what it is that's not happening anymore."

I sighed and went to sit between them.

"Jules, I'm going to tell you something in confidence, and you're going to do your best to forget it as soon as you hear it, okay?"

She nodded, obviously curious.

"Like I told you, I was crushing on somebody. But after thinking it through, and talking to Seth, I've decided it would be insane to act on it. So I won't be needing a makeover anymore, I guess."

"Oh no you don't—you're not getting out of your makeover that easy." Julia laughed. "But come on, spill—what's the big deal with the crush?"

"It's a big deal because the object is Jaden," I admitted.

Julia's perfect mouth formed a round 'O' of surprise. "Ouch, that is a dilemma," she finally said.

We rehashed my decision to ignore my feelings. They understood, though neither of them seemed to think my crush was as calamitous as Seth had. Maybe, in similar circumstances, their families would have been more accepting. It was hard to tell, since they weren't faced with my situation.

"You know, this is actually the perfect time for you to have a makeover," Julia told me thoughtfully. "It will be a distraction, plus, looking good will make you feel better. And you'll attract so many boys that before you know it, you'll be saying, 'Jaden who?'" I had to smile at her enthusiasm, though somehow I doubted I'd ever be saying that.

We made plans to go shopping so that I could update my wardrobe. And accessories, since apparently those were important.

"I don't want to see you wearing any more of Seth's T-shirts," Julia told me severely. "And work on evening out your tan, will you? That farmer tan will *not* work with the outfits you'll be wearing."

"How am I supposed to do that? I don't exactly have a ton of free time, Jules."

She rolled her eyes at me. "You work outside, T. Just teach some lessons in a bikini top."

"I can try," I said skeptically. I didn't think it would go over too well with Dec, though. Teri was excited about the makeover too, and I started to get interested despite myself. It *was* a good distraction—and if I was being honest, I did want Jaden to find me attractive, even if I could never, ever admit my feelings to him.

Nine

Jaden showed up for lunch on Tuesday, and the plan was for me to accompany him to the polo club that afternoon so I could have my first lesson. There was just one slight obstacle that I hadn't foreseen.

"Hold on a second here." Dec frowned when Jaden and I started making plans. "Tea, you're grounded, remember?"

I looked at him in alarm. "Yes, but... I'm supposed to be training Schweppes. I can't do that if I don't know how to play the game."

"You'll just have to do what you can from here, because you're not leaving the property." He was impassive, and I felt my chin set stubbornly. This was ridiculous.

"Dec, be reasonable," I began heatedly. I felt someone nudge me under the table; when I looked round Jaden gave a tiny shake of his head. I locked eyes with him for a second, debating whether to argue, but as his gaze held mine my breath caught and my stomach jumped. I looked away quickly, completely distracted.

After we cleared the dishes Jaden gestured for me to get out of the kitchen. I grabbed Seth and we made our way down to the barn. Jaden sauntered in ten minutes later, looking smug.

"Okay, we're cleared for take-off. You can go to the club, as long as you're with me, and we keep the time to a reasonable minimum."

"And you have to ensure that I don't have any fun, I suppose?" I asked him, grinning.

The ride to the club went quickly as we caught up on news. The trail opened onto the back of the polo grounds, which were fantastic: a huge expanse of perfectly mowed emerald grass, stabling for eighty horses, and turnout paddocks. I'd spent most of my previous visit in one large barn. Now I saw that most of the stabling consisted of smaller, three-season barns—basically groups of roofed stalls without outer walls, because polo ponies were either turned out or playing in warmer climates during the winter. José set me up with a blue roan mare called Maya. I was riding one of the club's horses so I wouldn't have to worry about scaring Schweppes while I learned.

Jaden started off showing me the basics: how to hold the mallet and the double sets of reins, and the more common swings. I tied hard to focus only on what he was teaching me, and not pay attention to the other details trying to impinge themselves on my consciousness, like how perfect his face looked behind the dark sunglasses, how powerfully graceful his movements were, or how sexy I found it when his arm muscles jumped as he moved.

When he was done demonstrating, Jaden threw down a white ball. It was about three and a half inches in diameter—not very big when you considered it was usually hit at a gallop. In other words, at about thirty-five miles an hour.

"Try hitting it using a half-swing," he instructed.

I walked Maya toward the ball, trying to time my swing so I'd hit the ball when it was level with my stirrup. It was a lot harder than it looked. I practiced the different swings; the one I had the most trouble with was the full swing, where your arm arcs around in almost a full circle before striking the ball. It's an important shot in polo, and the one that delivers the most power, but I just couldn't seem to get it right.

"Do you want to take a break and rest your arm?" Jaden asked after we'd been working at it for a while.

"No, I want to learn this shot," I said. I was frustrated at my lack of success, and as usual, my frustration was making me stubborn. I tried again. And again, I barely clipped the ball.

Jaden rode over and held out his hand. "Give me your mallet, Tea," he said firmly.

I handed it over with a questioning look.

"I can see you arm shaking," he explained. "You're going to hurt yourself if you keep pushing now."

We walked our horses side by side around the field, while I massaged my forearm and flexed my fingers. I had to admit, they were sore. It was a perfect spring day, sunny and a little breezy, and I began to relax and enjoy my surroundings. Especially one aspect of my surroundings.

"How is Schweppes coming along in the barn?" Jaden asked.

He rode closer to me as I answered, until our lower legs were pressed together. I tried to tune out the fact that his leg was rubbing against mine while I answered, but the feeling was starting to distract me. He seemed completely unaware of our physical contact—how could he not notice, I wondered. It felt so good to me, dangerously good... it was probably fortunate that he didn't enjoy it the same way I did. Probably.

"What else is new?" he was saying now.

"Dec's mad at me," I sighed.

Jaden's carefree laughter surprised me. "What did you do this time?"

I looked up in annoyance, about to protest his insulting assumption, but when I found his face my breath caught in my throat and I couldn't speak. His smile was so playful, his light-flecked eyes so warm and teasing... with the sun shining on his honey-brown hair, his whole being seemed to glow with warmth. After a long beat, I felt a wide answering smile spread across my face, all indignation forgotten.

When I was rested we tried again. After about an hour I was making contact with the ball quite frequently, even sometimes at the trot and canter. Jaden was gentle but persistent as a coach—he was free with his praise but made me correct my mistakes, too.

"You really are a quick study, aren't you," he said as we headed back to the barn. I shrugged. I was a bit disturbed by the joy I'd been feeling from his praise; it was a clear indication I wasn't squashing my emotions down enough. I made up my mind to try harder.

When we got back to the barn Stephanie was grooming Gracie, her Belgian Warmblood. They were well-matched; Stephanie was tall, her long brown hair only a shade lighter than her mare's liver chestnut coat.

"Your ribs are still hurting you," she remarked as I was untacking Schweppes. She didn't phrase it as a question, and I looked at her inquiringly.

"Sometimes... how did you know?"

She smiled. "It's my job. You're welcome to come and see me, you know. I can probably help with the pain. Are you getting headaches, too?"

"Okay, now you're just freaking me out," I said. I *was* still getting headaches, but few people knew about it.

"Here." She handed me her card. "Make an appointment, and we'll get you all fixed up for the show season."

Julia had decreed that a shopping trip in Toronto was called for; we'd already snuck in some shopping locally—and my summer

137

wardrobe was looking significantly better—but she wasn't satisfied. And since I needed a dress for Stacey's upcoming party, Dec had agreed to let me go, eventually.

"Why can't you go into Paris or Burlington?" he had asked suspiciously, naming two closer towns.

"I want to get something nice," I replied innocently. "And I need Julia's help for that." Dec understood my limited interest in fashion; I'd owned the same two dresses for years.

"Here," he capitulated finally, handing me some money, "go ahead, then."

Teri came too, and we found the perfect dress. Julia also insisted on trying half the cosmetics counter on me. I didn't see the point of most of the products but on her advice I ended up bringing quite a few home. I felt conflicted about it—as if trying to make myself attractive went counter to my promise to Seth. When I confided my worries to Teri and Julia, they dismissed them, reiterating that the makeover was all about me, and I used their arguments to quell the whispers of doubt. Not for the first time, I wished I'd inherited the same genes that Seth had from our Swedish mother, so that I could be tall and fair and beautiful, too. It seemed to me that I wouldn't need to go to nearly as much trouble to be attractive if only Nature had been a little more accommodating.

I saw Stephanie that week, and true to her word, she did wonders for my injuries. Physically, I was feeling better than I had in months. Mentally, I was also recovering my equilibrium, and catching up in school. My emotional state, however, was a mess, thanks to the confusion and guilt I was feeling over Jaden.

It was mid-May, and the pace of work at the barn had picked up significantly. I was teaching more, and faced the challenge of scheduling my weekend lessons so they wouldn't interfere with polo practices. Jaden was spending increasing amounts of time at our place, and despite the uneasy feelings he created in me, I liked having him around. Life was different when he was there. We ate better, for one thing, as Seth happily pointed out. Dec barbecued a lot during the summer, and even the standard of our barbecues was elevated by the addition of things like marinated vegetable brochettes, something that Seth, Dec and I never would have done if left to our own devices. Another improvement was in Dec's mood. He was happy to be seeing more of Jaden. And the amount of heavy work I did decreased significantly when he was nearby; I would pick up a haybale or a jump standard only to find it lifted out of my hands, usually accompanied by his sigh of frustration.

May also brought a new pony for me to ride. Emma, my beginner student, had been riding with dedication for almost a year, and her parents had succumbed to her pleas. Soon after I'd put the word out, Karen called to say she had found the perfect large pony. Cameo came off the trailer looking like a fat, grey furball, but underneath it all she had beautiful conformation and a divine personality. She'd been a young and promising show pony when she was sold to a rich family; the daughter had ridden her a few times before losing interest, and Cameo had spent the next two years living in a field. Emma's parents, the Tremblays, wanted me to train and show Cameo this year so that hopefully, she and Emma would be ready to compete together the following year. So, despite not having my own horse to show, I was kept busy.

I had learned enough polo by now to ride in my first practice match—or at least, in one chukker or period of it, since I only had one horse. I was pretty excited about it when Jaden and I discussed it the day before; we were in the barn, getting our equipment ready.

"I'll get you a regulation helmet and kneepads," he said, "but you might want to wear a body protector, too, in case you fall off."

"That's not an issue—I don't come off," I told him confidently.

"That's a bit cocky, don't you think?" He was frowning.

"It's not cockiness if it's true," I retorted. I crossed my arms, frowning back. Seth muttered something that sounded like 'here we go again' and wandered off.

Jaden gave me a stern look. "You're going to have to change that attitude on the polo field—if you're not on guard against falls you'll get injured. And bumping is perfectly allowable, though no one will do that to you at our club." His expression made it clear they'd better not.

I pursed my lips. "How about we try right now? Let's mount up, and feel free to try and get me off."

"Be serious, Tea," he rolled his eyes at me. "I've got almost a foot on you in height, and I'm close to twice your weight. I'd flatten you."

"Not unless you took my horse down first," I said with assurance.

He narrowed his eyes. "That's just the point, Tea. Your horse *could* go down, it happens."

"Fine," I muttered. "I'll wear a body protector. But I won't need it."

I shaved off Schweppes' mane the day before our practice game, all except for a tuft at the base, near his withers. Jaden had been telling me to do it for weeks, but I'd been putting it off, and he finally dug out the clippers and said he'd do it himself if I didn't.

"But his hair's so *pretty*," I whined. "Can't I just braid it instead?"

"Sorry, but no," he insisted. "It's a safety issue; you can't be getting things caught in his mane during a match."

Schweppes' neck looked very bare during our ride to the club. Jaden rode Piba and led Kermit alongside her, and along the way he reminded me of the basic rules and talked about strategy. I remembered when he'd first started explaining the game, a couple of weeks before.

"A game is usually four chukkers," he had said.

"Each seven minutes long," I added.

"Let me guess—you did some research?" he said. "Okay, tell me what you know."

I told him what I had read about the players and their positions.

"Out of the four positions, you'd normally play number three, right?" I guessed. "Because you're the playmaker, the strongest player."

I watched the smile grow on his face as I went on to describe the basic rules. Since then he had taught me a bit more, but today would be the first time I would have to remember any of it under pressure.

At the club we dismounted and Jaden introduced me to Jennalyn, his long-time groom. Jennalyn was... well, hot. There really wasn't any other way to describe her. Of average height, but with the kind of luscious, curvy figure that I could dream of, but would never have. She was stylish, too, naturally, as though the multi-toned brown hair and stunning yellow-and-grey eyes weren't enough. Despite that, though, I liked her right away, because she was also incredibly nice. I also knew that Jaden thought highly of her—and he had high expectations.

I was getting to know many of the faces at the club, and Jaden gave me some background on the people we met. As we neared the main barn a man with somewhat long, wavy black hair came out. I remembered Jaden pointing him out; his name was Mateo, he was from Argentina and he was the club's other hired professional. At the sight of us he stopped dead and said something to Jaden in Spanish. He smiled at the end, but it wasn't a pleasant expression. Though Jaden's answer sounded relaxed, when I glanced at him his jaw was tight and his shoulders stiff.

Mateo's groom, a busty blonde, rode up and handed him his horse. I looked at Jaden inquiringly; he shook his head, but the scornful look Mateo gave me reinforced my impression that he'd been talking about me.

"Jennalyn?" I turned to her.

"Don't mind him, Tea," she said soothingly, "there's no love lost between him and Jaden."

"But what did he say?"

She hesitated, glancing over at Jaden, who was getting on Kermit.

"He told Jaden that he should leave his little dolls at home where they belong, not bring them onto the polo field."

I leveled a glare at Mateo, grabbed the remaining handful of Schweppes' mane and vaulted into the saddle without touching the stirrup. He turned his horse away with a last supercilious look.

"That's my girl," Jaden encouraged as he rode up alongside me. "Show him what you're made of."

My girl. My heart swelled irrationally at his words; I was suddenly and passionately in love with the phrase. It's just an expression, I reminded myself ferociously. It means nothing. But the words echoed endlessly through my head, filling me with a fierce, mournful longing. We rode to the field side by side, but I had no awareness of my surroundings. Until the chukker started, that is.

Trying to play on a team was very different from practicing alone with Jaden. There was so much going on, and everything moved so fast. Schweppes was overwhelmed, too; he wasn't used to being bumped and crowded. However, my teammates were all very supportive, especially Jaden's friend Dan, whose two kids were about my age. On the opposing team I recognized Mateo, a tall man called Lucas, and Davis, a player that I knew Jaden didn't like. Jaden was one of the umpires. My teammates passed me the ball several times, but almost every time Mateo was there, bumping into Schweppes and riding me off the ball. I gritted my teeth; this was getting personal. There was a lot of yelling in Spanish between Jaden and Mateo. I got the impression that Jaden was trying to assign penalties for the bumping, but as he had warned me, it wasn't against the rules.

A polo field is enormous, about the size of nine American football fields, and the play was moving rapidly from one end to the other. At one point Schweppes and I trailed behind, away from the pack. I spotted Mateo galloping our way—and the ball on the grass between us. Without thinking, I flattened myself onto Schweppes' neck, urging him into a gallop. Mateo was bearing down on us, bucketing along at full speed, but I refused to deviate.

"Hold steady, baby," I whispered to Schweppes. He proved his courage—even though Mateo's horse was bigger than him and had already bumped him several times, he didn't waver. With a yell of frustration, Mateo swerved and I hit the ball. The whistle blew immediately, of course; it was a foul. I had suspected as much when I went after the ball. I could hear Mateo ranting in Spanish as Jaden rode up to me.

"Didn't you hear me shouting at you?" he asked.

"No," I said, not meeting his eyes.

"It's just as well," he sighed. I looked up to find him grinning. "It's also just as well that you don't understand Spanish, or you'd be adding a lot to your vocabulary of curses right now."

The chukker ended, and I was about to head back to the stables, but to my surprise Jaden suggested that I ride Kermit in the next one.

"You'll learn a lot more by riding an experienced horse and following his lead," he said. It was true; I often told my students the same thing, so I accepted gratefully, if a little nervously. Kermit was Jaden's number-one horse, and Jaden was a world-class player. I didn't want to screw up.

"Don't even try to hit the ball," Jaden instructed once I was mounted. "Just take note of where Kermit goes and how he positions you. Oh, and watch the goalposts, he's hit them a few times and he'll swerve very abruptly to avoid them."

From the instant the ball was thrown in, everything was a blur. Kermit was very fast, and he certainly knew what he was doing—I was always in the thick of things. Fortunately, I was able to stay balanced and follow his sudden movements because I wasn't trying to hit the ball. The whistle blew for a foul, and the instant play resumed Kermit took off galloping for our opponent's goal. As I neared it I saw the ball—it was lying a few feet away from the goalpost, and we were far ahead of anyone else. I swung Kermit around in an arc, my mallet raised. He was going at a nice controlled gallop; this was going to be an easy shot. I leaned out of the saddle, started my swing, and the next thing I knew the ground was rushing up to meet me. By the time I looked up Kermit was galloping down the field, keeping pace with Mateo, who now had the ball.

I got to my feet and dusted myself off, and straightened to see Jaden cantering up to me. I had to admire Piba's schooling as she dropped from a canter to a walk in one fluid stride, then halted next to me. Jaden reached down; to his credit he was only wearing a small smile.

"Not a word," I warned him.

He withdrew his hand.

"Would you rather walk, then?" he asked angelically.

I sighed, handed him my mallet, and held up my left hand. We grasped each other's wrists; there was no perceptible signal, but our timing was perfect—he yanked as I sprang, and I flew easily onto Piba's back behind him.

"You don't weigh anything at all—no wonder you came off so easily," he commented.

I groaned. "I thought you weren't going to say anything."

He pulled Piba to a halt. "You're still free to walk."

"Fine," I muttered. I stayed put.

Piba resumed moving.

"Will you listen to me next time?" His tone was benign.

"Yes," I replied humbly.

The next day was Sunday, and I went to help groom at another match, this one in Alliston. At the polo grounds I saw Caley walking past while I tacked up Piba.

"Hey, Caley!" I waved to her, and she wandered over.

"Hey kid, how's it going?" She seemed a bit subdued, not her usual hyper self at all.

"Great. It's so good to see you again; I can't wait to watch you play," I said enthusiastically, and I meant it. It was inspiring to see good female players.

"Cool. How did you like the party?"

I didn't get a chance to answer because suddenly, Jaden appeared.

143

"Is Piba ready?" he snapped. I looked around in surprise—he wasn't usually this impatient. He didn't acknowledge Caley, and she kept her eyes down, her face turned away from him... an angry suspicion flared in my head.

"Jaden—tell me you didn't..." He shot me an icy look and I quailed.

"Caley," I pleaded, "What's going on? Did Jaden-"

"That's between you two," she interrupted. "See ya around, Tea." The look she gave me was somewhat cold, and it saddened me. I really liked Caley, and I'd hoped to count her as a friend.

I whirled around and glared at Jaden, but he held up a hand, his face implacable.

"Not now. I've got a game to play."

"Fine," I snapped, turning back to Piba, "But you are *so* telling me afterward."

A hand grabbed my shoulder and spun me around. He leaned his face close to mine; his eyes were burning with anger.

"Don't forget who's in the wrong here, Tea. You were the one buying the drugs, not me—I don't have to justify anything to you."

He released me and stalked off. I was floored by his outburst. I felt tears well up and turned around quickly, struggling to keep them contained. I hadn't known that he was harboring that level of ill-feeling toward me; the discovery was surprisingly painful.

When he returned five minutes later I handed him the reins without looking at him. I felt his hand, warm and calloused, on my cheek. He didn't say anything, and neither did I, but the ache in my chest eased.

Jaden was in a better mood on the drive home. His team had won, naturally. I got the impression that he was barely trying on the field. I was looking forward to watching him in the year's first big tournament at the end of May, where he would perform against players closer to his own caliber.

"Jaden... about Caley," I began hesitantly. I was nervous about bringing it up, but felt I had to. It wasn't right for me to be damaging their friendship this way. He glanced over at me; I noticed his hands tighten on the steering wheel.

"What about her?" His tone wasn't encouraging.

"Please don't stay angry with her. She was trying to do us a favor... and she's been your friend for a long time. My bad decisions shouldn't be coming between you."

"She endangered you, Tea," he said vehemently. "I'm not sure I can count her as a friend anymore after that."

"*She* didn't endanger me—I'm responsible for my own actions. Caley was great, she was looking out for us all night."

"She wasn't there when some strange boy had his hands all over you," he growled.

I glanced at him, startled, and tried hard to squash the little tendrils of hope that were unfurling inside me. Jaden almost sounded jealous—something that I should *not* be happy about. Though I was. I took a deep breath and pushed the thought away.

"Jaden Foster, are you telling me that you would write off a friendship over one mistake?" I asked him severely.

It was his turn to look surprised. "Tea, what she did-"

"Was not such a big deal," I interrupted firmly. "She gave me what I asked for, and was very kind about it, too. Not everyone's going to be as overprotective as you are." Thank God for that.

He met my eyes for an instant, the conflict in his plain to see. I was suddenly, inordinately touched that his concern for me was so great that he would create a rift with his old friend. Touched, and guilt-ridden.

"Please..." My voice was gentle this time, and warm from the dangerous emotions pulsing through me. "I feel so bad about coming between you. It was my doing, Jaden... forgive her."

He gazed at me, long enough that I began to worry about the road, and the frustration on his face was gradually replaced by a lopsided smile. He reached over and squeezed my hand; my heart faltered, then drummed loudly inside my chest. I had to look away from him.

"All right," he agreed quietly.

We spent the rest of the drive in comfortable silence. Even though he released my hand after a few seconds, my skin continued to tingle for a long time.

After a bit of grumbling from Dec—and some threats of dire consequences if my grades didn't improve—it was agreed that I could play in another practice match the following Saturday. I'd be playing in two chukkers, the first and the last, so Schweppes wouldn't get too tired. Jennalyn was in the barn getting Jaden's horses ready, and as she worked she give me the scoop on people at the club. I liked her version as she provided details Jaden didn't.

"No one likes Davis because he thinks his money will buy him acceptance," she confided. "He's obnoxious, he cheats, and on top of that he can't play. And Jaden thinks he treats his horses like machines."

I nodded; I'd heard that complaint from Jaden. "What's the deal with Jaden and Mateo?"

Jen hesitated. "I'm not sure," she hedged, but I could tell she knew. "Mateo was a pro at the Toronto club last year. They seemed to get along fine at the beginning of the season, but by the end they were barely civil toward each other."

I wondered at the intrigue as I rode onto the field for the final chukker. Whatever the feud was about, Mateo's dislike for Jaden apparently extended to me. He had never spoken to me. He was riding his own horse, a gorgeous bay Thoroughbred named Belita; I'd heard she was fantastic. I didn't get a chance to watch her, though, because as usual once play commenced everything happened so fast I could barely follow it. A yell made me look up. Belita was streaking down the field, her graceful long legs a blur of movement against the emerald grass. Davis cut in front of me and galloped straight toward Belita; trying to steal the ball, I thought. I slowed Schweppes to a canter as I watched Davis's mallet go up, so we'd be ready to shoot off in a new direction. It was only at the last second that I realized something was amiss—the angle of Davis's mallet was wrong. I watched with horror as it swung into Belita's legs with a sickening thud.

I felt a split second of cold shock. Then everything was red. Red blood roared in my ears and a red haze covered my eyes as I shrieked and rocketed down the field. I wasn't aware of having asked Schweppes to gallop, but he knew what I wanted, and he must have called on his Quarter Horse blood because I felt a sudden burst in his already fiery pace. I dropped my mallet; I wouldn't need it for this. We had almost caught up to Davis's chestnut gelding. I kicked out of my stirrups and as I drew level I used the pommel of my saddle as leverage to yank my feet up. Davis's horse was bigger than Schweppes, I needed the extra height... I crouched for a nanosecond, my feet on the seat, then launched myself at Davis with all of my might.

My mid-air tackle worked perfectly—I knocked him sideways out of his saddle and he was still floppy with surprise as I crashed on top of him with a satisfying *whump*. I rolled off him, onto my knees in the damp grass, breathing hard. Davis didn't move, and I had just become aware that I was shaking violently when Jaden galloped up. He leaped out of the saddle before Kermit had even stopped, landed agilely and took two running steps toward me.

"Tea!" His voice was wild; he was panting.

I looked up at him, suddenly apprehensive. The reality of what I'd done was just starting to sink in. Sure enough, as I watched, the frantic expression on his face hardened into one of cold fury.

"What the hell was that?" He bit off each word distinctly. His voice wasn't loud, but the ferocity of his tone was enough to make me cringe back.

To my relief, Davis chose that moment to groan and roll over, and seconds later his teammates converged on us. There seemed to be a lot of yelling, some of it in Jaden's voice, but I didn't pay attention. I was still on my knees, bracing myself on the grass with my hands and trembling with reaction. I kept my head down until the voices and hoofbeats faded away. My shivering was under control now—the adrenaline must have been used up.

"Get up." The words were forced from between Jaden's clenched teeth.

I hazarded a nervous glance up at him; he was towering over me, his entire frame quivering with what I could only assume was rage. I noticed with mild surprise that, for the first time I could remember, he didn't have a hand extended to help me... maybe because both of those hands were tightly clenched into fists, the skin white over the knuckles. I scrambled to my feet, feeling the dull throbbing in my head that was the aftermath of my own rage. I didn't want to meet his eyes, but I could feel them burning into me.

"Get off the field and wait for me." The whole sentence was a growl.

I fled without looking at him. To my relief I spotted Dan leading Schweppes my way.

"Now *that* was the most incredible piece of riding I've seen in a long time." He laughed as he handed over the reins. "You should consider a career as a stunt rider."

Schweppes nudged me in the stomach happily.

"Yes, you were wonderful," I praised him, stroking his golden neck. "Thanks," I added to Dan. I tried to return his smile, but my nerves with still jangling. He indicated Jaden with his thumb and looked at me sympathetically.

"He's giving you grief?"

147

I nodded glumly.

"Well, don't take it to heart. The rest of us thought that rocked."

He held his hand up for a high five, and I slapped it before trudging over to the stable area. Despite Dan's encouraging words, I didn't feel much better. 'Don't take it to heart' was a phrase that simply couldn't apply with regards to Jaden; everything he did affected my heart. That was the problem—I couldn't seem to build adequate defenses against him. For every brick I mortared onto the wall, he somehow took two down.

When I reached the barns I saw Mateo and Belita outside and hurried over to check on her.

"How is she?" I inquired anxiously.

Mateo was icing Belita's leg just above the knee while his groom, Sharleen, held the lead rope and fed Belita carrots. He rose and gave me an inscrutable look.

"She will be okay. He did not hit the knee, that..." he called Davis a few choice names and I grinned. Suddenly he grinned back; his teeth flashed brightly against his dark skin and his eyes crinkled up at the corners. I felt a shock of surprise that I had never noticed how good-looking Mateo was... but then, I only seemed to notice one man these days. One who certainly didn't notice me, at least not in that sense.

"Thank you, muñequita," Mateo said warmly. "You are small as a kitten, but brave as a tiger." He grasped my shoulders and kissed me on both cheeks. I beamed, happy at his sudden approval.

"Mateo," a familiar voice snarled.

I dropped my gaze quickly.

"The chukker is over. How's Belita?" Jaden sounded less angry now, the words barely clipped.

"Okay, I think. The vet is on her way." I felt Mateo's eyes on me; I was sure my posture betrayed my trepidation. "Don't be too hard on our little tiger."

I was oddly touched that he was looking out for me. It made me feel, for the first time, like part of a team. A team whose captain was snarling again.

"That's my business, Mateo. Tea, let's go."

I tightened Schweppes' girth and mounted, my heart accelerating. We headed for the trail home. I was braced for the onslaught of Jaden's wrath, but he didn't say a word, and I fell in behind him, not wanting to feel his furious glower at my back. We had gone about halfway—fifteen minutes or so—when the silent treatment started to wear on me.

"Jaden..." I began tentatively.

"Hush." It wasn't quite a snap.

I resigned myself to a quiet ride, and passed the time replaying my impulsive act of revenge in my mind. In retrospect, it seemed far more daring than it had felt at the time; I'm sure I wouldn't have done it if I'd stopped to think it through. My left cheekbone was throbbing—it felt a bit swollen, I seemed to remember it hitting Davis' helmet—and my right elbow was skinned, but other than that I was remarkably unscathed. I started to feel a bit irritated with Jaden for overreacting.

We were almost home when he wheeled Kermit to face me and rode up so we were knee to knee. His fury had cooled, but his eyes glinted with steel and his jaw was tight. It was hard not to look away.

"If you *ever* do anything even *remotely* like that again, you will be banned from the club, and I will never coach you again. Is that clear?"

I blinked in surprise, and tried not to show how much those words hurt. I knew he was angry, but I hadn't known that anything could make him mad enough not to teach me anymore. I nodded mutely, keeping my face carefully composed.

We made our way to the barn in silence. I took my time cleaning Schweppes up, and after checking his legs carefully I rubbed them with liniment. I was starting to feel like I could use a rubdown myself; various aches and pains were beginning to emerge from my tumble. Lucky I'd had Davis as a pillow, I thought to myself with a smile. The smile faded fast, though. The more I thought about Jaden's reaction, the more irritated I got. Not only was he blowing this whole thing out of proportion—our teammates' responses were proof of that—but to threaten never to teach me again? That was downright petty. And mean. If I were being truthful with myself, I might have admitted that I was mostly angry that he had the power to hurt me so easily. I decided truthfulness was overrated.

After getting Schweppes comfortable I went and hid in my room, and waited as late as possible to go help with dinner. I sighed with relief when I walked into the kitchen and saw Jaden wasn't there.

"Hey dude, how was the practice game?" Seth called over his shoulder.

It looked like we were having pasta—good, something simple and quick. I'd eat a few bites, then make my escape. I started making a salad.

"It was... interesting. I'll have to tell you later." I gave him a significant look; Dec was just walking in. Seth's face was bright with curiosity, but his brows drew together as he examined my face. I felt my cheekbone. It was definitely tender.

Jaden walked in right after we sat down. He took his usual spot across from me, but I didn't look at him.

"How was practice?" Dec asked. "Is Tea coming along?"

Jaden didn't answer; he was staring at his plate, his jaw clenched tight. Dec looked at me questioningly.

"Um, the game was cut short. Mateo's mare was injured," I explained.

"Oh, that's too..." Dec trailed off, looking at me. "What happened to you?"

I could feel Seth's eyes on me too.

"I, um, had a little spill," I explained lightly. "It's nothing."

Which wasn't really a lie. I kept my eyes carefully away from Jaden and prayed that he wouldn't tell the truth. I was sure it would go over about as well with Dec as it had with him.

"Why, what happened?" Dec insisted.

It wasn't surprising that he would ask—I really hadn't been as cocky as Jaden thought when I said I didn't come off. I rode a lot of horses, some of them very difficult, and aside from the tumble off Kermit my last involuntary dismount had been almost two years ago. So it wasn't surprising, but it was inconvenient, because now I had to lie.

"Someone cut in front of us, and Schweppes had to swerve really fast." I was trying to come up with a plausible scenario, but it was hard under pressure.

"I thought you were taking care of her?" Dec turned to frown at Jaden, and I made the mistake of following his gaze. Jaden was glaring at me through narrowed eyes.

"Taking care of her," he spat, "would be a much easier task if she had *any* sense of self-preservation whatsoever."

All the slowly building anger I'd been feeling toward him burst forth.

"It wasn't about *self*-preservation—did you even see what Davis *did*?" I was leaning across the table toward him, almost yelling.

"Hey! Easy, you two," Dec admonished, glancing back and forth between our angry faces.

"Excuse me," Jaden stood abruptly and stalked out.

Dec watched him go with a frown, then looked back at me. I wanted to excuse myself too, but I knew I wasn't getting away that easily.

"Tell me what happened to your face, Tea." Dec's voice was quiet but grim.

My eyes flashed up, startled at his tone.

"I fell off." I could hear the false note in my voice as I was caught by surprise.

"Tea... I haven't seen Jaden this angry in a long time." He was speaking slowly, watching me. "You two have obviously had some sort of fight again."

I could feel the blank look on my face; I didn't know where he was headed with this. He dropped his voice lower.

"Did... he didn't hit you, did he?" I couldn't remember ever seeing Dec look so nervous.

"What? No, of course not!" My shock was genuine; Dec looked relieved. "How could you even think that?"

I was upset on Jaden's behalf—no matter how angry I was with him right now, I didn't want people thinking that of him... thinking he'd be capable of hurting me.

"I had to check, kiddo. He—well, he has something of a history."

My face went rigid with anger.

"You are underestimating him so much it's insulting—he would never do that! He was madder today than I've ever seen him, and he didn't touch me," I growled. "I doubt that you would have shown as much restraint."

Dec's eyes flashed. I expected anger, but instead, for the first time, I saw hurt on his face. I instantly regretted my words; it was a low blow, and I knew it. Dec had really changed over the last few months, he was obviously working hard at improving our relationship, and I was quite sure that throwing the past in his face was not only unfair but unhelpful.

"Sorry," I said meekly, ducking my head.

I was going to have to tell the truth, that much was obvious. More equivocation would only increase the tension at this point. I relayed the story quickly, making it sound as tame as possible. A fair bit of yelling later, I bolted to the barn. Seth, bless him, had volunteered to do the dishes so I could escape Dec's considerable ire.

I went to check on Schweppes, and petted him as he nosed through his hay. I suddenly felt such a fierce ache for Blaze that I sagged against the wall; I slid down it and sat in the corner next to Schweppes' hay. He continued eating, nudging me occasionally—he was an angel in the barn now. There was no sign of his former aggression.

I was surprised when Jaden appeared. I thought he'd gone home. I didn't look at his face, just watched his feet advance toward me.

"Don't," I said in a strangled voice.

The feet stopped. I hugged my knees and stared at the wood shavings. "I can't take any more today."

He sat right next to me. I could feel the heat from his body reaching my arm.

"I just came to offer you a shoulder to cry on, if you want." His voice was quiet.

I frowned at him. "No lecture tucked up your sleeve?"

He half-smiled; his eyes were warm again, and slightly... remorseful? That couldn't be right.

"No. Just the shoulder."

He slid his arm around my shoulders. My heart flew into a sprint, and I felt suddenly warm, and slightly dizzy. I hid my face in my knees; it was getting worse. Jaden had always been affectionate, but my response to his touch was getting more and more frenzied. I didn't know what to do—obviously I shouldn't be feeling this way, but I couldn't exactly avoid him. And even if I could, I didn't want to. He was way too important a part of my life.

"About today," he began. "I may have overreacted a bit."

"Ya think?" I mumbled sarcastically into my knees.

He gave my shoulder a squeeze; my heart stuttered and I inhaled sharply.

"You nearly gave me a heart attack, Tea. I thought I was going to find your mangled body." His voice was starting to sound clipped again. I tossed a dirty look his way.

"Hey, no lectures," I reminded him.

He nodded, pressing his lips together. The sight of his mouth did strange things to my stomach; I averted my eyes again.

"Well, you'll be happy to know I'm grounded. Again." I didn't even sound bitter, I was still too preoccupied by my body's betrayal.

"Why?" He sounded shocked. "And why would I be happy about that?"

I turned my face to his, frowning. "I thought... well, don't you think I deserve it?"

He didn't answer the question. "How did Dec find out? I wasn't going to tell him, Tea." He looked upset, which confused me. And I wasn't about to tell him the truth, obviously.

"I... well, it sort of slipped out. I wasn't doing a good enough job fabricating, and I tripped myself up."

"Kind of like now," he said grimly, frowning at me.

I had to look away again. I noticed he kept his arm around me.

"Dude," Seth exclaimed, spotting me as he cruised past Schweppes' partly-open door.

I exhaled noisily. "You know, a stall is just not the private retreat it used to be," I grumbled.

Jaden removed his arm. I felt cold without it.

"So what was all that about?" Seth stepped inside too as he studied both of our faces.

"Don't, Seth," I warned him.

He looked stubborn. Jaden turned and questioned me with his eyes.

"It's nothing," I assured him. "Come on, Seth." I held my hand out so he could help me up. "Let's go watch TV, I'm dead."

Jaden put his hand on my forearm and pushed it down.

"What are you not telling me?" The steel was back in his voice.

I just shook my head, preparing more denials, but Seth spoke up.

"He has a right to know, Tea." He turned his warm blue eyes on Jaden; they were serious, for once, and full of questions. "Dec thought... when he saw the bruise... well, he asked Tea whether... you hit her." He ended in a whisper.

I felt Jaden stiffen next to me. I searched his eyes, expecting to see shock and hurt, but instead I found shame, and more than a hint of anger.

"That's why you told him," he said through gritted teeth.

153

I put my hand on his arm, igniting showers of butterflies in my stomach.

"I'm sorry," I whispered. "I told him you would never do that."

Jaden's face was cold as he shook my hand off.

"That's where you're wrong though, Tea. Dec knows me better than you do." He got up and stalked out, his long stride pulling him quickly out of sight. Seth and I stared at each other, stunned. After a minute he came to sit beside me.

"Why did you tell him?" I asked him, anguished.

"I thought he had a right to know what Dec was thinking about him. But I didn't think... wow."

"Is that really the only reason?" There was a slight edge to my voice.

He turned his head to stare at me. "What are you suggesting? That I hurt him on purpose, because I found him with his arm around you?"

He looked angry, the expression out of place on his face. I felt immediately contrite—of course Seth would never do anything so hurtful.

"Sorry, Moo," I breathed. I squeezed his hand; his face flowed from angry to worried in an instant.

"So why *did* he have his arm around you?" He sounded only slightly accusing.

I shook my head. "It was purely comforting, Seth. He did it the same way you would. Nothing more."

"Maybe to him. But what about you? Bet you didn't feel the same as when it's my arm." The accusation was more definite now.

I went back to examining the shavings. "I won't act on it, Seth. I told you."

As soon as we got back to the house, I confronted Dec.

"I'd like the truth, Dec," I said with no preamble when I found him at the kitchen sink. He looked slightly surprised at my directness, but nodded.

"I know a bit about Jaden's 'history'," I started slowly. His look of surprise deepened. "I know he got into some fights, and that he was once arrested for assault. But what makes you think he would hit *me*?" I felt a twinge as I said it—the mere suggestion was painful.

"I don't know." He answered me slowly, thinking through his response. "I suppose it's partly that I haven't seen him that angry in a

154

long while. And during the time in his life when he did get that angry, it was rare for him to reach that point and *not* hit something. Or someone."

"But did he ever hit a girl?" I persisted.

Dec looked uncomfortable. "I don't think so."

"I'd be willing to bet anything that he never has. And it's unfair to him to even raise those kinds of suspicions." I looked him in the eye. "He knows what you suspected of him, Dec. I'm sorry it slipped out, but it did, and I think... I think you owe him an apology." It was my turn to feel uncomfortable; I'd never presumed to tell Dec what he should do before. Nor would it have gone over very well in the past, I was sure. He considered me for a minute, then nodded slowly.

"You're right. I'll tell him the next time he's here."

Ten

As it transpired, however, 'the next time' was a long time coming. Jaden didn't show up the next day, which didn't really surprise me. But after three days, I began to worry; that was the longest he'd stayed away since school had let out. I called his cell a few times, to no avail. I considered calling the club to see if Jaden had been there, but I didn't want to raise questions if he wasn't going to work. The thought that he might drive all the way down there and not even see me was unexpectedly hurtful. I resolved to put some more emotional distance between us—this wasn't healthy. I'd start right after I saw him again.

On Wednesday I sent him an email. I kept it short, the tone light, but he didn't respond, though I knew he read his mail on his phone throughout the day. My worry grew. His Facebook status hadn't changed. I stayed signed in to Messenger as much as possible, but Jaden was never visible. I texted him once, too, in case he was having Internet issues, but I knew that was a stretch.

Then, on Friday night, he suddenly appeared on Messenger. I waited.

Jaden Foster says:
how's the bruise?
Tea says:
gone. like u. where u been?
Jaden Foster says:
around
Tea says:
i'm going 2 practice with Lucas tomoro

There was a long pause, and then:
Jaden Foster says:
calling

I stared at the word for a minute before getting up and pacing by the phone. It rang a second later; I picked up on the first ring.

"Hi." I sounded breathless.

"Hi." His honeyed tones were smooth, as usual.

I hesitated, unsure of what to say. He spared me the trouble of finding something.

"Why are you practicing with Lucas?" There was a hint of disapproval in his voice, enough to make me defensive.

"Gee, I don't know, maybe because my regular coach has been AWOL for the past week? I've still got a horse to train, you know. What have you been doing all this time, Jaden?" My voice was subdued now, almost pleading.

"I've been thinking." His voice was quiet, too.

"About...."

He got even quieter. "The risks I'm taking, mostly."

My feeble store of patience ran out.

"Oh, for crying out loud! So you got mad and thought about smacking me—I hate to shatter your illusions, but that hardly makes you special. *I* think about hitting *you* all the time. And at this rate, I may well do it when you finally show yourself. But it doesn't make me run and hide and abdicate all my responsibilities." It came out louder than I'd intended.

There was a long silence. I closed my eyes, cringing. I'd gone too far, again... I heard a small chuckle, then what might have been a sigh.

"Don't leave without me tomorrow."

Jaden showed up early the next morning. I was sweeping up after the morning feed when he strolled in.

"Hi," he said, sounding perfectly normal. The shadow of an impish smile was on his face. "Should I duck?"

I smiled despite myself. "I'll let it go this time."

I hadn't fully realized how much I missed him, but now that he was in front of me I had to stifle the urge to throw my arms around him. I told myself to get a grip. His eyes grew pensive as he watched my face.

"Sorry," he said quietly.

He put his hand on my shoulder, and without thinking I covered it with my own. I heard my heartbeat go up in volume.

"I'm sorry, too." My sincerity must have shown on my face; for once, I truly regretted my recklessness. "What I did was really stupid."

"No," he said softly, "what you did was... well, it was you."

His mouth tugged up at my uncomprehending look. "Tea, the fact that you can't see injustice done without being galvanized into action—even if it is ill-considered, dangerous action—is not a character flaw. On the contrary, it shows how compassionate you are."

"One could argue that I didn't show much compassion for Davis." I was joking, trying to distract myself from my racing heartbeat. I liked what he was saying far too much; I was afraid he'd be able to read it on my face.

He grinned and took his hand back. I drew a shaky breath, saddened and relieved at the same time.

"You'll be glad to know that Davis has been officially expelled from the polo club. I suspect quite a few people will thank you for that."

"Jaden, do you think... will I be kicked out, too?" I asked him anxiously. I'd been worried about that, in the lulls between worrying about Jaden's absence. A maneuver like mine was completely unacceptable in polo; normally, a player would likely be banished for attacking another player as I had done. Another thing I hadn't thought of, at the time.

"No. Even if they were so inclined, I have some pull with the owners. You're safe." He winked at me.

Even though we were speaking again, I barely saw Jaden that week, as he was teaching a clinic at the Toronto Polo Club. Stacey's party was on Sunday, and the Saturday before I went to get a haircut—the final step in my makeover. Julia had insisted that I go to her hairstylist, so Teri and I drove all the way to Oakville. We picked up Julia and cranked the tunes on the drive.

Julia's stylist was in a trendy salon. When the hairdresser was done I turned my head, admiring my new cut from all angles. It was short and funky, parted on the side, with long bangs that fell just over my right eye. A few soft tendrils curled around the top of my neck, which was otherwise completely exposed—quite a change, since my hair had flowed halfway down my back when I came in.

"Wow, Tea, you look like a Manga character," Julia breathed.

"So you like it?" I asked the girls a bit anxiously.

"I love it!" Teri exclaimed. "It's totally you."

Julia nodded, grinning. I heaved a sigh of relief. Regardless of the awkwardness of having to distance myself from Jaden, at least I would face the party tomorrow with my head held high.

Julia spent the night at my place to help me get ready. She didn't trust me to do my own makeup, which was probably wise, since I rarely wore any. She and Teri went for a trail ride in the morning while I taught my lessons; by one o'clock, though, she dragged me into the house.

"Why do I need two hours to get ready?" I grumbled.

"You'll thank me later," she answered firmly.

Two hours later, I did see her point. After showering I had donned the pale yellow dress we had found; Teri tied the halter top into a flat bow on the back of my neck, and I examined myself critically in the mirror. Though the makeup Julia had applied was very light and barely noticeable, it seemed to highlight my features just right—large eyes gazed back at me from a small, elfin face with high cheekbones. My mouth looked fuller, softer, and shone petal pink. The fabric of the dress clung to my admittedly unimpressive curves, at least making it appear I had some. My shoulders and back were bare almost to my waist, showcasing my now-uniform tan. I watched a smile grow on my reflected face; I hardly recognized myself. My girlfriends were right— looking good did make me feel stronger. Like maybe I could handle seeing Jaden, and have the strength to shut him out.

We went downstairs. I guess I wasn't the only one to register Seth's open-mouthed expression because Teri and Julia both sported huge grins as they said goodbye. Seth looked me up and down carefully, taking in everything from my makeup to the anklet of small white stones above the pink-painted toenails.

"What's going on, Sis?" he asked suspiciously. "Why are you all... done up?"

"The girls thought it would make me feel better," I explained.

"Make better bait, more like," he muttered.

I grinned. "Is that a compliment, baby brother?"

He smiled back reluctantly. "Okay, so you look good. Way too good, in fact."

Dec blew into the room in his usual last-minute rush. "Are you ready? Let's go before-" He stopped in mid-sentence when he caught sight of me; I felt myself flush and fidgeted nervously while he absorbed my appearance. I looked down at his approach.

"Tea... honey, you look..." He cleared his throat. "Is that the new dress you bought?"

"Yes." I looked up at him, feeling uncertain; the expression on his face was one I'd rarely seen there. It was... tender.

"I wish your mother could see you now," he said, his voice husky.

I felt my throat constrict; I wished for the same thing. Almost daily.

He placed his hand on my shoulder somewhat awkwardly. "I can't believe how grown-up you look. And how... well, you look really nice."

I got increasingly nervous as we approached Stacey's. I told myself I was merely concerned about potential reactions to my new look, but in truth I was only worried about one relative's reaction. To add to my nerves, I was also feeling guilty about caring what he would think, and hoping that I could act natural around him. We followed the interlocking stone path into the backyard. Fortunately it was a warm day for May, and I was comfortable in my light dress.

Stacey was having a separate, much bigger sweet sixteen party for her friends, so this one was mainly family. About a dozen people were already in the large yard, including my uncle Peter. I felt my gorge rise; since hearing about how he had treated Jaden as a child, I felt a strong antipathy toward him. Jaden was nowhere in sight. I noticed everyone was fairly dressed up—a lot of summer suits and dresses—and was very glad I'd had Julia's and Teri's help to get ready.

Stacey rushed up to me.

"Omigod Tea, look at you! You look amazing!" Her enthusiasm was so genuine that I felt a pang of remorse for the condescending way I sometimes thought of her. Who was I to judge her for being interested in things I considered shallow? I was obsessed with my own cousin; I wasn't in a position to judge anyone. As Stacey grilled me about my new look we were joined by her cousin from Uncle Robert's side of the family. I remembered him vaguely from another gathering.

"Hey Stace, are you going to introduce me to your friend?"

"Ethan, silly, it's Tea! My cousin, remember? Which makes her your second cousin, so don't get any ideas." She giggled.

"Tea, seriously?" He smiled at me. "You've certainly changed since the last time I saw you."

Ethan was cute. He was a darker blond than Seth, somewhat stocky, and a few years older than me. We had just started talking when I felt something behind me—my hairs stood on end; I knew without turning that Jaden had arrived.

Stacey looked over my shoulder. "Aunt Paloma!" She went to greet her, and as I turned to follow her progress I caught sight of Jaden.

He was staring at me. His eyes traveled slowly down my body, then back up; I felt flooded with heat, and yet a shiver passed through me. As I watched, his jaw clenched, his eyes narrowed, and his hands balled into fists. I was confused by his response but had no time to ponder it, because Aunt Paloma came right over to hug me hello.

"Tea, darling, you look wonderful!" She kept one arm around me as she turned to her son. "Jaden, you didn't tell me what a lovely young lady Tea's grown into," she chided him. "All he talks about is what a natural you are at polo," she confided, rolling her eyes.

"Oh... well, I do love polo," I said inanely, stealing a glance at Jaden. I felt uncertain after his odd reaction; the anger was no longer obvious, but he was undoubtedly tense, still standing a good six feet away from us.

"Aren't you going to say hello?" his mother asked him.

"Of course," he said, sounding very natural. He loped over smoothly; as he bent to kiss my cheek I met his eyes—they were burning with some intense emotion, and it wasn't a good one. I dropped my eyes quickly, flustered. His nearness and irresistible scent did nothing to help my nerves, either. I was rigid with tension as he walked away.

"D'you want to get a drink?" Ethan asked.

I agreed with a sigh of relief. I had no idea what had just happened, but I felt weak in its aftermath.

Keeping my distance from Jaden turned out to be easy—he was avoiding me. That was the only conclusion I could come to. I hung out with Ethan, Stacey and Seth; when I stole glimpses of him, Jaden seemed completely absorbed by other family members. Once or twice I thought I caught him just looking away, but that could have been my imagination. I tried hard not to look his way too often.

It wasn't until after dessert that we even spoke. The temperature was dropping as the sun slowly sank toward the horizon.

"Are you cold?" Ethan asked, noticing that I was hugging myself.

At my nod, he took off his jacket and draped it around my shoulders. I'd been noticing this odd phenomenon all afternoon—even though I was the same person I'd been yesterday, ever since I had shown up with my newly feminine appearance, people had been treating me differently. As if I were suddenly fragile. Even Dec was more solicitous than usual, to my utter astonishment.

"What made you cut your hair short?" Stacey asked.

Jaden's eyes came to rest on me; I tried to focus on Stacey while I answered.

"I donated it. I discovered this organization that makes free wigs for kids with hair loss... it seemed like a good cause to go short." I kept my gaze away from Jaden, but I could feel his lingering on me.

"Are you coming on Friday?" Dec asked from the next table, drawing Jaden's attention away. I relaxed as Jaden shook his head.

"Not until late, a friend of mine is opening an exhibit at a gallery." He looked at me. "It's Ryan, actually," he told me with seeming reluctance.

"Oh. Well, wish him good luck for me," I told him.

"I will." He watched me for minute, his eyes reserved. "Would you like to come?" he asked abruptly. "You and Seth, I mean," he glanced over at Seth.

"Really?" I was surprised he would ask, considering he hadn't said a word to me all evening. He noticed my hesitation and sighed. "I know he'd be glad to see you again. And his work is worth seeing."

I shrugged. "Well, I'd like to, but we may have to talk Dec into it."

He gave a ghost of his normal smile. "Leave it to me." He went to sit by Dec.

By the time we left it was all arranged. I said a warm goodbye to Ethan, who hugged me tightly. Without his company as a distraction the party would have been even more uncomfortable. I couldn't believe I had hardly spoken to Jaden at all—my plan to distance myself from him was obviously working, but my success left me feeling painfully empty.

There was only a month of school left, so in theory I should have been studying a lot more, but I was hopelessly distracted that week. I only saw Jaden once; he dropped in on Wednesday before heading for the club to play in the weekly practice game, or club chukkers, as they were known. We exchanged a few polite words, hardly looking at each other.

"Well, Tea," Dec announced during dinner, "you'll be happy to hear I'm taking your advice and building more paddocks. Including a pasture with a run-in shed, so we can keep some horses outside during the winter."

"That's good news," I told him, perking up.

"And Jaden is helping," Dec added. "So he'll be staying here four or five nights a week."

My stomach plummeted.

"It's the least I can do, since you refuse to accept board money for my horses," Jaden told him.

I felt Seth's eyes on me, but I couldn't look at him. I was too afraid my face would reveal my dismay. Jaden in my house five days a week—how was I supposed to keep a safe distance from him *now*?

After a phone consultation with Julia, I decided to wear my edgiest top and jeans to the art gallery. Seth drove into the city; I probably wasn't very good company, as I was still preoccupied with the coldness I'd felt from Jaden on Sunday. It was strange, we'd been so close these past few months—had I imagined the distance on Sunday? I shook my head, I'd find out soon enough.

The art gallery was a long, narrow space. I found myself scanning the room for Jaden as soon as we were inside, but I didn't see him.

"Hi there," Chris greeted us, smiling. "Thanks for coming, Ryan will be happy to see you." My return smile was genuine. I'd forgotten how friendly he was.

"I'm so glad to be here, I can't wait to see his work. Oh, this is my brother, Seth." I remembered to introduce him after he elbowed me.

"Can I get you some wine?" Chris offered.

Seth grinned down at me, and answered for both of us. "Sure."

We weren't of age, but it wasn't as though this was a bar. An art gallery wasn't going to get raided for fake IDs.

Chris was back in minutes with two glasses of white wine. I didn't really like wine, but hey—I was in the city on a weeknight, at an art gallery, seeing an exhibit by an artist I actually knew. Those were some pretty exciting firsts for me; I wanted to do the other new things that went along with them. Seth and I started off at the front of the gallery, while Chris wandered off to mingle. I quickly realized that Ryan's work was incredible. We were admiring the third painting along the wall when a long arm reached over my shoulder and plucked the wineglass out of my hand.

163

"I doubt Dec would be very impressed if I brought you home drunk," Jaden said.

I spun around, my heart racing. I noticed my mouth was dry too—when had Jaden's presence started making me nervous? I'd gotten used to his touch making my body overreact, but he wasn't touching me now... this was getting downright ridiculous.

Jaden looked phenomenal. He was always frustratingly gorgeous, but I usually saw him at the barn, when we were both working and dirty. Tonight he looked like he belonged in a magazine spread for urban fashion.

I closed my mouth with some effort. "Hi."

He smiled at me, but it wasn't with his usual warm affection. His eyes remained cautious, appraising. They flickered quickly over my clothes, and I felt suddenly self-conscious about what I'd worn—I hoped I looked okay.

"Hand it over, Seth." He held out his hand for Seth's wine. "One of you has to drive home tonight, and I took responsibility for the pair of you, remember? I should have my head examined." The grin he gave Seth seemed totally natural, I noticed with a pang.

He wandered off, drinking the confiscated wine and stopping here and there to chat. He seemed to know a lot of the people here... people who were all older and more sophisticated than me, I thought wistfully. Seth and I turned back to the canvases, but it wasn't long before his attention wandered. I could see him shooting glances at a girl sitting on a circular leather couch in the middle of the gallery; she was probably in her early twenties, and very pretty. She looked at home in an art gallery. I smiled. Seth didn't have a physical 'type', but a girl like this one would naturally capture his interest. The fact that she was older, and in a unique—for us—setting would just make the challenge that much more fun for him.

I nudged him. "Why don't you go talk to her?"

"You don't mind?"

"'Course not."

He flashed me a grateful smile before heading off. I did feel a bit self-conscious once he was gone, and scanned the room for Jaden again, but I didn't see him. I couldn't help thinking that the fact he hadn't returned yet meant that our presence—well, my presence—wasn't that important to him. Which was a good thing, I tried to tell myself.

Chris returned then. "Where's your brother?"

I pointed him out, cozying up to the pretty girl on the couch. "He saw something he liked."

"Well, he's a real cutie, I'm sure he'll have no trouble making friends," Chris laughed. He linked his arm through mine. "C'mon, I'll show you around. Ry wants to see you, too."

Going through the gallery with Chris was fun. He was good-looking, chatty and gregarious; he introduced me all around and made me feel at ease. When I confessed that I didn't know anything about art, he laughed and threw his arm around my shoulders.

"It's nice to have someone admit they don't know about it for a change, we get so many posers coming to Ry's shows." His eyes were a very light brown for someone with an obvious Asian background. I was wondering about his ancestry when I felt eyes boring into me. I turned around. Jaden was across the room in a small knot of fashionable people—mostly women, I noticed. I gave him a tentative smile, and he half-smiled in return. Chris, his arm still wrapped around me, followed my gaze.

"Speaking of works of art..." He grinned, trailing off.

I tried to hide my sinking feeling. It was true, obviously, but that's not what made Jaden so incredible. Well, it wasn't the only thing—but it was the one element that ensured he would always be surrounded by girls, most of whom would be more beautiful, exotic, or accomplished than me. Not that it mattered, I reminded myself.

Chris resumed towing me around, and we found Ryan.

"Tea's worried that she doesn't know anything about art," Chris informed him after we'd said hi.

"You don't need to know about it to appreciate it," Ryan reassured me. He was soft-spoken, and I liked his unassuming manner, especially considering how unbelievably talented he was. "You just have to know what you like."

"Well, I love everything here. You're now officially my favorite artist," I said. Ryan walked me around and talked about his creations; I found myself having a good time, even though Jaden's conspicuous absence was always on the periphery of my awareness. And then, suddenly, he was there. With a blonde.

"Ry, you remember Summer?"

Summer.

The infamous ex-girlfriend. I tried hard not to let my face betray my shock as Summer air-kissed Ryan. She was stunning, of course. Tall—maybe five foot nine—and slender, with the kind of soft physique you only see on someone who has never developed their muscles. Her light ash-blond hair fell straight past her shoulder blades, and large grey-blue eyes dominated the pretty face. Her whole appearance, from makeup to clothes, was very polished.

Jaden turned his gaze onto me. I couldn't read the look he gave me—it seemed almost angry, though I had no idea what I could have done to deserve it.

"And this is my cousin, Tea," he introduced me. I felt the weight of his stare as I shook hands with Summer; I had no clue what I said to her. Summer flitted off to join some friends.

"I invited her because I thought she could help you," Jaden said to Ryan. "She has a lot of social contacts—gallery owners, agents. She'll do you a favor, for my sake."

I'll bet she will, I thought bitterly.

I had a hard time concentrating after that. I hung out with Ryan, and occasionally Chris, and tried to deny how bothered I was by Summer's presence. I watched surreptitiously as Jaden joined her in a circle of what were surely mutual friends of theirs. He brought her a glass of wine; the smile she gave him as she took it was almost giddy. Luckily for me, Chris and Ryan were both very easy to be with, and didn't seem to notice my distraction.

Toward the end of the evening Ryan and I were collapsed on the round white sofa where Seth had earlier joined the pretty girl. They had long since disappeared somewhere—probably downstairs; it turned out there was another floor to the gallery, where more of Ryan's brilliant works hung in various rooms. Ryan and I had really bonded that evening. He was so kind, with an unexpected, barbed sense of humor. Even though he was in his early twenties, he looked much younger with his dimples, big curls and bright new-penny eyes. I glanced over at him and smiled. My smile dissolved, though, as I caught sight of Jaden over his shoulder; at the look on my face, Ryan swiveled around too.

Jaden and Summer were in the corner. As I watched, he put his hands on her small waist and drew her toward him. The look on his face was one I'd seen only once before—with Brianna. I sat frozen, feeling the blood drain out of my face, as he lowered his head slowly until their lips met. She seemed to respond with enthusiasm and soon had her arms wrapped around his neck. I tore my eyes away, feeling an echoing tear somewhere deep in my chest. I was gasping, staring at the fists clenched in my lap; my entire body, though shaking, felt leaden and cold. How could I have been such a complete, total, deluded idiot?

Ryan put his arm around me.

"I thought he was your cousin?" he asked quietly.

I looked up at him, blinking back tears. "He is."

"Well, that sucks ass," he said with feeling. "C'mon, let's go get drunk. I'm sure there's some wine left."

I nodded gratefully, and we headed for the makeshift bar at the back of the room. I was halfway through my third glass, and feeling pretty tipsy, when I found it being pulled away yet again. This time, however, I held on.

"Let go, Tea," Jaden said impatiently.

I wish I could, I thought to myself. The sight of him caused the pain in my chest to flare fiercely; I was going to be stubborn but Ryan came to my rescue again.

"It's best to humor him when he gets like this, sweetie," he told me conspiratorially. He gently took my glass away and handed it to Jaden, giving him a cold look for good measure. Jaden's eyes widened in obvious surprise.

"Where's your brother?" he snapped at me.

I shrugged. "I don't know, I'm not his keeper." I giggled at my own weak joke—wow, I must have been tipsier than I'd thought.

"Great," he growled. "Stay here." He jabbed at the spot where I was standing with his finger and turned on his heel, presumably to find Seth.

I turned to Ryan, despair welling up inside me. "That went well."

Jaden eventually came back with a chastised-looking Seth trailing behind him. He walked us to our car without saying a word. Once I was buckled into the passenger seat, though, he leaned down and inspected me, frowning.

"Will you be okay? You look kind of green."

"I'm fine," I said shortly. I was starting to feel pretty nauseous, truth be told. I thought he was going to berate me for drinking, but he straightened up silently, looking troubled.

It was a tortuous drive home. I tried to be happy for Seth, who'd had a great time and was hoping to see the gallery girl again, but my thoughts were roiling muddily. Jaden was following behind us in his car; he was spending the night, which meant I would have to face him in the morning. My stomach curled with anxiety at the thought. Jaden was right—I needed therapy, but not for the reasons he thought.

I awoke feeling awful the next morning. And it wasn't just because my head was pounding and my stomach queasy, either. I'd managed not to throw up until after we got home, and had crawled into bed exhausted, but sleep had eluded me... and even though I hadn't been thinking too clearly, I had reached a conclusion about Jaden's distant, cool behavior of the past week. An appalling, humiliating conclusion, but one that made sense. He must have realized how I felt about him. It wasn't surprising, really—my body gave me away every time he came near me. So, having guessed my totally inappropriate feelings for him, he was pulling away from me. I wasn't sure whether he was simply upset, or whether he was making it clear that—obviously—there could be nothing between us. Either way, it would explain why he kissed Summer right in my line of sight. Not that he needed any excuses, I remembered, cringing.

I was utterly mortified at the thought that Jaden knew. I wanted to avoid him, to hide, but we were playing club chukkers that afternoon. I considered faking illness, but then he'd think I was ducking out because I was hung over, which was a weak and pathetic excuse. Crazy as it seemed, I still didn't want him thinking badly of me. Thinking worse of me, I should say.

I stayed in bed as long as I could before tottering to the washroom. The morning dragged by; I didn't see Jaden, which was a relief, but I knew I couldn't avoid him all day. He was in the kitchen when I went in for lunch. I said hi without meeting his eyes.

"How are you feeling today?" he asked.

I glanced up; his face was reserved, unsmiling.

"Fine," I responded.

We treated each other very politely as we got lunch together. I wasn't very hungry—my stomach was still uneasy, as was I. Jaden noticed my lack of enthusiasm.

"You won't have the strength to play if you don't eat more than that," he admonished. He sounded so much like his old self that I glanced up with a smile half-formed on my face. Our eyes locked for a brief second, and I was taken aback at the unhappiness I saw in his.

After lunch, I was in the barn tacking up Schweppes when Jaden came in.

"I'm going to drive," he said abruptly. "Piba's sore, and I don't need Kermit today. I'll meet you there."

I nodded, surprised. We had always ridden to the club together, and I couldn't imagine why he was giving Kermit a day off on a weekend. He must really want to avoid being alone with me. I felt hot with embarrassment as I finished bridling Schweppes. Well, I wouldn't impose my presence on him. I resolved to be as indifferent toward him as possible—that should help restore his peace of mind.

I only played in the first chukker, and it didn't go well. I was distracted, my head hurt, and I felt weak, but worse than any of those was the shame I felt at playing so badly in front of Jaden. I was relieved to ride off the field when it was over.

"You look sad, muñequita," Mateo commented. He was riding a horse I didn't recognize. I had discovered that 'muñequita' meant 'little doll'. I was less than overjoyed with the nickname, but I didn't want to antagonize Mateo by saying anything.

I shrugged.

"Do you want to come for some stick-and-ball practice with me?"

I looked up at him, surprised. Mateo had warmed up to me considerably since I'd avenged Belita, but this was the first time he'd actually sought out my company.

"All right," I agreed. I needed the extra practice, for sure.

We rode around the thin line of trees to the practice field. We started hitting the ball up the field, taking turns, though I missed a lot more than he did. Mateo turned out to be a good coach; he was harder on me than Jaden was, but I appreciated that. I was used to demanding teachers, and I liked to push myself.

"You're bending your elbow again!" he reproved me, when I'd hit the ball only to see it, once again, roll only a few feet. "You won't get any force behind your swing like that. Here." He rode up and demonstrated a full swing. "You see how I lean to the right? Do that, and keep your arm straight."

I tried again, at the walk. The ball left the ground and flew twenty feet.

"Yes! You got it in the air!" he congratulated me. He rode up for a high five. I had just slapped his hand, grinning broadly, when Jaden rode up. His expression was stony.

169

"Mateo, we need you in the next chukker," he said curtly.

"Okay," Mateo replied lazily. He looked over at me and winked. "See you later, chiquita."

"Shouldn't you be going home?" Jaden's words were clipped, his face tense... what was he mad about *now*? I hadn't done anything.

"I was just getting in some extra practice," I said defensively.

"With help from Mateo." The angry mask slipped for an instant, and I thought I saw hurt in his eyes before he looked quickly away.

"Jaden..." His name was a plea; I hated the tension and awkwardness between us. His golden-brown gaze met mine, and in that instant I could have sworn he hated it, too. Then the hardness returned.

"You'd better get home, or Dec's going to change his mind about allowing this."

I nodded slowly and turned Schweppes toward home.

The year's first big polo tournament was the following Sunday, and our whole family, as well as our friends, were going to watch Jaden play.

"There's a dress code," Jaden reminded us over lunch on Wednesday. "You'll have to wear a dress again, Tea." The look he gave me was carefully neutral.

"So what's your handicap now, anyway," Dec asked, spearing a piece of broccoli.

"I'm an eight," Jaden said casually.

My fork fell onto my plate with a clatter; at the same time I felt my mouth drop open. Jaden gave me a startled look.

"I wasn't aware that would mean something to you," he commented.

"Of course it means something to me—I'm learning the game, aren't I? I've been doing some-"

"Research, right," he finished for me with a small smile. "And what have you learned?"

"Lots of things. Including the fact that the highest-ranked player in Canada has a handicap of six goals."

He shrugged. "Well, I've mostly been playing abroad. Maybe that causes some confusion, but now that I'm here..."

"You're the highest-ranked player in the country," Dec finished, looking impressed. Well, that's just great, I thought sourly. Just when I thought it couldn't get any more impossible to ignore him.

Kabir and Teri rode with us in Dec's truck on Sunday, and Julia met us there. The facility, just north of Toronto, was easy to find, but parking was a mite harder. We circled amongst the Jaguars and Porsches for a few minutes before finding a spot.

"Wow, I've never seen so many high-end cars in one place," Seth said excitedly. "Did you see the Maserati, Sis?"

"Probably," I laughed. I wouldn't recognize it, though.

I was wearing a pretty, summery dress that Julia had lent me, but when we found her she took one look at me and towed me to the washrooms to put some make-up on.

"Why didn't you do it at home?" she scolded, "that's why we bought it."

Fortunately my short hair didn't require much styling, or doubtless she'd be re-doing that, too. When she was satisfied with my appearance we joined everyone at the table that Jaden had reserved for us under a large white tent beside the polo pitch. Stacey and her parents were already there, along with Gran and Aunt Paloma.

"There he is," Stacey exclaimed, jumping up.

Jaden was winding his way between the tables, stopping occasionally to shake hands with various people. He was wearing a navy polo shirt with a white '3' on it, along with the required white pants and brown boots. He looked stunning.

When he got to us he wound his arm around Stacey.

"Tell us, dear," Gran said, "are you representing the Killean club?"

Jaden shook his head. "No, I'm playing for a team I rode with last year, the Davenport Daemons. David Davenport is the patron, and he hires a couple of pros for every tournament."

I became aware of a familiar sound; it was getting louder but before I could identify it Jaden continued, "There he is now."

I swiveled around to follow his gaze as a helicopter landed in the adjoining field. All eyes in the spectator tent turned toward it as Summer Davenport and her father climbed out and headed our way.

I didn't want to watch, but it was as though I couldn't help myself. An inexorable force drew my eyes to Summer as she approached Jaden. She started to put her arms around him; he kissed her cheek quickly and deftly stepped around her to shake hands with her father. David Davenport was older than Dec, his hair mostly grey, but he gave an impression of fitness and energy. Jaden introduced us all before the Davenports left to mingle.

As he was turning to go Jaden said, "Oh, if anyone has questions about the game, ask Tea—she can probably answer you." He faced me for the first time that day. I strove to keep my face expressionless as he scanned me briefly before wheeling abruptly and leaving the tent.

Teri and Julia looked at me; I'd already shared the details of my evening at the art gallery with them.

"Wow," was all Julia said.

It wasn't until Jaden left that I realized I'd been digging my nails into my palms. I looked around the tent, trying to distract myself. The aura of wealth and privilege was unmistakeable. This was Jaden's milieu, and he was clearly at home here. He had gone to private schools and played polo throughout high school... even though we were members of the same family, we moved in very different social circles.

"So what's the big deal about Jaden being ranked 'eight'?" Seth interrupted my train of thought.

"Well, polo players are ranked on a scale of minus two to ten goals," I started explaining, feeling a bit shy as everyone's attention focused on me. "It's called a handicap. But ninety percent of players are ranked between minus two and two goals, and most players go pro once they've reached a rank of three. Eight is actually very high."

As if to underscore my words, the announcer started to introduce the teams. The players rode forward one by one as their names and numbers were called, but when he got to Jaden the announcer deviated slightly.

"In the number three position, we are very fortunate to welcome back to Canada one of our own—I know that many of you are looking forward to watching and learning from him this year. Please welcome back, our international star, Jaden Foster!"

A rousing cheer went up, not only from the spectators, but also the players on the field and the grooms on the sidelines. I scanned the grounds; people were genuinely excited at the prospect of seeing him. He truly was a star—I realized that I had never before appreciated the magnitude of his achievements. And polo wasn't nearly as big a sport in Canada as it was in some other countries. I could only imagine the kind of reception he enjoyed there.

The game started, and watching Jaden play was a revelation. I'd always sensed a certain fierceness in him, simmering just below the surface; now it exploded into action, and seeing it uncontained was awe-inspiring. His ferocity cut a swath through the opposition, and my heart alternately stuttered and surged as one seemingly impossible maneuver followed another. He leaned so far out of the saddle that I felt as though only my prayers were keeping him mounted, he rode everyone off the ball, made shots that defied the laws of physics, and generally created total havoc for the opposition. My heart hammered throughout the entire first chukker; I was relieved when the riders went to switch ponies. I needed a chance to catch my breath.

I was somewhat calmer for the second chukker when, halfway through, a horse suddenly slipped, fell, and rolled right over her rider. Dec's grip on my wrist was the only thing keeping me in the tent. The mare staggered to her feet soon afterward, but it took the rider considerably longer. Replacements were called in, the chukker resumed, and it was announced that neither horse nor rider was seriously injured. We breathed a collective sigh of relief.

At halftime the spectators poured onto the field for the customary divot-stomping. This involved searching out the clumps of grass that had been unearthed by the ponies' rapid stops and starts, and then toeing those clumps, known as divots, back into the ground. It was a nice break, and a chance to stretch our legs.

The third chukker was almost without incident, except at one point I could have sworn I saw Jaden drop forward on Piba, clutching his right arm. The play was moving too fast for me to be sure, though, and he went on to take a savage swipe at the ball and score a goal, so I thought I was mistaken.

We were nearing the end of the fourth chukker; the game was almost over. The ponies thundered to one end of the field, and my heart nearly stopped as some of them collided—I couldn't tell if Kermit was one of them. Suddenly several mallets went up. A horn blew, and some of the players jumped off their ponies. One of the opposing team's players was on the ground, not moving. Medics ran onto the field, but as it turned out he was quite gravely injured and play didn't resume until after an ambulance had taken him away. The game was wrapped up quickly after that, with the Davenport Daemons winning by a considerable margin.

We headed down to the stable area to see Jaden. He was standing by the trailer with two rather glamorous-looking girls, and handed them a piece of paper just as we arrived. They seemed to leave reluctantly.

"Was that your autograph or your phone number?" Seth joked.

"Both," Jaden winked at him.

I felt my teeth snap together. People were walking by, some patting him on the back as they passed.

"So, what did you think of the game?" he asked us expansively.

"You're even better than the last time I saw you," Dec said enthusiastically as he clapped him on the shoulder. "It was great to watch you play again."

"Yeah, I had no idea polo was so *fast*," Seth said. I tried not to feel irritated at his slightly awed expression.

Jaden's eyes moved to my face. They were cautious, as usual these days. I crossed my arms and surveyed him narrowly.

"Well, one thing's for sure, I'm not taking any more crap from you about how reckless *I* am," I said.

He laughed—his real laugh, warm and carefree, and in an instant I felt my defenses evaporate. He was so utterly irresistible in that moment. He started to reach for me and for a second I thought he was going to hug me as he would have done so naturally, just two weeks before. Then he caught himself, and the cautious mask fell back into place. I felt the smile freeze on my face as a new tear further damaged my chest.

We saw Jaden again on Tuesday. It turned out I'd been right about seeing him clutch his arm—a massive bruise covered his biceps from shoulder to elbow. He'd gotten hit by the ball, which can reach speeds of one hundred and ten miles an hour. Dec shook his head and gave me a significant look.

Later, I found myself briefly alone with Jaden in the tackroom.

"Remember that time I was being cocky?" I asked him.

"You'll have to narrow it down a bit for me."

"When I said I didn't fall off, and challenged you to get me off my horse?"

"Oh, that time. What about it?"

"I was an idiot. Thanks for not taking me up on it."

He nodded. "I would never do anything to hurt you, Tea." He said it softly, holding my gaze. I ripped myself away and went back to work, shaken. I was obviously reading way too much into his words.

Eleven

Early June brought the first authentically beautiful days of summer. My long term under house arrest was finally over, and I took advantage of my newfound freedom to go to the polo club and practice whenever I could. Mateo and Dan both helped me a lot, and under their tutelage I began to see some improvement in my skills.

Jaden was teaching a clinic at the club one morning, and I decided to head over there to practice. And to be near Jaden... as awkward as things were, I still preferred being near him to being away from him. Maybe I was turning into a masochist, I thought grimly as I rode onto the field. It was a perfect day, not a cloud in the sky, and though it would likely be hot later I was comfortable in my T-shirt for now.

There were four students in the clinic, three men and one woman. I was practicing nearby, so I could watch discreetly, hoping to pick up some tips. After a while, though, I turned and watched more overtly. I couldn't believe what I was seeing—I couldn't believe the difference in Jaden. He cajoled, threatened, encouraged, or yelled at his students, as needed. But in every case, he pushed them; he got every last ounce of performance out of those players. He was as tough as Karen. This was in a different league from the coaching I'd been getting, and I soon wheeled Schweppes away. Did he not think I was worth teaching? Was I was so lacking in potential that he wouldn't even expend the effort? I headed home, fuming.

At the dinner table that night the talk turned to Schweppes.

"He's really coming along well," I told Dec proudly, "even though it isn't ideal for us to be learning together." It was usually a good idea for either the rider or the horse to have experience in whatever discipline they are attempting.

"Maybe you should let me ride him in our next practice," Jaden suggested.

I thought about it. Jaden had obviously done a great job schooling his own horses, and he knew a lot better than I did what was required of a polo pony. But he was also a more aggressive rider than I was—not mean, but more demanding. All of his aids were applied harder, something that Schweppes had hated when he was a school horse. I didn't want Schweppes to have any negative experiences with polo so early in his training; I was worried that if he didn't like Jaden's riding it would put him off the game.

"Thanks, Jaden, but I think it's too soon for that. He's just getting comfortable with me."

He leaned across the table toward me.

"Tea, you know as well as I do that in order to get the best out of someone—human or horse—you sometimes have to push them out of their comfort zone."

I nodded; that was perfectly true. "You don't seem to be applying that rule to me, though," I pointed out.

He looked at me suspiciously.

"You're way harder on your other students than you are with me," I accused him, also leaning forward. I was still irked by my discovery, and it must have shown on my face.

"I thought you just wanted to train that pony, not kill yourself," he snapped back.

"That doesn't mean I don't want to learn to play as well as I can!" I raised my voice to match his.

"Now, now," Gran soothed.

Jaden lowered his voice. "So now you're angry because I'm not hard enough on you?" he asked, incredulous.

"I just want you to treat me the same as your other students."

"Well, don't worry," he said ominously. "I'm done taking it easy on you."

Jaden was true to his word. We hardly spoke during our ride to the club the next day, and once on the field Jaden did all the talking. Only he was mostly yelling. He had me practice the different swings over and over, especially the full swing, which was still my weakest shot. He kept me moving all the time, until I was exhausted and my arm was shaking. I gritted my teeth and kept going; there was no way I was going to complain, not when he was finally taking me seriously.

Thankfully Dan and Lucas came out on foot and asked if we'd be up for a little two-on-two game. We agreed, and while they went to collect their horses I dismounted and sat on the grass to rest, Schweppes grazing happily next to me. Jaden disappeared into the stable area. I felt a brief, sharp sadness that he didn't stay with me, but

I smothered it quickly. He returned only when Lucas and Dan did. I ended up paired with Jaden because I was the least experienced. Any team he played for was always unbalanced, because his handicap was so high.

The game was brutal. I started off tired, and the other players were all out of my league. Not that they didn't make allowances. Jaden did pass me the ball frequently, though I suspected he could have won against the three of us without much effort.

"Tea! Pay attention! That was an easy shot, I know you could've made that!" he yelled when I missed a second pass in a row. My temper flared; I shot up the field, rode Dan off the ball, and hit it. The surge of adrenaline that followed was a lifesaver, and kept me fired up enough to get through the rest of the chukker. I was hugely relieved when it was over, and I'm sure Schweppes was, too—he was breathing hard and his neck was lathered.

I had a quiet ride home, as Jaden stayed at the club. I couldn't help thinking about the state of our relationship; it had only been three weeks since Stacey's party. Before that, we'd been so close... okay, so our friendship had been tainted, on my side, by the attraction I couldn't help feeling toward him, but the underlying connection was strong. Now it seemed as though we barely spoke unless we were arguing. I sighed; I didn't know how to fix it. I did know, though, that I was going to improve at polo or die trying, because there was no way I was getting yelled at like that for the rest of the summer.

After dinner I went and sat on the porch steps, rotating my right shoulder, which was killing me, and trying to stretch out my arm. My wrist hurt, too. It was a quiet evening. I loved this time of year, with its lush floral and green smells, long days, and warm, fragrant nights. Schweppes and Starlight were in the small turnout paddock to my left and I watched them lean together, tails swishing against the emerging mosquitoes. They used to get turned out with Zac, until Anne objected, and the three of them had been fast friends. I wondered if they missed hanging out with him, and decided they probably did. Horses have long memories.

Jaden came out and sat at the other end of the step, two feet away from me.

"Don't you ever use the chairs?" He indicated the chairs on the porch.

"Nah." I shrugged, wincing slightly.

"Does your shoulder hurt?"

"No," I lied.

He didn't look convinced. "It's very common, in the beginning. You'll get some forearm and wrist pain, too. You might want to try wearing a brace for a while."

"I'll let you know if I need it," I said, tilting my head slightly to look at him. That was a mistake—he was staring at me, his remarkable eyes intense, and once they caught mine I was trapped. I felt like a rabbit in front of a snake, and I stared back, immobilized. I don't know how long we stayed that way; the sound of the screen door behind me broke his hold and I looked away quickly, relieved. My heart was beating as though I was back on the polo field, and I was rocked by confusing emotions. That afternoon my anger and determination had kept all other feelings at bay, but the look Jaden had just given me... dammit, get a grip, I told myself firmly. He was off-limits, and he had no interest in me. It wasn't his fault that his presence threw me into complete disarray.

"Skooch down," Seth said behind me.

I moved down a step, and he sat behind me and started rubbing my shoulders. I leaned into his hands gratefully—there was no point in lying to Seth, he always knew. Out of the corner of my eye I saw Jaden smirk.

"How's the bad shoulder?" Seth asked.

The smirk disappeared, replaced by a frown.

"Do you have an injury you didn't tell me about?" Jaden demanded.

"It's nothing, it's an old one," I told him. I examined the ground while Seth continued to smooth the knots from my muscles.

"I'm not surprised she didn't tell you," he snickered, "it wasn't exactly her brightest moment."

"Seth..." I said warningly.

"I'd like to hear it," Jaden said quickly. "It might help me understand what I'm dealing with."

I wasn't sure if he meant my shoulder or my attitude, but I wasn't about to ask. Seth launched into the story of the day I went to my friend Maddie's place, where they had a herd of horses turned out onto a large pasture at the back of their farm. It was a beautiful pasture, fifty acres of rolling green hills, and the horses had wandered far away. Maddie and I were on foot, and the plan was simply to shepherd them back toward the barn, which they would then willingly enter. For some reason, though, I was in a hurry, and I thought herding them on horseback would be faster. Maddie was carrying a lead rope, so we caught a little chestnut mare, and I vaulted up to start playing cowgirl.

The plan seemed to work swimmingly at first, and within minutes I had the herd thundering toward the barn. We started galloping down a hill—and my mount put her head down and bucked. At the best of times, that's a tough move to handle, but unprepared, riding bareback, with only a lead rope for control, I didn't stand a chance. I flew off, arcing up a good ten feet from the ground, and when I came to I was face-down on the ground, with my right shoulder rolled sickeningly underneath my body. It turned out my shoulder was dislocated. It healed, but had never been the same since. Seth finished the story; I could see Jaden's scandalized expression in my peripheral vision.

"Don't you have any sense of danger at all?" he huffed.

I glared at him. "It was a long time ago. I don't see how my childhood indiscretions are any business of yours."

"If you think that's bad, have you heard about the time she got caught hitchhiking?"

I spun around to turn my glare on Seth. He was grinning broadly.

"Stop it, Seth," I hissed between my teeth.

"Hitchhiking?" Jaden sounded utterly shocked. I didn't look at him; I smacked Seth on the arm and stomped into the house. I knew what he was doing—he was telling stories that would paint me as reckless and immature. I couldn't believe Seth would stoop to that, though; I'd already given him my word, and I was sticking to it.

I went to my room, fuming. That hitchhiking story sounded worse than it actually was; it was more embarrassing than anything. When I was fourteen, I went to a friend's house, and we had a big argument. Her place was only about a mile from our house, but Dec wasn't home so I didn't have a ride. I stormed out, intending to simply walk home. After a while, though, it seemed silly not to try and catch a ride, so I stuck out my thumb... only to have a white pickup pull over. Dec's white pickup. Needless to say, my one-time foray into hitchhiking came to a painful and immediate conclusion.

I heard the stairs creaking and peered out my door; it was Seth.

"Get in here," I growled at him.

He sauntered in, but looked a bit wary all the same.

"What's up?" he said with false flippancy.

"What's going on, Seth? Since when do you try to make me look bad?" I asked angrily.

He stared at me for a minute.

"Since he's looking at you like...like..." He bit off his retort and looked away, scowling. His hands were jammed in his pockets, his shoulders hunched. I hated that we were at odds over this; we rarely fought. Sure, we argued sometimes over stupid things, but this was different. Abruptly, I felt as though Seth's prediction was coming true already—the mere fact that I was attracted to Jaden was causing discord in our family. Discord with my own brother, my only blood relative in the world. Or the only one that I knew personally, anyway, which amounted to the same thing. I collapsed onto the bed and dropped my face into my hands.

"You were right," I groaned.

"About...?" He came and joined me.

"It's insane for me to have feelings for Jaden," I said vehemently, "look at what it's doing to us." I gave him a beseeching look. "I'm trying to stop, I swear."

He watched me seriously for a long moment.

"It's not just you," he said finally. "I think he's into you, too."

My heart instantly ballooned at those words—I couldn't help it—but I made a huge effort and squashed it down firmly.

"I think you're wrong about that," I said, frowning. "But in any case, it doesn't matter. I gave you my word. It's too dangerous, Seth, you said so yourself."

He nodded. "Sorry, Sis," he said quietly. "I shouldn't have done that. When I saw how he's acting around you—well, I sort of panicked."

He patted my knee before leaving. I lay awake for a long time that night, trying very hard not to think about how I felt when Jaden looked at me, or about what Seth had said.

I developed a new strategy after that day. I went to the polo fields with Jaden a couple of times a week, when he'd coach me. He continued to be very demanding, and I determinedly kept trying, though I wasn't playing well in front of him. I couldn't seem to get Seth's words out of my head, and the thought that Jaden might possibly reciprocate my feelings left me tense and confused—not an ideal state of mind for optimum performance. So as often as I could, I went to the club without him. When I practiced on my own or with other club members I played much better, and I incorporated all the new skills Jaden was teaching me.

It was mid-June, and the show season was in full swing. I tried not to think about what I'd been doing at this time last year; that weekend I was going to a show with Cameo, her first big, official competition. She was performing wonderfully at home, and you couldn't help but love her, with her little grey ears always pricked forward and her kind, willing attitude. She was a dream pony. I couldn't believe that someone had willingly parted from her. Teri was going to the show too, and competing in the same division; it was the first time in years that we'd ride against each other, and we were looking forward to it.

We arrived at the showgrounds Friday evening, got the horses settled in their temporary stabling, and got all the gear unpacked before heading to the motel. The usual party atmosphere reigned as we got junk food and sat on the beds talking until Karen yelled at us to go to bed. I felt myself slowly unwinding. I hadn't realized just how tense I was becoming, with Jaden always around. It felt good to be with the girls, and even better to be showing again, although I couldn't watch the jumpers. That was still too painful.

Emma and her parents arrived on Saturday morning. In many ways, they were ideal horse show parents—they wanted Cameo to do well, but they didn't pressure Emma or me in any way. They trusted me to get their daughter and her pony ready to compete together, and I appreciated it. It made me even more determined to do well with their child's pony.

Unfortunately, despite an auspicious beginning, I made a foolish mistake in the second class and we were eliminated. I was embarrassed beyond description, and felt terrible that I'd let the Tremblays down, although they were very gracious about it.

We got home late on Sunday, and I dallied in the tackroom after everyone left. Everything was put away, but I was in no hurry to go into the house and explain my disgrace, so I paced back and forth, getting madder and madder, though I couldn't have said why.

"Aargh!" My frustration erupted, and I spun, aiming a blow at the nearest wall. But instead of the hard surface I expected, my fist smacked into a hand—a familiar hand. Dual jolts shot through me: one from my captive fist, and one that speared right through my heart. I wrenched my hand free without looking at him.

"Do you want to talk about it?" There was an undertone of strain in his voice; I wondered what this exchange was costing him.

I shrugged. "There's nothing to talk about. It makes me feel better."

"*Hitting* something makes you feel better? That sounds dangerously familiar." The strain in his voice was gone, replaced by a sharp edge.

I looked at him then. His expression was carefully controlled, but his eyes were judging me.

"The difference being, only inanimate objects will suffer from *my* wrath," I threw at him without thinking.

A flicker crossed his face and I bit my lip, hard. I had wanted to lash out... but not at him. I never wanted to hurt Jaden. I dropped my eyes, and was about to apologize when he spoke quietly.

"You're not an inanimate object, Tea. I don't want to see you hurt." The last words were fervent. He wasn't just referring to this.

My eyes flashed to his face. It was more open than it had been for a long time—I could see the confusion and worry there. I tried in vain to swallow the ball in my throat, and felt moisture prick the corners of my eyes. Even if he didn't care the way I did, he did care, and I'd been cold and distant toward him. I just hadn't realized how much it was hurting him, too.

"Sorry." I wasn't even sure what I was apologizing for, exactly. I sank down onto a bench. "There was a journalist at the show yesterday," I admitted. "She wrote a magazine article about Blaze and me last year." I really didn't know what it was about Jaden that made me confess these things to him. Things I didn't want to talk about.

He sat next to me, not close, but near enough for my entire body to feel electrified.

"That's why you forgot your course," he said, understanding. I glanced over; his face was sympathetic.

"Word travels fast. Yes, that's why. It's still no excuse, though."

"You're way too hard on yourself, Tea. Even great athletes make mistakes."

I shrugged.

"Did you keep a copy of the article? I'd like to read it, if you don't mind."

I nodded. "It was entitled 'A Blaze in the Jumper Ring: Hot New Talent Setting Courses on Fire'." I smiled a bit at the memory.

We sat for a minute; I could feel his eyes on me.

"What else is going on?" he asked finally.

I was instantly tense. Was he asking what I thought he was asking? I looked up cautiously; I was far from ready to address this. His lovely eyes were also wary... I couldn't introduce any more tension now. Not when we were actually talking, really communicating, for the first time in weeks. For the moment, I was incredibly happy just to be near him, so I brought up another issue—one that undoubtedly troubled me, but which was nothing compared to the dilemma Jaden presented.

"This is my last year as a junior." I sighed. "Last year I had two jumpers on the circuit, and I was attracting a lot of attention. The good kind. And this year... I've got nothing. Next year I'll be eighteen, and I can't compete as an amateur. I'm afraid I'll be out of my depth, riding against the pros. Assuming I even have a horse to ride."

He nodded. I appreciated the fact that he didn't try to dismiss my worries.

"Do you have a plan for next year?" he asked.

I shrugged. "If I could think of a way to earn a pile of money, I'd buy another jumper prospect. But I haven't had any brainwaves, and Dec doesn't want to buy any more horses right now. So, no."

There was a way I could triple my earnings for the summer—by doing what Teri was doing, working at the racetrack. At the show she had announced she was working as an exercise rider for the summer; I was envious, not of the job, but of the money. I was paid for the lessons I taught and the training I did, and when we sold a horse I'd schooled Dec usually gave me some money, too. But it didn't add up to much compared to the track, so I might have sounded a tad bitter when Seth and I discussed it in the barn the following night.

"Wish I could work at the track. But that's not happening," I grumbled.

He snorted. "Well, duh."

I laughed at his goofy expression. Seth had changed over the past few months, gotten more serious; I was happy to see some of his natural silliness re-emerging.

"What's new with Melissa?" I asked him as we started feeding. He had kept in touch with the swimmer from Montreal; it was the first time he'd had a completely non-physical relationship with a girl.

He sighed. "She's got a boyfriend now."

"Oh. Sorry, dude."

"It's okay, she lived too far away, anyway. I kind of wish the girl from the gallery had called me back, though... I feel so used." He said it jokingly, but I could sense an element of truth to his words. It was probably the first time in Seth's life that a girl hadn't called him back, rather than the other way around. Life was changing for Seth, too.

My brief tackroom conversation with Jaden made me miss him even more when things went back to normal. The new normal for us— distantly polite. On Wednesday Gran made an unexpected midday visit and brought lunch with her, and I was sent to fetch Dec and Jaden.

I walked past the big grass paddock in front of the barn, toward the row of new posts poking out of the churned-up grass. Once I got close, though, I stopped dead. Dec was nowhere in sight, and Jaden was working with no shirt on. I remembered seeing him bare-chested the year before, but the effect it had on me now was markedly different. I watched him wrestle a post into a fresh hole in the ground for a minute before he looked up and saw me. I blushed and looked away even as I started walking forward; I didn't want him to think I'd been... well, watching him. Although I clearly had been.

"Lunch is ready," I muttered, barely glancing at him.

When he thanked me I fled with a sigh of relief. I really didn't know how I was going to survive the summer.

It was chilly when I went to do the last check of the barn on Thursday night, and I wished I'd worn a sweater instead of just running outside in my t-shirt. Everyone seemed comfortable until I got to Piba's stall—what I found there made me instantly tense.

Piba looked unhappy, and as I watched she turned her head, looked at her flank, then stamped her hind leg a few times. Uh-oh. I quickly checked her feed bowl, and sure enough, there was some grain left in there. I went in and took her pulse; it was forty beats per minute, on the high end of normal, but since Piba was such a fit horse, I suspected that number was high for her. Her neck was slightly damp too. I checked her gums; at least they were pink and moist, and the color returned quickly when I pressed my finger against them.

I thought for a minute. Normally, if there were people around, I would take steps to treat the colic first, and call the vet if it showed no signs of subsiding. But I was alone, and Piba already seemed quite uncomfortable, so I decided to call her right away.

"Hold on, sweetie, I'll be right back to take care of you," I reassured Piba with a quick pat. I ran to the tackroom to call. The answering service told me that Kathy, our vet, was with a foaling mare, and her partner was away at a conference. They agreed to send Kathy over as soon as possible.

I collected a blanket on my way back, because it was chilly outside and Piba was already sweaty. After putting the blanket on her I brought her outside to walk. We slowly followed the perimeter of the big sand ring; I shivered and tried to hug myself close to Piba's body. Normally I would walk a colicky horse for about twenty minutes out of every hour, but I didn't have a watch on, so I would have to guess. Piba wasn't getting any better, she didn't pass any gas or poop, and occasionally she would stop to kick at her belly. I was getting worried. The word 'colic' is enough to make any horseperson break into a cold sweat. Colic is the number one killer of horses—it's truly remarkable what sensitive digestive systems equines have. And the fact that they are completely unable to vomit makes digestive upsets even more likely. The trouble was, without knowing the exact nature of the problem, it wasn't safe to try to treat her.

After what I thought was twenty minutes I put Piba back in her stall and tried calling the vet again. Kathy was still with the mare. I found a jacket and put it on gratefully before going back into the barn.

"Piba, no!" I cried as soon as I spotted her.

She was lying down, trying to roll. My worry exploded into outright fear; this was the most dangerous possibility with colic—the horse rolls to try to relieve the pain, and sometimes they move so violently that they cause an abdominal torsion. Those twisted guts are what killed horses most of the time. If it happened Piba would need immediate surgery in order to survive.

I ran into her stall, my heart beating hard, and started trying to get her up. I yelled, pushed, and yanked on her halter, and finally she heaved herself to her feet with a groan. I quickly clipped on the lead rope and brought her back outside, shaking with relief. My heart was still pounding—I couldn't leave her by herself, and I had no way of knowing whether the vet was on her way. I needed help.

I brought Piba into the barn, tied her next to the tackroom doorway so I could watch her, and called Jaden's cell. It went to voicemail right away so I left him a message, trying not to sound too panicked, but asking him to come to the barn as soon as possible because Piba was colicking. I didn't bother trying the vet again, and Dec had left his cell in the house, so there was no way for me to reach him.

We went back to walking. Once in a while I would allow Piba to rest—I didn't want to exhaust her—but she often tried to lie down when I did, so I'd have to cajole her into moving again. I had to admit she was being amazingly cooperative. Horses are often in so much pain with colic that they scarcely notice their surroundings; they will walk into walls or crush the people around them. It was the only time I would hit a horse—to force him or her to stay on their feet and keep moving. But Piba summoned her courage and responded to my requests; I didn't have to resort to violence.

After about an hour I went back inside and called Jaden again, and left another message when there was no answer. I tried the vet's office again too, and felt a rush of relief when they said she was on her way.

"Good news, sweetie, the doctor's coming for you," I told Piba as we headed back outside. It felt as though we'd been circling that ring for hours in the starry darkness, but I was developing a real affection for Piba. She had astounding heart to still be cooperating when she was suffering so much.

When headlights came up the driveway I turned to Piba and hugged her.

"Hang in there, girl," I said as I brought her into the barn.

"Wow, you look like I feel," the vet commented as she began her exam. "How long have you been walking her?"

"I'm not sure, but it's been a while—she kept trying to go down," I explained. As it turned out, it was one a.m., so I'd been walking Piba for close to three hours. And I wasn't done yet. After examining Piba, Kathy suspected an impaction, so she administered mineral oil and then it was back to slowly circling while we waited for it to take effect. At least Piba and I weren't alone, though—Kathy sat on the wall jump and kept us company. It took about an hour before Piba suddenly stopped, lifted her tail, and produced a huge poop. The obvious relief on her face made me laugh; I patted and hugged her before turning to Kathy.

"Is that it? Can she go back in her stall now?"

"Should be, but you'll have to keep an eye on her. Are you on your own? Where is everyone?" she asked.

"They went out. It's okay though, I'll stay with her."

187

Piba looked as happy as I felt to be heading inside. She had a drink of water and lay down with a sigh, but didn't try to roll. I left Jaden one last message, telling him that Piba had been treated and would be okay.

Once Kathy left I got a horse blanket and laid it down at the edge of Piba's stall. I sat and watched her, taking comfort from her obvious relaxation. My eyelids grew heavy, and though I fought them for a while, eventually I lay down, and must have drifted off to sleep.

A soft rustling woke me. I opened my eyes a crack to see Jaden kneeling by Piba's head, his face distraught. She was still lying down, but looked comfortable. When she raised her head Jaden put his arms around her, and she rested her face against him, taking solace from his presence. I felt my eyes well up and closed them quickly; I didn't want tears giving away the fact that I was awake, and I didn't want to intrude on their moment, either.

After a few minutes I heard movement, and peeked for a second—Jaden was headed toward me. I kept my eyes shut as he settled on the blanket near my head. He stroked my hair very lightly, while I prayed that I wouldn't tremble. When he got up and left I felt a bewildering mix of relief and despair, but he was soon back. A weight settled over me, and he resumed his position by my head. I hadn't realized that I was cold, but as the warmth from the blanket seeped through me I drifted comfortably back into sleep.

I woke up in my own bed. I blinked groggily; the light streaming around the curtains was too bright. I should have been at school by now. I got up and staggered to the bathroom for a shower even though I was late; I'd slept in a stall the night before, after all. I was headed downstairs, still yawning, when the sound of arguing made me pause.

"They're seventeen, they're old enough to be left alone for a few hours," Dec was saying.

"I don't care how old she is, Tea shouldn't have had to deal with that on her own," Jaden countered heatedly.

"She wasn't on her own, Seth was here. And horses get sick, son, you know that as well as I do. Why are you so worked up about this?"

"Because it isn't fair, Dec. On the one hand, you treat her like a kid. Yet at the same time you've given her adult responsibilities—too much for her to carry, and-"

"All right, I think that's enough." Jaden's argument was cut off abruptly by Dec's warning.

I walked into the kitchen, trying to look nonchalant.

188

"Morning," I said, stifling another yawn and heading for the coffeepot. I stole furtive glances at Jaden while I poured my coffee. I was bemused by what I'd heard.

"How's Piba?" I asked him.

"She's much better this morning, even ate a bit of hay. How do you feel?" he asked solicitously. "Don't you want to sleep a bit more?"

"I can't," I replied at the same time that Dec said, "She's got school."

Jaden threw him a disgusted look. I was startled, and a bit nervous, when he told Dec, "I think she should stay home today."

"No, it's okay," I said quickly. I could just imagine trying to relax while Dec paced disapprovingly downstairs.

"Her grades have dropped considerably," Dec said by way of explanation. He looked at me uncertainly. "Unless... are you really too tired?"

"No, I'm fine," I assured him. I saw Jaden's disbelieving look out of the corner of my eye.

"I'll drive you, then," he said quietly.

I tried not to sigh at the swirl of contradictory emotions within me. Joy that I would be near him, and fear of the pain his nearness would surely cause. Happiness at the prospect of his company, sadness and doubt because I knew it wouldn't mean anything to him. Dammit, I was too tired for this.

And so irritation was my dominant emotion as we set off for school.

"You shouldn't antagonize Dec like that," I warned Jaden. "He's been in a bad enough mood lately."

"Why, are you worried about backlash?" he asked, frowning.

"No, I'm simply pointing out that it's not smart to poke an irate rhinoceros with a stick," I said shortly.

"All right," he sighed. He looked over at me. "Where was Seth last night?"

I'd obviously given away too much during my stressed messages the night before.

"Where were you?" I countered. I immediately wished I hadn't; I was pretty sure I didn't want to know where he'd been.

"I went out. I had my phone turned off."

I remembered my foggy impressions from the wee hours. Jaden had been well-dressed, and he'd been wearing cologne, I'd caught a hint of it when he sat by me. I tried really hard not to let my mind imagine what he'd been doing that would make him turn his phone off. I had enough to deal with.

"Seth went out," I said brusquely.

"Well, I'll be having a word with him about that," he said, the anger in his voice unmistakeable.

I turned on him in aggravation. "No, you will not. He asked me if I minded, and I didn't."

"What did he have to do that was so important he had to leave you alone all night?"

I glared at him. "The same thing you were doing, probably. And that Dec was doing too, for that matter." I was the only one without a sex life, apparently.

Jaden flinched. He turned his face back to the road, but I could feel his tension. A minute later he pulled over. He took his seat belt off and faced me squarely. I couldn't look him in the eye, though.

"I'm sorry," he began. "I feel guilty about not being there last night, but... I shouldn't be blaming anyone else." He leaned toward me; the urge to touch him was so strong that I actually cringed back a little.

"Tea." He waited until I lifted my eyes to his; my breath caught. I couldn't look away.

"Thank you," he murmured. His hand found mine, and a wave of heat washed over my body.

"You're welcome," I managed after a minute. I looked away as I pulled my hand back—I was imagining things in his eyes that would only cause me more suffering later.

We drove in silence until we were almost there.

"What does 'Piba' mean?" I asked as we were pulling up.

"Uh... it means 'chick'."

"Chick as in a baby bird?"

"No... it's Argentinean slang. 'Chick' as in a girl." He looked faintly uncomfortable. "Because she's so girly, you know."

I nodded. It suited her. "I only ask because she's so brave. I thought her name might reflect that."

"The two of you have that in common," he replied. "You should ride her when she's better. I think you'd get along."

I might have been exhausted, but I started school that day with a smile on my face.

After Piba's colic, Jaden stopped yelling at me. He did continue to coach me, and between that and the help I got from Mateo and Dan, I improved immeasurably. There were some small, low-goal matches coming up, and my teammates were all urging me to play. So when Gran came over to cook dinner on Monday, which always made everyone happy, it seemed like the perfect time to ask Jaden to let me play in a real match. Unfortunately his reaction left much to be desired.

"No," he said flatly.

"Why not?" I protested.

Jaden looked frustrated. "This isn't the jumper ring, Tea—polo is a rough sport. These guys are all bigger, stronger, and faster than you, and they'll use it. You're tiny, you could get hurt."

"So you won't let me play at all?"

"Not in official matches, no." He was unapologetic.

Gran clucked her tongue. "That's enough, now. Eat your dinner, both of you."

Seth snickered; I looked over angrily, but couldn't stay mad in the face of his infectious smile. I took a deep breath and turned back to Jaden.

"Did you know that women make up twenty-five percent of all polo players?" I asked him. "They're the fastest-growing segment of the sport. There are even women pros—not many, I'll grant you, but they're out there."

Jaden watched me, looking torn between exasperation and amusement.

"Not only that, but the highest-ranked woman in the U.S. had a handicap of five goals at the height of her career. That's higher than Mateo's."

"What's her name?" Jaden asked suddenly.

"Sunny Hale... why, don't you know that?" I asked, confused.

He grinned. "Oh, I know it. I've met her, in fact. I just wondered how far you'd gone in your research."

"Come on, Jaden." I leaned toward him. "There are plenty of girls playing polo, even at our club. Why not me?"

"The girls at our club have all been playing for at least a year, not a month, like you. And none of them are my cousin, so-"

"So," I interrupted, "you don't get to make sexist and biased decisions about their playing."

"Tea," Dec interjected tiredly.

Jaden gave me an icy stare. "You're not ready," he said flatly.

"And even if you were, you wouldn't be playing," Dec said with finality.

I turned to him in surprise. "What? Why?"

"Because Jaden's right. I've spent the past ten years watching him limp home sporting one injury after another. I won't go through that with you. I have enough to worry about with you riding jumpers."

And now I wasn't even doing that, I thought bitterly. I gazed at my plate. This was an unforeseen hurdle, but one way or another, I was determined to play in a match.

Twelve

I was in the barn the following afternoon chatting with Lisa, one of our boarders, when Karen came in. Lisa was a surpassingly sweet, motherly woman. She often brought Seth and I treats from home, and she had been a great help and comfort to us during our mother's fight with cancer, as well as after her death. I offered Karen one of the brownies Lisa had just given me—they were extra chocolaty, just the way I liked them.

"Did you hear about the show?" Karen asked, helping herself to a brownie. She had been to an A-rated show over the weekend; I hadn't gone because Cameo wasn't quite ready to compete at that level.

"No, I haven't seen anyone yet," I replied curiously. "What happened?"

"Well, Stephanie and Gracie won everything in sight, but Marty dumped Jennifer in the ring," Karen said, shaking her head. "She's getting nervous about riding him. Can you get on him sometime?"

"Sure, I can do it today, if you want." I was happy at the prospect of riding a jumper again. It had been far too long.

As soon as Karen was out of earshot, Jaden strode over, frowning. He'd been around the corner with Piba, and as always, I'd been aware of his presence.

"Why are you getting on that horse?" he demanded. "He doesn't belong to the barn, and you're not even showing him. So why are you assuming the risk of riding him?"

"It may surprise you," I spat at him, affronted, "but when I'm not on the polo field I'm considered a pretty competent rider. Karen's my coach, we do each other favors. And it's not risky for me."

His eyebrows crept up at my tone. "He threw Jennifer off, didn't he? She's a good rider too."

"He won't dump me," I said with certainty. I prayed that he wouldn't, or there would be no living with Jaden.

"Well, I don't think you should do it," he said, crossing his arms.

"Then I'm glad it's not up to you," I said as I turned away. I knew he wouldn't stop me, much as he might want to; we were very careful not to touch each other anymore. I marched off angrily, insulted by his lack of confidence.

"Your cousin really cares about you," Lisa commented as I brought Marty out. She was smiling.

"He's got some way of showing it," I muttered sullenly, "he's always mad at me."

"Well, now, that's just how men are," she said soothingly. "It's hard for them to admit when they're worried. My husband's the same way with me and our girls."

I thought about what Lisa had said while I tacked up. I had gotten used to Jaden and I being angry with each other; it was easier to be around him that way. It kept him at a safe distance. The fact that he might be worried about me was hard for me to contemplate—it set my chest to aching and my throat to tightening. I crumpled the thought up in my mind and tried to focus on Marty.

He was an interesting little horse. He belonged to a wealthy actor from Toronto who almost never rode him, but who liked to watch his horse compete at shows, so Karen had various students ride him. None of them lasted long, however, because Marty had an unfortunate habit: he liked to buck. And like most good jumpers, he was an excellent bucker; he got most of his riders off, though I didn't think it was intentional.

We went to the main ring and started warming up. Marty was a Thoroughbred, but he wasn't very tall, only 15:3 hands high. He had a surprisingly big jump in him though, and a long stride—he reminded me of Northern Dancer, the famous racehorse, who stunned the world with his incredible speed despite his small size. They even looked a bit alike, although Marty was a darker bay and had only one white sock.

When Karen came into the ring I was surprised to see Jaden with her. I thought he was due back at the club. Though I couldn't help being aware of his presence, it didn't throw me into turmoil the way it did on the polo field. This was my arena, after all—I was able to tune him out, for the most part.

"I'm trying to figure out what the trigger is," Karen was saying as she set up a combination. "He seems to buck mostly as he's landing after a line of fences, but it's not consistent, so we'll try a few things and see what sets him off."

I trotted the combination a few times, and Marty jumped it cheerfully. He didn't seem at all tired from the show two days before. I was having fun; I hadn't jumped much over the past few months, other than with the school horses and Cameo, and they couldn't handle very big fences. Karen soon asked me to jump a course. It was almost four feet high, big enough that I had to pay attention.

I picked up a canter and headed for our first line. Marty jumped it beautifully. His canter was so smooth and rhythmic that he was easy to set up properly for the takeoff, but there was still a powerful thrust to his jump. Then, after the second fence, he exploded into action—he hadn't even taken a stride after landing, he just erupted, rounding his back and then pistoning his hind legs up so high behind him that we were almost vertical. I braced myself, leaning backward, and jerked on one rein to try and get his head up. After about five bucks he finally lifted it and I slowed to a walk, panting.

Karen laughed. "You rode that beautifully," she said, shaking her head in apparent amazement. I grinned at her, happy with her unequivocal praise. It wasn't easy to earn. My gaze was drawn to Jaden, who was standing tense, fists clenched at his sides. His face was pale.

"Relax, cuz—I'm still on, see?" I winked at him. He took a breath and ran his hand through his hair; the familiar gesture sent a ripple of pain through my chest.

"Okay, let's try again. Start with the triple bar this time, then do the rest of the course," Karen instructed.

I did as she said. I was flying, thrilled to be in my element again, doing what I loved, what I was good at. Marty didn't try bucking again until after the last line, and I managed to get his head up after three bucks this time.

"I don't know what's setting him off, Karen, but I can tell you this—he isn't trying to buck me off." I could sense the occasional filament of Marty's feelings intersecting mine, and there was no malice there. He was happy.

I was happy too that night, but Jaden was subdued. For once, though, it didn't affect me—usually I was such a sensitive barometer of his emotional state that I had a hard time being happy if he was down. But I felt alive, as though I'd just woken up and remembered who I really was after a long spell of amnesia. I was already making plans to find a jumper to ride; there had to be a way, somehow, for me to start competing again. The fire within me, the one I thought had been extinguished by Blaze's death, had been rekindled.

195

My good mood carried over to the next day. Jaden was teaching a clinic in Alliston, so I wouldn't be seeing him; things had been so tense between us that his absence was actually something of a relief. Since it was Wednesday I headed over to the club after dinner to play in the club chukkers.

It was the last chukker of the evening, and I was on Schweppes again. I'd ridden Maya, the club pony, for the last chukker. Even though Maya was more experienced than Schweppes, I was happier riding my little golden horse. We were forging a real bond while learning the game together, and I loved feeling his joy and enthusiasm for his new career. It buoyed my spirits, too, though I hardly needed it today.

The chukker started off fast. The ball switched directions a few times in rapid succession; it was hard to keep track of the play among eight galloping horses and the mingled yells of their riders. Suddenly, I saw Dan, who was on the opposing team, hurtling down the field with the ball. Mateo noticed too; as I watched he tried to ride Dan off the ball... Mateo's pony barged his shoulder into Dan's mare's, Mateo hit a beautiful backhand, and the ball was ours again. Or rather, mine—it came straight at me. I hit it as hard as I could and galloped up the field after it.

"Come on, Schweppes," I whispered as I leaned over his neck. He put on another burst of speed, and he was fast—the other horses were hard-pressed to catch him when he galloped all out. As we drew level with the ball I leaned out of the saddle, glanced at the goalposts for a split second, and executed a strong full swing. The mallet struck with that satisfying 'thunk' of perfect contact, and the ball arced up and flew through the goalposts. I had scored.

It was my first goal. I was elated, even though it was just a practice game. I turned Schweppes to find everyone converging on us, my own teammates and those from the 'opposition'. We were all in the same club, after all. Everyone congratulated me; I was patted on the back and high-fived by all. Mateo had just leaned over to kiss my cheek when a movement on the sidelines caught my eye—a tall, lean, long-strided movement. Jaden.

He stood perfectly still now, watching me. I wondered how long he'd been there as I walked Schweppes over to him. He wasn't smiling.

"Hi," I said tentatively.

He nodded. "That was quite a shot," he said casually. "A perfect shot, in fact."

Mateo drew level with me. "She plays much better when no one is screaming at her, no?" he asked Jaden smugly. "Come on, chiquita, it's time for the throw-in."

I turned back to the game. My elation over my first goal had almost completely evaporated, leaving confusion in its place. The rest of the chukker went smoothly, even if I never regained the momentum I'd had before seeing Jaden. Our team won.

After the game we gathered at the picnic tables with drinks and snacks. Most of the players were having beer, but I was celebrating my first goal with a can of Coke.

"Tea, I think you should play with us in the tournament next weekend," Caley said suddenly.

"Oh... thanks, Caley, but I don't think I'm quite ready for a tournament match yet," I told her haltingly. I was acutely aware of Jaden's eyes trained on me from the adjoining table. He didn't say anything.

"Well, we all think you are. You'd be doing us a favour... you and Schweppes look so small and sweet, the other team will never see you coming. Your speed and aggression will catch them totally off guard— we'll have a huge advantage. For the first chukker, at least," she grinned at me.

I smiled back, but I couldn't help shooting an anxious glance over at Jaden. He was still watching me quietly. Caley followed my gaze.

"Is that what's worrying you?" She chuckled and turned to Jaden. "All right, J, stop being an overprotective idiot and tell your cousin she can play." A chorus of agreement seconded her; my friends were all rooting for me, and razzing Jaden for trying to keep me under wraps. I smiled suddenly, feeling a glow of acceptance and encouragement from them.

"What do you plan to tell Dec if you play?" Jaden shot at me.

I hadn't thought about that. Dec had made his feelings perfectly clear—no real matches.

"He doesn't have to know," I suggested hopefully. The minute the words were out of my mouth I regretted them; I didn't want to set Jaden off. But to my amazement he just nodded thoughtfully.

He was in the barn waiting for me when I got home. It was almost dark and the stable was empty of other people. He didn't say anything right away, just started helping me untack Schweppes. I stole fleeting glimpses of him while we worked—I couldn't believe things had gotten this uncomfortable between us. I missed our easy friendship, but the fact that my body was so vibrantly aware of his presence almost guaranteed we couldn't go back to it. I sighed as we started grooming.

"Tea."

I met his eyes over Schweppes' back, and felt a moment of surprise; they were soft.

"When I saw you play today, it made me I realize how much I must have been intimidating you... I've been harsh."

I was already shaking my head. "No, you haven't. You've taught me so much, and I appreciate it. Really." I could scarcely admit that turmoil caused by his mere presence made me play badly around him.

"Well, after what I saw today, I have to agree that you're ready for a low-goal match. So if you want to play in the tournament next weekend—you're in."

"What about Dec?" I checked cautiously.

"I can keep a secret."

I felt a smile grow slowly on my face. "Thanks."

He nodded, and left me to finish putting Schweppes away on my own.

Even though he had relented enough to let me play, it turned out that Jaden had conditions. He insisted on being on my team, for one thing.

"You're going to spend the entire match galloping around trying to keep people away from her," Caley predicted, shaking her head. "You'll drive everyone crazy."

"Too bad," Jaden responded grimly. "If Tea's on the field, then so am I."

"I thought you were umpiring?" Dan pointed out.

"I'll umpire the other matches."

"But how can you play in a low-goal game?" I asked in confusion. "You're practically a medium-goal team all on your own."

A match was considered low-goal if the total of all four players' handicaps was under ten. Since Jaden's handicap was eight, I didn't see how that was possible. Especially since Mateo was also supposed to play with us.

"That's why Lucas is on the team," Jaden explained. "Since he's ranked minus two, like you, our total handicap will be eight."

It didn't sound quite fair to me, but I was happy just to be included, so I kept mum.

The tournament was in Alliston. Another of Jaden's conditions was that I start off riding a more experienced pony in the first chukker, so we brought Maya, the club pony.

The first chukker went swimmingly; in fact, if I hadn't been so nervous at playing in my first match, I might have been bored. As Caley had predicted, Jaden rode like a demon, keeping a space cleared around me and passing me the ball occasionally, when I'd have an easy shot. It was almost embarrassing.

I was happy to get on Schweppes for the second chukker.

"Jaden, try to relax a bit, okay? I'm fine on my own," I urged him.

He didn't answer, just turned and headed onto the field for the throw-in.

It all happened in a flash. One minute I was galloping down the field, the sound of hoofbeats thundering in my ears, and the next I was on the ground, and the hoofbeats were in my head. From a great distance, I heard the collective gasp of spectators, Mateo's enraged roar, and, seconds later, Jaden's frantic voice in my ear.

"Tea! Are you all right? Can you hear me?"

"You, and the cavalry pounding through my head," I said weakly. I tried to push myself up, but his hands restrained me.

"No, don't move yet, sweetheart. The medic's on her way."

He held my hand. I was lying on my side, and I shifted experimentally—nothing seemed damaged except for my head. I was having trouble breathing; when I touched my face my hand came away covered in blood. My right cheekbone, eye and nose felt like they were on fire.

I let go of Jaden's hand reluctantly as he made way for the medic.

"Can you speak, dear? Can you tell me where it hurts?" It was a woman's voice. Gentle hands began probing the back of my neck.

"I'm okay," I said. It sounded like I had a bad cold. "I think only my face is hurt."

"Let's get her helmet off," the medic said.

I recognized Jaden's hands as he carefully took off my helmet, supporting my head like a baby's. I rolled over slightly and was finally able to see. The medic had a kind, grandmotherly face framed by white curls. I looked to my right and found Jaden. He looked stricken.

"Am I that hideous, then?"

He didn't answer, but took my hand in his again. I swallowed, the metallic aftertaste of blood strong in my mouth.

The medic spoke up. "The injuries seem limited to your face. Let's get you to the first-aid tent and see what we can do for you."

I started to move, but Jaden was too quick for me; he picked me up and started walking, cradling me in his arms.

"I can walk," I protested. The motion was making my head pound; I felt a bit sick.

"Will you please not argue with me for once," he said, but his tone was gentle. My head was resting on his shoulder, and his voice vibrated pleasantly in his chest. He smelled good, too. How was that possible, when he'd spent the morning in the barn and a half hour sweating on the polo field? It was so unfair. I put my free arm around his neck and pulled myself a little closer—might as well enjoy the cessation of hostilities while they lasted. Jaden murmured something in Spanish.

"Did you just call me a baby?"

He chuckled quietly. "Something like that."

When we got to the first-aid tent he laid me down carefully on a gurney. Two medics converged immediately. Now that my head was back, though, I couldn't breathe—blood was running into my mouth from the back of my nose. I struggled to sit up and my head spun dizzily.

"Easy, now," the male medic cautioned, steadying me.

He performed the standard head injury assessment, and then the grandmotherly one started palpating my face. I clamped my teeth together to keep from whimpering; Jaden held my hand again.

"Why are you still here?" I asked, the words distorted from sliding through my teeth. "You've got to finish the game."

"I'm staying with you."

"But we'll forfeit!"

"Then we forfeit," he shrugged.

I stared at him in amazement. Jaden was very competitive—despite his status, I doubted most people realized just how competitive he was, because he didn't flaunt it. It wasn't hard for me to recognize the signs, though, since I was the same way.

"Just go, Jaden," I urged him.

He looked stubborn, but the medic broke in before it could escalate into an argument.

"Well dear, it doesn't look as though there's any serious damage, but you should get an X-ray to make sure there's no fracture to your cheekbone. You're very lucky," she smiled and handed me an icepack. It felt absolutely blissful.

I felt another trickle of blood from my nose; before I could ask, Jaden was there with a tissue. He wiped the blood away gently, his face close to mine, his hand on my shoulder to steady me. Our eyes met, and my already obstructed breathing staggered and stopped. The wall that I had carefully maintained for over a month crumbled in seconds, and I felt naked and vulnerable. He cupped his hand to the uninjured side of my face; he was so close now that I could feel his breath brushing my cheek.

"Your beautiful face, Tea... I'm so sorry," he murmured.

He didn't look away, and I couldn't even breathe, let alone move. He tilted his head slowly, and I felt a tremor go through me.

"What's going on here?" Mateo joked. He bounded in with Lucas on his heels; Jaden jerked away from me. The sudden rush of air into my lungs brought me back to reality.

"How's the patient?" Mateo continued.

"Impatient to go," I told him.

"Well, you won't have long to wait. Our game's over, thanks to Mateo," Lucas complained with a smile. "He decided to take out the jackass who hit you, and they don't have a replacement."

Mateo looked proud of himself; I expected Jaden to jump down his throat but to my shock he just nodded and bumped fists with him. Today was full of surprises.

Jaden scooped me up again and started toward his car.

"Please let me walk," I pleaded. It wasn't only pride that prompted me this time; being so close to him was painful now that my defenses were down. I knew the closeness couldn't last. I had to go back to shutting him out—it was the only right thing to do, I reminded myself frantically. I had to ignore the thought that I wanted to stay nestled in his arms forever.

Jaden wanted to drive me straight to the hospital, but I needed my health insurance card, and I thought Dec would be less likely to overreact if I didn't call from the emergency room. When we got home, I was insistent.

"You have to let me walk this time. I don't want Dec thinking it's worse than it is."

He walked me inside, supporting me by the elbow, and sat me on the couch. He disappeared and came back a minute later with a new icepack; mine was starting to melt. I heard the screen door as Dec came in, and I steeled myself—he'd been unusually irascible the past few weeks.

He froze as he spotted my face, then came quickly to kneel by me. I removed the icepack—might as well get it over with. I heard his sharp intake of breath before he stifled it.

"I had a little accident," I explained needlessly.

"What happened?" His light blue eyes darkened with concern as they perused my battered face.

"I got hit by a mallet."

"She needs x-rays," Jaden added quietly.

Dec nodded. "Okay, honey, where's your health card?" We were pretty used to this drill; when you worked with horses occasional injuries were a fact of life. And when you happened to have a risk-taking personality, like mine, they happened a bit more frequently.

"In my wallet, on my desk."

He went upstairs, and I leaned gratefully back into the couch. It was getting hard for me to keep my eyes open; the right one was almost swollen shut. I closed them with a sigh.

"Jaden." Dec's voice came from a few feet away. He sounded grim.

Next to me, I felt Jaden rise silently.

"What in blazes happened? Why was she playing?" Dec demanded. He kept his voice low, but he was definitely angry—unfortunately my clothes were a dead giveaway that I'd been on the field.

My left eye flew open, and I managed to coax the right lid apart a few millimetres. Jaden was facing Dec; he hung his head before answering.

"I'm sorry, Uncle Dec." His voice was subdued. It was the first time I'd ever heard him call Dec 'Uncle'; it made him sound younger... vulnerable.

"Hey, hold on a minute," I said, pushing myself up.

"Sit down," they ordered in stereo. I feigned deafness and joined them, trying to ignore the violent tattoo beating in my right cheek.

"Dec, you can't possibly blame Jaden for this-"

"Yes I can, actually," he interrupted harshly, "you were his responsibility."

"He's right, Tea," Jaden agreed quietly. His palpable sadness pierced through me, more painful by far than the injuries to my face.

"No he isn't! I'm not anyone's responsibility but my own. I'm the one who demanded to play; I couldn't find my own helmet, so I borrowed one. It didn't have a faceguard, but I didn't care-"

"And you didn't notice that?" Dec demanded, glaring at Jaden.

"He has better things to do than worry about my equipment—he's got the whole team to look after!" I snapped at Dec. "And anyway, look how successful you've been at getting me to wear a helmet."

Okay, so maybe that was going a bit far, given what a sensitive subject helmets were around here. Dec's eyes narrowed dangerously.

"Sorry, I didn't mean..." I backpedalled cautiously, "I just meant, we all know how careless I am when it comes to things like safety. You can't expect Jaden to change seventeen years of dedicated recklessness overnight." My attempt to lighten the mood worked. Dec shook his head with a half-smile and Jaden guided me back to the couch and, thankfully, my icepack.

"Can you take care of things here while I take her to the hospital?" Dec's voice was barely clipped now, and Jaden looked relieved. He nodded.

"I'll bring the truck around, kiddo." Dec squeezed my shoulder on his way out.

Jaden observed me thoughtfully. "You defended me."

"Of course. But why didn't you defend yourself?"

He made a face. "Because I deserve it."

"That's ridiculous!" I almost yelled, and it hurt. I was getting well and truly mad now. "Don't you realize how patronizing that is? I'm not a child, Jaden. If you want to blame someone, blame me. Or even better, that moron riding with his stick out."

He stared at me for a moment, but averted his eyes before speaking.

"I know you're not a child, Tea. Believe me, I know."

Nothing was broken, as it turned out. Jaden wasn't around much that week, but Jennalyn came by, and she was well versed in natural remedies; between the ointments and oils she brought me the swelling in my face went down rapidly. I took it easy, teaching my usual lessons but only lightly schooling Cameo, and by the next weekend I was feeling—and looking—considerably better.

The Davenport Daemons were playing in another tournament that weekend, and Julia came along with my family to watch. Teri, sadly, had to be at the racetrack. I missed her; we'd been inseparable every summer for years.

Dec was concerned we'd be late, but he needn't have worried—we arrived before Jaden did. Julia and I went to the stable area. Jennalyn had Piba all warmed up and ready to go, but there was no sign of Jaden. Mateo was M.I.A., too.

"Don't worry, they'll turn up," Jen said calmly. "They went to a big fundraiser last night, they probably just got in late."

Or not at all. Jen had barely finished speaking when a limousine pulled up; the door was flung open and Jaden, Mateo, and David Davenport spilled out. They were all wearing tuxes, and even unshaven, with the jacket open and no tie on, Jaden could have passed for a tuxedo model as he loped quickly up to Jen.

"Hi, Jen. Where are my clothes?"

"In the truck."

"Thanks." He glanced at me; a flicker crossed his face. "Hi," he said curtly before setting off. His abruptness hurt, even though I tried to tell myself to welcome it.

The match was action-packed, but free of calamity. I would never have guessed that Jaden and Mateo had been up all night; they both played superbly, and were obviously able to set aside their mutual animosity while they were on the field. The Davenport Daemons won again.

After the game Dec headed for the washrooms while Seth, Julia and I hurried down to the stable area. We caught sight of Mateo and Jaden dismounting. I only had eyes for Jaden, but Mateo intercepted me first, grabbing my shoulders and kissing me on both cheeks.

"Congratulations—you were fantastic," I told him sincerely.

"Gracias, chiquita." His smile was warm.

I glanced over at Jaden, but he was taking Kermit's bridle off; I wondered where Jennalyn was. Up close, Jaden looked rough. Somehow, dammit, it only made him hotter.

Mateo was looking inquiringly over my shoulder, and I turned to make introductions.

"Mateo, this is my brother Seth, and my good friend Julia," I indicated them in turn.

Mateo shook Seth's hand and kissed Julia's, giving her the usual appreciative look. Then he turned back to me and took my hand, lifting it above my head and twirling me in a circle while he gave a low whistle. I caught sight of Jaden as I spun—he was watching with eyes narrowed and jaw clenched. I was wearing another dress of Julia's; it was pale grey with pink cherry blossom branches growing up from the hem.

"You are muy beautiful in that dress, chiquita. You will come to the after-match party with us, yes? All of you." He waved his hand toward Seth and Julia.

I didn't get a chance to respond; Jaden's voice was icy as he answered for me.

"She's seventeen years old, Mateo. We're not bringing her to a party with a bunch of drunken polo players looking to score."

I flinched at his words. Was that what he did at those parties—get drunk and finally oblige all those blond, long-legged polo groupies who always seemed to be throwing themselves at him?

"She will be with me, no? I will protect her." Mateo laughed, his eyes crinkling. He turned to convince Julia and Seth to join us. Kermit was still wearing his saddle; I went over and started loosening the overgirth.

"Let me do that," Jaden said impatiently.

"I don't mind."

"You'll get your dress dirty," he insisted. He stepped in and took over unsaddling.

"It's not like I'll be wearing it anywhere," I said in a low voice. I knew I sounded petulant, but I couldn't help it. I felt as though something cold and heavy had settled in my stomach; there was no way I was going to a party to watch Jaden carousing with—or worse, leaving with—another girl. And I wouldn't impose my presence on him when he so clearly didn't want it.

"Tea," he said, sounding frustrated.

"Should you really be going to another party tonight?" I asked sullenly. "You look like you're still drunk from the last one."

"And?" he demanded angrily.

I ground my teeth together, staring at the grass. I had no right to question his actions, no say in what he did. So I said nothing.

He spoke lower this time. "Tea, look at me."

I raised my eyes to meet his tense ones.

"Going to these parties is part of my job. The patrons expect it, and people who put money into the sport want to rub shoulders with the players after big matches. I'm going because I have to."

"And you don't want me there."

He looked directly into my eyes for a long moment, not answering, and I felt a swooping sensation in my stomach. He moved in closer, until I couldn't see anything except his face, and those unbelievable eyes staring into mine... Dec's voice made me jump.

"Great game, son." He patted Jaden on the shoulder. Jaden looked startled, but recovered himself quickly as he turned to Dec and started discussing some of the plays. I went back to Seth, who thankfully wrapped his arm around me; I was cold. He was wearing an odd expression, but I was too preoccupied to wonder about it. After a bit more match analysis with Mateo, we were ready to go. Dec had firmly nixed any party ideas, so Julia headed home in her car and Seth and I climbed into the pickup. I sat in the back; I didn't have the energy to fake a happy expression.

When we got home Seth offered to check the barn so I wouldn't have to change. I was just pulling on my PJs when he spoke softly at my door.

"Hey, can I come in?"

"Sure."

He came and sat on the bed. He looked tense.

I sat next to him. "What's wrong, sweetie?" I asked, concerned.

"I think I was wrong, Sis."

"About what?"

"About you and Jaden."

I could feel my eyes widen in surprise. "Okay, you're going to have to spell this out for me, because you can't be saying what I think you are."

He took a deep breath. "Ever since you told me how you feel, I've been imagining the two of you as a couple. Not that I wanted to. I couldn't help it, it's like telling someone not to think of elephants. And the thing is—I think he suits you."

I stared at the ground, my jaw and my fists both clenched tight. This wasn't something I wanted to hear, not now.

206

"It's not only because you have so much in common," Seth went on. "It's also... well, he can handle you."

"What's that supposed to mean?"

"Come on, T, we both know you're a bit wild. Much as I love Kabir, I know that after a month with you he'd be curled up, rocking back and forth in his happy place. But Jaden isn't fazed by your stunts."

I thought of Jaden's reactions when he had caught me doing drugs downtown, and when I had tackled Davis on the polo field. I didn't think 'unfazed' quite captured his response. However, it was a moot point, I reminded myself.

"It doesn't change anything, though, does it?" I asked Seth quietly. "The risk is the same, and everyone might end up hating me if I even admit how I feel."

He shook his head slowly. "I don't know, Sis. I've been watching you. You're miserable. And Jaden's no better. How long can you go on this way?"

"As long as I have to," I said determinedly.

And for the next few days, at least, it was easy, because Jaden was teaching at the Toronto club, and he stayed at his place. I thought constantly about what Seth had said, try as I might not to. No matter how I circled the idea, I couldn't fathom Jaden having any interest in me. But if he did, it would only make things even more disastrous.

Thirteen

Everything changed on Wednesday.

The day started normally enough; I worked throughout the morning, and went into the house for a drink before my afternoon lesson. Blue was standing outside the office, staring at the door and whining.

"D'you want to go in?" I asked her. I strolled over to open the door, and that's when I heard it. The unmistakeable 'thwack' of leather meeting flesh. For the barest instant I stood frozen in shock, and then I hurled myself through the door, my heart hammering. I didn't pause when I got inside, so I only half-registered the scene: my brother, standing with his shirt off, his back criss-crossed by red lines. Dec with his arm upraised, about to create another one. The blow never landed; I catapulted myself at him, hitting him blindly over and over.

"Tea! Stop it!" he yelled, trying to fend off my flailing arms.

"You fucking bastard!" I screamed. "How could you! How can you call yourself our father? A real father would never do this—mom would hate you if she saw you now!" I could barely see through my tears, so the stinging slap caught me by surprise. I staggered sideways; when I recovered and turned back toward him I found Seth blocking my way. His back was to me, and his fists were up. My breath jammed in my throat—I felt as though my very heart had stopped. Seth had filled out over the past year, and he was taller than Dec, but there was no question that Dec was much, much stronger. He could crush Seth, if it came to that.

"Seth, no." I couldn't seem to get my voice over a whisper; it was like one of those nightmares when you want to scream, but all that comes out is a frightened squeak. I clutched his arm before noticing Dec's posture. He wasn't defensive or aggressive. His arms were hanging by his sides, and though he was breathing hard he was looking back and forth between Seth and me with an expression bordering on panic.

"Get out. Both of you," he snarled at us.

We fled. Seth followed me up the stairs, and I led him straight to the bathroom and found the can of topical anesthetic spray we kept there. He turned around and braced his hands on the counter; my own hands were shaking as I started to carefully spray the emerging welts. It wouldn't numb the pain completely, but it took the edge off. I surveyed the damage as I worked—the skin was broken in a couple of places, but overall, it could have been worse. I was still in shock. This was beyond what we were used to. Dec had never made Seth take his shirt off, or lashed his back before.

"Dammit, Tea, why did you come in?" Seth growled at me as I sprayed.

My eyes flew upward, startled, and met his in the mirror. "What do you mean, why? He was hurting you!"

"He caught me smoking."

Understanding dawned, and I hesitated for a second. "Well, that doesn't matter. It's still not justified, Seth... he shouldn't be doing that." I heard the echo of Jaden's voice in my head as I said it. I finished spraying the anesthetic.

When Seth turned around I was shocked to see anger on his face.

"He was almost done; now he'll only be madder. And what if he'd really hurt you?"

Seth's uncharacteristic anger threw me off; my voice was uncertain as I answered. "He wouldn't. And... well, I don't think we should stand for him hitting us anymore."

"What's our alternative, Sis? Move out? In case you've forgotten, we're still in high school. We've got no money, and nowhere to go. And you wouldn't want to leave anyway, you'd miss the horses too much. So why are you pissing him off?" He stalked out.

I was crying in earnest now, and wanted to go sob in my room, but suddenly remembered I had a lesson to teach. I was afraid to run into Dec downstairs—not afraid in the physical sense, I just didn't want to face him. But I had to go. I pulled myself together as best I could, washed my face, and crept carefully down the stairs. The office door was closed, and I slunk quickly outside.

Seth didn't come out at feeding time, which almost made me start crying again. He'd never stayed mad this long before. When I was done feeding I trailed slowly back to the house, my heart beating with trepidation. I wasn't interested in dinner, but I couldn't hide in the barn forever. I didn't see anyone when I came in, and headed straight to my room. No one came looking for me. When it got late I wondered if I should go do the bedtime check of the barn, but decided to skip it. If Dec saw lights on he'd surely go and do it.

I slept fitfully, which wasn't a surprise. By six-thirty I was wide awake. As I headed to the bathroom I realized I hadn't sprayed Seth's back again last night. I kicked myself; he'd probably had a rough night. I grabbed the can of anesthetic and went and tapped quietly on his door.

"It's me."

"Yeah, come in," he said tiredly.

He sat up in bed as I walked in.

"How's your back?" I asked tentatively.

"It's been better. How's your face?"

In truth, I had completely forgotten that Dec had slapped me the day before. I felt my left cheek; there was nothing there to remind me. The right side, of course, was still patterned in fading bruises from the mallet.

"Completely fine."

I held up the spray bottle, and he turned sideways on the bed.

"Sorry I forgot last night," I said as I began spraying.

"'sokay. Sorry I was such a jerk yesterday. Did you eat last night?"

"No. You?" It was rare for Seth to miss a meal.

"I snuck downstairs and had a midnight snack." He turned around and gazed at me somberly. "Have you seen Dec?"

I shook my head.

Seth stayed in his room, and I went out to feed the horses. As I was hurrying through the living room Dec's voice rang out from the kitchen.

"Tea."

I stopped reluctantly and turned toward him, but I didn't look him in the face.

"Eat something first." He walked past me and headed upstairs.

I moped into the kitchen and found a granola bar and some coffee. I felt awful. I wanted to go after Dec and say... well, I didn't know what I would say. But he sounded sad.

After feeding and teaching a lesson I went back to the house for another coffee; I was tired. There was no sign of either Seth or Dec—they must have been avoiding me, as well as each other.

I had a huge pile of laundry to do, but I didn't want to be in the house, so I decided to clean out the horses' automatic waterbowls. It was a tedious job and should take a couple of hours. Unfortunately it wouldn't keep my mind very busy, but I doubted if anything would provide enough distraction for me at this point. I gathered my supplies and started in Zac's stall. I turned the knob on the pipe that supplied his waterbowl. Then, with the water shut off, I scrubbed out the metal bowl with a sponge and dish soap before rinsing and refilling it. Zac was good company, nudging me with his nose and occasionally resting his chin on my shoulder the way he loved to do. I still missed him.

I had only done four stalls when I heard a familiar voice down the aisle, and sighed. Ever since I'd been hurt during the match, something had changed between Jaden and me. I couldn't seem to maintain the same distance that I had before the accident, with the result that his presence now caused me actual pain—a dull ache in my chest that occasionally spiked into a jab when he looked at me or talked to me a certain way. All in all, something I could do without today.

"Good morning." He spoke through the bars of Gracie's stall. His smile was almost normal, but his eyes were cautious. I wasn't the only one who had noticed the change in the tenor of our relationship.

"Hey," I said listlessly. I met his eyes for the barest second before dropping them back to the waterbowl.

"What's wrong?" he asked immediately.

"I don't really want to talk about it," I replied in a low voice, but even as I was uttering the words I knew they weren't true. What I desperately wanted was to talk to the old Jaden, the one who was both family and good friend, the one that existed for me before the curse of physical attraction ruined everything.

Jaden stepped into the stall. Thud, thud, thud went the ache in my chest. I exhaled sharply. Honestly, I didn't need this today.

"Can I help?" he asked quietly. Yes, I thought savagely, you can help by staying away from me. But I knew I didn't really mean it.

"No," I said, paying careful attention to my scrubbing.

"Tea..." He was standing right next to me now. He'd been careful not to touch me since the day of the accident, but I was afraid he would surrender to his habit of making me face him when I didn't want to. So when he moved again, I cringed away from him. I glanced at his face just long enough to register his hurt expression. I felt the first jab in my chest.

"Tea, what's going on? Is this about..." he hesitated, and I looked at him, curious. He didn't finish, but I had made the mistake of locking

211

eyes with him. I don't know what he saw in mine, but it was enough to make him half-reach for me. He caught himself; there was an edge to his voice when he spoke again.

"Up to the hayloft. Let's go."

I didn't resist—I knew that tone well enough by now to know that I'd be carried if I didn't walk. I led the way into the feedroom, drying my hands on my jeans, and slowly climbed the ladder to the loft. I didn't sit down, but turned to face him with my arms hugging my chest.

"Out with it," he ordered.

I took a deep breath. I didn't know how to explain why everything was in such chaos; it wasn't as though Seth and I had never dealt with a beating before. It wasn't such a big deal, usually... but this time was different.

"Dec caught Seth smoking," I began in a low voice. He winced; he understood immediately.

"Damn."

I nodded mutely.

"Is Seth okay?"

"He's-" I hesitated. Jaden didn't need to know the gory details; sadly, he probably knew all too well how Seth was. "Yeah, he's alright."

I saw anger flash in Jaden's eyes, but he controlled it quickly.

"What else?" he pressed.

"That's not enough?" I asked impatiently.

"I want to know what's made you this upset," he insisted. "Tell me the whole story."

I swallowed. I didn't even know where to start.

I heard him sigh. He came and guided me over to some haybales, his hand on my back. I expected the jab in my chest, but it still hurt. We sat down and he took my hand, moving deliberately to give me the chance to pull away. I didn't. Jab, jab.

"Now please tell me," he said quietly.

I studied the wooden boards under our feet as I spoke.

"I interrupted him. You know what a foul mood Dec's been in lately. He was—well, it was bad. I couldn't believe it, and... I don't know how he can even blame Seth for smoking, we've all gone through a rough time this year... anyway, I just lost it. I basically attacked him."

I heard Jaden catch his breath as his hand tightened around mine. My voice was as soft as breathing when I went on.

"Then Seth turned on him, and it almost came to a fight."

There was a pause.

"Did he-" His voice shook, whether with anger or some other emotion, I couldn't tell. I knew what he was asking, and I shook my head quickly, not looking at him. His grip was almost painfully tight now, and when I glanced at him his eyes were closed.

"No," I lied. "But now... now none of us are talking to each other. I said some really mean things to Dec, and Seth's mad at me, and... it's my fault."

Tears were burning my eyes, and I fought to hold them back. Jaden's arms went around me; he rested his cheek on my hair. One hand rubbed my arm.

"Nothing's your fault, Tea. Not one bit of blame for this whole sorry mess is attributable to you. You have to believe that."

I didn't say anything. I was too busy fighting to breathe, a task made challenging by the constant jabbing in my chest.

He coaxed my face up gently with his warm fingers. As I met his beautiful brown-gold eyes my heart gave one hard punch against my ribs. And the truth exploded inside me—I loved him. Not as my cousin. Not as the close friend he'd certainly become. I loved him as a man. I'd been fooling myself by thinking this was an attraction I could ignore.

"Why didn't you call me?" His face was tight with distress.

"I guess... I didn't think we had that kind of relationship anymore," I answered carefully. I was stunned by my new awareness; I felt like I couldn't think.

"We *always* have that kind of relationship, Tea. No matter what," he said vehemently.

I sensed an opening, but hesitated. What if he didn't feel the same way? That seemed more than likely, and I'd suffered enough pain for a while. The knowledge of my true feelings had come to me at the worst possible time. Or maybe it was a good time—I had nothing to lose, at this point. I steeled myself and looked him in the eye.

"Jaden—do you ever think that we're, um, very... close, for cousins?"

His expression tensed. Oh no, he doesn't feel that way, I thought wildly. Of course he doesn't—he's incredible—brilliant, talented, kind, generous, not to mention gorgeous... what would he want with me, an average girl with a minor talent for riding? My eyes returned to the floorboards.

"What are you asking me, Tea?" His voice was soft.

"Nothing." I wanted to laugh at myself; what had I been thinking?

"Do we have to go through this again? Tell me."

I gulped. "Do you remember when I got hurt?"

"Only too well."

"When you were wiping my face... well, for a second there, I thought... I thought you were going to kiss me."

I wasn't sure whether he could hear my barely whispered words over the sound of my heart battering itself against my ribs. There was a long pause, but I was too afraid to look at him. I might be too mortified to ever look at him again. Then he whispered back.

"For a second there, so did I."

Shock swept through me. The battering in my chest didn't abate. I realized I'd been holding my breath and drew in a faltering lungful of air. Then another.

I raised my eyes to his slowly; the incredulity must have been plain on my face.

"So... you... I mean, you're..." I couldn't form a coherent thought, let alone a sentence.

He understood, though. "Of course I'm attracted to you. How could I not be?"

I bit my lip. I could think of lots of reasons why he wouldn't be, personally. He leaned toward me, and I could read regret in his eyes.

"But I will never act on that attraction," he said gently.

A dozen questions and arguments elbowed each other in the race to my mouth, but the only one that slipped out was a whispered, "Why?"

Jaden squeezed my hand between both of his. My pulse bounded in my veins, and my hand tingled; I tried to ignore them so my face wouldn't betray how hopeless my obsession was. He watched me steadily with those unbelievable eyes, which did nothing to help me stay calm.

"Because it would be wrong," he said firmly.

I looked away.

"It's not only that it would create scandal," he said, "though trust me, in our family, this would be a scandal. We could seriously jeopardize family ties if we tried to have a relationship."

My stomach reacted to the very words, but I nodded. Seth and I had reached the same conclusion, after all. Jaden was still holding my hand; I squeezed his tighter, part of me already grieving at the prospect of letting it go.

"But it's not all about our family. It's also for your sake... you've been through a lot this year. A sordid relationship with an older relative is the last thing you need to deal with right now."

I had to smile a bit at his choice of words. "You make it sound like you're a doddering old uncle. There's only six years difference between our ages, Jaden."

He smiled a bit too, but his smile was sad. "And in ten years' time, that difference won't matter in the slightest. But right now, it does."

I started to argue, but he put his hand on the side of my face. I was stunned into silence, my face now tingling to match my hand. He looked into my eyes.

"Forget about me, Tea. Find a boy your own age to date—since I'm your only male cousin, you should be pretty safe on that front."

"You're not ruling out Ethan, then?" I couldn't help joking feebly.

His face tightened, and I felt immediately sorry for bringing it up.

"It's your choice, naturally... but if you would do me a favor, please don't date Ethan. I'm not sure I could handle having to see that."

I nodded, wide-eyed.

He let go of me; I felt a tangible sense of loss already. We sat in silence for a few minutes, gathering our thoughts, but the day's upheavals were far from over.

"Where's Dec?" he finally asked quietly.

"In the house, I guess—why?" My heart rate shot up in anticipation of his answer.

"Because I'm going to talk to him." He stood up; I jumped to my feet in front of him.

"No! Jaden, you can't-"

He misunderstood.

"He won't hurt you, Tea." The words were almost a sob. He held my shoulders tightly, and I shook my head quickly, wanting to explain.

"No, that's not why... I'm not worried about him hurting me."

Jaden let go of me; that did hurt.

"What is it, then?" He still looked upset.

I sighed. "I think he already feels bad," I admitted, my head hanging. "And he's been working so hard in therapy... if he knew that I told you, I think he'd be embarrassed. Ashamed, even."

"He should be," Jaden said harshly. "Let me get this straight—you don't want me talking to him because you're trying to protect his *feelings*?" I could hear the suppressed anger in his voice.

"Yes." I looked up. Knowing my feelings were reciprocated changed everything; when I saw his face soften, it was twice as difficult as before not to reach for him. I clenched my hands into fists.

"Well, nothing's going to get resolved by silence. Everyone's going to have to come out of hiding sometime and discuss this, and I'll be staying here until that happens."

I couldn't shake his resolve, but when we went to the house Dec wasn't there, and his truck was gone. Jaden went to Seth's room while I went into mine for a change of clothes; the weather was hot now. Within minutes I could hear them laughing, and I had to grin. Those two could joke about anything. They came in a minute later, Seth plopping onto the bed while Jaden took the chair.

"So, T, have you heard that Jaden's volunteered to be our bomb defuser?"

"Yup. Told you he was unbalanced," I kidded. I had changed into a light pink tank top and grey shorts; Jaden's eyes seemed to linger on my body for a minute before he determinedly looked away. I felt a flutter in my stomach.

"How do you feel, Seth? Are you going to do any work today, or what?" I asked to distract myself.

"I feel hungry," he complained.

I gave him a shove; we grinned at each other and went to make lunch. Seth and I were good again—that part was easy.

We were in the barn when Dec came home, and Seth and I stayed there while Jaden headed for the house. Since school had ended, Seth and I did the morning and evening feeds on weekdays. We had time to finish feeding all thirty-eight horses before Jaden came to get us. We walked back to the house together; I didn't even realize that I was shaking until Seth put his arm around me and I felt the tremors. Unless they were his.

Dec was in the living room. At our entrance he walked slowly up to Seth and gripped his shoulders.

"I'm sorry, son." He looked him in the eye; I wondered if my expression was even half as shocked as Seth's was. Being Seth, of course, he recovered quickly.

"Okay. But this is the last time," he joked, quoting what Dec always said when we apologized to him.

We all chuckled; now that the tension was broken we found seats. I made sure I wasn't next to Jaden.

"I have something to tell you," Dec began. "I've been keeping certain things to myself in an effort to protect you, but Jaden seems to think we'd benefit from being a little more open with each other, and I'm willing to give it a try if you are."

Seth and I nodded.

Dec took a deep breath. "Please realize that I'm not offering this as an excuse. It's just an explanation for why I've been... a bit tense, lately." He paused, looking at our faces. "I promised your mother I'd take care of you. That I'd provide for you, and do my best to keep you safe, even though lately I feel as though you both do whatever the heck you want. But now... well, I'm being sued, kids. Remember that project I worked on last year, the one so big I had to get a partner? Well, he falsified some of the data we used, without my knowledge. The trouble is, if I lose this lawsuit all my assets could be seized to pay the debt. Including this property—the house and barn."

Seth and I stared at each other in astonishment for a minute before I leaned against him. I hadn't expected anything like this. No wonder Dec had been so cantankerous lately.

"Like I said," Dec went on, "it's not an excuse. And I'll keep you posted on what's happening."

Dec was sitting on the loveseat by himself. He had a dejected air, and I felt bad for him suddenly, as though we were a sentencing jury. I went and sat next to him. He put his arm around me and pulled me closer.

"I'm sorry about what I said," I murmured.

"Don't be, honey. You were right," he replied. He brushed my cheek briefly. "I'm sorry, too," he added in a mutter.

I looked down, but not before catching sight of Jaden's eyes-narrowed expression. We went to make dinner, and it wasn't as awkward as I would have thought.

When I went to do the bedtime check of the barn Jaden followed me out.

"Why didn't you tell me the truth?" he asked quietly. He was standing close, but was careful not to touch me now. I felt a jab in my chest anyway.

I shrugged. "I knew it would upset you. And I didn't want to add fuel to the fire."

"Protecting everyone else, as usual," he said softly. "But who's protecting you?"

"You are," I reminded him. "As usual."

He nodded slowly. "I haven't been doing a very good job, though."

"Are you kidding me? No one's ever taken care of me the way you do, Jaden," I told him with feeling. It was the truth.

His eyes tightened in pain. I reached for his face—I couldn't help myself—but before I made contact he caught my hand.

"I meant what I said, Tea. We can't be anything more than family." He said it gently enough, but I could already see the colder, harder persona of the last month re-emerging. My chest constricted, and I pulled my hand out of his grip.

"No problem," I said matter-of-factly. I walked away before my face could betray my anguish.

It *was* a problem, though. Jaden stayed for a couple of days. Aunt Paloma came over the following day, and she and Dec spent a lot of time closeted together. Dec was being unusually affectionate with Seth and me; I could tell he sincerely regretted falling off the wagon, and a tenuous new closeness was emerging between us. Between Jaden and I, on the other hand, things were even more strained than before, which was saying something.

We went back to our standard of careful non-contact, and we spoke to each other politely when necessary. Only now that I knew the truth, it was even more difficult to be near him. Thankfully he had a polo tournament that weekend, so I got some respite from the tension.

On Tuesday Jaden was back. Everyone else showed up that day too, even Teri. It had been a sweltering, muggy morning, the sky almost white with heat. No one was very inclined to ride or work, so we spent most of our time in the relatively cool tackroom. Jaden was working on the fencing, but he came in occasionally, and whenever he made an appearance my entire body seized up and I could barely speak. This was going to get old pretty fast.

I was lounging against the wall when a deafening bang made us all jump. I exchanged a frightened look with Seth, and we ran outside, followed by Kabir, Julia and Teri. We ran back in just as quickly; raindrops the size of golf balls were dive-bombing us. The bang we had heard must have been thunder. As I watched through the open doorway an enormous fork of lightning speared the sky.

"Quick, we've got to bring in the horses," I yelled. I ran and grabbed a handful of lead ropes. As I was tossing one to each person Jaden appeared and took one. We set off running through the rain; luckily, with six people helping it only took minutes to get the horses safely inside. By the time we were done the storm was already abating, and we were all laughing as we tried to shake the water off.

I almost ran headlong into Jaden as I was going into the tackroom. I stumbled back, carefully avoiding his outstretched hand. Pain flashed across his eyes.

"I'm going to check on the horses in the pasture," I mumbled.

Jaden had completed enough pasture fencing so we could turn horses out there. It was a bit far from the barn, but that suited me perfectly.

I squished my way through the water-soaked grass to the pasture. The sudden downpour had already cooled the air, and I shivered slightly in my wet clothes. The worst of the storm seemed to be over, and when I reached the pasture fence I paused, debating whether I really needed to bring the horses in. The rain had dwindled to a fine mist, and there hadn't been any lightning or thunder since I'd left the barn. It was so nice to be away from the tense atmosphere there that I lingered, leaning on the fence and watching the dark wet patches creeping down the horses' coats.

I didn't hear the footsteps until they were directly behind me. I knew whose they were without turning; only Jaden's presence would raise the hairs on my body like that.

"Tea," he said my name like a caress.

I was about to duck away, but he knew me too well—his hands shot out and gripped the fence board on either side of me. He was so close now that I could feel the heat from his body searing the back of mine, but this heat made me shiver all the more.

"How long are you planning on not talking to me?" His voice was subdued.

I shrugged. I felt, rather than heard, his sigh.

"You're angry with me."

He was wrong about that. It wasn't anger that was making me avoid him, it was self-preservation.

"I don't blame you. I know I've made a mess of things. I came to give you a choice... I was planning to leave at the end of the season." He paused, but my brain was already frozen. He was planning to *leave*? "But if you'd rather I left now, I'll understand. I'll find a spot for my horses closer to Toronto."

Like at Summer's father's barn, I thought, anguished. My chest constricted painfully, and my breath started coming in sharp, raw gasps. Either way, he would be gone. My only option was whether to prolong my suffering. It was the same impossible choice: the pain of his presence versus the torture of his absence. I didn't say anything; I don't think I could have spoken even if I'd wanted to.

"Let me know what you decide," he continued quietly. He hesitated, then dropped his head close to mine. I felt the *zing* of current from my face down to my shoulder, though he didn't touch me. He whispered his parting line in my ear.

"I miss you."

I waited until his footsteps faded to surrender to the wracking sobs, and they shook me for a long time before I pulled myself together and went back to work.

Jaden didn't come back for three days. My friends couldn't help but notice my despair as I trudged miserably around the barn, and I told them it was my unrequited crush that was bringing me down. Teri and Julia agreed with Seth—they thought that at this point, Jaden and I being together couldn't be much worse than our being apart, but I couldn't agree. I spent the time trying desperately to convince myself that I would be fine once he was gone.

He reappeared on Friday; I pounded down my joy and relief at seeing him as best I could. We exchanged a few polite words, then went back to ignoring each other. Julia, Teri and I were in the main aisle grooming that afternoon, after going for a long trail ride.

"Have you ever thought about getting a tattoo?" Julia asked as she picked out Jasmine's forehoof.

"Uh-uh," Teri shook her head emphatically. "That's not for me."

They looked at me.

220

"Well, I've thought about it, but it would be such a waste of money." They waited expectantly. "Because I would spend so much to get it done, and when I came home Dec would skin me alive, and I'd lose the tattoo along with the cash," I explained, laughing at their grins of sudden understanding.

I saw Jaden out of the corner of my eye, in the adjoining aisle with Kermit. Our conversation had captured his interest, though he tried not to show it. I ignored the now-routine jabbing in my chest. What I do from now on is none of Jaden's business, I reminded myself fiercely.

"What about piercings?" I asked, and saw Jaden's back stiffen. I knew I was goading him, just a little.

"Oh yeah, I definitely want to get my bellybutton done," Julia said enthusiastically.

"I'd rather get my upper ear done, I think," Teri said.

I thought of how I had admired Caley's look. "I think I might get my eyebrow pierced," I said.

"You don't think Dec would mind?" Julia asked doubtfully.

"Oh yes, I'll be just as dead," I admitted cheerfully. "You should have seen him when I got my ears pierced—he was apoplectic. I had to hide out for a while, even with the unassailably logical argument I had."

Teri was chortling; she remembered this story.

"Tea wanted to get her ears pierced," she explained to Julia, "and Dec said yes. So she came home with a nice earring in her right earlobe—and three in her left."

"You're awful," Julia giggled.

I caught a glimpse of Jaden; his expression was enigmatic. I turned away quickly, breathing slowly to control the jabs.

I was in the feedroom that evening when I heard him behind me. His quiet tread brought him close—too close, when I turned I felt the wall against my back. My heart flailed in protest at his nearness. Jaden's expression was carefully controlled as he trapped me with his gaze.

"Tell me you're not putting a needle through that face," he exhorted.

I was struggling to keep my face smooth, not to betray the pain in my chest. It made me defensive.

"Why do you care? You won't be seeing it," I muttered callously.

The hurt in his eyes made me regret my words instantly, but before I could open my mouth to make amends, his expression hardened.

"Have you thought about what I asked you?"

I swallowed. I didn't know what to tell him; it seemed like either choice would leave my heart in tatters.

"I—I think you should do whatever's easiest for you." My voice was thick with suppressed emotion.

He grimaced. "I want to know what *you* want," he insisted. He leaned forward in his intensity, planting one hand on the wall by my head. His nearness was overwhelming; his scent and the heat from his body were too much for me. I began to tremble. I wanted to fling my arms around him and beg him not to leave... but instead, I just told him the truth. I selfishly forgot about my obligations to my family, about the risks we would take. My heart was hurting me so much that, finally, its call was the only one I heeded.

"You know what I want." My voice was raw with pain.

"Tea... we can't. You *know* we can't," he groaned. His face twisted with grief, his eyes pleading for understanding. I felt my own overflow with silent tears.

"Don't cry, sweetheart, please..."

My eyes were locked on his face; I read his intention even before he began to close the distance between us. My stomach flipped right over.

"Don't," I choked. If he kissed me now my fragile heart would splinter into a thousand piercing shards. Of that I was sure. He stopped, his lips an inch away from mine, and questioned my certainty with his eyes.

"Please don't," I breathed.

His face closed off, and he withdrew suddenly and loped away, fists clenched at his sides. I sagged against the wall and slid down to the ground, my tears accompanied by sobs now. How had things grown into such an impossible mess? I'd managed to hurt him again, despite my best intentions.

Half an hour later I shuffled into the tackroom, where Julia, Teri and Kabir were hanging out with Seth. I had tried to pull myself together but apparently I hadn't done a very convincing job, because I drew looks of concern as I slumped down on a bench.

"What's wrong, hon?" Teri came and sat by me.

I shrugged one shoulder. "Nothing." Nothing new, at any rate.

"Jaden again?" Julia guessed sympathetically.

I nodded listlessly. "We had a... a talk."

Kabir frowned. "Is he being a jerk to you, T?"

I looked at him in surprise. "No, not at all."

"Then why does he keep making you cry?" he insisted. "Is it just that he's saying no to you? Because he doesn't feel the way you do?"

"It's not that," I shook my head. "He... he does feel the same way." My voice was hushed, my eyes on the floor. I heard several gasps, so I assumed my friends had heard.

"He what? Why didn't you tell us? What are you going to do?" Their startled questions bounced around the tackroom.

"He's... attracted, but he feels the way we did at first, Seth." I looked at my brother as I spoke. "That it would be weird. And wrong. And upset the family. And he's probably right, and I'm an awful person for not even caring." I dropped my face into my hands, and Teri patted my back comfortingly.

Julia came and sat by my other side.

"You don't think he'll reconsider?" she asked gently.

I shook my head. "He told me to go date a boy my own age. And he's going to move his horses out soon; I've literally driven him away. Dec's going to flip, he was thrilled to have Jaden here."

"That doesn't sound like a very bright move." Seth frowned. "He's still working at the polo club, right? And he's building the fencing, he wouldn't bail on Dec in the middle of that."

"I guess he wants to minimize his time here," I mumbled. I felt another spasm in my chest.

"Of course he does," Julia said thoughtfully, "because it's difficult for him to be around you now. Just like it's hard for you to be around him... he really does have feelings for you."

I recognized the scheming look on her face; it had gotten us into trouble more than once.

"No, Julia. Whatever you're planning, I'm not doing it."

"Why? Don't you even want to *try* to change his mind?" she asked innocently.

"No, I don't. He doesn't want me, and I'm going to respect his wishes. I don't want to play any games," I told her impatiently.

"But that's not exactly right, is it?" Teri said. "He does want you—he's just scared. Same as you were. But you came around, and so did Seth. Maybe with time, he'll come around too."

"Time, or the right incentive." Julia grinned. "Which brings us back to my proposal." Everyone looked at her, waiting. I groaned and dropped my head into my hands again.

"If he wants you to date a boy your own age, then I think you should do just that," Julia began.

I looked up in confusion. "Jules, I have zero interest in dating right now. Less than zero."

"Well, you don't actually have to date anyone. Just make it seem like you are. Once Jaden sees you with someone else, maybe he'll realize it's not what he really wants."

"So, in a nutshell, try to make him jealous," I said in a flat voice.

Julia nodded.

"No way," I said emphatically. "I'm not doing that; it would be... mean."

"Why, hasn't he been dating all this time?" Kabir demanded.

I flinched as I thought about the night of Piba's colic. "Maybe," I conceded.

"And do you remember how you felt when he was making out with his ex right in front of you?" Teri added.

"Yes, I do. And I don't want to hurt him like that," I said miserably.

Seth snorted. "He's hurting himself; he's being an idiot. I mean, look at the two of you—you're both miserable. Dec knows something's going on, which makes him suspicious, which makes it a lot harder for me to get away with anything. Does Jaden not care what this is doing to *me*? That's just plain selfish."

I smiled a little in spite of myself. "Look, guys, I really appreciate what you're trying to do... but the only thing I'm going to do now is try to get over him."

Kabir got up and stretched. "Well, if you change your mind, you know who to call if you need a volunteer." He winked at me. He went home, and Julia and Teri left soon after.

Seth slung his arm around my shoulders as we walked to the house. "You're being very mature about all this, T. Way more mature than I would be." He laughed.

I didn't answer, but I didn't think my behavior was the result of maturity. It was the result of love.

Fourteen

We played club chukkers the next day. Jaden and I had an awkward, quiet ride to the club, but practice went well. It was another hot day, so when the game was over I decided to give Schweppes a quick shower.

A girl I didn't recognize wandered past as I was scraping the excess water off Schweppes. A groupie, by the looks of her—too manicured for a player or groom. I glimpsed long, light brown hair and pretty blue eyes as she scanned the stable area.

"Hey, isn't that the girl Jaden hooked up with at the party?" Sharleen's voice floated out of the barn.

"Yeah, looks like," Jennalyn's voice answered cheerfully.

"What I wouldn't give to be in her shoes," Sharleen sighed wistfully.

My stomach plunged past my knees. My heart started pounding painfully, but I couldn't hear it over the roaring in my ears. I bent forward, trying to get the blood back to my head, and leaned against Schweppes for support. I tried to take deep breaths, but I couldn't seem to control my panting.

After a few minutes I was able to straighten up, though I was still shaky. Schweppes turned his head to look at me inquiringly.

"I'm okay," I whispered to him. It was a lie, though. I looked around, but I didn't see the girl. I set off with Schweppes to find her, although I was far from sure that I wanted to. I didn't have to go far; as I came around the corner of the barn I saw her standing with a group of people. She was next to Jaden. I walked forward woodenly until I was right behind them. Mateo spotted me.

"Hola, chiquita," he said. "Are you ready for the barbecue?"

I carefully kept my eyes on Mateo's face.

"Actually, I'm going to head home. I, um, have a headache," I told him haltingly.

"Are you okay?" Jaden sounded concerned, and I allowed myself to look at him, finally. The stab of pain that went through me almost made me gasp aloud.

"Yes, fine," I said faintly. "Nothing an aspirin won't cure." My eyes flickered over to the girl, who was smiling. She was beautiful, of course, but she didn't look at me. Her eyes were on Jaden.

"I'll come with you," Jaden was saying. "You shouldn't-"

"No!" It came out sharper than I'd intended; surprise crossed his face. "I'm okay, really. I'm just going to ride home slowly and lie down. You stay. Have... have fun." My sentence ended almost in a whisper, and I stumbled away, my arm around Schweppes' neck for comfort.

I did ride slowly, but I couldn't keep my mind from racing. It seemed that Kabir was right. Jaden had been dating, after all. Apparently, just because he was—or claimed to be—attracted to me, didn't mean he wasn't still interested in others. Every thought lanced through me, sharp and white-hot. Sharleen had said they'd hooked up at the party. She had to mean the party after the last big match... was that why he hadn't wanted me there? Maybe he'd had plans to see the girl all along. That thought brought the first embers of anger glowing to life within me; I encouraged them, fanning them with more thoughts of Jaden's possible duplicity. It felt better to be mad than so utterly, horribly empty.

The evening was awful. I used my headache excuse to get out of eating dinner, but then I had to stay in my room, and I was too wound up for such a small space. I paced the three strides back and forth along its length over and over. I reminded myself several times that I had absolutely no right to feel angry or jealous, but, though my brain believed me, my heart wasn't buying it. I was inordinately relieved to hear Jaden come home at our usual time—he hadn't gone anywhere with her, then. But when I heard his footsteps on the stairs, I panicked; what if he came to check on me? I slapped the light switch off and dove into bed fully dressed, pulling the covers up over my head. Sure enough, a quiet knock sounded on my door a moment later. I ignored it, and heard Jaden's footsteps recede down the hall to the guestroom. I flung the covers off angrily; it felt childish and pathetic to be hiding like this.

The next morning I didn't go outside until the last minute, knowing that Jaden would have to be at the club. I had barely slept, so I had a rough morning, but I made a decision—I wasn't going to play in the club chukkers that afternoon. I felt slightly less pathetic after I'd called the club and told them I wouldn't be there. It seemed I'd finally gotten the incentive I needed to distance myself from Jaden.

He showed up for lunch, and other than asking me how I was feeling, we didn't exchange a word, though I could feel him shooting glances my way. I volunteered to do the dishes; Dec and Seth headed out.

"I'll help you," Jaden sighed, "otherwise we'll be late."

I turned to face him.

"Actually, I'm not going today." I was impressed with how steady my voice was.

His eyebrows rose in surprise. "Why? Are you still not feeling well?"

"I feel fine," I said coldly. "I just have other plans. There's more to my life than you and polo, you know."

A shadow of pain crossed his face, and I felt an answering ache deep within me. Then he nodded slowly.

"Good," he said quietly. He turned and left before my tears spilled.

Jaden didn't come home that night.

I tried not to jump to the conclusion that he'd gone out with the blue-eyed girl, but it was hard. I felt absolutely wretched; I couldn't even put a name to the bitter emotions that washed over me. Every second seemed to last an hour as I tried frantically not to think of him. Finally, I couldn't take it anymore and called Teri.

"Hey. Were you sleeping?" I belatedly realized that I'd forgotten to check the time. It was almost midnight and Teri was usually up at four-thirty to go work at the track.

"Kind of," she yawned, "but it's okay, I've got tomorrow off. What's up?"

My pain poured out in a torrent. Teri listened quietly, offering the occasional murmured word of sympathy.

"Why don't we go out for breakfast tomorrow?" she suggested. "That way we can talk without worrying about being overheard. I'll send Julia a text, too."

"I'll do it, Ter, you go back to bed. And thanks for not telling me to shut up and let you sleep."

After I texted Julia I went to bed and lay awake for another hour before falling into an uneasy sleep. I dreamt of Jaden, and woke up with tears on my cheeks. It was still early, but I got up and showered.

Julia actually made it down for breakfast, to our shock—she wasn't a morning person. Seth and Kabir came too, and my spirits lifted marginally at my friends' show of support. I told them the story of the blue-eyed girl, and how wounded I felt, and how Jaden couldn't be very interested in me, after all. Which, I pointed out, was a good thing—it should make it easier for me to disregard him until he was gone. The searing pain in my heart seemed to disagree, but I ignored it.

The first thing I noticed when we got home was Jaden's car. My pulse immediately stepped up its pace. He came down the steps of the house as Seth and I got out of the car, and my heart hammered even harder as he stopped in front of us.

"Hi," he said carefully. He looked tired. As though he hadn't gotten much sleep, I thought bitterly.

"Hey dude," Seth replied. "Off to the club?"

"No, I'm working on the pasture today," Jaden told him. He glanced at me before striding away. It was a look of pity.

That was what pushed me over the edge. I could take being rejected, but I was damned if I was going to be the object of anyone's pity. Especially Jaden's.

"Kabir!" I marched over as he got out of his car. "I'm going to need you to kiss me."

We spent considerable time planning, and decided that the barn wall, facing the main riding ring, would be the most conspicuous. Jaden usually walked around the far side of the ring on his way to the house for lunch.

Kabir thought I should stand against the wall, but the others overrode him, not only because I had to be visible—and Kabir was big—but because I could more clearly demonstrate my willing participation in the kiss by leaning into him, rather than the other way around.

"Should we practice a bit first?" Kabir suggested jokingly once we were outside. At least, I hoped he was joking.

I gave him my most serious 'be serious' look. "I don't think that will be necessary."

"Sorry," he said quietly. "I know this isn't exactly fun for you. It's not quite how I've imagined kissing you, either."

I frowned. He had imagined kissing me?

"Kabir... are you sure you're okay with this? I mean, you do realize that I'm basically using your body, right?"

"You think I mind you using my body?" He gave a comical leer. "Please, Tea—help yourself." Then he grinned at me, his normal, friendly grin, and I relaxed somewhat. Kabir was an old friend, and I trusted him.

We got into position. He leaned back against the wall and I faced him uncertainly. His big arms closed around me, but he was tentative, barely touching me.

"You feel even smaller than you look," he murmured. "I'm almost afraid to break you."

I couldn't help flashing him a quick smile, despite my pounding heart, because I had just been thinking the opposite. He was much bigger up close, at least twice as broad as me. I felt completely engulfed by his embrace.

"Try to relax," he suggested, "you're as stiff as a board."

He was right; even my face felt stiff.

"I don't think I can," I whispered. Now that I was actually doing it, I was liking this idea less and less, and I wasn't sure why.

"Come here," he said, guiding my head onto his burly shoulder.

He patted my back with one hand. I closed my eyes and sighed as I realized why I was so uncomfortable—I felt like I was cheating. On Jaden. Which was obviously ridiculous, since he didn't want to be with me, and never would. If Jaden had his way, my life would be spent doing this... kissing someone other than him. My resolve strengthened. I put my arms around Kabir's neck.

"He's coming," he whispered, looking over my shoulder. He glanced down at me, his dark brown eyes uncertain. "You want me to take the initiative?"

I nodded slightly; my mouth was dry. Kabir looked nervous too, but he bent his head and lightly touched his lips to mine. I didn't move.

"Come on, Tea, this isn't going to convince anyone," he whispered.

He pulled me closer, pressing me against him, and covered my mouth with his again. I squeezed my eyes shut and tried to pretend he was Jaden. I felt our lips move, and I didn't resist.

I heard a powerful engine roaring to life, then the crunch and spray of gravel. I ripped away from Kabir and ran around the corner of the barn in time to see Jaden's car spin sideways, fishtailing, before he recovered it and went tearing down the driveway. In the instant I saw it, his profile looked rigid. And flawless. And furious.

I sagged back against the barn and covered my face with my hands. I was shaking. Kabir put his arm around me and pulled me close to his side, supporting me.

"Come on, sweetie. Offhand, I'd say that was a complete success. Let's go get the debriefing over with."

I felt wretched. Seth and our friends thought the kiss had accomplished its purpose: it was now clear that I wasn't simply sitting around pining for Jaden. But I was despairing because, in the end, I'd made him suffer—and I couldn't help but be hurt by his pain. I wished I could take back my impulsive action; I was ashamed of what I'd done. I thought about calling him, but this wasn't the kind of conversation you could have over the phone. I knew what I had to do. Luckily it was Monday so I had no lessons to teach; I got into the car and headed for Toronto.

I wasn't sure he'd be home, but he answered right away. My heart was racing as I stepped through the doorway. I sidled over two steps and hunched against the wall, not watching as Jaden shut the door. He stepped back, putting some space between us. I glanced up at him—his hair was tousled, his face expressionless except for a tightness around the eyes. Those eyes bored into mine and I looked down quickly, unable to hold his gaze as shame coursed through me afresh.

"So," he said, his voice flat.

I studied the scuffed toes of my paddock boots as I spoke.

"Jaden, I—I'm so sorry," I stammered. I waited for the anger to come, for that look of fury he'd worn when I'd seen him last, roaring away in his car.

"Why are you sorry?" His voice was unexpectedly gentle.

I looked up in surprise. "Because I kissed Kabir," I said, stating the obvious.

He managed a small, rueful smile. "You're sorry for doing as I asked—forgetting about me, and finding a boy your own age to date?"

"Yes. I mean no... Kabir and I aren't dating." I swallowed hard and forced myself to meet his eyes before whispering the truth. "I was trying to make you jealous."

Shock crossed his face for an instant, quickly followed by the anger I'd expected. He stepped closer; I resumed my shoe inspection.

"Why?" he demanded, his voice rough. "After everything we've talked about, why would you even attempt that?"

I felt my face reddening, and was glad he couldn't see it. "Okay, it was stupid, I get it..." My voice trailed off as his fingers lifted my chin. I felt defiance mix with my embarrassment as I found his eyes again. They were intense, smoldering in a way I'd never seen before.

"It *was* stupid," he growled softly, moving even closer. "But it worked." I blinked, my brain stalling just as my heart began hammering fiercely. My eyes widened as he ducked his head and whispered in my ear, "You're in a lot of trouble."

Part Two: Fruit

Fifteen

I stood frozen as Jaden's lips brushed my earlobe, then slowly kissed my neck. The kisses continued down to my shoulder, leaving a burning path in evidence of their passing. He slid his hands lightly down my arms, and I trembled, my breathing accelerating wildly. Strong, warm hands suddenly gripped mine, which felt cold and clammy.

"Are you okay?" his low voice breathed.

I opened my eyes to find his face inches from mine. His molten gold-chip eyes were worried.

"Fine." My voice came out in a whisper, and I laughed weakly. "Actually, much, much better than fine."

His lips curved upward, transforming his face, and I felt warmth flush my cheeks. God, he was beautiful when he smiled like that. He took my face in his hands, his eyes holding mine with burning intensity. Slowly, watching every flicker of emotion on my face, he bent his head and brushed his lips against mine. Hesitantly, I slid my arms around his neck. He kissed me again, more firmly this time, and I felt his breathing speed in time with mine. Our lips were moving together now; warmth flooded my body, and I pulled myself tightly against him. His arms dropped down to my waist, and I gasped as his hands found the bare skin there. I'd forgotten I was wearing a short halter top... his touch felt hot, feverish. He groaned as he pulled me even tighter against his hard body.

"I remember the first time I saw you wearing this... this fragment of a shirt," he murmured against my cheek. "I was so angry—I wanted to march you right back into the house and make you change."

I pulled back slightly so I could see his face. "You were *angry*?" Not exactly the reaction I'd been going for.

A small, wry smile tugged at his mouth. "Of course I was. You made me want you. When I saw you coming down the steps with your whole midriff exposed..." He shook his head slightly, his voice husky. "I couldn't deny anymore that I wanted you. I wanted you so badly, no matter how wrong it was." His hands tightened convulsively on my

233

back, and he kissed me again, harder this time, more urgently. I molded myself to his shape, my hands sliding into his hair. I had forgotten we were still in the entrance—in fact I barely remembered my own name—until Jaden grabbed my waist and lifted me so our faces were level. I felt the wall against my back; he held me there by leaning the entire length of his body against mine. Every inch of our bodies were pressed together now, but insanely, I wanted him still closer. His lips parted; I followed his lead and felt his tongue caress mine. I heard a low moan, and was surprised to find it came from me. Too soon, he pulled away, lowering me gently, and we leaned together with our chests heaving.

When we had somewhat caught our breaths he chuckled quietly.

"I haven't even asked you in—where are my manners?"

He guided me to the couch in the living room. I was shocked to note that part of me wanted to go the other way, toward the bedroom. We sat angled toward each other, and he held my hand in both of his. I felt almost shy, looking at him now. He started caressing the nape of my neck. Shivers ran down the length of my back at his touch.

"I would never have guessed that I'd like your hair short," he murmured, smoothing a lock behind my ear, "but I love it. It shows off your long, slender neck."

He leaned in and kissed the hollow behind my ear, then followed my hairline, one slow kiss at a time, to the nape of my neck, his arms sliding around me and supporting me, which was a good thing as my body seemed to have turned to jelly.

I sighed shakily, and Jaden shifted around so he was looking me full in the face.

"Is this... weird for you?" he asked carefully.

"No, not weird, more like—surreal. I can't believe we're actually doing this." I smiled at him tentatively. "But I'm so glad we are."

He pressed his lips softly against mine, and my stomach swooped like I'd missed a step going downstairs. I pulled him toward me, wanting to feel his body on mine again. I slid back further and further, until I was half-lying on my back, with Jaden pressed deliciously against me. After only a few seconds, though, he pulled us both into a sitting position, chuckling.

"Let's not rush things," he said. "I suspect we have some things to discuss first."

"All right," I agreed, trying not to pout. "What would you like to discuss?"

"Well, for starters... am I a better kisser than Kabir?" He said it lightly, but he was watching my face carefully.

For a minute, I was speechless—I just stared at him blankly.

"I don't know," I finally stammered. "I wasn't really paying attention with Kabir, to be honest."

"Hmm... then I guess I have my answer." He gave a quick smile, which disappeared as he leaned in and held me with a penetrating stare.

"Look, I know you kissed him for my benefit—but please don't do that again. I really hated it."

"Okay." My mind was still reeling, refusing to cooperate while I was trapped in his gaze. I tore my eyes away. To my relief, my brain started up again.

"While we're on the subject of kissing other people," I ventured, "what about Summer?"

He didn't say anything right away, and I studied his face while he was thinking. His jaw was tight, and he was frowning, though he held my hand and was absently tracing circles on the back of my wrist with his thumb. I tried fruitlessly to ignore the tingling from his touch. Finally he looked at me, his face unhappy.

"If we're going to make this work-" My heart leapt and it must have shown in my face, because he smiled slightly. "If we're going to be... involved, then I want us to be honest with each other. No secrets. Agreed?"

I nodded. Jaden was looking uncharacteristically nervous; he licked his lips and averted his eyes.

"I've been trying to deny that I was attracted to you. I tried to distract myself by seeing other people." His voice was quiet.

I felt crushed, the tears threatening to flow, but I fought back my emotions. This was obviously hard for him, too, and he was only being honest. And after all, until today I really didn't have any kind of claim here.

So I kept my face composed as I asked, "The girl at the polo club?"

His eyes returned to mine. "What girl?"

"The one standing next to you on Saturday. Sharleen said you guys hooked up at a party." It was my turn to look away; I was afraid of what his face would reveal.

"Is that what you thought? Why you left early that night, and didn't play yesterday?" He sounded... relieved. I peeked at him cautiously. "She had too much to drink at the party, and I drove her home. That's all. I don't even know why she showed up on Saturday."

Well, I knew. "If not her, then who?"

"I'm not sure that matters. Tell me, did you really think I would have been picking up girls two weeks ago? What kind of man do you take me for?" He was frowning; he sounded upset.

"The kind who's trying to distract himself," I reminded him. "So you weren't? Picking up girls?"

He looked away again, but squeezed my hand. "I was dating earlier this year. Starting with Brianna."

I swallowed hard. "How many others?"

"One. Well, two if you count Summer, although we didn't date, we just had the one... relapse."

I winced, but didn't say anything. I was definitely counting Summer.

"Look, Tea, I'm a man, not a kid, and..." He sounded defensive.

"Let me guess," I said bitterly, "you have 'needs'-"

"That's not what I was going to say-" he interjected.

"Did you sleep with them?" I pulled my hand away from him and clenched my fists in my lap.

"No."

I glanced at him, and though his brow was furrowed, his eyes met mine calmly, hiding nothing. I believed him. Although I couldn't help thinking that I could never have dated anyone but him these past few months.

"Did you kiss them?"

"Yes."

I wasn't really surprised, but it still hurt. I blinked back tears angrily; I didn't want to cry. I felt Jaden's hand on my face, gently trying to make me face him, but I resisted.

"Tea." His smooth voice was very soft. I wished I didn't love the sound of it so much. I kept my eyes resolutely away from him.

"Tea, look at me."

I slowly lifted my eyes to his. He wiped away my tears with his thumbs.

"I know you're hurting right now, but hear me out. First of all, you need to know that those other kisses were nothing like the ones we just

236

shared. What we just did..." He exhaled hard. "Well, I've never felt anything like that before."

A swell of joy coursed through me. "Really? I mean, neither have I, but you've probably had a bit more experience than me."

"Maybe a bit." He smiled. "Second, I was unattached at the time—in terms of relationships, I didn't think of you as an option. Sometimes, in a moment of weakness, I'd consider the possibility... but I suppressed those hopes quickly, because I knew they were wrong."

I opened my mouth to argue, but he held up a finger to silence me. His face grew stern.

"Third, I haven't kissed anyone recently. *I'm* not the one who was kissing someone else this very afternoon."

"I—but—that's totally different," I spluttered.

He gave me a look that clearly indicated he didn't think so.

"Now that I think of it, my kissing Summer was very similar," he said. "I wasn't trying to make you jealous. Rather, I was trying to convince myself I didn't care that I wasn't with you."

I thought about it for a minute, then cocked my head and considered him. "Okay, how's this—I'll forgive you for Summer if you forgive me for Kabir."

"Deal."

We shook hands, and he pulled me forward and crushed me to his chest. "It's so good to finally hold you," he whispered.

"It's even better to finally be held," I replied. That was such a gross understatement it was almost laughable; I couldn't remember ever being happier. I never wanted to move.

As though reading my thoughts, Jaden asked quietly, "How long do you have?"

I sighed. "Not long. I told Dec I had to help Teri with a personal crisis."

We drew back and assessed each other. I knew we were wondering the same thing.

"Shall we keep this quiet for now?" he asked.

"Yes." I hesitated. "But, Seth knows about... well, he knew why I was kissing Kabir."

A flicker crossed his face. "Well, I didn't expect Seth to stay in the dark for long," he conceded.

"And, um," I continued uncomfortably, "Teri also sort of knows... and Julia."

He raised his eyebrows. "Does everyone know that you've been, uh-"

"Lusting after you?" I supplied, grinning.

He laughed. "Oh, is that what you're doing?"

We grinned at each other, but my smile soon faded. "We can't tell Dec," I said quietly.

"I suppose there's no reason to say anything yet," he agreed, "though I don't like lying to him. Eventually, though, we'll have to tell him." The prospect seemed to worry him.

I was secretly thrilled at this mention of the future. I was so happy that I didn't even worry about breaking the news to Dec; after all, who knew what tomorrow would bring? Jaden walked me to my car, holding me close all the way. He kissed me goodbye far too briefly— though it was probably several minutes—and I drove away.

I was up early the next morning, even though I had barely slept. I'd been far, far too excited. I kept reliving every moment I'd spent with Jaden, every touch, every word. I wondered if I had dreamt the whole thing, but the look he gave me when he arrived the next morning made it clear everything had been real. We decided to go for a ride, after Seth agreed to teach my one morning class. They were beginners, and they would have fun with Seth, although they might not learn much.

We spoke very little on the ride. I led the way, taking Jaden to a little copse that I had discovered. It was a short distance from the regular trail, the trees surrounding it were very dense, and inside it was a small clearing. We dismounted and led our horses across the long, gently waving grass.

Once the horses were secured I took off my chaps; it was getting hot already. Jaden took my hand and led me into the shade of a large tree, and we faced each other, finally alone. I felt a bit tongue-tied as I watched his eyes roam over my face, pausing on the dark circles under my eyes.

"You look tired." He smiled knowingly.

"So do you." I smiled back.

He rested his hand on my cheek, softly brushing the dark smudge under my eye with his thumb. His touch was a balm; I leaned into it, feeling all the hurt and uncertainty of the past few months evaporate, like dreams touched by the morning light.

He watched my face as he put his other hand on my waist and inclined his head slowly. He meant to be gentle, to ease into our kiss as he had yesterday. I could tell that was his intention—but when our lips met, it was a flame meeting gasoline. His mouth came down hard on mine; my arms snaked around his neck as I flattened myself against him. I was yanked off the ground as he clamped his arms around me, and my legs wound around his hips of their own accord. I could hardly breathe, blood was roaring in my ears, and for a long time all I could feel and taste and smell and see was Jaden. Eventually I felt a shift and realized we were lying on the grass, his weight binding our bodies even more tightly together. His lips traveled all over my face, my neck, my shoulders, while his hands caressed every part of me they could reach, and I clutched him to me with all my strength, gasping. When his mouth finally returned to mine it was softer, more patient. He kissed me deeply; I felt a moan in my throat and with the same sense of shock as the night before, I understood that I wanted him. I wanted us to strip off our clothes and make love right then and there. I was taken aback by the intensity of my desire. It was an entirely new thing in my experience.

"Jaden..."

It wasn't the first time I'd said his name, but he sensed the difference and pulled back immediately.

"No, wait—don't get off me," I protested, drawing him back in.

He returned his body to mine with a slight smile, though he didn't rest his full weight on me, I now realized. He looked somewhat apologetic.

"Sorry, that was a bit-" he started to say.

"Don't," I interrupted softly. I stared into his light-flecked eyes. "That was the best... interlude of my life. Don't say anything against it."

He exhaled in relief.

"Me too," he murmured, nuzzling my cheek. "The best by far."

I was thrilled beyond belief at his words. I knew Jaden had had other girlfriends, at least one of them serious, and he was twenty-three, after all—I was sure he had slept with some of them. The fact that our little romp could make him as happy as it did me was just unbelievably reassuring.

"The best, really?" I smiled at him a bit shyly. "Even though we're not... we didn't..." I couldn't quite bring myself to say it.

"It's all about who you're with," he murmured, winking.

I felt like it was only his body lying on mine that kept me from floating away.

"You know," I began hesitantly, not sure how to bring it up. "If you want... um, we could-"

He eased off me, his expression tightening slightly.

"Is something wrong?" I asked worriedly.

"No, querida," he reassured me quickly. He brushed my cheek with his fingers, studying my face, and then pulled me close and kissed me gently. I was all for getting carried away again, but he pulled back, grinning.

"Easy, Sparky."

He knew how much I hated that nickname—I swatted at him and he sprang away, laughing. I had barely begun to give chase when he turned and caught me up in his arms. He carried me back to our shade tree and sat down under it, leaning his back against the trunk and settling me sideways in his lap. I nestled against him. He had one arm around my shoulders, and his other hand went to my bare legs—I was wearing shorts. He made a sound low in his throat, almost a sound of pain.

"What?" When I looked at him his eyes were closed.

"You have the softest skin of anyone I've ever known," he explained, his voice rough. His eyes locked onto mine; they were smoldering. My stomach fluttered madly in response, but I must have still looked puzzled.

"It's very arousing," he explained.

"Oh." I didn't know what to say to that.

"Maybe a little too arousing," he continued wryly. He took his hand off my leg.

"Oh, that's right," I laughed, "because we're trying so hard not to turn each other on today."

He laughed with me, squeezing me tighter against him. The smile lingered on his face, but his eyes were serious when he spoke again.

"I still can't believe that I'm touching you like this." His fingers trailed up and down my arm, and I tried to ignore the thrill that shot through me, so I could concentrate on what he was saying.

"You don't know how long I've waited for you to do that," I confessed, turning my face into his neck to hide my blush.

"It can't be as long as I've wanted to." His voice was almost bleak. "I tried to deny it for a long time; I was so ashamed of myself for thinking of you that way."

"Why?" I asked softly. "I mean, I had reservations too, but you seemed more-"

"Stupidly stubborn?"

I kissed his jaw.

"I think 'troubled' is more accurate."

He sighed. "Tea—you're my little cousin." He didn't flinch away from the word, as I sometimes did. "I thought of you as someone I was supposed to protect, and help, and love like a sister."

"And now?"

He cupped my chin with his hand. His eyes were unapologetic; they held mine steadily as he bent his head and kissed me slowly. The butterflies invaded my stomach again, and I wondered idly how long it would take before my heart stopped trying to fling itself out of my chest every time he touched me.

"I've surrendered," he said somewhat grimly.

I made a sound of contentment and melted against him. I reveled in his closeness; I ran my hand slowly over his chest, his shoulder, and down his arm. His forearms were detailed like a Thoroughbred's, and I traced my fingers over each distinct muscle and vein. I felt a shiver go through him, and he caught and held my hand. I pressed my lips to his neck, inhaling the addictive scent of his skin; it made me want to get even closer. Maybe Jaden was getting similarly distracted, because he spoke again.

"So, when did you know, exactly?" he asked quietly.

I understood right away what he meant.

"It was that night I went downtown with Ter and Jules," I admitted somewhat hesitantly. I didn't want to remind him of how childishly I had behaved just two short months ago. As if to confirm my fears, I thought I saw him wince.

"The night I manhandled you and made you cry." His voice was flat.

I stroked his cheek, wanting to comfort him.

"That's not the way I remember it," I said. "It was so confusing at first... I did my best to ignore my feelings, but—well, we both know how well that worked out," I finished wryly.

He ran his hand down my back, pausing midway and following the curve of my ribs forward. My breathing got shaky as his hand trailed down to my stomach.

"You're thin again." His eyes were liquid with remorse.

"You're not to blame for my inability to feed myself."

In answer, he kissed each of my eyelids. "I'm sorry for every tear I made you shed."

"None of them were your fault," I protested. "I'm just not as self-sacrificing as you are. I was selfish enough to want you, no matter what the consequences."

"Disregarding consequences does sound like your m.o.," he agreed, his mouth tugging up a bit.

I felt his smile drawing me in—it made me want to touch him, kiss him again, but there were questions that I'd waited too long to have answered. I didn't want to get sidetracked, so I shifted off his lap and sat on the grass. He kept my hand in his.

"What about you? When did you know?"

"The night of that party, I already suspected that my feelings for you weren't what they should be, but I managed to justify them to myself." He glanced down at me, his eyes unreadable. "I had to make an effort not to hurt that boy, you know. The one who was plastered against you."

I tried to hide my surprise. I hadn't realized to what extent that scene had bothered him.

"But I told myself it was only natural that I felt protective of you—after all, you're young, and you had placed yourself in what was potentially a very dangerous situation." He squeezed my hand with a small smile, letting me know it wasn't a rebuke.

"Did you end up admitting it that night?"

"No, I managed to delude myself a bit longer. Until the day you tackled Davis, in fact."

His body tensed, and a shadow crossed his face. I couldn't bear to see it. I kneeled in front of him, straddling his legs, and took his face in my hands.

"Don't be sad," I whispered. I knew he was blaming himself for something he had only considered. The fact that he had never acted on the impulse didn't seem to matter to him; I didn't know what to say to make him feel better. A sudden question distracted me. "Wait—is that why you stayed away so long?"

He took my hands and held them in his.

"Yes. I was trying to get a handle on my feelings. It was my reaction that day that finally convinced me; I was so terrified you'd been hurt that I was shaking. After that I couldn't keep pretending I didn't care more than I should."

I lowered my eyes; the memory of my idiocy—and of his fury—made it hard to look at him. I studied our hands. He raised one of our entwined pairs and brushed my cheekbone with his fingers.

"I want you to know—I never thought about hurting you, querida," he said quietly. "And thank God, or I wouldn't deserve you. I'm sorry I let you believe that I did."

My eyes flew to his; a smile was growing inexorably on my face. "I *knew* it! I knew you wouldn't do that—you're way too chivalrous to ever hit a girl."

"Chivalrous?" He raised a brow.

"Don't bother denying it." I grinned at him. "But then why..." I lapsed into thought, wondering at the lie.

"Dec had already jumped to that conclusion," he explained. I could see how the thought hurt him, though he tried not to show it. "It was easier to just go with it... after all, what other explanation could I offer? I couldn't admit the truth. And in the end, I made the same decision you did, and tried to subdue those feelings."

"You still touched me, though," I said slowly. I saw surprise flit across his face. "The day you came back, you put your hand on my shoulder."

"You remember that?" He sounded amazed.

I gave a short laugh.

"Jaden, your touch is not something I can forget. Or ignore." His eyes were starting to smolder again, and I felt my pulse react. "You only stopped touching me after Stacey's party," I remembered.

"Ah, yes. Stacey's party." If those words were terse, the next ones were a growl. "I've been meaning to talk to you about that."

I was still straddling his lap; he raised his knees and I slid forward, thudding into him. His arms snaked around me, holding me fast. He rubbed his cheek against mine.

"How dare you," he growled softly in my ear, "come to a family event looking so utterly desirable, and then proceed to ignore me for the duration?"

I didn't get a chance to answer because his mouth came down on mine, the frustration he had felt that day still evident in his kiss. I was soon reciprocating just as intensely; the feeling of his body against mine had me unhinged in minutes.

We stopped to catch our breath, leaning our foreheads together.

"It seemed wiser to avoid you," I said when I could speak, "considering that what I wanted to do was this..."

I wove my hands into his hair—it was surprisingly soft—and he leaned his head back against the tree trunk, closing his eyes.

"And this..."

I kissed his eyelids, his cheekbones, his jaw. His breath was coming fast again, but then, so was mine.

"And especially, this..."

I pressed my lips to his, trying to emulate the way he had kissed me the day before. It wasn't long before we were rolling onto the grass again; I ended up lying on top of him.

"You know, I was under the impression you didn't like my new look that day," I said.

"Are you serious? Tea, when I walked into that yard and saw the girl in the yellow dress, I was attracted to her. My body reacted to hers. When you turned around, and I saw it was you, I couldn't believe it. I'd worked so hard to convince myself that you were too young—even if you weren't my cousin—and then you show up, looking not only years older, but also... delicious. I was going out of my mind."

"Delicious, really?" I brushed my lips against his; he clamped his arms around me and set about proving his words. He was very convincing—I believed him.

We lay side by side on the grass and talked. I could still scarcely believe that I could touch him anytime I wanted, and Jaden seemed similarly bemused, because he was constantly reaching for me as we spoke, stroking my hair, my face, my arms.

"What does 'querida' mean?" I asked. I'd started picking up some Spanish on the polo fields, but that wasn't a word I'd heard before.

"It means 'beloved'; I guess we use it like 'darling'," he said tenderly. I smiled; I had a new favorite word.

"What time do you need to be back?" Jaden asked finally.

"I don't have a lesson until two... it can't be that late yet." I didn't want to leave. Ever. But my traitorous stomach had other plans, because right on cue, it growled.

He laughed. "Come on, let's get you home so I can feed you."

"No," I protested, "I'd rather stay—who knows when we'll be alone like this again."

"You are not missing another meal because of me," he said. He was already getting to his feet, pulling me with him. He put his hand on my cheek. "We have all the time in the world, querida. Now that I have you, I'm not going anywhere."

Sixteen

I floated through the rest of the day without any idea what I was doing. Jaden went to the polo club, but was due back for dinner, and it was incredible that after waiting all these months, I didn't know how I was going to survive the few hours until I saw him again. Unfortunately when I did see him, we couldn't be alone. Dec was home and it was time to eat.

"So, kiddo, what's this I hear about you and Kabir?" Dec asked after we sat down. "Have you finally relented, then?"

"There's more gossip than riding going on in this place," I grumbled. It was hard not to look at Jaden, since he sat right across from me. I caught a glimpse of his face; he looked amused and aggravated at the same time. Beside me, I could feel Seth carefully not looking our way.

"Is it true?" Dec pressed.

I sighed. "No, Dec, nothing's going on with Kabir. The whole thing's been blown way out of proportion."

"Well, you could do worse," Dec asserted. "Kabir's a great kid."

Aggravation was winning out over amusement on Jaden's face now, and I gave him a small, apologetic smile when Dec wasn't looking. His answering smile was so dazzling that I was glad I was sitting down.

Later that evening we snuck out to the shed. Jaden went first; I followed a few minutes later. After bolting the door I turned to look at him hesitantly, but he opened his arms and I threw myself into them joyfully.

"Sorry about that," I murmured.

"I have only myself to blame," he sighed, holding me tight. "If I hadn't been so stubborn you wouldn't have had to resort to drastic measures."

"You know what I think?" I asked, looking up at him seriously.

"What?"

"I think it's been far too long since you've kissed me."

"An egregious lapse," he agreed.

I tilted my head up, but he didn't start with my lips. He kissed my forehead, my temple, the corner of my eye, my cheekbone, then trailed slowly down to my jaw. My arms were around his waist; I started to pull them free but he tightened his hold so I couldn't move an inch.

"Patience," he breathed in my ear, a hint of a smile in his voice.

There was a workbench along one wall; he picked me up easily and strode over to sit me on it. My arms were still captive but I wrapped my legs around his hips, pulling myself close. He brushed his cheek against mine, then took my earlobe into his mouth, and I felt his teeth press into it gently. Something between a sigh and a gasp escaped me, and I pressed myself against him as hard as I could. My heart was thudding, and the desire to feel his mouth on mine was already becoming overpowering. His mouth moved to my neck, and his tongue traced circles down to my collarbone. He kissed the hollow at the base of my throat; I could feel his warm breath on my skin, and my own was coming in shallow gasps. He skimmed his face up my throat and kissed my chin. Our eyes locked as he moved to the corner of my mouth. My lips trembled, and he finally covered them with his, kissing me softly, slowly, and relentlessly, until I thought I would faint.

When he set me back on the ground my legs were shaking.

"I think I need to sit down," I said. I couldn't believe the reaction he'd been able to evoke in me—I was in even bigger trouble than I'd thought. He gave a throaty chuckle as he supported me over to the old tack trunk in the corner.

"I must have done a good job," he said, pulling me onto his lap. His eyes were dancing.

I stared at him in outrage.

"You're a—a tease!" I accused him.

He flashed a wicked smile before murmuring in my ear, "Anticipation is half the fun."

I shot him a doubtful look before nestling my head into his shoulder. He smelled wonderful.

"I don't know how I'm going to stay in my own room tonight." I sighed.

His sigh echoed mine. "That's going to be a challenge for both of us," he agreed, "but I won't touch you in Dec's house."

"In that case, I'm glad we have a shed." I smiled at him.

"It's completely arbitrary, I know," he said. "It's bad enough we're carrying on in here."

He felt guilty, that much was obvious. I was suddenly worried.

"Are you having second thoughts?" I whispered.

"No, mi corazón," he murmured, kissing my hair.

I looked at him quizzically.

"It means 'my heart'," he said softly. "I have no regrets—we can't go back to how things were. You are my heart now."

The lump in my throat didn't allow me to speak, but I held his face in my hands and kissed him. I'm sure I was a lot less skillful than him, but he seemed to enjoy it all the same. Afterward we sat, contentedly silent, until my burgeoning anxiety prompted me to speak.

"Why do you feel guilty?"

He considered for a moment, his fingers doodling aimlessly on my shoulder blade. He answered my question with another one.

"Do you know why Dec would approve if you chose Kabir?"

"Sure—he's intelligent, respectful, obedient... Dec's probably hoping some of that would rub off on me." I snickered.

He watched me with only the ghost of a smile. "You forgot one."

"What?"

"He's seventeen." His eyes tightened with worry, and his hand seemed to go to his hair of its own accord. I reached up and took it in mine.

"I fail to see how that's in any way significant," I told him firmly.

"You're young, Tea. Sometimes... I feel like I'm taking advantage of you."

"Taking advantage of me to do what, exactly? To give me what I want most in the world, the chance to be with you?" I was speaking passionately now, needing to convince him. "Jaden, if you weren't twice as strong as me, I'd be taking advantage of *you* right now."

His brows lifted. "Twice as strong?"

"What—too high?" I teased.

He was still laughing as he carried me to the door.

I floated through the rest of the week on a cloud of happiness, living for my few stolen moments with Jaden each day. For people living in the same house, it was surprisingly difficult for us to find time alone together. For one thing, I had never before fully appreciated the extent to which the barn rats—the dedicated lesson kids—trailed behind me. They followed me constantly, and I had to develop ploys, like sending them on time-consuming errands, in order to get away.

The kids also loved Jaden; he played with them, teased them, and helped them in almost equal measure, and as a result they were dogging his footsteps, too. And naturally, we had to be extremely careful whenever Dec was around. The one time of day when we did usually see each other was during the final check of the barn at bedtime; Seth would come out with us as a cover, and Jaden and I would climb into the hayloft for a few minutes alone. But while those moments were blissful, I craved far more.

That weekend Jaden went to a polo tournament, and I took Cameo to her first big A-rated show. We were gone for the entire weekend. Teri came too, and I was overjoyed to spend time with her. She was dating Rob, the exercise rider who'd helped us the previous fall, and was very happy. I missed Jaden atrociously over the weekend, but my overall joy was so great that it seemed to buoy me through everything—Cameo couldn't put a hoof wrong and won Champion of her division. Emma and her parents were delighted, but their pleasure was nothing to mine when we got home and I spotted Jaden's car in front of the shed.

He came out to help with the unloading, and we couldn't wait—as soon as the horses were safely in the barn we stole away to the hayloft. There was enough commotion, with everyone unpacking and getting the horses settled, that our absence would likely go unnoticed.

We didn't speak for the first few minutes. When we eventually unglued our bodies we got comfortable on some haybales.

"How was the show?" Jaden inquired. He was holding my hand.

"Excellent. Cameo won Champion."

He smiled widely and leaned forward to press his firm lips quickly against mine. "Congratulations."

"How was the tournament?" I asked him.

"Great, we won every match I played in."

I rolled my eyes. "There's a surprise. You always win."

"Not always. You're my lucky charm, now that we're together I feel like I can't lose."

It was my turn to smile and kiss him. I felt exactly the same way. A knock on the trapdoor made us both jump, and I looked at him in alarm while Seth called out in a hushed voice.

"Heads up—Dec's in the barn."

"I'll go first and distract him," Jaden said quickly. I waited a few minutes before climbing down. Dec and Jaden were nowhere in sight, but my heart continued to race for a long time. Obviously, we'd have to be more careful.

Jaden left on Friday—it was Chris's birthday and they were going out, along with Ryan, to celebrate. He wandered back in on Sunday afternoon, and I could have sworn I felt his presence before he was even in the barn. I peeked around the corner when I heard him talking to Dec. He was clutching a coffee and sported two day's growth of stubble on his jaw, and although his eyes were hidden behind his shades, I got the feeling they were scanning the barn for me.

I walked into Jaden's line of sight. He kept talking, but his mouth lifted a little at the corners.

"I'm going to get changed." I heard him tell Dec. I waited a few minutes after he left before hurrying out.

I slipped into the shed carefully; there were lots of people around on the weekend.

"Corazón," Jaden breathed as he drew me into his embrace. After two days apart, I wasn't prepared for the effect of his proximity—his scent, his touch, his voice, were even more overwhelming than I'd remembered. I felt myself go weak as his lips met mine; only his arms, clasping me tightly to his body, kept me upright. By the time the kiss was over I couldn't even look at him, so I just rested my head against his chest and fought to catch my breath.

"Is my arrogance leaving you breathless again?"

I don't know why I was surprised that he recalled the incensed comment I'd flung at him last Thanksgiving; I knew by now how good his memory was. I felt his knuckles brush my cheek, and looked up to find him grinning wickedly. Somehow his gum had ended up in my mouth, and I chewed it for a minute, inhaling the scent of mint.

"I missed you," I said when I had regained my composure. "Did you have fun?"

"Some. But I missed you like crazy. I wish you could have come with us."

"Yes," I replied, laughing, "and me disappearing with you for an entire weekend wouldn't arouse Dec's suspicions in the least. Not to mention I can't even get into a bar."

"True," he admitted. "Though if I had you to myself for an entire weekend I wouldn't let you out of the house, anyway."

My stomach swooped, and I had to lean against him again. I loved the feeling of his soft cotton shirt layered over the hard muscles underneath; the combination was very seductive, somehow. As I slipped my hands under the hem I felt the thrill of electricity that contact with his skin always seemed to bring. I felt, more than heard, the sound of happiness he made low in his throat.

"I spent twenty-three years blissfully ignorant of the effect of your touch, and now two days without it feels like torture," he said, his voice rough.

"I know exactly what you mean," I said. "I think my body knew I was in love with you before I did."

He drew back, a slow smile growing on his face.

"No, wait—that came out wrong," I gasped.

He skimmed his hand from my jaw to the back of my neck, holding me in place.

"Meaning," his lips murmured against mine, "that you're not in love with me?"

I couldn't answer, mostly because he kissing me very, very tenderly. When he finally released me he looked at me expectantly.

"Well?"

It took a few minutes for me to recover enough to understand; when I did I sighed and rested my head on his chest again.

"Of course I'm in love with you, Jaden. Isn't it obvious?"

"It's still nice to hear." He took my face in his hands and pulled away just enough to capture my eyes with his molten ones.

"I love you, Tea Everson."

Dec headed into the city early the next morning because he had to be in court for the lawsuit proceedings. Jaden had a coaching gig at the Toronto club, and before he left we hid in the shed to say goodbye.

I'd been replaying Jaden's declaration of love almost continuously in my head since the day before, so I suppose it wasn't surprising that the thought arose. It was a bit awkward, though, that it occurred to me while my arms and legs were wrapped around him.

"It's a good thing we don't have the same last name, isn't it," I mused, "because that might be a bit weird."

I was sitting on the workbench; Jaden leaned back so he could see my face. He kept his hands on my hips.

"I suppose—but why would we?"

"There was some talk about it, when Dec adopted us."

His eyebrows shot up. "Dec adopted you?" He backed up a step, pulling out of my embrace and taking his hands off me.

"Well, yes... during the year my mom was sick. They thought it would make things easier, you know, in case..." I swallowed, staring at the floor. "I thought you knew."

For a second all was still, and then his arms went around me. He held me tightly; I felt his lips press into my hair.

"I didn't know," he murmured after a minute.

I wound my arms around him and hid my face in his neck. He was obviously bothered by the news, but I didn't understand why.

"It doesn't change anything, though, does it?" I hated that I felt the need to ask.

He took my face in his hands; his eyes were soft as they held mine.

"Preciosa, nothing can change my feelings for you. I'm just making a few mental adjustments, that's all. Like to the fact that legally, Dec is your father, not your stepfather."

I shrugged. "Yes, but we'd been calling him our stepfather for four years by then. It was easier to just stick with it."

"I understand. But it also means that under the law, we really are first cousins."

"So?"

"So," he said, his voice very quiet, "in some places, an intimate relationship or marriage between first cousins is illegal."

I thought about it for a minute. "In that case, I've never looked forward to breaking the law so much in my life," I said, pulling him closer. I wasn't too worried about it, and judging from the enthusiasm of his kiss, he wasn't, either.

After Jaden left, Seth and I had a relatively quiet day, since it was Monday. Dec called to check on us around nine that night, and I was just wrestling Seth over the t.v. remote when Kabir called.

"Hey, I'm heading over to Kyle's, you guys wanna come?"

Kyle was a good friend of Seth's, and was also the only boy I'd ever dated. It hadn't lasted long, and we remained friends. We joined Kabir at Kyle's for a movie marathon, and by the time we checked the clock it was two a.m. It was a half-hour drive back home, and we had to feed the horses at seven. But my heart lifted as we came up the long, treed driveway that gave the stable its name—Jaden's car was parked by the garage. I peeked through the door of the guestroom and found him asleep. I managed to resist waking him; he had been annoyingly firm in adhering to his rule of no touching in the house, and with Dec away, the temptation would be triply hard to withstand, so I went to bed.

The next morning didn't start well.

"Seth! Tea! I want you down here *now*," Dec roared.

I knew Seth's alarmed look mirrored mine. Dec's temper had been much milder of late, but if he was as angry as he sounded then I, for one, didn't trust him not to fall off the wagon. Not yet.

He was in the living room, hands on his hips and nostrils flaring. We slunk up to stand in front of him.

"I just checked my messages—I had four calls from your Gran. Apparently she came by last night to check on you, and the house was empty. She stayed until midnight waiting for you and no one showed up. She was frantic." His voice was quiet now, but with an edge of menace that boded ill for us. The barn was never supposed to be left unattended. "What do you have say for yourselves?"

"They were with me, actually," Jaden appeared in the kitchen doorway; my heart strained toward him. He loped over and faced Dec, edging casually in front of Seth and me. "I'm sorry we worried Gran, I'll call her to apologize. I suppose I should have called you, too—it was an oversight," he lied smoothly. He seemed perfectly at ease, his rueful smile totally authentic.

Dec was taken aback. "But... where were you all?"

"We went into Cambridge to meet some friends of mine, and we lost track of time."

"Well, you two should have known better." Dec shot Seth and me one last glare. "Next time, I expect a call *before* you go out, and I want you home by midnight at the latest. Ten on school nights."

"Yes, sir." We nodded dutifully.

"And Tea, would you call Kyle back, he called three times yesterday alone," he added, disgruntled. Jaden absorbed this news and turned to consider me. He looked upset.

"I'm going to call your Gran." Dec stalked to his office.

"Whew! Thanks, dude." Seth grinned at Jaden as they bumped fists. "You got this, Sis? I'll take care of the barn."

I nodded faintly, avoiding Jaden's eye.

As soon as Seth was gone Jaden faced me. "I'll see you in the shed in a minute," he said, his voice without inflection.

I got to the shed without anyone seeing me, and once inside I started pacing. I felt oddly nervous, for some reason... if I hadn't known better, I would have said that Jaden was jealous. Which was ridiculous, of course—I didn't even notice the existence of other boys since Jaden had come into my life. Still, butterflies fluttered in my stomach as the door opened and he stepped quickly inside. He slid the deadbolt into place before turning; he was expressionless as he came to stand before me.

"Is there something you'd like to tell me?" he asked.

I swallowed, not knowing quite what to say. He sighed, then took my right hand in his, interlacing our fingers. He moved our interlaced hands behind the small of my back and pulled me against his hard body. His other hand cupped my chin; his eyes were tight as they bored into mine.

"First of all, where were you last night? Gran wasn't the only one looking for you, you know."

"We went and chilled at Kyle's—we didn't think anyone would miss us. Nice cover, by the way. Thanks."

His face didn't relax. "Next time, make sure you've got an alibi, okay? And don't stay out so late. We'll be outed if I have to keep running interference with Dec."

I tried to nod, but he was still holding my chin.

"Second, why does your ex-boyfriend keep calling you?"

I managed not to laugh, though the idea of Jaden—wonderful, kind, sexy Jaden—feeling threatened by this geeky teenager was ludicrous. I couldn't contain the small giggle that escaped, though; the arm behind my back relaxed slightly as his look turned quizzical.

"He wants me to see a movie with him, that's all. No one knows I have a boyfriend, remember? And I guess he still has kind of a... a thing for me," I explained haltingly.

"And how do you feel about him?" His eyes never released mine.

"Seriously?" I was getting impatient now. "Jaden, I honestly can't tell you how I feel about Kyle because I haven't thought about him in months. You're all I think about. I love *you*."

His face relaxed, and he closed his eyes and touched his forehead to mine.

"Sorry," he whispered as his arms enfolded me, "jealousy's not very attractive, I know." I breathed in the intoxicating scent of his skin, and thought that I didn't really mind a bit of jealousy.

"Actually," I said slowly, "I find everything about you attractive."

His arms tightened around me, and he kissed my temple.

"I don't understand, though," I admitted. "Why are you jealous?"

He hesitated, and watched my face carefully as he spoke. "Partly, I suppose, because you're young. Long-term relationships aren't exactly a hallmark of the teen years, and I shudder at the thought of losing you. And your beauty will always place temptation in your path." I rolled my eyes at that patent untruth. "Mostly, though, it's just me... it's my issue. I'm working on it, I promise." He gave me a small, contrite smile, and I actually felt weak in the knees. I laughed at myself privately. I had always ridiculed the whole concept of swooning, and here I was, practically the poster girl for Swooners Anonymous. I gazed up at him.

"If I could make a suggestion, I believe your interrogation technique leaves something to be desired," I said with mock seriousness.

"Is that so?"

"It's quite lacking in kisses, for instance."

A gleam came into his eye, and he reached over slowly. Even before his skin met mine, my pulse pounded away like a racehorse out of the gate. He captured both of my wrists behind my back in one of his strong hands, and twined the other into the hair on the back of my head. He inclined his face slowly toward mine, the anticipation building until it was almost painful. When his lips finally met mine they were urgent, demanding. I responded eagerly; he soon freed my hands and I ran them up his back, under his shirt, feeling his muscles work as his hands also began roaming. They traveled from my shoulders, to my waist, to my hips—then suddenly, he slid them into the back pockets of my jeans and pulled me more tightly against him. My heart sputtered spastically. I stopped kissing him—a first—and hid my face in his chest.

"Are you okay?" He sounded concerned, and I noticed how quickly he went into 'soothing mode'. He pulled his hands out of my pockets and instead started patting my back and smoothing my hair. And I understood—he was afraid he'd spooked me, pushed me too fast. I sighed.

"Jaden, when are you going to sleep with me?"

I felt him stiffen.

"You're still young, Tea. What's your hurry?"

"I don't think I am hurrying. All of my girlfriends have already had sex-"

"Both of them, you mean?" He chuckled quietly.

"Hey, I know other girls. But it's not just them; Seth's already slept with half the swim team, for crying out loud. The entire female half."

He frowned. "Sounds like I need to have a word with that boy."

"About what, being safe? 'Cause I already give him that speech about once a week, and so does Kabir. I think he's pretty careful. As careful as Seth ever gets."

He shook his head impatiently. "It's not only about the physical risk. Your body isn't something to be shared with just anyone; if you do that—well, I think it devalues the experience."

I felt amazingly uplifted at hearing his views, as though a weight I hadn't known I was carrying had been lifted.

"Does that mean you haven't been with very many people?" I asked shyly. I couldn't look at him.

He stroked my cheek. "I thought I was conducting the interrogation here?" I could hear the smile in his voice.

"Meaning?"

"I'm not sure this is something we should discuss right now." He didn't look happy. "And in truth, the number doesn't matter, because everything's changed now. I love you."

As always, every cell in my body seemed to inflate at those words, though I noticed he still hadn't answered my question.

"Tea!" a voice yelled from outside.

I groaned. "Oh, no, it's Karen. I didn't think it was so late. She's gonna kill me, she hates it when we're not ready."

"Come on, I'll help you." He seized my hand and towed me to the door. Before opening it, he kissed me softly, then raised his eyes to mine.

"Querida, you may not be my first, but I'm hoping you'll be my last."

The subject came up again sooner than expected. Seth had a swim meet in Toronto later that week, and attending it provided the perfect cover for Jaden and me to spend a few hours alone. After dropping Seth off at the pool, Jaden and I headed to his place. It felt good to be back there, in my place of sanctuary.

We ended up talking about school. For the first time ever, Seth had gotten better grades than me in everything except chemistry and math.

"How do you get away with missing so much school?" I grumbled to Jaden, remembering how often he'd been at the barn.

"Easily," he said smugly. "I have excellent recall."

"Is that a fact?"

I was on the couch; he came and leaned across the back of it, and spoke low in my ear.

"Yes. For instance, I still remember every bad name you called me when I had you over my shoulder at the track."

I blushed at the memory. "Oh, right... sorry about that."

"I had it coming. Still, I have to admit I was surprised at your vocabulary. Or is Dec not as opposed to that kind of language anymore? I learned to duck after cursing around him."

"Trust me, he's still just as weird about it," I assured him fervently.

"In a way, I appreciate it now," he mused. "It made me find more creative ways of expressing myself."

"And look where that's gotten you—law school, eeww." I laughed and faked a shudder.

He made a grab for me, but I'd spent a lifetime dodging Seth's long arms, and I rolled off the couch and danced out of the way easily. He soon caught me, though, and proceeded to tickle me mercilessly. I tried to retaliate between shrieks but he wasn't ticklish at all... just my luck.

We tumbled back onto the couch, still laughing. Jaden pulled himself into a sitting position; I was on my knees next to him, and impulsively I straddled his lap, facing him. His startled look morphed into a hungry one as I ran my hands from his shoulders, down his chest, and over his muscular stomach. As I lifted his shirt, though, he caught and held my wrists.

"Let's keep our clothes on for now, shall we?"

"Why? I've seen you shirtless at the barn before."

"It's not the same, and you know it," he chided.

I gave a mental sigh. I had never been in a rush to have sex—I hadn't been in love, or felt the supposed peer pressure, nor been pushed by boys to accommodate them. And now that I had finally found someone I desperately wanted to make love to, his overprotective tendencies were standing in the way. So, in typically reckless fashion, I decided to embellish a bit. Okay, a lot.

"You know, Jaden," I said slowly, looking down at my captive wrists, "I think you may be under a misapprehension... about me not having sex before." I phrased it carefully so it wasn't an outright lie.

I felt him tense slightly.

"Reaaally?" He drew out the word. "Well, this is something of a surprise."

I chanced a look at his expression—it did hold surprise, but there was something else in his eyes, something I couldn't identify.

"When did this happen?" he asked conversationally.

"Um, last year... with a boy from school," I manufactured.

"I thought you and Kyle weren't serious?" he demanded. Oops—I'd forgotten about Kyle.

"We weren't. I was mostly curious; I wanted to see what all the fuss was about," I said. Which was perfectly true, in a sense—I did want to see what the fuss was about, now. "So, if you're worried about me, well, you don't have to," I finished lamely, staring at my hands again.

"I see," he said. I peeked at his face; he looked thoughtful. "Well, that changes things."

He stood suddenly, cradling me in his arms, and carried me down the hall. We were in the bedroom before I clued in; excitement coursed through me, along with a touch of apprehension, which I tried hard to keep from my face.

He deposited me on the bed, hesitating by the edge. Slowly, he stripped off his t-shirt, while I watched, my heart thudding madly. His torso was even more impressive up close, and I admired the play of muscles under his skin as he moved to lie next to me, wearing only his jeans. We locked eyes as he leaned in to kiss me, caressing my face with his hand. Our lips had barely met when he rolled on top of me; as always I loved the feeling of his body pressed into mine, but this time, in addition to my racing heart, I felt my mouth go dry. Jaden's kisses were usually slow and lingering, but his mouth was already moving down to my neck, and one hand trailed down over the swell of my breast. My breath caught in my throat. I pulled his face back up; I needed to feel his lips against mine as his hand continued downward. He had gotten as far as my zipper when he rolled us back onto our sides.

"Just how far are you planning to let me go with this?" he inquired casually.

I blinked, confused. His eyes seemed to look right through me, and his expression was exasperated.

"I—I don't know what you mean," I countered, though I was afraid that I did.

258

"Tea, look me in the eye and tell me you're not a virgin," he ordered.

I stared at him defiantly, willing myself to say the words, but once his eyes caught mine I just couldn't do it. I turned my face into the pillow, embarrassed.

We lay without speaking for a moment, until he stroked my hair and sighed, "Are you all right?"

"That depends," I mumbled into the bedding.

"On?"

"On how... easy, or not, this is for you," I said awkwardly. I hazarded a look at his face—torn between concern and confusion—and had to smile, albeit tremulously.

"I know, that barely even made sense to me," I said.

Jaden was lying with his head propped on his elbow. He leaned forward and kissed the outer corner of my eye, then skimmed his face down to my ear.

"I understand," he murmured, his voice husky, "and for the record, it's far from easy."

The tightness in my chest eased, and I threw my free arm around him and pulled myself close, burying my face in his neck. He ran his hand down my back, and as I kissed his bare shoulder I felt his heart accelerate against my chest. His lips found mine again, and although they moved slowly, gently, this time the fireworks within me ignited even faster. I mashed myself against him, hitching my knee over his hip even as I wondered whether he would object. He didn't—instead he wrapped both arms around me, holding me fast, and I felt his hips move against me, nearly driving me out of my mind.

"I want to feel your skin against mine," I whispered. He gave his head a small shake against my shoulder. I managed to wriggle my arms down to my waist, and started pulling up my shirt. He froze.

"I'm not undressing," I promised breathlessly, "just lifting it a bit... please?"

He didn't protest further, so I quickly yanked the thin fabric out of the way, and with a sigh fused the bare skin of my belly to his. He groaned, his face buried in my neck, and after only a few seconds, to my dismay, he disengaged himself gently.

"We're getting a little carried away," he warned, still breathing hard.

"I don't mind," I told him, grinning.

259

"You're unbelievable," he complained. His reproving tone probably would have been more effective if his eyes hadn't been shining so tenderly, and his hand hadn't caressed my arm so softly.

"Tell me something," he said, "what if I had believed you earlier? What if I had gone ahead and... Weren't you nervous?" His eyes were serious now.

I held his gaze. I wanted to deny it—my nerves weren't going to help my case—but I also felt a new compulsion to be truthful with him.

"Yes, I was. Very."

"But you wouldn't have stopped me." It wasn't a question.

"No."

He leaned in, suddenly intense, and cupped my face with his hand.

"Tea, that's crazy. We're together now; there's no need to hide your feelings from me anymore. And you don't have to trick me to get me to sleep with you. In fact," he laughed softly, "it may be quite a trick for me to wait."

"Why *are* we waiting, then?"

He studied me, the same tender expression he'd worn earlier warming his face. "For one thing, we haven't been together long. There's no reason to rush the physical aspect of our relationship."

I nodded; that seemed reasonable. Frustrating, but reasonable.

"For another," he said, hesitating, "I've never been anyone's 'first' before. I want to do it right." He watched me, slightly anxious, as though confessing to a major shortcoming. Joy swept through me at his revelation.

"Really?" I smiled, kissing the corner of his mouth. "So—in a way—it's a first time for you, too." I felt his lips pull up into a smile under my mouth.

"Yes, it is," he murmured. "A very momentous 'first', because I hope to be making love to you for a long time to come."

At that I started kissing him in earnest, wrapping my arms around his neck and rolling him onto his back. Something wasn't right, though, and as we broke apart I rested my head on his shoulder, sighing as I identified the source of my discomfort. I was ashamed—Jaden had obviously deliberated this question, and his reasons for waiting were perfectly valid. I felt not only immature but almost... treacherous, for having tried to deceive him. I placed my hand on his chest, over his heart.

"I'm sorry I lied to you," I said in a small voice. "I won't do it again."

His hand covered mine. "I know," he said simply.

There was a pause.

"So, um, how long do you think..."

He laughed. "When the time is right, we'll know. But for now," he sat up, pulling me with him, "we'd better get off this bed. I think we've courted temptation enough for one day."

Seventeen

We were off to another show that weekend, and Seth had gotten into the finals at his swim meet. Which was great, except that he was supposed to be helping at the show.

"Why don't I come help you?" Jaden offered, when I complained I'd be short-handed.

"Are you sure?" I asked doubtfully. "It'll probably be boring for you."

A day of hard work at a horse show was a far cry from Jaden's usual role when playing polo. At the tournaments, he hopped onto horses that were groomed, tacked up and warmed up for him. All he had to do was ride onto the field and play, and afterward go hobnob and drink champagne.

"I'll be there," he assured me.

Jaden arrived in time to watch Emma win third place in her equitation class.

"Can you help Emma put Chip away?" I asked him. "I've got to get ready for my classes with Cameo."

When Cameo was ready I went into the tackroom of our temporary stabling to find my riding jacket. Julia was lounging on one of the folding chairs, yawning. I was just pulling on my jacket when Jaden walked in; he stopped dead at the sight of me. I sighed.

"I know, it makes me look about twelve," I grumbled. "Karen insists that I wear them in the pony divisions, she says it's more appropriate than breeches and boots." I was wearing jodhpurs and paddock boots, the garb that children traditionally wear.

"Karen likes it because it makes the judges think you're younger," Julia said placidly. "It works, don't you think?" She directed her query at Jaden.

He swallowed. "Yes, definitely. I feel like a pervert for ever even thinking you were hot," he said to me.

"And yet he's still checking out your ass," Julia stage-whispered to me, giggling.

Outside, Jaden gave me a leg up onto Cameo. "Good luck, little girl." He grinned and winked at me.

Jaden's wish for me came true; Cameo was fabulous, and won Reserve Champion. The only ones to beat us were Teri and Picasso, so my mood was jubilant when I ran into Robin on my way to the washrooms.

"Tea, you're just the girl I was looking for. Could you catch-ride a horse for me?"

Robin was a friend of Karen's. She was a good coach, but she and Dec didn't get along—I had a feeling there was a story there, although I wasn't privy to it. He wouldn't be happy if I rode one of her horses... still, it couldn't hurt to find out more.

Robin filled me in on the details on our way to the schooling ring; the horse was entered in the 1.25 meter jumper class. Most of the older coaches still talked in feet and inches, but all horse shows were now metric to conform to international standards.

"His rider just got hurt, but I'll hop on and show you how he goes, and then you can decide," Robin said cheerfully.

She rode up a minute later on a massive bay horse with three flashy white legs and a stripe down his long nose. It quickly became apparent why his rider might have been hurt; it had been a long time since I'd seen such an intractable horse at a show. He threw up his head and shied, tried bolting, and pranced sideways when he should have been walking. I was about to tell Robin to forget it when she started jumping him—and then I couldn't speak, because my mouth was hanging open. He was enormously powerful, his hind legs propelling him upward like rockets. He overjumped everything by a mile, and he wasn't particularly tight with his legs, but then, he didn't need to be because there was no chance of him touching the fence. This horse had potential stamped all over him in neon.

"What do you think?" Robin chirped as she pulled up.

"How long do I have before his class?" I needed time for some schooling with this horse.

"About an hour."

"Okay, I'll do it. I'll be right back."

I ran back to our stabling to make sure my students were taken care of, and to let Jaden know I'd be gone for a while.

"Hold on a second," he said, frowning. "What do you know about this horse?"

"I saw him go, and I know his rider's coach. It's okay, Jaden. I take catch-rides sometimes, it's extra money."

"I'll come with you."

I hesitated. "You don't need to, really. The kids need you here." Before the words were out of my mouth I knew I'd said the wrong thing; he stared at me suspiciously, saying nothing.

"Fine, then, come on," I muttered.

Robin was still riding the bay horse when we got back to the schooling ring.

"That's your catch-ride?" Jaden turned on me in disbelief. "That snorting, plunging monster?"

I nodded.

"No," he said flatly.

I bristled. "What do you mean, no?" I demanded.

He crossed his arms and stared at me in frustration. "Do you remember when Karen asked you to ride that bucking bronc? I wanted to say no to you then, Tea. I wanted to have the *right* to stop you."

"And you think you have that right now?" Because I certainly thought differently.

"At the very least, I deserve a say when you make a decision to risk your life," he said, his voice sharp.

"I already told her yes. I'm not backing out now."

He glared at me.

"What was I supposed to do, Jaden? Run all over the showgrounds looking for you so I could ask your *permission*?"

He flinched. "It's not like that. I just don't want you to get hurt."

"Yeah, thanks for the vote of confidence," I said bitterly.

"Don't take that tone with me," he snapped, angry now. "I'm not casting aspersions on your skill. It doesn't matter how good you are, you don't have enough time. You can't retrain the horse in the schooling ring."

"You're right—time is short. So I'd better go."

I turned and headed toward my mount, feeling deflated and small after our argument. A hand on my elbow turned me around; he studied me silently for a moment before speaking.

"Just promise me you'll withdraw if he's too much for you," he said. "There's no shame in that."

For you, I thought, but I nodded. He gave me a lopsided smile that wreaked immediate havoc with my body—I wished so much that I could kiss him. Worry was still clear in his eyes.

"Don't worry on my account." I grinned at him. "I hear only the good die young."

He rolled his eyes, but looked marginally more cheerful as he headed back to supervise my students.

I had no time to dwell on Jaden's unhappiness, because the horse—whose name, appropriately, turned out to be Hades—required every last bit of my strength and skill to manage. The shying and jogging and head-tossing I could handle, but he had one habit that repeatedly threw me off balance, and it was something I'd never encountered before. Every so often he would grab the bit and wrench his head downward, jerking me violently forward. He was a huge horse, with a tremendously powerful neck. I had no hope of stopping him, and not much time to convince him to trust my hands enough not to yank on them. I tried, though—I rode him as gently as I could, keeping a very soft contact with his mouth. When I started jumping him I nearly laughed aloud; the feeling of barely contained power exploding underneath me was unbelievable. Even Blaze hadn't had this kind of voltage.

My number was called far before I felt ready. I rode past Alex at the in-gate; I'd barely seen him this season but we'd exchanged a few words earlier.

"Good luck, Tea," he called out. He looked concerned.

I went into the ring with my heart racing. Hades snorted and raised his head as I pointed him toward the first line of obstacles. He jumped it fantastically, but on landing he wrenched his head down hard and I felt a ripping pain in my right shoulder. I had to ignore it, though, because our next fence was coming up. We raced through the rest of our course; I could barely steer Hades and I couldn't slow him down, because my shoulder didn't seem to be working properly, but we stayed on course and, thanks to his incredible thrust, we didn't have any rails down. I gritted my teeth to keep from crying as we walked out; now that the class was over he seemed perfectly relaxed, and cruised out quietly on a loose rein.

The rest of the afternoon was very busy, and I was able to hide my injury until we got home. As I was unloading Splash from the trailer he pulled my arm, and a whimper escaped me before I could quash it.

Jaden's head whipped around. When he noticed that I was holding the lead rope in my left hand he came and grabbed it huffily. I followed him into the barn as he led Splash to his stall, furtively rotating my shoulder to assess the damage. Jaden emerged still scowling, and planted himself in front of me with his arms crossed.

"You do realize this is precisely what I was worried about, don't you?" He kept his voice low, but I was upset by his anger—I had gotten used to Jaden comforting me right away when I was troubled or hurt. I spun around and stomped away. Jaden fell into step next to me; he put his hand on my good shoulder but I shrugged him off. I was marching to the house as fast as I could, yet he kept pace with me casually.

"Why don't you leave me alone," I snapped.

"I want to check your shoulder," he replied easily. He was already over his fit of pique.

"And you happen to have an x-ray machine in your pocket?" I grumbled. I wasn't really angry anymore, though. My shoulder hurt, and I wanted to be alone to lick my wounds.

"You know I've had some experience with shoulder injuries."

"Fine," I conceded with poor grace.

We went to the upstairs bathroom and inspected my shoulder; it didn't seem serious, but something was definitely pulled. Only afterward did Jaden notice I was still wearing gloves.

"Don't freak out," I said pleadingly as I slowly eased them off.

He winced when he saw my hands, but to my relief, didn't say anything. I started running cold water over the skinned and bleeding parts of my hands—I'd forgotten to wear gloves while riding Hades, and the braided reins had done some damage. Jaden rummaged in the medicine cabinet. When I was done washing, he applied ointment and bandages more gently than I would have thought possible. He didn't say anything until he was done.

"Why didn't you pull up when you got hurt?"

I felt the weight of guilt pressing down on me at the thought of my broken promise.

"It didn't happen until the end."

"Liar," he said without heat. He started to pull my chin up, looking for my eyes. I jerked it away, annoyed.

"Why do you always do that?"

"Because," he said with perfect confidence, "your eyes can't lie to me."

266

Which was entirely true. I just wished he hadn't noticed.

"It happened right after that first line—you know, when he almost yanked me out of the saddle in the corner," I admitted.

"I was with your students, remember?"

"Liar," I said softly. I looked up at him. "I saw you watching my round." A small, tender smile grew on my face. His own softened in response and his hand brushed my cheek, seemingly oblivious to the open bathroom door.

"And you kept going because..." he prompted.

"Come on, Jaden," I said, gently reproving. "We're both athletes—you can't tell me you've never pushed through pain before."

He watched me stubbornly for a minute, then sighed and gingerly took my hand.

"All right, I have. But I find the thought of you doing it frankly disturbing. Besides which, it was entirely unnecessary today. That wasn't even your own horse, you didn't have anything to gain."

"I gained six hundred dollars, doesn't that count as something?"

"Money is nothing compared to your safety," he stated emphatically. He was starting to look decidedly huffy again. "Anyway, if you need money, you can always come to me, Tea. You know that, don't you?"

I shook my head. "Thanks, but I don't want your money, Jaden."

He closed his eyes. "Is it really necessary to argue with me about everything?"

It was my turn to sigh. I'd upset him enough; it was time to be honest, no matter how it rankled. I placed my hand on his cheek, and he opened his eyes reluctantly.

"You were right," I said sincerely.

His expression brightened; I had to smile a bit at his reaction.

"I can't tell you how it thrills me to hear those words coming from your lips," he said, "but about what, precisely?"

"Pretty much everything," I conceded. "That horse was too strong for me. I didn't have enough time to work with him before going into the ring. It wasn't safe..."

For a second, he seemed to be trying to contain his delight at my admission. Then, to my shock, he leaned over, closed the bathroom door, and locked it. He then sat me on the counter, wrapped his arms around me, and kissed me. Deliberately. Inside the house. The shock quickly gave way to other, warmer feelings, but when I wrapped my legs around him he pulled away.

"Why don't you stay here and rest your shoulder," he suggested, "and I'll go back to the barn and help the kids."

The horses' shipping bandages needed to be taken off, they had to be fed, and the equipment had to be put away.

"Thanks," I said. I leaned forward and stole a quick kiss before sliding to the floor. "But it would make Dec suspicious if I didn't go back."

"Why? Aren't you going to tell him what happened?" He frowned.

"Well, there doesn't seem to be much point... I mean, it's done with now, it would only upset him unnecessarily." I looked at him hopefully.

"You know, querida, if you and Dec are going to develop a new dynamic, at some point you're going to have to start trusting him."

"I know. And I realize that he won't react the way he used to, but he'll still be mad, and I'm too tired to deal with that tonight."

"All right," he said, resigned. "I won't say anything."

I knew he disapproved, but he didn't show it. I thought about that as we made our way to the barn. Jaden had trusted my judgment today, twice. He was changing, growing into our relationship. I wasn't sure I could say the same.

I managed to keep my injuries inconspicuous while we were in the barn. However, we had barely sat down to a late dinner when Dec noticed my bandaged hands.

"What happened to your hands, kiddo?" he asked, taking one of them and turning it over to view the damage.

I didn't look at Jaden. I kept my eyes squarely on Dec and told him matter-of-factly.

"I got a catch-ride at the show today. The horse was a bit strong for me, and I didn't have gloves on. He tugged on my bad shoulder a bit, too."

Dec looked startled, though whether by the information or my candor, I didn't know. To my right, I could feel Seth stiffen. Gran was shaking her head and tut-tuting.

"But... why'd you take it, if the horse was too much for you?" Dec asked.

"Mostly because I miss the jumper ring," I said. "But I thought it would be easy money, too."

He frowned at me for a moment, his eyes appraising. There was an edge to his voice when he spoke again. "We've talked about this, Tea. Karen wasn't there to advise you—you should have been with your students, not out taking risks on strange horses."

I nodded. "I know. It was bad judgment on my part," I admitted.

Dec couldn't hide his surprise this time, but after surveying me with raised brows for a minute, he turned to Jaden, frowning again.

"Where were you while she was engaging in this foolishness?"

"He was with the kids," I answered quickly. "He didn't know what I was doing."

I allowed myself a glance at Jaden. His eyes held mine for an immeasurable moment, but I couldn't fathom the expression in his. Whatever he was feeling, though, it was powerful.

I turned back to Dec.

"So how did you do in the class?" he inquired.

He was perfectly calm. His tone was conversational, curious. I blinked in surprise before answering.

"Um, not bad... we were third. Out of thirty-four."

"And the money?"

"Six hundred dollars." I grinned.

Dec nodded thoughtfully. "Just make sure this is the last time, Tea."

"Yes, please be more careful, dear. You've been injured quite enough," Gran added worriedly.

"Okay," I told them as normally as possible.

Seth kicked me under the table and gave me an 'I can't believe you pulled that off' look. Jaden's face, though, was still inscrutable.

After dinner I went to check on the horses we'd brought with us that day. They were all content, munching their hay and relaxing. Even though it was already dark, it was a balmy evening and several boarders were still in the aisles, so I didn't pay attention to the footsteps until hands came from behind me and caught my shoulders.

"Just wait until I get you alone," Jaden breathed into my ear.

My stomach wobbled.

"I'll be in the shed," he added. I listened to his footsteps fade before turning around.

I waited a minute before following. When I peeked through the front door some boarders were standing next to their cars chatting, and I fidgeted anxiously while waiting for them to finish. It seemed to take forever. When they finally drove away I hurried over to the shed, looking over my shoulder, but no one else appeared.

I slipped through the door. Before I turned around I felt his hand on the nape of my neck; I had barely faced him when his lips found mine. He pulled me close, and for a minute kissed me so lovingly that I felt like I would melt and form a puddle on the floor. When he stopped I opened my eyes slowly. He was looking at me with the same intense expression I'd noticed at the dinner table.

"I'm proud of you," he said, caressing my cheek.

I leaned into his hand. "Tell me—was the kiss my reward for good behavior?"

"You could say that," he allowed with a smile.

"I told the truth about my shoulder too, did you notice? Though I didn't have to..." I hinted.

"Hmm, that's right," he murmured.

The heat in his eyes made my breath catch. He cupped my chin in one hand, and used the other to brush the hair back from my face. He kissed my forehead, and I closed my eyes. I was already trembling in anticipation. The kisses followed my hairline, but from my temple, all of a sudden, his mouth was at my ear, hot, whispering my name.

"Tea..."

I exploded.

I threw my arms around his neck and crushed my lips against his, pressing my body into him as hard as I could. Fortunately he lifted me up; I think I would have climbed his body otherwise. My legs wrapped around his waist. My lips parted, and when his didn't follow suit right away, I traced the tip of my tongue along them until he succumbed with a moan. After a few minutes he sat me on the workbench, and we leaned together.

"Ow." The throbbing pain in my shoulder intruded on our moment, and I rubbed it ruefully.

"Querida, I'm so sorry, I forgot," he said, immediately contrite.

I chuckled. "I'm the one who practically assaulted you," I reminded him.

He kissed my shoulder, looking worried. "Let's get you inside and get some ice on it."

"I'd rather stay here with you."

In answer, he set me carefully on the ground, took my hand, and headed for the door.

Between repeated applications of Jen's homeopathic remedies, a treatment from Stephanie, and a week of rest, my shoulder was well enough for me to play in one chukker of the next weekend's practice game. It was a casual, slow chukker, and at one point Mateo took a wild swing, completely missed the ball, and almost whacked his pony in the head.

"Hey Mateo," I yelled, laughing, "como se dice 'that shot really sucked' en Español?"

He turned and galloped straight at me; before I knew it he had yanked me off Schweppes and was cantering off the field with me. I was getting really tired of polo players with forearms like iron bars—I was going to have bruises on my ribs. We were both laughing, though, as he conceded to bring me back to my pony.

I suspected Jaden would have something to say about the incident, but his comment wasn't what I expected.

"Have you been learning Spanish from Mateo?" he asked casually after the game. I could see the effort he expended not to seem bothered.

"A little, here and there," I replied carefully. In fact I'd been learning as much Spanish as I could, both at the club and online.

Jaden faced me; I froze as he held me with that powerful, unwavering gaze of his.

"*I* can teach you Spanish, Tea."

"I know you can, querido, but you have far more compelling things to teach me," I reminded him. "You're showing me things I can't learn from anyone else."

His eyes went from worried to molten in an instant; it looked as though a lesson would take place that very second. I felt myself flush in response, and was about to throw myself at him when I remembered where we were. Still on the polo grounds, surrounded by witnesses. I restrained myself with difficulty; I was already growing weary of all the subterfuge.

A few days later, Seth dropped a magazine on the kitchen table in front of me. It took me a second to realize why he did; it was one of those magazines you see in supermarket checkout stands—the kind I never read. My eye was caught by the small picture inset on the cover, under the headline, "The Hot Men of Polo, p. 24". It was a picture of Jaden.

I flipped quickly to the article. It gave only a superficial rundown of the sport, but gushed at length about the men who played the game. It was followed by a short biography of ten top players, including a picture and some vital stats. Jaden was the only one I knew.

He got back from the club soon afterward, and found Seth and I in the living room.

"Jaden, can I talk to you for a minute?" My jaw was clenched; the words came out distorted.

"Uh-oh," Seth advised Jaden under his breath, "I've seen that look before... I'd run if I were you, bro."

Jaden punched him on the shoulder. "Thanks for the confidence," he said drily.

He motioned me to the door, letting me lead the way to the shed. I turned on him the second the door was bolted.

"Don't you think a little heads-up was warranted here?" I demanded, brandishing the magazine.

He shrugged. "I forgot about it."

"You *forgot* you were interviewed, photographed, and going to be featured in a magazine?" I said incredulously.

"Yes," he replied a touch impatiently, "I forgot. We did the photoshoot months ago, and in case you haven't noticed, I've had other things on my mind."

He held his hands out, palms up, and tilted his head a bit, a heart-stopping smile on his face. I could feel the charm being turned on; it was an almost irresistible magnetic force, drawing me in, but I held fast. I crossed my arms, eyes narrowed, and glared at him. He sighed.

"Tea, I don't understand. It's just an article; it's not my first, and it probably won't be the last. What's the problem?"

"The problem," I hissed, "is that under 'status' it says 'single'. As if you don't have enough groupies flinging themselves at you already!"

"You have a few groupies of your own," he pointed out, frowning slightly.

"My groupies are all girls!" I almost shouted.

He flashed his wicked smile. "So are mine."

"Oh, this is *so* not funny!" I growled at him.

"I think it is, actually." He closed the distance between us, grinning. I spun around, turning my back on him. I wasn't ready to be appeased yet. He held my shoulders, pulling me back against him, and spoke low in my ear.

"I thought I was the jealous one." It sounded like he was still smiling. He ran his hands slowly from my shoulders down to my wrists, and back again. His hands left a trail of heat on my skin; I could feel myself softening, melting back into him.

"It's just... those girls are so beautiful. I know you must get propositioned all the time, and now everyone will think you're available, and it will get even worse," I tried to explain.

He wound his arms around my waist and started kissing my neck. I tilted my head to give him better access before I caught myself.

"Stop cheating," I protested feebly, "this is no way to fight."

"I don't want to fight," he murmured against my skin between kisses. "I want to remind you that you have nothing to worry about, from groupies or anyone else."

He was kissing my jaw now, and moving toward my ear. Little shivers of pleasure were making it hard for me to concentrate.

"And why is that?" I managed to ask eventually.

"Tea." My name came out in a sigh. He turned me around so I was facing him. "Don't you know me better than that by now?" His tone was gently chiding. "Sometimes the attention is flattering, I won't deny it. But that's not why I play. I'm *yours*, Tea—yours only—and I'll be yours for as long as you want me."

His eyes were intense, willing me to believe him. Relief washed through me. Hearing him state things so plainly erased all my doubts— Jaden wouldn't lie to me. I knew that the way I knew the sun would rise in the east.

"You weren't done reminding me, were you?" I murmured, pulling his face down to mine. He resisted for a minute, teasing me, gliding his hands slowly up and down my body.

"Don't make me come up there," I threatened.

"First jealousy, now threats," he chuckled. "I'm seeing a whole new side of you today." He sat me on the workbench, smiling at the worried look on my face. "I like it," he whispered against my cheek.

I wrapped my arms and legs around him, pulling him as close as I could. He spent a few more minutes being very, very convincing; by this point I was breathless... and wanted more. I lifted my shirt, then his, just enough so I could feel the bare skin of his hard stomach against mine. To my chagrin, he tensed and pulled away almost immediately.

"You know what the feel of your skin does to me," he reminded me, disapproval clear in his voice.

"Yes, I do," I agreed angelically, "and thank goodness, otherwise you'd have *all* the power."

The following week we went to play club chukkers, and the ride gave us some private time to talk. Dec had just finished a big project, but he'd immediately taken on another contract, and was away a lot during the week.

"Sometimes I feel as though I'm living with the embodiment of the two major male stereotypes," I sighed.

"Which are?"

"That guys think mostly about their careers, and getting laid. Not necessarily in that order."

"That's very flattering, Tea," he said drily. "Though I can see how Seth and Dec might leave you with that mistaken impression."

I smiled and reached over to take his hand off the reins. "*You*, on the other hand, are the most multi-faceted man I've ever met. In fact, you're such a Renaissance Man that you're giving me a complex."

Because of the club chukkers, we did the bedtime check of the barn late that night, and the minute we stepped inside, I knew something was off. I hesitated, listening—then I ran toward the sound of acute respiratory distress. I pinpointed it in Casey's stall and flung open the door. His head was hanging, and every breath was obviously taking enormous effort—he was sweating, and his limbs trembled. He gave a labored cough.

"Damn," Jaden said, "I'll call the vet." He took off for the tackroom.

I felt along Casey's throat for obstructions, not really expecting to find any. I'd suspected for a while that he had breathing issues, but I'd never seen such a bad respiratory attack.

Jaden ran back. "She's on her way."

That was good news, but Kathy's office was twenty minutes away. I sprinted to the medicine cabinet and quickly scanned the medications... there was nothing for asthma attacks, but I had a flash of inspiration. I grabbed a bottle and syringe and dashed back. I drew the fluid into the syringe and tapped it, making sure there were no air bubbles inside.

"You'll have to try to hold him steady," I said.

"Wait—what are you giving him?" Jaden asked.

"Bute." Bute was short for Phenylbutazone, a common medication around stables.

"But that's a painkiller!" he said worriedly.

"It's also an anti-inflammatory, and the only one we've got that will be fast-acting, because I'm injecting it," I muttered as I pressed my thumb into the jugular groove on the neck. I waited for the swelling that would indicate blood pooling above my thumb.

"Are you sure about this?" he pressed.

I met his eyes. "No. But I don't think he can make it until the vet comes. Hold him, please."

I gave mental thanks for Jaden's strength as he supported Casey's head and, despite Casey's continued coughing, managed to keep him fairly still while I inserted the needle into the vein. A burgundy ribbon flowed over my hand; I attached the syringe, pulled back the plunger and checked that blood flowed in. Then I depressed the plunger slowly. I don't think I breathed until I withdrew the needle.

We patted Casey as we watched for any change. It seemed to take a very long time, but was probably only two minutes before he shook his head. He coughed again, then straightened up his stance somewhat and looked at me.

"Whew," I breathed. "You scared us, buddy." My hands were still shaking, but Casey was definitely improving now. I smiled up at Jaden, and found him gazing at me with a look of wonderment. He pulled me into a hug.

"Whoa! Careful," I warned, quickly moving my hand. "I'm still holding the needle."

He chuckled and released me. "I can't believe you just did that. Where did you learn to give IV injections?"

"The vet showed me."

When Kathy arrived she examined Casey while we explained what had happened; when I got to the part about injecting the Bute she laughed.

"You have good instincts, Tea. It's probably the one thing you could have done, given what you had to work with."

Casey's close call kept me up that night. I kept imagining how Dec would react if he discovered my secret. That the news might incite him to violence was something I'd already considered, and accepted. My worries this time went beyond the joined bubble of Jaden and me. What if Dec tried to forbid the relationship? I couldn't imagine leaving the barn; I loved every one of those horses like my own. Sure, Seth and Dec would meet their basic needs if I were gone... but I was the one who gave them special treats, coddled them when they were sick or injured, and understood their relationships with each other. I was the one who was good in an emergency. Dec could make my life miserable at home, but if I left, I wouldn't be the only one to suffer.

It was August, and suddenly every day felt like a clock ticking down to the dreaded time when school would dictate that I only see Jaden on weekends—if that. We spent every possible minute together, although our need to be discreet made it challenging. So when Dec went out one afternoon and told us not to expect him until late, we headed straight for the hayloft, to the corner that Jaden had cleared out for us behind a big pile of bales. It gave us an extra measure of privacy; if anyone climbed up we would hear them, but they wouldn't be able to see us unless they searched somewhat. There was a flat area made up of a few bales, and my pulse spiked upward when I noticed the addition of a blanket. I gave Jaden a questioning look.

"Your skin's so delicate," he explained, "I noticed you got scratched last time."

"And... my skin will be exposed?" I hardly dared believe it; I searched his face carefully.

"Don't get carried away," he chided. He smiled at my look of frustration, and took my face in his hands. "I was thinking of your arms and legs, since you persist in wearing as little as possible around me."

"It's summer," I reminded him. "Besides, I've got to use whatever meager weapons I have at my disposal."

He raised a brow as I wound my arms around him.

"Weapons? Are we at war, then?"

His beautiful face was getting closer; my heart galloped faster with every inch of approach.

"Not war, more like a minor conflict. One in which you always have the upper hand," I said, only mildly sour.

"Well then," he whispered, "let the battle begin."

We sank onto the blanket-covered bales, and I had to smile at the thought that even indoors, we always seemed to be lying on grass. We didn't touch in the house, of course, and the shed was even less comfortable than the barn. What little time Jaden and I spent horizontal was either out in the fields or in the hayloft.

My musings were cut short as Jaden trailed his hand slowly up my arm, over my shoulder, to the back of my neck. I closed my eyes with a shiver; all the hairs on my body were already standing up. I felt his lips on my shoulder. He lowered me onto my back as his mouth followed the line of my collarbone. I wove my fingers into his hair as he kissed the hollow above the bone and started moving up my neck. My breathing was growing uneven, and I was already growing desperate to feel his body against mine. I freed my hands from his hair and tried to pull him on top of me, but he didn't budge.

"A little longer, querida," he murmured.

"Tease," I accused him, smiling against his cheek.

His hand was on my hip, and on impulse I took it and slid it under my shirt. It wasn't there a second; before I could blink my arms were above my head and one of Jaden's hands was clamped firmly around my wrists.

"Naughty," he admonished with a trace of a smile.

We locked eyes as he lowered his head slowly, pausing when he was so close I could feel the warmth of his lips above mine. I'd had enough; I arched up and closed the distance. It seemed that Jaden had reached his limit, too—the instant my mouth met his he covered me with his body, freeing my hands, and I used them to pull him against me as hard as I could. My pulse was loud in my ears, and for a few endless minutes all that existed, all that mattered, was Jaden.

When we were both panting he rolled us onto our sides. I caressed his face; I felt like I was melting with love.

"Te quiero, Jaden," I murmured.

His eyes burned into mine. "I love you too."

"You know what I find interesting about 'te quiero'," I said as casually as I could, "is that it's used to say 'I love you', but it also means 'I want you'."

He smoothed my hair back from my face, and let his hand rest on my neck.

"It depends on the context," he agreed.

My heartbeat got louder. I swallowed nervously.

"I want you, Jaden." My eyes never left his; I saw the flare of answering desire dilate his pupils before he squeezed his eyes shut and pulled me against him.

"We've talked about this, Tea," he whispered against my hair. "It's too soon. I don't think we're ready for that yet."

"Speak for yourself," I grumbled. "I couldn't be more ready. And it doesn't help that you're always leading me on, either."

"It will be worth the wait," he purred. He gave me a look of such scorching promise that my stomach lurched and I was flooded with longing for him again. I pulled away from him and dropped onto my back, covering my face with my hands.

"Aargh."

He tugged one of my hands away and held it in his. "I guess the blanket was a bad idea," he said ruefully.

"What? No... it's nice to be comfortable." Not that I really noticed where I was, when I was pressed up against him. "How come we never go to your place anymore?" I asked suddenly. Now that I was thinking of comfort and Jaden in the same sentence, it seemed the obvious answer.

"We haven't really had time," he said evasively. He didn't meet my eyes.

"We could make time."

He hesitated, looking torn.

"I don't think us going to my place would be wise right now," he admitted finally.

Understanding came to me in a rush.

"You've been avoiding it," I guessed, and saw the truth of it in his eyes. "Because... you're as tempted as I am." I could hardly believe it.

His eyes held mine wordlessly for a minute, before one corner of his mouth tugged up slightly. "Possibly even more so."

"Then, why..." I was too shocked to even finish my sentence.

He pulled me close again before answering.

"For all the reasons we've discussed. You're young. So is our relationship. We have the stress of keeping it secret to deal with. And... you've had a difficult year, mi amor. A sexual relationship brings with it a whole new set of concerns; you don't need anything extra to deal with right now."

"Making love to you can only improve my year," I said with certainty.

His expression softened, and he kissed me sweetly for a moment. Which, of course, only made me want him more.

"Far be it for me to pressure you," I sighed.

Jaden was playing in another tournament at the Toronto club, and since it was a rare weekend with no show for me, I went to watch him. It hadn't occurred to me, however, that Summer might attend for the same reason.

I was with the grooms before the match, so I looked on from a distance as Jaden kissed Summer's cheek. She put her arm around his waist, and I gritted my teeth before he disengaged himself smoothly and headed toward her father. I was across the field, but I could see clearly when Summer stopped Jaden by putting her hand on his arm. He leaned toward her, and she spoke close to his ear. He didn't pull his arm away, I noticed bitterly. I wondered if this went on at every match—I wasn't usually there to see it.

I didn't say anything about it, but I didn't go back on Sunday, using backed-up lessons as an excuse. It wasn't that I was jealous, exactly, but I didn't want to watch their exchanges, and I couldn't distract Jaden by asking about it while he was in the middle of a tournament. So the question only came up on Sunday night, when we were finally alone in the hayloft. Jaden was tired from a hard weekend; maybe that's what made him sound so impatient when I asked him.

"David is the team patron, the whole team depends on his support to play, and it's my livelihood. I need to use a certain amount of discretion when it comes to dealing with his daughter."

"Which means what, exactly?"

He hesitated. "I think that Summer is hoping we'll resume our relationship."

I broke into a sweat; my heart constricted, but it managed to race all the same. "And what have you told her about that?"

"I haven't said anything—I haven't encouraged her in that belief, if that's what you mean." He was frowning.

"You know," I said slowly, "it occurs to me that you're a very good liar, especially for someone so averse to dishonesty."

He just waited, brows pulled together, for me to go on. I swallowed; I wasn't sure that I even wanted an answer to my question.

"So I'm wondering," I continued softly, not looking at him, "who are you lying to? Summer, or me?"

"What kind of question is that?" he demanded. "I've never lied to either of you."

"You lied to her with your body, Jaden, when you kissed her at the gallery. And when you don't pull away from her, all those times she touches you." My voice was even quieter now. "Either that, or it's me you're not being honest with."

My voice broke then, and I spun away from him, but he caught my wrist and yanked me back. I thudded against him; the hardness of his body still sometimes surprised me, especially when it was coiled, as now, with tension. Or was it anger? I raised my eyes to his warily. I felt his hand on the back of my head, twining into my hair.

"Do not," he growled fiercely, "suggest to me that I don't love you. After everything we've been through, everything we're risking to be together—don't you *dare* suggest that."

His eyes sparked with anger, but the love shining behind it was unmistakable. That look was impossible to doubt, and the rush of emotion that swept over me at the sight of it left me weak. I put my free hand on his cheek; he was still gripping one wrist tightly.

"Lo siento," I said softly. I could feel the remorse in my eyes.

It felt more appropriate to apologize in Spanish. I wanted him to be unable to doubt my sincerity, as I no longer doubted his. For a second his eyes widened in surprise. Then he trapped my face in his hands and kissed me in a way that left no room for uncertainty of any kind. When I was completely breathless he released me. I sat on a bale, but Jaden was too wound up; he started pacing.

"I didn't mean to upset you," I said quietly.

"I'm not upset. It's just that... Tea, for you to harbor doubts about something so basic means you have no concept of my feelings for you. I was with Summer for a year, I thought I loved her, but you..." He paused, and his hair suffered in his agitation. "There's no comparison. You were *made* for me, Tea; you're my perfect match. I love everything about you—your incisive mind, your compassion, your stubborn pride. I love the way you look like an angry urchin one minute and a beautiful woman the next. I love watching you press your lips together to keep from smiling when you're trying to protect my pride. Everything." He stood tense, watching me, but I was too stunned to respond. I adored Jaden, but I doubted that I could have expressed my feelings as eloquently as he just had. I went and wrapped my arms around him instead, and held him with all my might.

280

"I love you, too." That didn't even begin to cover it, but it was all I could manage around the huge lump in my throat.

That week Dec won his lawsuit, and the atmosphere at home lightened considerably. Aunt Paloma and Gran came over for a celebratory dinner one night, and I watched Jaden head into the kitchen, where Aunt Paloma stood at the counter. He sauntered up and tried to take a cracker from the plate she was arranging; she swatted his hand away, but then gave him one anyway. His impish smile made me grin in response, though he couldn't see me. He gave his mom a peck on the cheek before getting some glasses from the cupboard. I felt an unexpected twist of sadness at their warm, easy relationship. My mom and I had been close, but I knew that kind of parental relationship was lost to me for good—it was something Dec and I would never enjoy. And while I'd always felt that Aunt Paloma was someone I might confide in, now that I was in love with her son I felt reserved and cautious around her. It saddened me; she had always treated Seth and I like true members of the family. I was so afraid of losing her acceptance.

Eighteen

I brought Cameo to another show that weekend, and she won another championship ribbon. It looked as though I'd be going to the Royal with a pony this year. Which was still quite an accomplishment, as everyone pointed out—it just wasn't the one I was aiming for. So when Robin called that week to say that Hades' owners wanted me to take over his training, I was ecstatic. There was only one obstacle: Dec.

"No way," he said emphatically when I brought it up. "I won't have Robin on my property."

"But Dec," I pleaded, "she'd barely be here, she only coaches the owners once in a while. The horse is a bit much for them."

He frowned at me. "You know, Tea, you never mentioned Robin when you told me that story."

"I didn't think it was relevant," I said evasively.

"Uh-huh," he said, dubious. "Well, I asked around after you rode that horse, and from what I've heard, he's downright dangerous. So the answer is no."

I huffed in frustration; we couldn't afford to turn away a new boarder, especially one who would also bring in training fees.

"Come on, Dec, would you object to this if Robin wasn't involved?" I demanded, arms crossed.

Jaden's phone rang as I watched Dec's face set in familiar lines of resistance.

"Stop arguing with him, querida, you're making things worse."

It took a minute for the words to register, but when they did I nearly jumped in surprise before I realized that Jaden had spoken in Spanish. I understood the sentence almost perfectly; I glanced over and saw him lounging on the couch, continuing what I assumed was a fictitious conversation in rapid Spanish. As I watched he hung up, still without looking at me.

I turned back to Dec with a smile.

"Okay, Dec. And... thanks for worrying about me."

He seemed completely disarmed. "I—well, all right then," he muttered. He headed outside.

I went and sat next to Jaden.

"You made your phone ring?" I checked.

"'There's an app for that'," he quoted with a grin.

"I feel like a secret agent." I smiled at him. My hand was on the couch; he brushed his fingers lightly over mine.

"Let me deal with Dec, okay? The two of you just feed off each other's obstinacy."

I rolled my eyes. "Yeah, that should be a challenge. You guys are on the same side."

"No, we're not," he disagreed.

I looked at him in surprise. "But... you object to me riding Hades even more than he does."

"I'll admit that I did, at first. But not anymore. I've come to realize that it's not fair for my fears to hold you back, querida. I always want to lift you up, not keep you down."

"Though I don't actually mind when you hold me down," I reminded him suggestively.

He chuckled. "Well, for now, let's see what I can do about Hades."

Dec barbecued again that night, and we sat outside to eat. I had just absently pushed the rest of my half-eaten burger toward Jaden, ignoring Seth's affronted look, when the subject of Hades came up. I was a bit taken aback that the conversation started while I was around to witness it.

"When was the last time you watched Tea compete?" Jaden was asking Dec.

"I don't remember, but then, I see her ride almost every day."

"That's not the same thing. You have to watch her one of these days, Dec. She's incredible. She's one of those people who shines under pressure, who can pull everything together when it really counts."

I was gazing at Jaden in amazement, but he wasn't looking at me. His eyes were on Dec, who was frowning.

"It's not right to limit that kind of talent, Dec. Tea has world-class potential. She deserves a jumper of her own to ride."

Dec sighed. "That's just not in the cards right now. We don't have that kind of money lying around." He looked at me. "You understand, don't you?"

I gave a small nod.

"Well, her own horse would be ideal, but it's not the only option," Jaden said slowly. "Not if everyone's prepared to be a little bit flexible."

"I know where you're going with this," Dec warned.

"And you wouldn't consider it under any condition? For your daughter's future?"

Dec hesitated; he looked at me, and I knew we had won. He and Jaden hammered out the details while Seth and I did the dishes, and I couldn't stop smiling.

I had a quick shower, combed through my damp hair and donned one of my few dresses. A summery blue and white, it flowed simply down from spaghetti straps at the shoulders to end barely at mid-thigh.

I headed for the barn to say goodbye to Jaden. I didn't really feel like going out anymore, now that he had unexpectedly arrived, but I'd promised the girls, and it had been a while since we had done anything non-horse-related. I resolved to be cheerful and try to have fun.

Lisa emerged from the tackroom as I came in, her chubby form festooned by her saddle and bridle.

"My goodness dear, you look nice," she exclaimed, looking me up and down. "I think you've changed even more than Alyssa this past year." Alyssa was Lisa's daughter, and was my age.

"Um, thanks," I mumbled.

Jaden wasn't in the school horse aisle; we strolled around the corner.

"Dec must have his hands full trying to keep the boys away from you," Lisa teased, a twinkle in her kind eyes. I shrugged awkwardly as she started saddling her pinto gelding.

I spotted Jaden in Piba's stall; I was feeling distinctly uncomfortable as I caught his eye and mouthed, 'hayloft?' He gave a tiny nod. His expression was carefully smooth, the way he looked when he didn't want me to know what he was thinking.

I hadn't been upstairs long before his arms closed around me. I leaned back into him with a sigh, feeling that peculiar sense of relief that his touch always brought. I twisted my head up to ask how he was, but my question was lost as his mouth came down on mine. He kissed me slowly, his hands traveling up and down my dress. The heat from his touch seared through the thin fabric.

"Wow," I said shakily a few minutes later. "Now I really don't want to go."

He pulled me around to face him, wearing a slightly resigned smile.

"Go have fun with the girls. I'll be here when you get back."

"Really?" I brightened instantly. "I thought you weren't staying tonight."

"Do you honestly think I'd leave after seeing you dressed like that? I'm staying right here to make sure you come home safe. And alone." He smiled to let me know he was joking, but there was worry in his eyes.

I frowned. "Do you want me to go change?"

"Of course not—I adore that dress." As if to prove it, he ran his hands over it again, down my sides and over my hips, stopping at the hem.

"Good," I murmured, "because I only wore it for you."

I covered his hands with mine and slid them down, onto my bare thighs. He stifled a groan as his body tensed against mine, and I was grateful once again for the unexpected power of my skin. He quickly jerked his hands away and wrapped his arms around me.

"If you're trying to drive me out of my mind, you're succeeding," he growled softly in my ear.

"It's about time you learned how it feels," I teased, kissing his neck.

He pulled back to give me a mock insulted look. His eyes seemed to get pulled down to my body of their own accord; when they came up they were troubled again.

"What's wrong?" I whispered, touching his face.

He smoothed his expression quickly.

"Not a thing. You should go or you'll be late." He stroked his hands down my arms, making me shiver, and hesitated. "You look wonderful."

I took his face in my hands, feeling the thrill that never seemed to wane at the knowledge that this beautiful person was mine. This beautiful, sometimes jealous person.

"Jaden, I am *yours*," I reminded him fiercely. "My soul is yours already, and my body will be yours anytime you decide to avail yourself of it... maybe you should stop resisting."

"Now isn't the right time, querida."

"Why? I love you. I want to be with you in every way possible."

"In *every* way?" he said suggestively. "Well, that should keep us busy for a while."

I could see both humor and hunger in his eyes, along with something else I couldn't identify. He kissed my bare shoulder, his hands gliding again across the smooth fabric of my dress.

"If this is part of your continued attempts to heighten the anticipation, I think we've overshot the mark a bit," I told him breathlessly as the kisses trailed up my neck to my ear. It was so unfair—he had only to touch me for me to lose any hope of restraint. It was time to fight fire with fire. I tugged up my dress, found one of his wandering hands with mine, and placed it on the bare skin of my waist. The response was instantaneous; with a groan, his arms clamped around me, his other hand also snaking under the fabric to find the skin of my back. His lips crushed mine. As I was yanked off my feet I twined my legs around him; he loosened one arm from around my body to caress my thigh, moaning low in his throat. Then, abruptly, he stopped. He disentangled my arms and legs gently and set me on my feet, not meeting my eyes.

"You're still feeling guilty," I sighed.

He looked remorseful, but I didn't know whether he felt that way for stopping so abruptly or for allowing himself to get carried away in the first place. To my chagrin, I suspected the latter.

"Let's not talk about it now," he said quietly, smoothing my still-damp hair away from my face. "Go out, have fun. I'll see you later."

I nodded. I wanted to get to the bottom of this, but I was definitely late now. I stood on tiptoe to kiss him quickly before hurrying down the ladder.

I saw a good movie with Teri and Julia, and afterward we went to a coffee shop. Teri and Rob were going through a rough patch; Julia and I listened sympathetically as Teri described their problems.

"What about you, Jules?" I asked her. "Seems like you've been having a quiet summer on the dating front." Julia usually went through several boys in the course of a season.

"It just doesn't seem to hold the same excitement it once did." She shrugged.

"You sound like Seth," I told her. "Can you believe he's only dated one girl all summer? And she only lasted a few weeks. He normally has them lined up."

"No surprise there—have you looked at Seth lately, T?" Julia asked.

I was surprised at her comment, but to be honest, I hadn't noticed much of anything this summer, other than Jaden. I told the girls as much.

"So are you guys doing it yet?" Teri inquired.

"No," I admitted. It was getting frankly embarrassing. "He still wants to wait."

"Maybe he's waiting until you're eighteen," Julia suggested. "Then you won't be jailbait."

I considered the idea, but it seemed pretty far-fetched to me. I couldn't imagine that a few months would make that much of a difference to him. We moved on to new topics, like the fact that school was starting in a couple of weeks; it was a source of growing anxiety for Jaden and me. We had talked at length about whether we should disclose our relationship—after all, once school started, we'd need an explanation for why we were spending so much time together. But we worried that if our family didn't take it well, it would be that much easier for them to keep us apart, once Jaden wasn't living with us anymore.

I got home in time to do the bedtime check of the barn with Jaden; Dec had gone into town so we weren't rushed. We climbed to the hayloft and got comfortable.

"Now will you tell me what's going on?" I asked, taking his hand.

"Yes." He took a deep breath before speaking. "You know, in many ways, I'm closer to Dec than to my own dad," he said quietly.

I nodded. "I know that Dec thinks of you almost as another son." The thought made me uncomfortable, but it was the truth.

"Do you remember when I went to live with my father?"

"Not very well. I only remember it as the time we stopped seeing you." Seth and I had been eleven. I recalled that Dec was upset about Jaden moving, and him talking to my mom about it.

"Well, you know part of the story. I was sixteen and going through a rough time. I wasn't getting along with my mother... what I neglected to tell you before is that I wanted to come here and live with Dec."

He was watching my expression. His own was sad; it hurt me like a physical pain. We were sitting side by side on a bale, resting our backs against the green pile behind us. I straddled his legs so I could hug him.

"Don't be sad," I murmured against his neck. "Whatever's going on, whatever you need to be happy, we'll do it."

He held me tightly, his face in my hair.

"Do you realize, if I'd come to live here, I would have been like an older brother to you?" His voice was so quiet I could barely detect the strain in it.

I tried to pull back; it was a minute before he released me. I took his face in my hands.

"Are you torturing yourself over what might have been?" It came out sounding more severe than I'd intended, and I took a breath and tried again. "What I mean is, yes, things would have been different then—but you didn't come live with us, and we barely knew each other until this past year. Why is this suddenly relevant?"

His sadness was beginning to scare me.

"It's relevant because it illustrates that we're linked by more than just our love for each other. There's family history involved."

I waited; he sighed and went on.

"Dec welcomed me with open arms. I suspect he thought I needed the guidance of a father figure, or at the very least a firmer hand to control my growing wild streak. In the end, though, my mother wouldn't allow me to leave. She wanted me at home, with her. Dec wouldn't allow me to come without her permission... they argued about it, and it caused a rift between them for a time."

I made myself comfortable against his shoulder again. It was hard to stay nervous while I was safely tucked against Jaden; his familiar smell in my nostrils and his hand idly drawing circles on my back were too soothing. But I did feel a growing sense of unease.

"I ended up moving in with my father because he had no compunction about me leaving without my mom's permission. My mother fought with him about that. Then, as I got into increasing amounts of trouble, Dec began arguing with my dad as well. For years, they barely spoke—until last Christmas, in fact—because of me. Even Aunt Penny got involved and argued with her brothers."

I stroked his face, not knowing what to say to make him feel better.

"So as you can see, I've already been the source of considerable discord in our family-"

"And I thought I was the black sheep... I have a long way to go before I touch your record." I couldn't help the impish smile that followed that thought.

"Don't get any ideas," he growled, but his tone was lightened by the amused look on his face.

As always, his smile drew me in. I pressed my lips against his, and he responded, but something wasn't right. He was too hesitant, too careful. I drew back, my unease exploding into fear.

"What's wrong?" I questioned him anxiously.

His eyes were guarded. "Nothing, I just-"

"Don't say nothing—why can't you kiss me?"

My heart was racing now, my mouth dry with dread. I'd known he was uneasy, but now I suspected a much more serious problem. I just stared at him, wide-eyed, and told myself to be patient and let him finish speaking. Even though I was quite sure I didn't want to hear what he was going to say.

He averted his eyes and swallowed before continuing.

"I went to my mom's last night. I wanted to get a sense of how she would react to... to us. We talked for a long time. I tried to be careful about what I said, but she's very perceptive. I think she started to suspect what I was asking."

He looked at me then, and his eyes were pleading. I was still staring, my face frozen.

"Tea, my mother's Catholic. And she believes that, in the eyes of God, you are my cousin. Period."

Now I was not only scared, but perplexed too. Jaden had never given any indication that he was religious.

"I'm... confused. What does that mean?"

"It means that I don't think my mother will accept us being a couple. That if we persist in being together, I'll create more discord in this family, when I've already done enough damage. And that you'll be the focus of much of that tension, when what you need most right now is a calm, stable family life."

If. He'd said '*if* we persist'... he wanted to end it. I heard short, panting breaths coming from my mouth. I was hyperventilating.

"I have to go," I mumbled.

I scrambled up, my mind a panicked blank, feeling nothing but an overpowering need to escape. He caught me before I'd taken two steps, his arms winding around me from behind.

"Wait, Tea." I heard tears in his voice.

"For what? Divine permission?" I choked out. I struggled to break away from him, but his arms constricted like steel bands, crushing me, and he buried his face in my hair.

"Let go of me, Jaden." My voice was suddenly oddly calm. "I can't talk about this now. I'm past my limit. Just let me go."

He released me. For the first time ever, I was in a hurry to get away from him. I threw myself down the ladder, scraping my shins, and ran. It was dark outside, but I knew the trails well. I ran until I couldn't run any further, stumbling often in the darkness, and when I couldn't run anymore I walked. Walking was a Herculean task; I felt as though a gaping hole had opened up under my feet, as if the Earth itself had become unstable.

I moved numbly, with no destination in mind. My feet, of their own volition, followed the familiar trails that I'd been riding twice a week. Even with the nearly full moon, the woods were creepy at night, and as I became aware of my surroundings I increased my pace, trying to get out of the forest as quickly as possible. My feet hurt; fortunately I was wearing almost flat shoes, but they were not designed for running. I was sure I had blisters, and now that I wasn't running anymore I shivered violently in my thin dress.

The trail opened onto our practice field, and beyond it I could see lights on in the barn and Mateo's apartment. I'd never been inside, but I knew where it was, and I stumbled tiredly to the door. He answered after the first knock.

"Tea." His eyebrows shot up in surprise. He didn't wait for me to speak, but put his arm around me and led me inside, his eyes on my tear-streaked face. He led me to a small kitchen and sat me down.

"Are you okay?" He looked concerned.

I nodded, another violent shiver shaking my frame. He left and came back with a sweater, which I put on gratefully.

"Would you like some tea?"

"Please." It was barely audible.

After he'd made tea he sat in the chair next to mine.

"Would you like to talk about it?" he asked kindly.

I shook my head. "I just had a fight... with my family. I didn't mean to run so far." My voice sounded strange, as though it belonged to someone else. "Sorry for barging in on you like this."

He smiled warmly and patted my hand. "You are always welcome, chiquita."

I was finally getting warm, thanks to the tea and the sweater. I looked at Mateo; he was really very nice, I thought. I wondered why Jaden disliked him so much.

"How long have you lived here?" I asked. Anything to keep my mind off the horrible thoughts I couldn't yet face. We went through another two cups of tea, and it was only when he yawned that I realized it must be late.

"Can I use your phone, Mateo?"

He handed me a cell phone and walked into the other room while I dialed, giving me some privacy. The time on the phone said almost midnight. Somehow over two hours had passed since I'd gone out to the barn.

Dec answered on the first ring.

"Tea!" The relief was strong in his voice. "Are you okay? Where are you?"

"I'm fine. I'm at Mateo's." I swallowed against the lump in my throat. His obvious concern—with no trace of anger—was touching. "I'm really sorry, Dec."

"We'll talk about it later, kiddo." He still didn't sound angry.

I heard voices in the background.

"Jaden's coming to pick you up," he relayed.

"Wait—can you come instead?" I whispered. I wasn't ready to face Jaden yet. The very thought had my throat constricting and my heart hammering painfully against my ribs.

There was a pause. "Sure. I'll be right there." He sounded surprised.

Mateo wandered back in a minute later. We didn't talk much while we waited, but it wasn't uncomfortable. The barn dogs announced Dec's truck within minutes—he must have been speeding. Mateo walked me to the door and opened it so Dec could find us by the light spilling onto the ground. They shook hands.

"Thank you," Dec told him sincerely.

Dec was silent until we reached the road. It was quiet at this time of night, with only occasional headlights slicing through the gloom.

"What happened, Tea? I went to the barn to look for you, and found Jaden looking like someone had shot his dog. He nearly went berserk when I asked where you were; he thought you were in the house."

I really didn't want to talk about this, but I had no choice. I had to come up with some sort of explanation for my behavior.

"We had a fight," I said quietly.

"That much is already obvious." It wasn't said unkindly. He hesitated. "Is there something going on that I should know about, Tea?"

I was surprised by how calm he sounded, considering that my heart nearly exploded with fear at his question. I tried to think quickly, but my mind was numb and overwhelmed. This was my chance to finally tell him the truth—and I found, to my intense surprise, that I *wanted* him to know. I was tired of lying... but then a deep, aching pain reminded me that the need for secrecy was over. It seemed pointless to go through the drama of revealing our relationship on the eve of its burial. And it was safer to keep the secret, to be sure that Dec wouldn't disclose anything to Aunt Paloma; I didn't want Jaden to suffer unnecessarily. So I sighed, and tried to weave a lie from bits of truth.

"Jaden had a disagreement with his mom," I began, faltering, "and, well, I guess I wasn't very supportive. He was already upset, and I argued with him about how he should deal with her."

Dec nodded. Then he surprised me.

"Did it make you miss your mom?" he asked gently.

I thought of all the times I'd wished my mother had been there to help me through my relationship minefield. I was sure that if she'd still been alive, Jaden and I could be together openly. I knew she would have had no objections herself; she had been very open-minded. And she'd had a way of smoothing things over with Dec, so I was fairly confident he would have accepted the news coming from her. But tonight, during this time of crisis, I hadn't once thought of her. I wondered if that should bother me. I shrugged. He seemed to take it as assent; he reached over and put his hand on my shoulder. We were already pulling into the long driveway.

"I miss her too, honey." His voice was gruff. He added something in a voice too low for me to make out clearly, but it sounded like, "especially at times like this."

I trudged up to the house slowly, not wanting to confront what was inside. I was afraid the sight of Jaden's face would send me spiraling out of control, and walked through the door with my pulse pounding and my mouth dry.

He was across the room. I seemed to have caught him in mid-pace; I had a glimpse of wild eyes burning into mine before I looked quickly away. Seth called out from in front of the computer.

"Neeps, Sparky." He grinned, shaking his head.

I gave him a weak smile.

"I'm going to have a shower," I muttered to no one in particular. I bolted upstairs. I turned the shower on as hot as I could stand it, and stood without moving for a long time. I refused to allow myself to think, concentrating on every menial detail of showering, brushing my teeth, and dressing for bed. My feet were bleeding where my shoes had cut into them, and I carefully applied bandages, always ignoring the rock-hard clenching of my stomach, and the racing pace of my heart, which refused to slow.

I thought I would toss and turn for hours, but my mind, desperate for escape, fled into unconsciousness almost immediately. I was startled awake by a dark shape looming above me; my gasp was muffled by a familiar hand over my mouth.

"Shh, it's me."

And suddenly I was in his arms, and we were kissing each other through our tears. We kissed tenderly, carefully, afraid to hurt each other. I tasted the salt from our silent mourning. Eventually we lay down; he stayed next to me, on top of the covers, holding me in a tight embrace. He tried to speak only once, but I placed my fingers on his lips and he subsided immediately. I didn't want to hear what was coming, not yet. For just a few more hours, I wanted to pretend he was still mine. I didn't even worry that what we were doing was astonishingly risky, that we could so easily get caught if Dec came to check on me. I just settled my head against his shoulder with a sigh and fell asleep.

I awoke to bright sunshine the next morning. I was alone in bed, and it was late. I had a lesson to teach at nine, which meant I had ten minutes to get to the barn. I dressed and brushed my teeth quickly, but walked right past the kitchen on my way out—there was no question of eating with my stomach still so painfully cramped. When I got to the barn, Seth took one look at me and offered to teach my class. I accepted gratefully and went to find Jaden, trembling with apprehension.

I ran through scenarios as I walked. I had promised Jaden that I would do whatever it took to make him happy, and I meant it. If what he really, truly needed was for us to be apart—well, I would have no choice. I would make it as easy as I could for him. The very thought made my head spin, as though I was teetering on the brink of a vast abyss, but I choked back my sobs firmly. Hysterics would solve nothing; I needed to be able to think clearly. But mostly, I needed to see Jaden, to look into his eyes and find the truth hidden there.

I found him working on the run-in shed, and stood for a while, admiring the muscles rippling in his bronze back. Last night he'd been so vulnerable, so open... I was worried about what I might find this morning, dreading the return of the closed, guarded expression of yesterday's fateful conversation. Long before I was done watching him, he spotted me. He joined me immediately, the warm, somewhat worried smile on his face making me weak, as usual. I searched his eyes carefully—they held anxiety, and confusion, and pain, but I felt relief that he was allowing me to see it. Doubtless the same emotions were reflected back to him from my eyes.

"Good morning." His voice was smooth as honey.

I started to feel the predictable effects of his proximity, and to make matters worse, he was still shirtless. Without thinking, I placed my hand on his solid stomach. He covered my hand with his, squeezing it against him for an instant, then pulled it away and dropped it. I understood his warning look; we were quite far from the barn, but still visible.

"Can we talk?" he asked quietly.

At my nod, he turned and led the way down the narrow trail in the grass, pulling on his white T-shirt as we walked. Barely out of sight of the barn, he took my hand and held it tightly. We went to the edge of the field; it was a beautiful spot, dotted with wildflowers and ringed by tall leafy trees, but I wasn't in any state to appreciate its loveliness.

We sat in the long, slightly damp grass. I wasn't aware that I was clutching my stomach until Jaden put his hand on mine.

"Does your stomach hurt?" I saw guilt darkening his eyes.

"Not really," I lied, removing my hand.

"Did you eat?"

I gave my head a small shake. He didn't reproach me, for once. Instead, he cupped my face with one hand and kissed me. It was a soft kiss, but he lingered. I responded despite myself and before I knew it we were rolling onto the damp grass, limbs entwined, kissing with a passion that tasted of desperation.

"Wait," I protested breathlessly as the weight of his body pressed onto mine.

"Please, Tea," he breathed in my ear, "please, just let me be close to you."

It was a plea I almost couldn't resist. It was so difficult, in fact, that I hedged for several minutes, while Jaden's lips grew more insistent and his body moved against mine in new, more purposeful ways. He showed no sign of pulling back, as he normally would have by this point. That's what set off the alarm bells in my head—the fact that his behavior still seemed desperate. As though this was our last chance...

"Jaden, stop." It came out in a whisper.

He sagged against me, his breathing rapid in my ear. I felt a sudden stab of doubt. What if it *was* our last chance? Had I just given up my only opportunity to make love to Jaden? Regret began rising within me, but I suppressed it quickly. Things were confusing enough right now; I'd have plenty of time to suffer through it later.

He flung himself roughly onto his back and shielded his eyes with his arm. He lay there for a second, then reached for me and gathered me to his side, settling my head on his shoulder. His face was rigid, set.

"I'm sorry," he said stiffly. "As though I don't have enough to apologize for... we can add my behavior just now to the list of reasons why you'd be better off without me."

I exhaled sharply in frustration.

"Okay, time out," I snapped. I sat up, jerking out of his embrace. "Jaden, would you please tell me what the hell is going on?" It felt good to get angry; it burned away the feelings of sorrow and uncertainty and unworthiness. For now.

He sat up and faced me, but he couldn't meet my eyes.

"The only thing going on is my complete and utter inability to do the right thing by you," he said tersely.

"What does that even mean?" I threw up my hands. "Look, all I want to know is-" My voice broke, and I had to swallow hard before I could go on. "Is there any hope of us being together, or is it really over?"

His eyes snapped up then; they burned into mine while his hands grasped my arms so hard it hurt.

"What? Of course we're together—I thought-"

But I didn't get to hear what he thought, because right about then I started sobbing. He pulled me onto his lap, whispering words of comfort, Spanish interwoven amongst them.

"Mi bebé preciosa, I thought you knew... that after last night you would have known we were still together." He kissed my hair, my forehead, my face. "Tea, my resolve didn't last five minutes after you left."

It took me a few minutes to get my crying under control, and then I took what felt like the first real breath I'd taken since the night before.

"You scared me for a minute there," I said. The understatement of the century.

"Did you really think I would have touched you the way I just did, taken advantage of you like that, if we weren't together?" There was an edge to his voice—more than annoyed, almost angry.

"Would you stop saying that!" My anger, on the other hand, was fully present.

He was taken aback. "Saying what?"

"That you're taking advantage of me! How many times must I tell you that you *cannot* take advantage of someone who wants the same things as you?"

He shook his head, his brows pulling together. "I can't help it, that's the way it feels to me sometimes."

"That's because you're still thinking of me as your little cousin. As someone without the maturity necessary to judge for herself what she's capable of handling. In other words, you're not seeing me clearly." I twisted onto my knees in front of him and took his face in my hands. "If we're going to make this work, you need to start seeing me as just Tea. Tea, your girlfriend. Your lover. That is, if I ever manage to trick you into sleeping with me." I couldn't help smiling a bit at the end.

We lay back in the grass, his arms around me.

"So what happened, Jaden? What changed your mind?" I was watching his face carefully, so I noticed the flash of anger in his eyes, though it passed quickly. I blinked in surprise; anger was not what I'd been expecting.

"I didn't 'change my mind'," he said, his voice low. "My mind wasn't made up. I wanted to *talk* to you." He pulled my body closer to his; his arms were hard with tension. I could feel his fist against my back.

"Please don't run away from me again," he said.

"Is that why you're angry?" I asked quietly. "Because I ran?" My face was hidden against his neck, and he pulled away and put his hand on my cheek. He waited until I looked at him before answering.

"I'm not angry at *you*, Tea. You know that, right?" He was frowning. My expression must have shown that I didn't, because he

296

sighed and stroked my face before going on. "I'm angry at myself, querida. For hurting you. For putting you in this impossible position. For not being man enough to stay away from you in the first place."

I studied his face.

"Tell me something, my love—do you regret our time together?"

"Not one second of it."

"Well, neither do I. I've been happier with you than I've ever been in my entire life. I can't imagine life without you anymore. I don't care about anything else." I was laying bare my soul, and it scared the hell out of me, but if ever there was a time for honesty, this was it.

He pressed his lips to my forehead for a long moment before locking eyes with me.

"Tell me something. Yesterday, why did you immediately assume that I was... breaking up with you?" His face tightened with pain as he said it.

"Because I've been feeling it, Jaden. I've felt your hesitation, your doubt. Your reticence. Like in the way you won't have sex with me." I paused, searching for words to capture my nebulous feelings. "I know it would offend your sense of honor to sleep with me if you weren't going to stay with me... and you haven't wanted to sleep with me."

He opened his mouth as if to argue, then seemed to think better of it. Instead, he traced my lips with his finger, looking thoughtful.

"I'm not reticent anymore."

I felt my eyes widen; my heart rate doubled in an instant. I had no doubt he was telling the truth.

"So, what are we waiting for?" I smiled as I pulled myself against him.

"We need to finish this conversation, for one thing," he reminded me, but he was smiling too. His hand moved up and down my back, keeping my body glued to his.

"Which will never happen, if you keep doing that," I assured him, my breathing already uneven.

"Oh." He released me, and I reluctantly put a few inches between us. "All right. I'll give you my perspective, and then... well, we can discuss what we should do." His voice was quiet, strained. He put one arm around me again. "And no running." The last was almost a growl.

I nodded.

"If being with you means creating a rift in our family, I can live with that—for me. But not for you, querida. You need this family. And you need them without all the drama of another feud. I'm afraid that, by choosing to be with you, I'll be robbing you of any chance at a peaceful family environment."

"Is that it?"

He nodded, frowning.

"Well then, I've already answered you. I told you I don't care about anything more than being with you. I'll take the risk."

"What if you can't live here anymore? We both know Dec's old-fashioned... what if he gives you an ultimatum?"

"Are you telling me I'd have no place to go?"

"That's not the problem. I would love nothing better than for you to come live with me—but what about the barn? The horses? Seth?"

I felt a pang at the mention of my brother's name.

"Seth would want me to be happy. As for the rest... that would be hard. There's no question that I would be sad for a while if I lost those things, but I'd adjust. But Jaden, if I lost you, I don't know how I'd go on."

He pulled me against him then. "You can never lose me," he whispered in my ear. "These questions, they're worst-case scenario. I hope we'll never have to face them, but I wanted to make sure that you've thought this through. That you've considered the very high price you might pay to be with me."

"You're worth it at any price," I murmured.

We lay quietly for a while, and he started rubbing my back again. After a few minutes I felt the inevitable warmth rising from his touch. It reminded me of the conversation I'd had with Teri and Julia... was it only yesterday? It felt like ages ago. It seemed like such an unlikely idea that I was almost embarrassed to bring it up.

"Jaden," I began, faltering, "you're not trying to put off having sex with me 'til I'm eighteen, are you?" I didn't look at him.

He didn't answer for a moment; when I glanced at him he was watching me thoughtfully.

"I'll admit it's crossed my mind," he said quietly. I tried to hide my surprise as he explained. "It might be easier for me to look Dec in the eye if I could tell him I waited until his daughter was a legal adult before I-" He hesitated.

"Jaden Foster, tell me you weren't about to use the words 'took' and 'advantage' in that sentence," I said severely.

"I was thinking of going with 'defiled', actually." He grinned.

"It's not funny," I insisted, but I felt my mouth turn up a bit just the same. "You don't really think of it that way, do you?"

"Of course not. But I'm afraid Dec might, and I want to do what I can to protect my relationship with him."

"Okay, so if he asks we'll tell him we waited. Which I seriously doubt will happen—he's not going to want to know any details."

He shook his head. "I doubt he'll say much to you about it, Tea. I'm the one who's going to have to answer to him." He sounded worried.

I kissed his cheek, and murmured my next words against it.

"Don't worry, my love. It will all work out—have faith." And I did have faith that it would, somehow. I had to.

"So we'll *tell* him we waited, huh?" He gave the ghost of a grin.

"Yes... which conveniently relieves us of the burden of actually having to wait," I pointed out, sliding my lips down to his, "because frankly, I don't think I can make it."

"You're incorrigible," he sighed. But his hand moved to capture my face, and he spent a few minutes reinforcing my point for me.

Nineteen

The next week Jaden was going to Ottawa for four days to teach. We said goodbye in the shed the night before. I tried not to show how desperately I would miss him, but he held me so tightly I knew he felt the same way.

We emailed every day, but it was hard, and now that I'd had a taste of it, I was consumed by dread for the more permanent separation coming in September. We'd have weekends, in theory, but I had horse shows up until the Royal in November, and Jaden played polo until mid-October at least. And even on those rare weekends when we were both free, we would have to contrive excuses and sneak around. I was happy for the distraction of our club chukkers on Wednesday.

Mateo had been helping me with my Spanish; I had learned a lot but there were some verb tenses I still had trouble with. After our game I grilled him for a while at the picnic tables, but I couldn't stay late— Dec wanted me home earlier when I wasn't with Jaden.

"Why don't we go out for lunch tomorrow?" Mateo said. "We can practice more then."

I was happy to agree, not only for the help, but also to divert my attention from the constant low-level torment of Jaden's absence.

It was a very interesting lunch. I noticed for the first time how Mateo's fit body and self-assured smile drew female attention, but he was as kind as he had been the night I'd turned up on his doorstep. I hoped there was a way for him and Jaden to at least bury the hatchet, if they couldn't be friends. I knew that Jaden would be less than thrilled that I'd gone out with him, though. In fact I'd been surprised that Jaden hadn't made a fuss over the fact that I'd run to Mateo's, the night of our break-up scare, but he had a ready explanation when I brought it up.

"Even I have the sense to realize you weren't running to him, Tea. You were running away from me." The pain evident on his face made me change the subject immediately.

Jaden got back on Thursday night, and it wasn't until we'd spent half an hour reuniting in the shed that I could truly breathe again. The next day was quiet, and my friends and I decided to go for a ride. I was about to go find Jaden when he spoke right behind me.

"I know you're up to something."

I jumped and whirled around.

"Guilty conscience?" he asked, smirking.

"Not yet." I grinned.

He arched a brow, waiting.

"Are you up for some trespassing on private property today?"

He hesitated.

"I'll take care of you—trust me, this isn't something you want to miss. Ride Kermit," I instructed as he headed down the aisle. "Piba won't like this. And no saddle."

It was a sweltering late August day, and we rode slowly. Jaden was the only one not familiar with our destination; Teri, Julia, Seth and I went there regularly—it was one of our favorite haunts on hot days. We were walking down a wide, tree-covered trail when Seth rode up alongside me. The girls and Jaden were behind us.

"You must be happy that Seth's finally paying you some attention, aren't you, boy?" I reached over and patted Winter's neck; he was a wonderful horse, as easygoing and uncomplicated as his owner. He was named for the two dozen or so unusual, perfectly circular white spots on his chestnut coat.

"Hey, now, Winter knows he's my guy, even when I'm not spending all my time with him," Seth protested. He patted Winter's shoulder. "You're still the handsomest, smartest, fastest horse in the barn."

"Well, maybe not the fastest," I corrected, "'cause Schweppes could take him."

"Are you nuts?" Seth was incredulous. "Winter's bigger and has a way longer stride."

"And just what are you willing to bet on that?"

He considered for a minute. "A week of doing the dishes."

"You're on. We go to the end of this trail, then along the long side of the field."

I shortened my reins and shifted my weight, alerting Schweppes that a change of pace was coming.

"Three, two, one, go!" I yelled.

We thundered down the trail neck and neck. I leaned low over Schweppes' roached mane, almost laughing with joy at his speed. "Come on, baby," I whispered. We were pulling ahead; by the time we burst into the open field Schweppes was at least a length out in front, and his legs were still pistoning strongly.

Incredibly, I heard hoofbeats thundering up on my left. I flattened myself even further onto the golden neck beneath me, but the next second Kermit was pushing his shoulder in front of us; Jaden reached down, grabbed the reins and pulled both horses to an abrupt halt. The look he gave me was exasperated.

"Oh, come on—you can't tell me that wasn't fun." I grinned at him.

"Tea, you're bareback, and Schweppes doesn't even have a mane to hang on to," he chastised.

"And your point would be..."

Kermit's body sidled over and pressed against Schweppes so that our legs were trapped between our horses. Jaden's hand went to the back of my neck; he turned my head to look at him.

"My point," he said silkily, "is that you will *never* scare me like that again."

"I warned you about the worrying—I think I see some frown lines already," I teased. The corners of his mouth were curving up to match mine as our lips met.

"Okay, break it up," Seth's voice came from right next to us. I started, but Jaden's hand was firm on my neck, and he wasn't done; it was several seconds before he released me. I looked around, flushed and slightly breathless, to see Seth, Julia and Teri all grinning at me. It was the first time Jaden had kissed me in front of anyone, and I felt self-conscious. Jaden, on the other hand, looked very pleased with himself.

"Schweppes won," I said to Seth.

Jaden cleared his throat.

"Oh, all right," I conceded grumpily, "Kermit won. But you're still doing the dishes, Seth."

It wasn't much further to our destination: a pond in a rock quarry. Part of the quarry was still operational, so we were technically trespassing, but there wasn't usually anyone around. As soon as we arrived, Julia, Teri and I stripped off our shirts and our chaps; we were all wearing shorts and bikini tops underneath. Seth took his shirt off too; he was left with his jeans. Remembering what Julia had said, I tried to consider him objectively. I had to admit, I could see her point—all the swimming and heavy work at the barn had paid off. Seth had gotten... well, buff.

Jaden rode up facing me.

"I told you you wouldn't want to miss this." I smiled at him. "But if you want to be in our clique, that shirt's going to have to come off."

I rode past him and let Schweppes amble down the grassy bank and splash into the cool water. It was his first time here, and I didn't know how he'd react. Even though some horses don't like the water, most are strong swimmers, and as it turned out Schweppes fell into the latter category. He waded around happily; when he seemed comfortable I pointed him toward the center of the pond. The water level crept up my legs as the pond got deeper and deeper, until I felt Schweppes' motion change beneath me—he was swimming.

When I turned and headed back to the shallows Jaden and Kermit were in the water, and Jaden had elected to join our clique. I tried not to stare. The sunlight sparkling like tiny crystals on the wavelets, the trees forming a verdant frame for the cerulean, puffy-clouded sky... in my eyes, those natural wonders were nothing to his beauty. We spent the afternoon swimming—with and without our horses—and lounging on the bank. And laughing. I couldn't remember the last time we'd had so much fun together, and the fact that Jaden was now a part of our little group made everything perfect.

We decided to take the horses for a final dip before heading home. We were wading in deep water when Seth and I started trying to push each other off our horses; it was a game we'd been playing for years, and normally I was good at it, clinging like a burr to my mount's back. But Seth was a lot bigger than me now, and I soon found myself dunked into the pond, laughing so hard that I couldn't climb back on before Schweppes swam away. I watched him head for the bank as a muscular arm swung down to fish me out of the water.

Jaden sat me in front of him on Kermit, but I was facing the wrong way—I was facing him. There was a look in his eyes I thought I recognized... I didn't have time to place it, though, because he hooked his hands behind my knees and pulled me forward, draping my legs over his thighs. His gaze never left mine; my breath faltered.

I knew, suddenly, what his eyes reminded me of—a wolf's. And I was the small, furry animal frozen in the wolf's stare. I had never felt so much raw sexual energy from him; it rolled off him in waves. One might assume it was because he was half-naked and dripping wet, but I didn't think that was it. I thought it was simply the first time he wasn't clamping it down around me. He wrapped his arms around me, and the shock of my wet skin meeting his broke my trance.

"I've made a dangerous discovery," he murmured in my ear.

"What's that?" I managed to whisper. Barely. The feeling of his skin fused to mine was making it almost impossible for me to think.

"I like kissing you in front of other people," he said. To demonstrate, he laid a trail of kisses from my ear to my lips, where he tarried, kissing me very, very thoroughly.

"Hey!" Seth broke in.

I rested my head on Jaden's chest and offered my brother an apologetic look. He held my gaze for an instant, uncertain. Determination hardened his features as he rode Winter out of the water; he headed straight for Julia. He pulled up next to her, leaned over, and kissed her full on her surprised mouth.

"Julia Yamamoto, will you go out with me?"

Julia's startled look melted into a smile. "I thought you'd never ask."

Seth turned toward me; the look he gave me was questioning.

"It's about time, bro." I grinned at him.

Seth rode next to me on the way home. "Are you sure you don't mind?" he asked quietly.

"Really, Seth, how can you even ask, after everything I've put you through by dating our cousin? You and Julia are perfect for each other."

September was almost upon us. School was starting in a week, and Jaden and I still hadn't disclosed our relationship to our family. The stress was beginning to tell on both of us.

I was checking my email while Jaden arranged the entries for the following weekend's polo tournament. He was speaking Spanish, but I could understand most of it now. As he started listing the players I caught his eye and shook my head.

"Uno momento, por favor." He lowered the phone. "What is it?"

"Mateo can't go, he has an important appointment." He'd told me about it over lunch.

Jaden's eyes narrowed to virtual slits as he went back to arranging the entries; he didn't look at me. I sighed—I'd be hearing about this later.

"Wow, Tea, how much Spanish have you learned?" Dec asked.

"A fair amount, I guess. I hear a lot of it on the polo field." No need to mention why I was so motivated to learn.

"That's great," he smiled at me.

I nodded, and headed to the barn to prepare for my lesson with Karen. Jaden came in as I was cross-tying Marty.

"I need to talk to you." His tone was casual, but I knew him well enough by now to detect what was simmering under the surface.

"I'm kind of in the middle of something," I pointed out. I wasn't in a hurry to discuss Mateo, and I was feeling angry at Jaden's continued mistrust. I didn't think I could remain calm if we spoke now.

"Ahora mismo, Tea." He kept his tone light; unless they noticed his clenched jaw the people around us wouldn't be able to guess that he had commanded, 'right now'.

Fine, then. I shot him an irritated look—maybe it was time to have this out, once and for all. I went to the shed, not checking to see if Jaden was following or not, and once inside I paced impatiently until I heard the door.

Jaden strode over with a purposeful look and took my face in his hands. I was already thinking of arguments, and was about to launch into them—but just then he kissed me, and I stopped thinking altogether. He wasn't gentle, as he normally was. His mouth was rough; he crushed my lips with his, one hand moving to the nape of my neck, allowing no escape. His other hand ran down my back to my waist and yanked me hard against him. For the barest instant I hesitated; he had never been this demanding... but it was Jaden, and his body, his scent, his angry lips on mine, had me mindless in seconds. I kissed him back fiercely, flattening my body against his. The blood was pounding in my ears so loudly I could barely hear our ragged breathing.

After a few minutes—or hours, it was hard to tell—we broke apart, panting. It was a minute before I could talk again.

"Well, that was..." I cast around for a suitable adjective but I just didn't have the vocabulary for it.

"Are you speechless? That's a first," he said. He was breathing hard, and looking at me as though he'd never really seen me before. "I hope it's temporary, though, because I suspect you have something to tell me."

He let go of me while he was speaking, and I wished he hadn't—I would have preferred to hide my face against him as I told him. As it was, I stood awkwardly in front of him, with my hands shoved into my pockets. I felt like a guilty kid, which irritated me. I hadn't done anything wrong. Still, I faltered a bit as I told him about my lunch with Mateo.

"You went out with Mateo?" he spoke quietly, but the edge on his voice was one I'd never heard before, and it was razor-sharp.

"No—I mean, yes, we had lunch together, but... it was nothing. He just wanted to talk... you know, about polo and stuff." My nervousness had me floundering to express myself. I peeked at Jaden's expression, which did nothing to relieve my anxiety. His lips were pressed together, his eyes hard. I could see the muscle in his jaw bunching, a sure sign he was mad.

"If it was nothing, why did you feel the need to hide it from me?" he demanded. His hand ripped through his hair.

"I wasn't hiding anything! It just... didn't come up until now," I argued weakly. I hated that hard voice, that cold face—this wasn't the Jaden I knew.

"Right," he snapped, "it's a coincidence that you didn't tell me about going out with the *one* guy that you know I don't want you near."

A sharp pain sliced between my ribs, as though his words had cut me. I felt tears coming, and I didn't want to cry in front of him—not when I was this mad.

"You know what? I'm not doing this now," I said as calmly as I could.

I started toward the door; he caught my arm. When I glanced up at him his infuriated expression hadn't softened.

"What are you going to do, Jaden?" I asked him softly. "Force me to talk to you?"

He let go all at once and turned away. I trudged slowly back to the barn, my heart feeling like it weighed a hundred pounds.

I could barely follow the lesson. Afterward Teri, Julia and I sat at the picnic table, and the girls had lunch while I had a drink. As soon as they were done eating, Jaden appeared and sat next to me. I didn't look at him, and the girls soon excused themselves.

"I'm sorry about earlier. I shouldn't have been so rough with you." His voice was subdued. "I didn't mean to scare you."

I clasped my hands on the table in front of me and took a deep breath. "Jaden, you've made me feel a lot of things—many for the first time—but fear isn't one of them."

"The look on your face..." His eyes scrunched up against the memory.

"I wasn't afraid, I was just... hurt."

He watched me warily, waiting.

"You-" I swallowed, feeling a fresh slice at the thought. "You don't trust me." I wondered if he could hear the pain saturating each word as clearly as I did.

His eyes opened wide and he sat back, shocked.

"No—Tea, that's not true." He shook his head; his hand covered my clasped ones, and he gripped them as though he could force the truth through my pores. "Of course I trust you; I trust you completely."

I studied our hands. We shouldn't be touching like this, out in the open, but I didn't want to pull away. I wanted the reassurance of his skin against mine.

"If you did, you wouldn't care that I went out with Mateo. Jaden, if you really understood how I feel about you, you wouldn't worry no matter who I saw or what I did with them."

He flinched. "It's not that simple, Tea."

"It should be."

We didn't have time to talk more, because it was time to go to the club. We barely spoke during the ride, but where the trails allowed it we rode side my side and he held my hand, squeezing it tightly as though it might slip from his grasp. But then our practice started, and so did the screaming.

"Mateo! What the hell was that? An infant could've made that shot—if you play like this in our match we might as well forfeit now," Jaden yelled. He looked livid.

"You are crazy, no? Caley, she ride across my line!" Mateo screamed back.

Jaden cantered up to us, his face grim.

"He's right, Jaden, Caley totally obstructed him," I volunteered, shooting Caley an apologetic look.

Jaden glared at me. "I didn't ask your opinion," he snarled.

"It's not opinion, it's fact! I saw the whole thing," I yelled at him, stung.

"All right, we're taking a break," he called out, surveying our frustrated faces. "Tea, come with me."

"Why?" I demanded, my hackles up.

He rode closer, till we were knee to knee. I could almost feel the heat of his anger scorching me, and I realized suddenly that it had been a long time since I'd seen him that way. Well, apart from this morning.

"Come with me. Now."

I wondered fleetingly what he would do if I simply rode away. Surely we were past the point where he would carry me if I didn't listen... but just in case we weren't, I followed him, seething. I didn't need that kind of embarrassment.

We had barely handed our horses to Jennalyn when Jaden grabbed my arm and dragged me toward the stables. He turned on me the instant we were hidden behind the building. His eyes blazed furiously; I took an involuntary step back as I felt their impact.

"I'm the captain of this team, Tea," he snarled, "and I can't do my job if you undermine me at every turn."

"How am I undermining you?" I meant to shout, but it didn't come out that loud—his anger was intimidating me.

"Let's see," he said with mock thoughtfulness, "Mateo can do no wrong today, evidently. Every time I criticize him you leap to his defense."

"That's insane!" Now I did yell. "You've had it in for him all day, and all because of your completely senseless jealousy!"

A spasm crossed his face. "This is not about me!" he thundered.

I bit back my retort and we stood, breathing hard and glaring at each other. I took a deep breath; underneath my anger, there was pain—that sharp, slicing pain that his mistrust always brought.

"Jaden, I don't understand," I said more quietly. "What's really going on here?"

His jaw clenched. "Mateo likes you," he said tensely.

"Yes, because he's my *friend*. I like him, too. Why is that a problem?"

We were standing about three feet apart; I saw hurt flash across his eyes before he dropped them and half-turned, pushing the heels of his hands against them. I felt a wave of remorse. His anger I could take, though it hurt, but his suffering left me utterly defenseless. With a lurch I closed the distance between us and slipped my arms around him. He didn't respond at first, his body remaining tense. Then his arms closed around me. We leaned together, letting the anger dim, feeling our bodies soften and warm to each others'. I was relieved our fight was over, but worry gnawed like rats at my insides.

"Jaden," I spoke softly, "I'm out of my depth here. I don't know what to do. Do you want me to give up all my male friends?"

He took my shoulders and pushed me back so he could see my face; his looked appalled. "Of course not! I would never ask that of you—nor want it." He said it with a conviction I could not doubt.

"What about a situation like today's?" I asked nervously, not looking at him. "Should I stand idly by while you run roughshod over someone because you... have issues with them?" I shied away from saying 'because you're jealous'. I didn't want to provoke another fight.

His hand cupped my chin and made me face him. His eyes were tight, but they regarded me steadily as he took a deep breath.

"Tell me, what would you say if I answered 'yes' to those questions?" Neither his eyes nor his hand allowed me to look away; I couldn't prevaricate even if I'd wanted to.

"I'd probably say, 'Okay'," I whispered. "I mean, what else could I do? I love you. But I'd end up resenting you for it, and I'm not sure I could keep it up. You know me, I suck at following rules."

He nodded thoughtfully, released my chin and took my hands in his. My heart skittered in apprehension—he wouldn't really ask me to submit to something so draconian, would he? It seemed so unlike him, but then, I was only beginning to understand how powerful jealousy could be.

He swallowed hard. "Tea, I owe you a huge apology. You shouldn't have to deal with this. I've been a hypocrite—I've demanded that you not keep anything from me, but I haven't been completely forthcoming with you, either."

None of this was lessening my nerves any.

"There's something I haven't told you," he continued in a low voice. He hesitated. "While I was with Summer, she was unfaithful to me—with Mateo."

I gasped, stunned. The idea of anyone cheating on Jaden was beyond belief in itself, but for it to be with Mateo... all the pieces fell into place with an almost audible click.

"Oh Jaden, I'm so sorry," I blurted. I hugged him hard; I wanted to physically draw the pain from his body into mine, so as never to see that look in his eyes again.

"What happened?" I whispered against his chest.

"It's not that complicated," he said grimly. "Summer was angry with me; she slept with Mateo to teach me a lesson. I think she was hoping it would make me jealous, ironically." He laughed without mirth.

"Is that why you broke up?"

"It certainly contributed, eventually. But when it happened-" He paused, thinking. "I wasn't a very good boyfriend to her, Tea. I felt as though I'd driven her to it, so I forgave her."

And there it was again—the unimaginable depth of Jaden's goodness. I thought of how profoundly he had changed my life over the past year, of the innumerable small acts of kindness, and I felt absolutely flattened with love for him. Tears sprang to my eyes, and my throat constricted. I'd been watching his face while we spoke, but now I returned to the shelter of his embrace. He rested his cheek on my hair.

"What about Mateo? How can you be on the same team as him?" My voice was thick with emotion.

"He claims not to have known that Summer and I were together. In retrospect, I realize that she was always careful not to reveal our relationship around him... so he can't really be blamed." There was the barest trace of bitterness in his voice. Another piece of the puzzle fell into place.

"Jaden, you know-"

Hoofbeats interrupted me; as they rounded the barn I jumped guiltily out of Jaden's arms and whirled to find Mateo riding toward us. He looked from my distressed expression to Jaden's grim one and frowned.

"You are okay, chiquita?"

I nodded, then deliberately walked over and wound my arm around Jaden's waist.

"Sorry to keep everyone waiting, Mateo," I said as normally as possible. "We're just having a little lover's quarrel." I tried to look sheepish. I felt Jaden's eyes on my face as his arm wrapped tightly around my shoulders.

Mateo's face crinkled into a smile, and he wagged his finger at me playfully.

"Ah, so that is what you are hiding, little tiger! Well, time to kiss and make up, we have to finish practice."

His face grew serious as he turned to Jaden. Tthe two exchanged a long look before Mateo spoke in Spanish; most of it was too fast for me to follow. Jaden gave a curt nod. I turned to him questioningly, and had a brief glimpse of fervent joy in his eyes before he crushed me in his arms, lifting my feet right off the ground, and kissed me ardently. Mateo chuckled.

"Not too long, lovebirds," he called over the sound of retreating hoofbeats.

Practice flowed much more smoothly after that; the mood was jovial as the game ended.

"Does this mean we're coming out of the closet?" Jaden asked on the ride home.

I thought about it. Nothing had changed, really. His mother would almost certainly react badly to the news, and the odds were good that Dec would, too.

"I don't think we need to, yet," I replied. "The Argentineans are all leaving after next week—I'll ask Mateo not say anything. Unless... do you want to tell?" I watched his face as he considered; he looked almost as conflicted as I felt.

"No," he said finally. "I'm afraid they'll keep us apart."

I agreed, although I had additional motivation to keep things quiet. After what I'd felt from him in the pond, I knew that Jaden was serious when he said he was ready to make love to me. I didn't want increased parental scrutiny now, not when we were so close.

That Friday Jaden was leaving for a tournament at the Club Polo Nacional, near Montreal. He was due back on Labor Day Monday, but I wouldn't even see him then because we both started school the next day. We were facing an entire week apart, and I was numb with apprehension at the prospect. We didn't say much before he left, but clung to each other until the last minute. The way Jaden was running his hands all over my body made me want to consummate our relationship that second, but for the next few weeks, both of our schedules were insanely busy. It figured.

Jaden called from the road on Monday—the tournament had gone well, but he sounded exhausted. I wondered if he had done a lot of partying after the matches, but I didn't worry about it the way I used to;

now, I only hoped he'd had a good time. I had barely climbed into bed that night when I heard a voice downstairs—a voice I would know anywhere. I bolted down the stairs, but the sight of Dec made me brake abruptly, my legs locking on the bottom step. I grabbed the banister to steady myself, cursing internally.

"Hi," I said casually, barely glancing at Jaden. I examined Dec. If he was surprised at my hasty entrance, it didn't show. "How was the tournament?" I finally allowed myself to drink in the sight of Jaden; I had a feeling I was beaming, but I couldn't help myself.

"It was great, they have a very nice bunch of riders at the Montreal club. I just came to get the horses settled... Jen was too tired to drive by herself." A likely story. His eyes were locked on mine.

"Are you staying overnight?" Dec asked.

Jaden shook his head. "I have school tomorrow too."

"Then I'll go make you some coffee so you'll stay awake," Dec said, patting him on the back on his way to the kitchen.

We met halfway across the living room.

"Meet me in the shed after Dec's asleep?" he whispered.

"What if it's really late?" I asked. "You look so tired." I could barely refrain from caressing his face as I said it.

"I don't care. I have to see you."

I actually floated back up the stairs.

It was after eleven when Dec went to bed; his door had hardly closed before I threw on a hoodie and ran out to the shed. I flew into Jaden's arms the instant the door was bolted, and for a long while the only sounds were the small, happy moans and whimpers of our reunion.

Finally I leaned my head on his chest, the beating of his heart imbuing me with a profound sense of well-being.

"Did you miss me?" he murmured.

I shrugged one shoulder, blasé. "Enh, you know..."

My impudence earned me a playful swat. I wrapped my arms around his neck, laughing.

"Yes," I started to say, but he caught my upper lip between both of his, diverting me from my answer.

"I-" My bottom lip was next, halting my words again. When it was free, I tried again. "Did-" He ran his tongue under my top lip. "Are you going to let me talk at all?" I managed finally.

"No."

I gave up. Some time later, he stroked my face, sighing. "I'd better let you get to bed. You're going to be tired for your first day."

"Never mind me, I'll be fine. But you have a long drive ahead of you, are you sure you don't want to stay?"

"Querida, if I stay here tonight, neither of us will get any sleep." My stomach did a backflip at his words. "Can we find any time next weekend?" he checked.

"I'm at Palgrave Friday and Saturday; it's a big show for Cameo. And there's our match on Sunday," I reminded him. Dec had finally agreed to let me play, in part because it was at our local club. "I don't know how we'll sneak away with all of that."

He grimaced. "Well, at least I'll see you at our game on Sunday."

It was an exhausting week. The transition to school was always tiring, although at least Seth and I didn't have to feed anymore on weekdays, which meant two hours a day less work for us. Cameo was a superstar at the Palgrave show, winning reserve champion again, so we'd be going to the Royal for sure. Dec came to watch the polo match on Sunday; it was the first time he'd ever seen me play, and though he congratulated me on my skill he nearly went into cardiac arrest several times—Caley and I were on the same team, and we had a great time feeding off each other's antics. Jaden was umpiring; it was a close game, and I was bone-tired by the time we were done. Gran made dinner that night, to everyone's relief—the rest of us had been away all weekend. Seth had gone to another swim meet, and had done very well; his place on the team was secure.

As soon as we got to the barn that night, Jaden pulled me into a dark corner of the feedroom.

"You're quiet tonight. Is everything all right?" His arms encircled me. Tension that I hadn't even known I was feeling drained out of me, and I molded myself to his body with a sigh.

"I'm wondering about that penalty you gave Mateo... it seemed kind of harsh." I felt his body tense slightly. "I thought we were past that," I continued gently. "I thought we were solid."

"We are solid," he assured me.

"Good. Because I'd like to continue playing club chukkers on Wednesdays, and you won't be there," I said hesitantly, "and... Mateo will. He's not going back to Argentina this winter."

I watched his face carefully. His jaw tensed, and he stared at me for a minute before taking a breath and pulling me close again.

"Don't worry," he said. "I'm fine with it."

I was vastly relieved he'd agreed so easily. "Who knew you had the capacity to be so reasonable," I teased.

"Oh, I'm full of surprises," he murmured in my ear. "You'll see..."

My heart sprang into action at his suggestive tone; within seconds it was thudding hard against my chest. His lips brushed along my jaw. "Shall we visit the loft?"

In answer, I turned and headed for the ladder, his hand tightly clasped in mine. Once upstairs we nearly ran to our private corner. We'd had barely any time alone since our breakup scare, but I hadn't forgotten his promise—we'd be making love soon.

We had to shake the dust off the blanket before we sat on it. Jaden took my face in his hands.

"Maybe we should talk about-"

"Talk later," I told him, pulling his face down. His lips were curving up as they met mine.

Within seconds we were prone. I slid my hand under his shirt, and he didn't stop me. But the real shock came when I started lifting my own, and instead of halting me, he actually helped, taking it right off while I watched his face, my heart pounding.

"It doesn't seem fair for me to be the only one who's topless," I pointed out. He stripped his shirt off before pulling me back into his embrace. I luxuriated in the feeling of his skin against mine, pressing myself against him. When I turned toward him he knew just what I wanted, kissing me so sensually that I had to break away, groaning.

"I can't take any more," I panted. His eyes were amused, but I noticed his breathing wasn't too steady either. "Jaden, I'm going to implode soon. I'll self-destruct. Let's just do it now."

He shook his head. "Your first time is *not* going to be in a hayloft," he said. "And besides," he whispered in my ear, "we don't have any birth control."

"Oh." Only Jaden could make the words 'birth control' sound sexy.

"But... if you want, I'll try to make sure you don't implode, either."

I just nodded, suddenly nervous.

He resumed kissing me, and I pulled him against me; slowly, his hand migrated downward. He undid my shorts. Before long I was confirmed in my theory that Jaden was good at everything he did.

"You weren't kidding," he chuckled quietly as I lay in his arms. "Implosion was definitely imminent."

It wasn't the first orgasm I'd had with Jaden; such was the force of our attraction that even through my clothes, the touch of his body had been enough to push me over the edge a few times. But this was different—it was so deliberate. I finally understood why they called it 'being intimate'.

I traced the contours of his face, marveling for the thousandth time at my good fortune.

"You know, I think I'm less worried about my first time than you are," I told him.

"That's because you never worry about yourself," he said, frustrated.

I rolled over to kiss the crease between his eyebrows. "No, it's because I'll be with you."

His expression eased, though the frown didn't completely disappear. "I don't want to hurt you... you're so small."

"I'm not *that* small. And... well, I'm not expecting to be super comfortable, anyway," I admitted. Teri had said it hurt, I recalled, whereas Julia said it wasn't bad. Neither was exactly a ringing endorsement. "The point is, I trust you. I'll be happy no matter what, because it's you," I said simply.

He crushed me to him for a long moment before releasing me.

"I just want it to be a great experience for you. My motives are purely selfish, of course," he said with a sly smile. "If you have a good time, you might want to do it again."

"I don't think there will be any issues on that front—I want to do it now, remember? I always want you," I said, pouting.

Jaden took a deep breath and smiled at me crookedly. "Well, in that case, I guess we should organize a sleepover soon."

My mouth fell open. "Are you serious?" I breathed.

"Very."

I threw myself on top of him. I was filled with a fierce joy; I kissed him hard, passionately, and in response he groaned and pulled me forcefully against his body. We spent a few minutes with me happily getting carried away again. Jaden regained control first, of course—there would be no need for a sleepover if it were up to me—and pulled my face gently away from his. He was wearing a Cheshire cat grin.

"We need to go back inside," he reminded me.

"Hold on a second—have you not noticed the disparity here?" I inquired, indicating my semi-clad state. "I showed you mine..."

A flash of that wolfish grin, and then he guided my hands to his jeans. I was entranced at finally being able to touch him.

"You knew what you were doing," I whispered in his ear, "but I'm going to need some more coaching..."

I lay with my head on his chest afterward, cocooned in happiness. As I snuggled against him I thought of how unbearable it had been to be separated from him that week. As always, he seemed to guess my thoughts.

"It's only going to get harder, you know."

"It's going to get harder than *that*?" I joked. "Okay, now you're just bragging."

He stared at me in shock for a second, before my beloved wicked smile began tugging at his lips.

"Is that dirty talk I hear spilling from your sweet mouth?" he murmured. He leaned in and crushed my lips with his for a long moment. "God, I love you." The words were almost a growl.

I held him tightly. I never wanted to let go.

"Where were you last night?" Jaden asked. He looked upset.

After a seemingly eternal week apart, I had gotten home late Friday night to find Jaden at our place, asleep.

"Seth and I went to Ter's—didn't you get my email?"

"No, I'm having issues with my account," he grumbled. He perused my face, frowning. "You look like you spent the night in a bar."

"We didn't go there with the intention of drinking," I said a bit defensively, "we just went to hang out, but you know I have no tolerance for alcohol. A couple of drinks and I'm drunk."

"Hey," he said, pulling me against him. "I'm not judging. I was worried, that's all." His arms wrapped around me protectively. "It drives me crazy that I'm not here to take care of you."

I sighed as I relaxed against him. "I miss you, too."

We sat down on some haybales; we had snuck up for a brief visit in the loft before my morning lesson with Karen.

"Well, the timing for this couldn't have worked out better," he commented. He handed me a small, gift-wrapped box.

"What's this?" I asked in surprise.

"An early birthday present. I couldn't wait."

I opened the package slowly, feeling emotional. My birthday was October twenty-first, over a month away—I couldn't believe he was already thinking about it. I gasped when I saw the contents, and turned to him with a radiant smile.

"A phone! Oh, that's perfect!" I pulled it out; it was an iPhone like Jaden's, only mine was white.

"It's got even more features than mine," he said happily. "And I added you to my plan, so you'll never see a bill."

I flung myself at him. "Thank you, thank you, thank you," I said between kisses.

"I definitely need to shop for you more often," he said, laughing. He caught my face in his hands and kissed me in earnest; before I knew it I was on my back, Jaden on top of me.

"Ow," I said suddenly as my head pounded painfully.

"What's wrong?" he asked anxiously.

"My head hurts."

He pulled me up carefully, just as Karen's voice yelled my name.

"Uh-oh, gotta go," I muttered, scrambling for the ladder.

Teri and Julia were already grooming their horses. Marty had thrown Jennifer off again, and she had broken her arm, so I was riding him regularly in my lessons now. I cross-tied him facing Picasso; Teri looked only slightly better than I felt.

I felt increasingly lousy as I groomed Marty, and I was afraid that today's lesson would be memorable. In a bad way. Sure enough, when Karen walked in things only got worse. She took one look at Teri and me and shook her head in disgust.

"Were you girls partying too hard last night?" she demanded, surveying us through narrowed eyes. I'm pretty sure it was a rhetorical question, because as a former alcoholic, she probably recognized our symptoms better than we did ourselves. I couldn't believe that we hadn't considered our lesson with Karen while we were imbibing the night before. She had very strong feelings about overindulging—the predictable effect of having a brilliant career cut short.

"Umm..." Teri seemed too stunned to speak, so I groped around uselessly for a good answer, aware of Jaden's eyes on me. Of course 'yes' would be the smart way to go, since Karen obviously knew. The danger here was that Karen and Dec were friends, and I didn't know

317

how to go about asking her not to rat us out. I was considering begging when Jaden went to stand by her.

"Look at them, Karen. They're suffering—I'll bet they won't be repeating this mistake anytime soon," he told her in a conspiratorial tone. He smiled and went on in his most compelling voice. "But it might be best if Dec doesn't find out, don't you think? We all know how he tends to overreact... I'd hate for Tea to be forbidden from showing again." He was gazing into her eyes; she blinked before responding.

"Of course, we can keep it between us," she agreed almost eagerly.

It figures, I thought. Even the drill sergeant isn't immune. I never stood a chance.

Karen turned to us and said matter-of-factly, "It's bad timing on your part, though, because you're riding the entire lesson without stirrups today. I want you to take them off in the barn."

Teri and I couldn't suppress groans, and even Julia looked apprehensive, though she hadn't been with us the night before. Work without stirrups was hard enough when you were fit and healthy. Today, it would be nothing short of brutal. Karen apparently thought a hangover wasn't punishment enough.

Jaden disappeared while the girls and I finished grooming. I was positively dreading getting into the ring; I felt leaden-footed and weak, and a horrendous pounding was starting in my head. Teri and I exchanged a look of misery.

Jaden reappeared with two bottles of water. He gave one to Teri and handed me the other, loosening the cap first.

"Drink," he ordered.

He started saddling Marty. When he dropped the stirrups and leathers from my saddle onto the floor he leaned over and murmured, "Are you sure you want to ride today? It's going to hurt, you know."

I sighed. "I know. I don't have a choice, though."

"Yes, you do," he argued, "But if you choose to ride, you're bringing it on yourself."

I shrugged. I was irritated, but didn't have the energy to argue.

In the ring, Jaden gave us each a leg-up and went to work on the pasture. As I had feared, the lesson was awful. A jackhammer seemed to have gotten lodged in my head, my legs were burning from the effort, and the ring seemed unnaturally bright. By the time Karen started setting up the jumps I felt faint with weakness. I considered pleading for mercy, but my pride interfered, and in any event I knew it would be pointless. Karen was a great coach, very much in demand, and she could afford to be as exacting as she wanted with her students.

She started us over a small gymnastic combination. I was thankful for Marty's smooth movement as he popped over it easily. He was in a good mood that morning, very cooperative, and I patted his dark bay neck gratefully. Julia went next, Jazzy as elegant as ever, and then it was Teri's turn, Picasso pricking his cute pony ears throughout. He was clearly paying more attention than Teri, who by now could have passed for the Hulk's petite younger sister. Fortunately for her, Picasso—being a pony—couldn't easily manage the distances or heights in the course of jumps we tackled next, so Teri was excused and got to walk Picasso. She shot me a look of sympathy as I started my round.

My legs were screaming now, and I was focusing more on the pain than on Marty. He landed after the first line of fences, put his head between his knees, and did his patented rodeo bronc imitation. I didn't stand a chance; I flew off and landed with a thud on my right side.

"You okay, Tea?" Karen called.

I didn't move. In fact, I was more comfortable than I'd been all day. A nap definitely seemed in order. Trotting hoofbeats interrupted that happy thought as Ter and Jules came to make sure I was still alive. I staggered up, groaning.

"Shit, Tea, you scared us," Julia chided me.

"Sorry." I moved my limbs experimentally—everything seemed to be working. Painful, but working.

Karen led Marty over.

"Well?" She held out the reins, challenging me with her eyes to wimp out. When I took them she gave me a leg up without a word. I started riding the course again, this time staying tense and alert for any sign of bucking. It was hard to pull up Marty's head when I didn't have stirrups to brace against, but we managed a decent round. Julia went next, and I focused on not vomiting while I walked Marty.

I was just sighing with relief that the lesson was finally over when Karen said, "Tea, I want you to go once more. That horse is capable of jumping a lot bigger; I want to see how he goes for you over some decent-sized fences."

I didn't think I had the strength to even walk to the barn, but I nodded dumbly. Karen altered the course and raised the fences. They looked huge.

"Okay, Tea. It's just the two outside lines and the triple-bar on the diagonal."

I walked Marty in a circle, psyching myself up. Then I pushed Marty into his smooth, ground-eating canter and we jumped the course—and somehow, it really came together. Everything just flowed. I was almost as shocked as I was exhausted; Ter and Jules whooped as I pulled up and I grinned at them in gratitude. Karen was eyeing me with a very thoughtful look on her face.

"You could have kept him a bit straighter through your last line, but overall, that was excellent." Those rare words of praise from her made the whole miserable experience almost worthwhile. Almost.

As I was untacking Jaden materialized. He took the saddle out of my hands.

"I saw your last trip. I had no idea Karen would make you jump that high today, of all days." He sounded shaken.

I turned to him with a smile, my earlier irritation forgotten. Just being near him numbed my pain, and I was dying to flow into his arms and let his hands soothe away the hurt, as they invariably did. His answering smile froze on his face as he noticed the dirt all over my shirt.

"What happened?" he asked.

"Marty dumped me," I muttered, embarrassed.

"Are you all right?" He started to reach for me, but caught himself.

"Yeah, I'm fine. I'll be hurting tomorrow, though," I said ruefully.

He exhaled heavily. "I owe you an apology."

"For what?" I asked, surprised.

"For my fatuous comment earlier. You never deserve to be hurt, Tea."

"Well, you're forgiven," I said easily.

"You *could* make me work for it, you know... make me put away your horse, for instance," he suggested, his eyes dancing. "Then you could help Teri—she looks like she might not make it otherwise."

The following week brought several changes. For one thing, Hades arrived, and I was looking forward to starting his retraining. Even more exciting was Karen's call, asking me if I could ride Marty at a show in two weeks' time; she had spoken with his owner, who was happy to have me take over as Marty's new rider. Even better, Marty was already almost qualified for the Royal, so if we did well at the show, I'd have a shot at the big time in November. But those events, however noteworthy, were nothing compared to the biggest one.

Twenty

The following weekend was, very conveniently, Julia's birthday, which provided me with the perfect excuse to be away overnight. I planned my cover story carefully with the girls, and arrived at Jaden's on Saturday evening. I was spending the night.

We spent a long time saying hello.

"Would you like to go out for dinner?" he asked when we'd finally moved out of the entrance.

"I'd rather stay in, if you don't mind."

"Sure, I can make us something."

"Can we just order a pizza or something?" I said.

I only managed half a slice of pizza, though, before my stomach shut down. Jaden put down his slice and wrapped his arms around me.

"Nervous?" he murmured.

"A bit," I admitted.

"You know, it doesn't have to be tonight-" he began.

"Oh no—you're not backing out on me now."

"In that case, would you like to adjourn to the bedroom?"

I hesitated. "Can I have a shower first?" I'd had one that morning, but another one suddenly seemed like a good idea, and I thought it might help me relax, too.

"It's your night, querida," he assured me. "You can do anything you like."

I took my time showering and brushing my teeth. When I was done, I hesitated; it seemed silly to put my clothes back on. I settled for wrapping myself in a towel. When I stepped into the bedroom I stopped dead—every available surface was covered in candles, their warm glow dancing like wraiths on the walls. Music was playing, too, and I finally noticed Jaden. He walked slowly up to me.

"I don't have anything sexy to wear," I confessed. It seemed a foolish oversight, now.

"It's a good thing... if you looked any sexier, I wouldn't be able to control myself," he said huskily, taking my shoulders and pulling me against him. The towel soon slipped to the floor, and for the second time ever, Jaden scooped me up in his arms and laid me gently on his bed. My heart was thudding this time, too, but it was with anticipation. Mostly.

I watched him undress, admiring every line and curve of his body. No sooner had he settled his long body next to mine than I glued myself against him; I was shivering. He wrapped me tightly in his embrace.

"Te amo, Jaden." I was using the more intimate, romantic form of 'I love you' for the first time.

His eyes burned into mine for a long moment. "Te quiero, Tea."

It was blissful to finally have time alone, with no fear of being discovered or interrupted. We took our time, exploring each other's bodies in new ways, and it was much later when Jaden finally rolled on top of me and cradled my face in his hands.

He was looking right into my eyes as he moved into me. It was a tiny movement, but I felt my eyes go wide. I tensed up automatically; he stopped. I closed my eyes and felt his fingers and lips caressing my face.

"Are you all right?" His mouth was at my ear now, the words barely a whisper.

"Yes," I managed.

He nuzzled my cheek. "It's okay, baby. I won't move until you're ready."

I'd always heard that it was difficult for boys to stop once they got started, but then, maybe that was the difference between a boy and a man.

"Is this hard for you?" I murmured.

"Don't you worry about me," he breathed. "This is already the best night of my life."

My heart lifted, and I nodded slightly; his lips moved to mine. This kiss was a bit rougher than usual, which was good—it distracted me, and I was swept away, as always, by my overwhelming need for him. It wasn't long before I was pushing down onto him.

"You can move now," I whispered breathlessly.

He made a small rocking movement with his hips; there was pleasure, now, along with the slight discomfort.

"Keep going." I hid my face in his neck.

He kept going, with small, gentle movements, until I could feel him, deep in my belly.

323

"We're completely joined," he whispered, caressing my hair.

I clutched him tightly to me, but then felt him starting to pull out. "Wait... what are you doing?"

"I think that's enough for our first time, don't you?"

I shook my head. "I want you to... you know, finish."

He raised his head to look at my face; his was concerned. "I don't know, Tea. I'd have to move a lot more for that, go faster. I don't want to hurt you."

I took his face in my hands. "Will you try? Please. I promise I'll tell you if it hurts." Too much, I added mentally.

In answer, his mouth came down on mine again. His hips started rocking, slowly at first, until I was moving to meet him. His mouth moved down my neck, and I felt his teeth pressing into my shoulder. Although it wasn't the first time he'd ever done that, for some reason it was now incredibly arousing, and I wrapped my legs around his body. That was all it took; our groans mingled as I felt him surge inside me.

"Wow," I whispered, when I could talk again.

"Wow is right," he murmured, still breathless, near my ear.

He began kissing my face; his eyes flew to mine when he felt the wetness on my temples, from the tears now running into my hair.

"I'm happy," I explained quickly. "I'm so happy that it's you."

Contentment seeped through every particle of my being. Though I would never have admitted it to anyone, I felt like I was finally, completely his. And he was mine.

Twenty-one

A couple of weeks later, I strolled down to the barn absent-mindedly. The day was sunny and mild for mid-October, with that golden glow that only seems to exist amongst the warm colors of autumn. I was almost at the barn when my subconscious registered something out of the ordinary and I came out of my reverie enough to look around.

There was a horse in the large grass paddock to my left—but I didn't recognize him. I went and leaned on the fence. He was bright chestnut, his coat like flames against the grass. He was bounding with energy, and looked quite young. As I watched he trotted along the fence, snorted at an imaginary danger and took off at a gallop across the paddock.

"Nice horse, isn't he?" Jaden's voice came from right next to me; I'd been so absorbed in watching the new arrival that I hadn't noticed his approach.

"Yes, very. But who is he? I didn't know we were getting a new boarder."

Jaden shrugged. "You'll have to ask Dec," he said, motioning toward the house. Dec and Seth were on their way.

"What do you think of him?" Dec asked when they reached us.

"He's beautiful... a really nice mover, too." As we watched, the new horse gave a series of enormous, twisting bucks. "And very athletic, apparently. Who does he belong to?"

"He's yours," Dec replied quietly.

"I—what?" I whispered. My face was frozen in shock.

"Happy birthday." Dec smiled. Beside him Seth was grinning hugely.

I turned back to the fence, too stunned to speak. On my other side, I felt Jaden's hand brush my arm.

"I was going to let you find your own horse," Dec said, "makes more sense, of course—but then the opportunity to buy this one came along, and I had to act fast. I have a feeling you'll get along, though... he's Blaze's half-brother." He finished the sentence quietly.

I stared at him. "What?"

He nodded slowly, his pale eyes assessing my reaction. "They have the same mother. Can you see the resemblance?"

Now that I was looking for it, it was obvious. This horse was a bit taller and leaner, but the shape of the head was the same, and his movement, especially, marked him as Blaze's brother. He had the same raw athleticism. He had a stripe down his face, and a snip that went off to one side, along with one white sock on his left hind. He was gorgeous. And he was mine. I glanced at Jaden; this had his signature all over it.

'You?' I mouthed. He shook his head, grinning. I didn't fully believe him, though.

I turned back to Dec. "But Dec—how? He must have cost a fortune."

He shrugged. "When we sold Zac I put the money away for you, for school. But you need a horse of your own to compete with... so I guess you'll be working for your university education." He winked at me.

I threw my arms around him. "Thank you." I whispered it against his shirt, afraid my voice would break.

"Well... you're welcome, honey," he said, patting my back a bit awkwardly.

I turned back to my new horse, my heart inflating. "Does he have a name?" I asked.

"They were calling him Cal around the barn. Why, do you have something in mind?" Dec said.

"I like Cal. It can be short for Caliente." That was perfect, with his flame-hot coloring. "But I have a different show name in mind for him." I glanced at Jaden; he was watching me in that intense way of his that made me want to... I got a grip on myself. "I'm going to call him Renaissance Man."

I felt a movement next to me. I knew Jaden would understand who my horse was named for.

I slipped through the fence boards to go acquaint myself with Cal. I was almost in the center of the paddock when he wheeled suddenly and headed toward me at a full gallop; he bounced to a gangly, graceless halt a few feet from me.

"You're going to have to cut it a lot closer than that to impress me," I said, laughing.

After I'd put Cal in the barn Jaden pulled me into the feedroom. I looked at him questioningly; it was daytime—we couldn't hide in there with boarders in the barn. He handed me a camera, and I held it, confused.

"Consider this it on permanent loan to you," he said. He grinned at my look of delighted understanding. Months before, I had mentioned to him that I regretted not taking more pictures of Blaze while he was alive. The subject had only come up the one time... trust Jaden to remember. I turned the camera over in my hands; it was medium-sized, digital, and seemed to have a lot of controls. Well, I could learn. After all, I had the perfect motivation.

Marty qualified for the Royal, but my first classes there were with Cameo. The large ponies went on Saturday, so there were quite a few spectators, although thankfully the Coliseum was nowhere near its seating capacity of over eight thousand—I was nervous enough. I had a number of my own personal cheerleaders in the stands, and they got to see Cameo win Champion of her division. The Tremblays were thrilled; I was incredibly happy, and so proud of sweet little Cameo. I had a week to recover before competing again with Marty.

Everyone came to watch Marty's class, except for Uncle Peter, who was away on business. The rest of my family were present, as were Teri, Julia, and Caley. I felt fortunate to have ridden in the enormous arena the previous week with Cameo; it had given me a chance to get used to the lights, television cameras, and constant motion of spectators flowing in and out of the stands. Marty, however, hadn't had the same opportunity, and I prayed that he would take it all in stride and not succumb to his habit of bucking when he got emotional. Since it was a jumper class, my goal would be to get the fewest 'faults' by leaving all the rails up—but it was also possible to incur time faults, so if Marty bucked, I'd have to keep going as well as I could, because pulling up would mean losing the class.

I felt nauseous and weak as I walked the course with Karen beforehand; the fences looked huge, some considerably wider than I was tall. Karen kept up a stream of advice and warnings, but my mind had taken on sieve-like qualities and I couldn't absorb any of it. By the time we returned to the hitching ring I was shivering with nerves. I'd asked Jaden to stay in the stands so I wouldn't be distracted by his presence, but I suddenly wished he was here, warming me, as always, with his touch, his eyes, and his words.

We started warming up. The hitching ring was a large rectangle. The entrance from the Horse Palace was at one end, the in-gate at the other, and on one of the long sides was the mouth of a wide aisle lined by concession stands, through which people milled constantly. Marty didn't like the aisle with the people very much; the sudden movements and sounds drew his attention away from the fences, and I could sense his occasional surges of nervousness. I reassured him as best I could, and allowed him to take a good look down the aisle—the Coliseum was bound to be even more impressive for him.

I let Marty look around as much as I could after we entered the arena; my ears were buzzing so loudly that I barely heard the announcement of our names, "Tea Everson, riding Martinique" as we picked up a canter. As I'd feared, Marty was intimidated by the Coliseum—his head was high and he was craning his neck to ogle everything, rather than focusing on me.

"Listen to me, now, Marty," I told him sharply. "Come on, buddy."

He flicked an ear back, and brought his nose down just in time for our first fence. One, two, three... we jumped seven fences without incident when, with no warning, Marty plunged his head between his knees and started bucking. A collective gasp went up in the arena, followed by loud ooh's and aaah's as I threw my shoulders back, cursing. He bucked around an entire corner before I got his head up again, and I kicked him in frustration as we lined up our next fence. He didn't like my show of temper, and matched it with his own—he flattened his ears back and took off, galloping our next two lines barely under control. I was shocked not to hear any rails coming down, and from the sounds of things, so were the spectators.

"Okay, okay, I'm sorry," I panted as I coaxed him back to a reasonable pace. Our last two fences felt easy by comparison, and a cheer went up as we landed. By some miracle, we'd gone clear.

I jumped off in the hitching ring and, after lots of patting, handed Marty to Teri so I could watch the rest of the rounds with Karen. Only two other people went clear; Alex and a woman I didn't know. Since we were all within the time allowed, there would be a jump-off. I walked back to the hitching ring on shaking legs.

I rode Marty around the warm-up ring, trying not to panic as I remembered Alex's round with Moose. The horse was such a behemoth he made the jumps look small, and his stride seemed about twenty feet long. I didn't know how we could beat him in a class where speed was of the essence; he could cover the distances in about half the number of strides it would take Marty.

Karen was nervous too, but her nerves took the form of increased irritability. She yelled at me to jump the practice fence again. I didn't want to do it any more, I wanted to save Marty's energy for the ring, but I didn't dare contradict her. We picked up a shaky canter. As we passed the 'people' aisle I glimpsed a tall figure out of the corner of my eye—a fraction of a second was all it took to recognize Jaden. I pulled up immediately, ignoring Karen's bellow.

He patted Marty and leaned against my leg, getting as close as he could. His face clouded with concern in response to the expression on mine.

"I'm scared," I whispered. Some small corner of my brain still managed to register shock that I would admit fear to anyone.

"I know, corazón. But it will all work out—have faith."

I cracked a small smile at hearing him quote my own reassurances back at me, but it quickly faded. Karen was sounding increasingly choleric behind me.

"Karen giving you a hard time?" he asked.

I nodded mutely. He reached up and put his hand on my stomach; I hadn't been aware of how tightly clenched it was, but under the warmth of his touch it relaxed, and I was able to take a deep breath. His gorgeous sun-kissed eyes burned into mine.

"I know she's a great coach, Tea, but right now... I think you should ignore her. You've got incredible instincts; go into the ring and follow them."

He tapped his hand twice over his heart, reminding me, his eyes still holding mine. I nodded, not trusting myself to speak, and walked Marty over to the in-gate. When I glanced back Jaden was leading Karen away with his hand on her shoulder, and she didn't look unhappy.

"It's just you and me, buddy," I whispered to Marty as I patted his neck.

Jaden might have had faith in my instincts, but I felt very uncertain as Marty and I ventured forth for the second time. I had no idea what strategy to adopt, so I simply aimed for the obvious—go fast and jump high. The danger was that since I wasn't keeping him quite as controlled, Marty could easily turn our round into a rodeo exhibition, which would be disastrous. I sent up a silent prayer as we cantered around the first corner.

Maybe my prayer was heard, because Marty was phenomenal. He loved the speed and increased freedom of the jump-off, and got so involved that he forgot to worry about the crowd. I barely heard the exclamations from the stands as we raced around the arena; his smaller size allowed him to make sharp turns with ease, and I heard a roar go up as we landed after our last fence—we'd set a scorching pace. The woman had gone first and had a rail down; the pressure was on Alex now.

Moose jumped a beautiful round, but he couldn't touch our time— when the ribbons were called, Marty had won. I felt ten feet tall as we led the victory gallop around the arena. I let Marty have his head and pumped my fist into the air, grinning. I didn't care if he bucked now, I felt like I could fly.

Back in the hitching ring, I exchanged hugs with a jubilant Teri and Karen before handing Marty over to them. I was hot and breathless from exertion, and quickly stripped off my helmet and jacket. I looked up to find Jaden striding rapidly toward me, a look of blazing pride on his face, and I didn't think—I just ran. I threw myself at him; his strong arms caught me, and the cheers and whistles of the surrounding riders serenaded us as we kissed.

It was odd how among all that noise, the sound of one throat being cleared could echo so distinctly. I suppose it was because the throat in question was Dec's.

We froze for an instant, and then quickly broke apart, though Jaden kept my hand tightly in his. He pulled our hands behind his back, trying to move me behind him, but I stood my ground; I wanted us to face this hurdle together, as a team of equals. When he caught my eye I raised my chin a fraction, and he nodded before we turned to face our assembled family.

We advanced slowly, and stopped in front of Dec. His face was inscrutable. His eyes travelled quickly from Jaden to me, taking in our clasped hands, and returned to Jaden's face.

"Uncle Dec, we have something to tell you," Jaden said, squaring his shoulders. I was impressed with how natural his voice sounded, but his hand gripped mine even harder.

Dec's eyebrows crept up a fraction. He didn't say anything.

Jaden took a deep breath. "Tea and I are together," he said firmly. "What I mean is, we're involved. Romantically."

Dec raised his arm; I felt Jaden flinch slightly through our hands, but he didn't move as Dec dropped a hand onto his shoulder and gave him a light shake.

"Do you really think, son," he drawled, "that you've been that discreet?"

Jaden stole a glance at me; I'm sure my look of shock mirrored his.

I nervously scanned the faces of our friends and family. Caley was grinning widely, as were Seth and Julia, standing with their arms around each other. Stacey's mouth was hanging open; the look of scandalized-yet-delighted incredulity on her face contrasted sharply with the expressions of shock and consternation featured on both her parents' visages. Gran was tight-lipped. Finally, my eyes came to rest on Aunt Paloma. She was clearly both horrified and distressed; her eyes were shining with unshed tears. She didn't falter, though, as she stepped toward her son and slapped him hard across the face. She turned on her heel and walked rapidly away. Jaden turned to me in anguish.

"Go," I urged him, releasing his hand.

I watched him weaving through the crowd, until the weight of many eyes made me turn back to our family, my mouth dry and my heart racing. Seth came to my rescue.

"Hey, Sis, shouldn't you be getting Marty back to his stall?" he asked.

"Yes, I should," I agreed in relief, looking around for him.

"We should head home," Uncle Robert sighed. "Congratulations, Tea." He didn't smile at me, but I appreciated the sentiment.

"You'll keep us updated on this, uh, situation, Declan?" Aunt Penny asked, shooting me one last dismayed look.

After assuring her that he would, Dec headed toward the rest of us, now crowded around Marty. I averted my eyes quickly, feeling ashamed even as I did so. I walked through the echoing Horse Palace surrounded by Seth and my friends, receiving occasional pats on the back and congratulations on the way. Dec kept pace with us silently.

By the time we got to Marty's stall, the tension was palpable.

"Do you guys want to go with Marty to the shower stalls?" I suggested to Seth. He held my gaze for a moment, making sure, but at my nod he agreed, and he and Julia followed Teri and Karen, who shook her head at me over her shoulder, grinning.

I took a deep breath and faced Dec.

I opened my mouth, but found myself at a complete loss for what to say. I forced myself to meet his eyes. They were troubled but, to my relief, not angry.

"You could have told me," he growled.

"Yes. I should have," I agreed quietly.

"Hmpf." He crossed his arms. "How long has this been going on?"

I swallowed. "Since July," I admitted.

He nodded; he didn't look surprised.

We were interrupted by Jaden's arrival. I almost ran to him; by force of long habit, we left a wide space between us when we stopped. I examined his face—he looked devastated, but he recovered his wits first, and pulled me into his arms. I held him tightly, feeling Dec's eyes on us.

"Sorry I left you on your own," he whispered in my ear.

"No, it's fine, of course you had to go. What did she say?"

He tensed. "She wouldn't talk to me."

I pulled back so I could see him; when I caressed his cheek he leaned into my hand, his face tormented.

"Despite everything I put her through when I was younger, my mother never once raised her hand against me. She was always willing to listen, at least." He swallowed hard. "I don't know if she'll forgive me this time."

We both started as Dec spoke right next to us. "Give it some time. This has been a shock to everyone, your mother most of all."

We dropped our arms quickly, and Jaden faced him.

"I apologize for not being honest with you," he said quietly. No one could have doubted his sincerity.

Dec grunted. "I take it this is serious?" he asked gruffly.

Jaden reached for my hand before answering. "It's as serious as it gets."

A spasm crossed Dec's face.

"Do you remember when you picked me up from Mateo's?" I said hesitantly. "The questions you asked me... I thought you might have suspected, even then."

"Well, naturally I speculated; the two of you couldn't keep your eyes off each other all summer." He stared hard at Jaden. "When I began to suspect what was going on... well, I planned to confront you, at first. But I waited; I wanted to be sure before I started making accusations. And then a funny thing happened—everyone got really happy. It seemed as though every time I walked into the house or the barn someone was laughing; even the students and boarders were affected by the mood you two created." He looked at me, finally. "I haven't seen you like that since your mother died. After everything you've been through, well, I didn't want to take that away from you. So I lived in denial of what was developing in front of me; I found ways to justify your more dubious behavior to myself." He shook his head, doubtful. "I don't know if I did the right thing. Maybe, if this had been nipped in the bud..."

I made myself look him in the eye. "We tried, Dec. We really tried to stay away from each other. We spent months making ourselves miserable, but we're like magnets; once we get close, we just can't stay apart."

I stepped nearer to him.

"I didn't mean for this to happen, Dec, but please-" my voice broke, and I stared at the ground; I didn't even know what I was asking him, exactly. I felt his hands on my shoulders.

"We're going to have to talk about this a lot more, but I'm not handing down any final judgments." I hugged him quickly. "This is going to take some getting used to," he sighed.

I had barely turned back to Jaden when a man and woman I didn't recognize came forward.

"Hi, you're Tea Everson, aren't you?" the woman asked politely. At my nod, she went on, "I'm with *Horse Sport* magazine; I'd like to congratulate you on your double win this week. Could I ask you some questions for an article we're doing on emerging talent?"

"Um," I said brightly. My head was still spinning from the day's drama.

"Would you like me to deal with the press for now?" Jaden murmured.

"Yes, please." I gazed up at him gratefully. He had experience with this kind of thing, after all.

He handed the woman a card. "Call me, and we'll set up an appointment for an interview."

The reporter scrutinized his face. "You look very familiar," she said. "May I ask who you are?"

Jaden wrapped his arm around me and breathed a satisfied sigh. "I'm Tea's boyfriend."

CPSIA information can be obtained at www.ICGtesting.com
Printed in the USA
LVOW062013011111

253047LV00001B/272/P